'I always seize the latest Lee Child with **pleasure**'
PHILIP PULLMAN

'**Nothing** makes for a great weekend quite like **quality time** with Jack'
LISA GARDNER

'Jack Reacher is today's **James Bond**, a thriller hero we can't get enough of'
KEN FOLLETT

'Lee Child just gets better and better . . . **Whip smart**, always compelling, always fun, he is **dangerously addictive**'
PETER JAMES

'Everyone needs to **kick some butt** sometimes, even if it's just imaginary'
JOJO MOYES

'One of the **best**'
JONATHAN ROSS

D0993673

The Jack Reacher series

Killing Floor
Die Trying
Tripwire
The Visitor
Echo Burning
Without Fail
Persuader
The Enemy
One Shot
The Hard Way
Bad Luck And Trouble
Nothing To Lose
Gone Tomorrow
61 Hours
Worth Dying For
The Affair
A Wanted Man
Never Go Back
Personal
Make Me
Night School
No Middle Name (stories)
The Midnight Line
Past Tense
Blue Moon
The Sentinel

For more information see www.jackreacher.com

THE
SENTINEL

Lee Child
and
Andrew Child

CORGI BOOKS

TRANSWORLD PUBLISHERS
Penguin Random House, One Embassy Gardens,
8 Viaduct Gardens, London SW11 7BW
www.penguin.co.uk

Transworld is part of the Penguin Random House group of companies
whose addresses can be found at global.penguinrandomhouse.com

First published in Great Britain in 2020 by Bantam Press
an imprint of Transworld Publishers
Corgi edition published 2021

A CIP catalogue record for this book
is available from the British Library.

ISBN
9780552177429 (B format)
9780552177436 (A format)

Typeset in 10.12/12.88pt Times Ten by Jouve (UK), Milton Keynes.
Printed and bound in Great Britain by Clays Ltd, Elcograf S.p.A.

The authorized representative in the EEA is Penguin Random House
Ireland, Morrison Chambers, 32 Nassau Street, Dublin D02 YH68.

Penguin Random House is committed to a sustainable
future for our business, our readers and our planet. This book
is made from Forest Stewardship Council® certified paper.

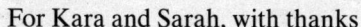

For Kara and Sarah, with thanks

ONE

Rusty Rutherford emerged from his apartment on a Monday morning, exactly one week after he got fired.

He spent the first few days after the axe fell with his blinds drawn, working through his stockpile of frozen pizzas and waiting for the phone to ring. *Significant weaknesses*, the dismissal letter said. *Profound failure of leadership. Basic and fundamental errors.* It was unbelievable. Such a distortion of the truth. And so unfair. They were actually trying to pin the town's recent problems on him. It was . . . a mistake. Plain and simple. Which meant it was certain to be corrected. And soon.

The hours crawled past. His phone stayed silent. And his personal email silted up with nothing more than spam.

He resisted for another full day, then grabbed his old laptop and powered it up. He didn't own a gun or a knife. He didn't know how to rappel from a helicopter or parachute from a plane. But still, someone had to

1

pay. Maybe his real-life enemies were going to get away with it. This time. But not the villains in the video games a developer buddy had sent him. He had shied away from playing them, before. The violence felt too extreme. Too unnecessary. It didn't feel that way any more. His days of showing mercy were over. Unless . . .

His phone stayed silent.

Twenty-four hours later he had a slew of new high scores and a mild case of dehydration, but not much else had changed. He closed the computer and slumped back on his couch. He stayed there for the best part of another day, picking at random from a stack of Blu-rays he didn't remember buying and silently begging the universe to send him back to work. He would be different, he swore. Easier to get along with. More patient. Diplomatic. Empathetic, even. He would buy doughnuts for everyone in the office. Twice a month. Three times, if that would seal the deal.

His phone stayed silent.

He didn't often drink, but what else was there left to do? The credits began to roll at the end of another disc. He couldn't stomach another movie so he retreated to the kitchen. Retrieved an unopened bottle of Jim Beam from the back of a cabinet. Returned to the living room and put a scratchy old Elmore James LP on the turntable.

He wound up asleep, face down on the floor, after . . . he wasn't sure how long. All he knew was that when he woke up his head felt like it was crammed full of rocks, shifting and grinding as if they were trying to burst out of his skull. He thought the pain would never end. But when his hangover did finally pass he found himself experiencing a new emotion. Defiance. He was an innocent man, after all. None of the bad things that had happened were his fault. That was for damn sure. He was the one who'd foreseen them. Who'd warned his boss about them. Time after time. In public and in private. And who'd been ignored. Time after time. So after seven days holed up alone, Rutherford decided it was time to show his face. To tell his side of the story. To anyone who would listen.

He took a shower and dug some clothes out of his closet. Chinos and a polo shirt. Brand new. Sombre colours, with logos, to show he meant business. Then he retrieved his shoes from the opposite corners of the hallway where he'd flung them. Scooped up his keys and sunglasses from the bookcase by the door. Stepped out into the corridor. Rode down in the elevator, alone. Crossed the lobby. Pushed through the heavy revolving door and paused on the sidewalk. The mid-morning sun felt like a blast furnace and its sudden heat drew beads of sweat from his forehead and armpits. He felt a flutter of panic. Guilty people sweat. He'd read that somewhere, and the one thing he was desperate to avoid was looking guilty. He glanced around, convinced that everyone would be staring at him, then forced himself to move. He picked up the pace, feeling more conspicuous than if he'd been walking down the street naked. But the truth was that most of the people he passed didn't even notice he was there. In fact, only two of them paid him any attention at all.

*

The same time Rusty Rutherford was coming out of his apartment, Jack Reacher was breaking into a bar. He was in Nashville, Tennessee, seventy-five miles north and east of Rutherford's sleepy little town, and he was searching for the solution to a problem. It was a practical matter, primarily. A question of physics. And biology. Specifically, how to suspend a guy from a ceiling without causing too much permanent damage. To the ceiling, at least. He was less concerned about the guy.

The ceiling belonged to the bar. And the bar belonged to the guy. Reacher had first set foot in the place a little over a day earlier. On Saturday. Almost Sunday, because it was close to midnight by the time he got into town. His journey had not been smooth. The first bus he rode caught on fire and its replacement got wedged under a low bridge after its driver took a wrong turn twenty miles out. Reacher was stiff from the prolonged sitting when he eventually climbed out at the Greyhound station so he moved away to the side, near the smokers' pen, and took a few minutes to stretch the soreness out of his muscles and joints. He stood there, half hidden in the shadows, while the rest of the passengers milled around and talked and did things with their phones and reclaimed their luggage and gradually drifted away.

Reacher stayed where he was. He was in no hurry. He'd arrived later than expected, but that was no major problem. He had no appointments to keep. No meetings to attend. No one was waiting for him, getting worried or getting mad. He'd planned to find a place to stay for the night. A diner, for some food. And a bar where he could hear some good music. He should still be able to do all those things. He'd maybe have to switch the order around. Maybe combine a couple of activities. But he'd live. And with some hotels, the kind Reacher preferred, it can work to show up late. Especially if you're paying cash. Which he always did.

Music first, Reacher decided. He knew there was no shortage of venues in Nashville, but he wanted a particular kind of place. Somewhere worn. With some history. Where Blind Blake could have played, back in the day. Howlin' Wolf, even. Certainly nowhere new, or gentrified, or gussied up. The only question was how to find a place like that. The lights were still on in the bus depot, and a handful of people were still working or waiting or just keeping themselves off the street. Some of them were bound to be local. Maybe all of them were. Reacher could have asked for directions. But he didn't go in. He preferred to navigate by instinct. He knew cities. He could read their shape and flow like a sailor can sense the direction of the coming waves. His gut told him to go north, so he set off across a broad triangular intersection and on to a vacant lot strewn with rubble. The heavy odour of diesel and cigarettes faded behind him, and his shadow grew longer in front as he walked. It led the way to rows of narrow, parallel streets lined with similar brick buildings, stained with soot. It felt industrial, but decayed and hollow. Reacher didn't know what kinds of businesses had thrived in

Nashville's past, but whatever had been made or sold or stored it had clearly happened around there. And it clearly wasn't happening any more. The structures were all that remained. And not for much longer, Reacher thought. Either money would flow in and shore them up, or they'd collapse.

Reacher stepped off the crumbling sidewalk and continued down the centre of the street. He figured he'd give it another two blocks. Three at the most. If he hadn't found anything good by then he'd strike out to the right, towards the river. He passed a place that sold part-worn tyres. A warehouse that a charity was using to store donated furniture. Then, as he crossed the next street, he picked up the rumble of a bass guitar and the thunder of drums.

The sound was coming from a building in the centre of the block. It didn't look promising. There were no windows. No signage. Just a thin strip of yellow light escaping from beneath a single wooden door. Reacher didn't like places with few potential exits so he was inclined to keep walking, but as he drew level the door opened. Two guys, maybe in their late twenties, with sleeveless T-shirts and a smattering of anaemic tattoos, stumbled out on to the sidewalk. Reacher moved to avoid them, and at the same moment a guitar began to wail from inside. Reacher paused. The riff was good. It built and swelled and soared, and just as it seemed to be done and its final note was dying away a woman's voice took over. It was mournful, desperate, agonizing, like a conduit to a world of the deepest imaginable

6

sorrow. Reacher couldn't resist. He stepped across the threshold.

The air inside smelled of beer and sweat, and the space was much shallower front to back than Reacher had expected. It was also wider, effectively creating two separate areas with a dead zone down the middle. The right-hand side was for the music lovers. There were a couple dozen that night, some standing, some dancing, some doing a bit of both. The stage was beyond them, against the far wall, taking up the full depth of the room. It was low, built out of beer crates with some kind of wooden sheeting nailed across the top. There was a modest speaker stack at each side, and a pair of metal bars hanging from the ceiling to hold the lights. The singer was front and centre. She seemed tiny to Reacher. Five feet tall at the most, and as thin as a needle. Her hair was in a perfect blonde bob that shone so brightly Reacher wondered if it was a wig. The guitar player was to her left, nearest the door. The bassist mirrored him on her right. They both had wild curly hair and high, sharp cheekbones, and looked so alike they could have been twins. Certainly brothers. The drummer was there too, pounding out the beat, but the shadow at the back of the stage was too deep for Reacher to see her clearly.

The left-hand side was for drinking. There were six round tables, each with four chairs, and four stools at the bar which was set against the wall, opposite the stage. It was kitted out with the usual array of beer pumps and bottle fridges and spirit dispensers. A mirror

7

ran its full width with a jagged star-shaped fracture midway up in the centre. The result of a bottle being thrown, Reacher thought. He liked the way it looked. It added character. But it wasn't enough to outweigh the biggest flaw in the place. The section of ceiling in front of the bar. Hanging from it were dozens of bras. Maybe hundreds. There were all kinds of styles and colours and sizes. Where they'd come from Reacher didn't want to know. It seemed sleazy to him. Unnecessary. And bad from a practical point of view. To get to the bar anyone reasonably tall would have to either push his way through or stoop down beneath them. Reacher waited until the band finished their last song then bent at the waist and pivoted around until he was close enough to snag a bar stool. He was the only one on that side of the room, and he couldn't tell from the bartender's blank expression whether that was a situation he was happy with or not.

'Coffee,' Reacher said, when the bartender finally acknowledged him. 'Black.'

'Don't have coffee,' the bartender replied.

'OK. Cheeseburger. Fries. No lettuce. No pickle. And a Coke.'

'Don't have cheeseburgers.'

'What food do you have?'

'Don't have food.'

'Where around here does?'

The bartender shrugged. 'Don't live around here.'

Reacher took his Coke and turned to look at the stage. He was hoping another band would set up but there was no sign of activity. Half the audience had drifted across and congregated around the tables. The rest had already made for the door. With no more music and no hope of food Reacher figured he might as well finish his drink and follow them out. He continued in the direction he'd been going before he was lured inside, but when he reached the alley at the far end of the building he heard a scuffling noise. He turned, and almost collided with the guitar player from the band he'd just heard. The guy took a step back, his eyes wide with fear and his guitar case raised like a shield. The singer almost piled into him from behind. Reacher held up his hands, palms facing out. He was aware of the effect his appearance could have. He was six feet five. Two hundred and fifty pounds. His hair was a dishevelled mess. He was unshaved. Children had been known to run screaming at the sight of him.

'I'm sorry, guys.' Reacher attempted a reassuring smile. 'I didn't mean to startle you.'

The guitarist lowered his case but he didn't step forward.

'Great performance tonight, by the way,' Reacher said. 'When are you playing again?'

'Thanks.' The guitarist stayed back. 'Soon. I hope.'

'Here?'

'No chance.'

'Why? Bad crowd?'

'No. Bad owner.'

'Wait.' The singer glared up at Reacher. 'Why are you here? Do you work for him?'

'I don't work for anyone,' Reacher said. 'But what's bad about the owner? What's the problem?'

The singer hesitated, then held up one finger, then another. 'He wouldn't pay us. And he ripped us off. He stole a guitar.'

'One of mine,' the guitarist said. 'My good spare.'

'Really?' Reacher stepped back. 'That doesn't sound like good business practice. There has to be more to the story.'

'Like what?' The singer looked at the guitarist.

'Like nothing,' he said. 'We finished our set. Packed up. Asked for our money. He refused.'

'I don't get it.' Reacher paused. 'A place like this, music's the draw. Not the décor. That's for damn sure. You need bands to have music. And if you don't pay the bands, how do you get them to play? Sounds like a self-defeating strategy to me. You must have done something to piss him off.'

'You don't get the music business.' The guitarist shook his head.

'Explain it to me.'

'Why?'

'Why? Because I'm asking you to. I like information. Learning is a virtue.'

The guitarist rested his case on the ground. 'What's to explain? This kind of thing happens all the time. There's nothing we can do about it.'

'Bands don't have the power.' The singer put her hand on the guitarist's shoulder. 'The venues do.'

'Isn't there anyone who could help you put things

right? Your manager? Your agent? Don't musicians have those kinds of people?'

The guitarist shook his head. 'Successful musicians, maybe. Not us.'

'Not yet,' the singer said.

'The police, then?'

'No.' The singer's hand brushed her jacket pocket. 'No police.'

'We can't involve them,' the guitarist said. 'We get a name for being difficult, no one will book us.'

'What's the point in getting booked, if you don't get paid?'

'The point is, we get to play. People hear us.' The singer tapped the side of her head. 'You can't get discovered if you don't get heard.'

'I guess.' Reacher paused. 'Although if I'm honest, I think you need to consider the message you're sending.'

'What message?' The guitarist leaned one shoulder against the wall. 'Suck it up. That's all we can do.'

'That's how we're going to make it,' the singer said. 'In the end.'

Reacher said nothing.

'What? You think we're doing the wrong thing?'

'Maybe I'm out of line.' Reacher looked at each of them in turn. 'But it seems to me you're telling the club owners it's OK to rip you off. That you're happy not to get paid.'

'That's crazy,' the singer said. 'I hate not getting paid. It's the worst.'

'Did you make that clear?'

'Of course.' The guitar player straightened up. 'I did. I insisted he pay us. He made like he was going to, and took me to his office. Only a guy was waiting there. The bouncer. He's huge. They must have planned the whole thing in advance because he didn't say anything. Didn't wait. Just grabbed my hand. My left.' He held up his left hand to emphasize the point. 'He grabbed it and pushed it down on to the desk where there's this kind of metal plate. It's all dented and stained. Anyway, he held my hand there, and the owner went around the desk and opened the top drawer. He took out a hammer. Used the claw thing to spread my fingers apart, then said I had to choose. We could have the money, and he'd break my fingers. One at a time. Or I could leave, unhurt, with no cash.'

Reacher was conscious of a voice in his head telling him to walk away. Saying this wasn't his problem. But he had heard how the guy could make a guitar wail. He remembered watching his fingers when he was on stage. They were the opposite of Reacher's own. Quick and delicate, dancing across the strings. He pictured the thug grabbing his hand. The owner, wielding the hammer. He stayed where he was.

'If you like, I could go back in there,' Reacher said. 'Help the owner see things from a different angle. Maybe get him to reconsider tonight's fee.'

'You could do that?' The singer didn't look convinced.

'I've been told I can be very persuasive.'

'You could get hurt.'

'Someone could. Not me.'

'He has a hammer.' The guitarist shuffled on the spot.

'I doubt the hammer will come into play. And there wouldn't be a problem if it did. So why don't I give it a try? What have you got to lose?'

'I'm not sure I'm—'

'Thank you.' The singer cut him off. 'We appreciate any help you can give us. Just please be careful.'

'I always am,' Reacher said. 'Now, tell me about the guitar. Your good spare. The guy really stole it?'

'The big guy did,' the guitarist said. 'Kind of. He followed me down from the office and snatched it. Then he tossed it down the stairs to the basement and looked at me all weird, like he was daring me to go get it.'

'You left it there?'

The guitarist looked away.

'Don't feel bad. That was the right move.' Reacher paused. 'Was it worth much?'

'A grand, maybe?' The guitarist shrugged. 'That's a lot to me.'

'And the owner, with the hammer. What's his name?'

'Lockhart. Derek Lockhart.'

'How much did he promise to pay you?'

'Two hundred dollars.'

'OK. And aside from Lockhart, the guy who was with him in the office, and the bartender, who else works there?'

'No one.'

13

'There is someone,' the singer said. 'A kid who busses tables. He's out back most of the time, smoking weed.'

'Anyone else?'

'No.'

'Have you seen any weapons on the premises?'

They looked at one another and shook their heads.

'OK then. Where's Lockhart's office?'

'Second floor,' the guitarist said. 'Stairs are past the bathrooms.'

Back inside, a solitary customer was nursing his last bottle of beer. The barman was shoving a threadbare broom across the floor between the tables and the stage. There was no sign of anyone else so Reacher made his way past the bathrooms and crept up the stairs. He saw one door leading off a narrow landing. It was closed. Reacher could hear a voice on the other side. It was male, he was sure of that, but he couldn't make out any words. They were soft. Rhythmic. Like someone counting. Probably checking the week's take. So they'd likely be locked in. Reacher took hold of the handle. Turned it. And simultaneously slammed his shoulder into the door. It gave easily, sending fragments of splintered wood spinning into the air.

'I'm sorry, gentlemen.' He stepped into the room and pushed the door back into its ruined frame. 'I didn't realize that was locked.'

The space was small. More like a closet than an office. Two men were crammed in behind the desk, shoulder to shoulder. The regular-size guy Reacher took to be

14

Lockhart. The other, a slack, flabby giant, would be the bouncer. Both were frozen in their seats. And the surface of the desk was covered with heaps of creased, greasy banknotes.

'Who the hell are you?' It took Lockhart a moment to find his voice.

'My name's Jack Reacher. I represent the band that played for you tonight. I'm here to talk about their contract.'

'They don't have a contract.'

'They do now.' Reacher took hold of a bentwood chair which was the only other piece of furniture in the room, tested its strength, and sat down.

'Time for you to leave,' Lockhart said.

'I only just got here.'

'You can't be here. Not during the count.'

'You didn't think that through all the way, did you?'

Lockhart paused, searching for a trap. 'What do you mean?'

'You said I can't be here. And yet clearly I am. Faulty reasoning on your part.'

'You can leave.' Lockhart spoke with exaggerated clarity. 'Or I can throw you out.'

'*You* can throw me out?' Reacher allowed himself a smile.

Lockhart's fist clenched on the desk in front of him. 'I can have you thrown out.'

'Are you sure? Where are all your guys?'

'I have all the guys I need, right here.' Lockhart pointed to his companion.

'Him? For a start, he's one guy. Singular. So you'd have to say "the only guy I need". But that's not right either, is it? Because he's obviously not up to the job. I could be asleep and he couldn't throw me out. I could have died of old age and he still couldn't do it.'

Reacher was watching the big guy's eyes throughout the whole exchange. He saw them flicker towards Lockhart. Saw Lockhart respond with the tiniest nod of his head. The big guy rose out of his chair. Reacher knew there was only one possible play that stood any chance of success. The guy could launch himself straight over the desk. If he was quick enough he'd arrive before Reacher was on his feet. But even if Reacher was already standing, the guy would still have his most powerful weapon. His weight. He had at least a hundred pounds on Reacher. Coupled with the speed he'd have gained diving forward, all those pounds would translate into some formidable momentum. There'd be no way for Reacher to counter it. He'd be knocked backwards on to the floor. Pinned down. Jammed in the corner, unable to bring his fists or feet or elbows to bear. And unable to breathe. Then all the guy would have to do would be wait. Physics would finish the fight for him. He could just lie there till Reacher passed out. It would be the easiest victory he ever won.

The guy made the wrong choice. Instead of diving over the table he tried to shimmy around it. That was a serious mistake for someone with his build. Reacher's goading had clouded his thinking. He wasn't focused on the win. He was picturing the pummelling he could dish out. Which gave Reacher time to scoop up the metal plate from the desk. Grip it securely with one edge against his palms. And drive it up into the guy's onrushing neck like a reversed guillotine blade, crushing his larynx and windpipe. Then Reacher shoved him square in the face and the guy fell back in the direction he came from and landed, choking and spluttering, in the corner.

'Normally I wouldn't have done that,' Reacher said, settling back in his chair. 'Not right off the bat. I'd have given him a chance to walk away. But then I remembered he was the one who took the kid's guitar, so I figured all bets were off.'

Lockhart was scrabbling for his phone. 'We should call 911. Quick.'

'Your friend will be fine,' Reacher said. 'Or maybe he won't. But in the meantime, while he's dealing with his breathing issues, let's get back to the band's contract. You promised to pay how much?'

'I promised nothing.'

Reacher ran his finger along the edge of the plate. 'I think you did.'

Lockhart lunged sideways, going for his drawer. Reacher tracked his movement and tossed the plate, spinning it like a frisbee. It caught Lockhart on the bridge of his nose, shattering the bone and rocking him back in his chair.

'I'm beginning to think this toy is dangerous.' Reacher picked up the plate and dropped it on the floor. 'You shouldn't play with it any more. Now. The contract. Give me a number.'

'Two hundred dollars.'

'Two hundred dollars was the original figure. But since it was agreed, you've revealed an interest in human fingers. Tell me, how many are there on a guitar player's left hand, for example?'

'Five.' Lockhart's voice was muffled thanks to his restricted airway.

'Technically there are four. The other digit is a thumb. But I'll take your answer. So two hundred dollars multiplied by five is . . . ?'

'A thousand.'

'Very good. That's our new figure. We take cash.'

'Forget it.'

'There's plenty of cash here. If counting is too difficult for you, maybe I should just take all of it?'

'All right.' Lockhart almost squealed. He selected two stacks of bills and slid them across the desk.

'Good. Now let's add your late payment fee. That's an additional five hundred.'

Lockhart glowered, and handed over another stack.

'We're almost done now. Next up is the equipment replacement surcharge. A round one thousand.'

'What the—'

'For the kid's guitar. Your buddy tossed it down some stairs. Get the money back from him if you want, but there's no way it's coming out of my client's pocket.'

Lockhart's eyes were flickering back and forth across his dwindling heap of cash. Reacher could almost see his brain working as he calculated how much he had left, and whether his chances of keeping

18

any would improve if he cooperated. 'OK. Another thousand. But not one cent more. And tell those kids if they ever come back, I'll break more than their fingers. And even if they don't come here, they'll never play in this town again.'

Reacher shook his head. 'We were doing so well, and you had to ruin it. You didn't let me finish. We'd covered the payments. But we hadn't gotten around to the incentives. This is important, so listen carefully. Every band member I represent has me on speed dial. If anything happens to any of them, I'll come back here. I'll break your arms. I'll break your legs. And I'll hang *your* underwear from the ceiling of the bar. While you're still wearing it. Are we clear?'

Lockhart nodded.

'Good. Now, incentive number two: other bands. Even if I don't represent them, I'm extending an umbrella agreement. As a courtesy. Think of it as my contribution to the arts. What it means is that if I hear about you ripping off another band, I'll come back. I'll take all your money. And I'll hang your underwear from the ceiling of the bar, same way as before. Are we clear on that, too?'

Lockhart nodded.

'Excellent. And in case you were wondering, I'll be carrying out random spot checks to test for compliance. Now, when is the next band playing here?'

'Tomorrow.'

'OK. I hope they're as good as tonight's. But even if they're not, remember. They get paid.'

19

TWO

Rusty Rutherford was not normally the type of guy who dawdled in his local coffee shop. He used to go to the same one every day. Always on his way to work. And purely for the caffeine. He didn't go in search of conversation. He wasn't interested in finding new company. His routine was always the same. He stood quietly in line and used the time to contemplate whatever problems were in store for him that day. He placed his order. Collected his drink as soon as it was ready. And left. The process was transactional, not social. Even after the week he spent isolated in his apartment it proved a difficult habit to break.

The adjustment process wasn't made any easier by the response he received from the other patrons. Normally his was a pretty neutral presence. People weren't pleased to see him. They weren't displeased. They displayed no curiosity. No animosity. He could have been a store mannequin for all the effect he had on the social interactions that occurred in the place. That

Monday, though, he felt like a magnet with the wrong polarity. He seemed to repel everyone around him. The surrounding customers left a bigger space than usual on either side. In the rare moments he was able to make eye contact the other person turned away before he could think of a way to start a conversation. By the time he reached the counter he still hadn't exchanged a single word with a fellow human being. But he had seen how the barista interacted with the two men in front of him when they stepped up to order. She smiled at them. And asked if they wanted their regular. She didn't smile at him. And she didn't say a word.

'My regular, please,' Rusty said.

'Which would be what?' she asked.

Rusty heard someone sniggering behind him in the line. He felt the urge to run. But no, he was there on principle. To fight for his rights. A little ridicule was not going to break his resolve. 'House blend, medium, no room for milk.'

'Two dollars even.' The barista turned, grabbed a to-go cup, and slammed it on the counter.

'No.' Rusty shook his head. 'I want to drink it here.'

The barista shot him a look that said *Really? I'd rather you didn't.*

'Oh, that's right,' she said out loud. 'I forgot. You lost your job. You don't have any place to go.' She tossed the to-go cup in the trash, took out a china one, poured, slopping coffee into the saucer, and slid it towards him, spilling even more.

*

21

The same time Rusty Rutherford was going into the coffee shop, a telephone was starting to ring. In a house a mile outside of town. In a room containing two people. A man and a woman. The woman recognized the ringtone the moment the phone began to chirp. She knew what it meant. Her boss was going to require privacy, so she stood up without waiting to be dismissed. Closed her notebook. Slid it into the pocket at the front of her apron. And made her way to the door.

The man checked that the *secure* icon on the phone's screen was green, then hit the answer key. 'This is Speranski.'

Speranski wasn't his real name, of course, but it might as well have been. He'd been using it professionally for more than five decades.

The voice at the other end of the line said one word: 'Contact.'

Speranski closed his eyes for a moment and ran the fingers of his free hand through his wild white hair. It was about time. He had made plenty of plans over the years. Been involved in plenty of operations. Survived plenty of crises. But never had the stakes been so high.

For him. Personally. And for the only person in the world he cared about.

The same time the telephone was being answered, Jack Reacher was getting into a car. He had solved his physics/biology conundrum to his satisfaction – and the bar owner's extreme discomfort – and begun walking back to the bus station. He had been planning to follow his time-honoured principle of taking the first bus to leave, regardless of its destination, when he heard a vehicle approaching slowly from behind. He stuck out his thumb on the off chance and to his surprise the car stopped. It was new and shiny and bland. A rental. Probably picked up at the airport. The driver was a tidy-looking guy in his early twenties. He was wearing a plain dark suit and the speed of his breathing and the pallor of his face suggested he wasn't far from a full-blown panic attack. A business guy, Reacher thought. Let out alone for the first time. Desperate not to screw anything up. And therefore screwing up everything he touched.

'Excuse me, sir.' The guy sounded even more nervous than he looked. 'Do you know the way to I40? I need to go west.' He gestured at a screen on his dashboard. 'The GPS in this thing hates me. It keeps trying to send me down streets that don't exist.'

'Sure,' Reacher said. 'But it's hard to explain. It would be easier to show you.'

The guy hesitated and looked Reacher up and down as if only just taking in his height. The breadth of his chest. His unwashed hair. His unshaved face. The web of scars around the knuckles of his enormous hands.

'Unless you'd prefer to keep driving aimlessly around?' Reacher attempted a concerned expression.

The guy swallowed. 'Where are you going?'

'Anywhere. I40 is as good a place to start as any.'

'Well, OK.' The guy paused. 'I'll take you to the

highway. But I'm not going far after that. No place you'd want to go, I'm sure.'

'How much further?'

'Seventy-five miles, maybe. Some small town near a place named Pleasantville. Sounds inspiring, huh?'

'Do they have a coffee shop in this town?'

The guy shrugged. 'Probably. I can't say for sure. I've never been there before.'

'Probably's good enough for me,' Reacher said. 'Let's go.'

Rutherford picked up the cup and realized he had another unfamiliar dilemma to face. Where should he sit? Deciding wasn't a problem, normally. He didn't stay. And he didn't have a dozen angry eyes probing him while he searched for an answer. He fought the urge to skulk at the back of the store. That would be the least uncomfortable option, for sure, but it would hardly serve his purpose. He didn't want a window seat either – he wasn't ready to put himself on display quite so prominently – so he opted for a small, square table in the centre. It had two chairs covered in red vinyl and its top had writing scrawled across every square inch of its surface. By previous customers, he guessed. There were song lyrics. Poems. Uplifting sayings. He scanned the words, found none he felt any connection to, then forced himself to look up. He attempted to make eye contact with the people at the other tables. And failed. Except with a toddler, whose parents got up and left when they realized what was going on. Rusty sipped at his coffee.

He wanted to make it last at least an hour. He worked his way down to the dregs. And still achieved no inter-action with anyone but the barista, who missed no opportunity to shoot him hostile glares. He refilled his cup and changed tables. Neither thing brought a change of luck. He stuck it out for another forty minutes, and then the barista approached and told him to either order some food or leave.

'I won't order any food,' Rusty told her. 'I'll leave. But I'll come back tomorrow. And the next day. And every day after that until everyone believes I'm innocent.'

The barista gave him a blank look and retreated to the counter.

Rusty stood up. 'Listen to me,' he said.

No one paid any attention.

'Listen to me!' Rusty raised his voice. 'What happened to the town totally sucks. I get that. But it was not my fault. None of it. The truth is I tried to stop it from happening. And I was the only one who did.'

No one paid any attention.

The barista leaned across the counter with a to-go cup in her hand. 'Take this and leave, Mr Rutherford. No one believes you. And no one ever will.'

The same time Rusty Rutherford was leaving the coffee shop, Jack Reacher was arriving in his town. Getting out of Nashville hadn't been a problem. Reacher had navigated using his instinct plus the landmarks he remembered from Saturday night's bus ride and had found the highway without getting them lost. Not so lost that the driver noticed, anyway. Once they were out of the city Reacher persuaded him to tune the radio to a local blues channel, then reclined his seat and closed his eyes. The music was half decent but despite that the guy wouldn't stop talking. About New York. The insurance company he worked for. How this was his first case after getting a promotion to Negotiator. Flying out that morning for a meeting at their field office. Getting lost on his way to whichever town had whatever kind of problem he was supposed to help solve. Something to do with computers. And foreign governments. And keys and portals and all kinds of other things Reacher had no interest in. He let the words wash over him and settled into a comfortable doze, only opening his eyes when he felt the car slow and they turned on to a state highway heading south. The half mile beyond the cloverleaf was teeming with restaurants and drive-throughs and car dealers and chain hotels. After that the terrain opened out. There were farmers' fields where the land was flat, stretched and warped into all kinds of irregular shapes by the sweeping contours, and groves of tall mature trees where the land was steep. After ten minutes they swung west again and continued along a steeper, twistier road for the best part of an hour until they entered the outskirts of the town. The guy kept driving until they found what Reacher guessed was the main street, then pulled over.

Reacher climbed out and took stock of his new surroundings. The place was unobjectionable, he thought.

A late nineteenth-century core supplemented by an influx of cash in the fifties, judging by the buildings. Some old ones weeded out. Some newer ones to fill the gaps, now showing their own age. The overall layout unchanged. A standard grid. Compact enough to require traffic signals at one intersection only. They were out that day, which was causing consternation among some of the passing drivers. But aside from that things were fine. Good enough for a pit stop, anyway. Reacher figured he could pass a half hour there. There was no ancestral connection. No intriguing name. No military significance. No interesting signs or structures. No link to any of his musical heroes. No reason to stay. No longer than it took to get coffee, anyway. Priorities were priorities.

Reacher was half a block from the intersection with the broken signals at the west end of what he figured was the town's main drag. There was a coffee shop diagonally opposite. There may have been others elsewhere in the town but Reacher saw no reason to check. He wasn't fussy. So he took advantage of the traffic chaos and started out across the street.

Reacher was heading for the coffee shop. Rutherford was leaving it. Reacher didn't pay him much attention at first. He was just a guy, small and unremarkable, holding his to-go cup, going about his business. Whatever that may be. But a moment later Reacher's interest ratcheted all the way up. He felt a chill at the base of his neck. A signal from some ancient warning system hardwired into the back of his brain.

27

An instinctive recognition. Pattern and movement. Predators circling. Moving in on their prey. Two men and a woman. Spread out. Carefully positioned. Coordinated. Ready to spring their trap.

Three against one. Not the kind of odds to worry Reacher. But Reacher was not their target. That was clear.

The men were positioned at each end of the block. One was pretending to look in a store window at the west end, right before the intersection with the broken signals. The other was at the east end, where the block ended at an alleyway, pretending to do something with his phone. An envelope of maybe 130 feet. The woman was stationed on the other side of the alleyway, at the start of the next block. Another ten feet away. There was a solid row of buildings to the north of the sidewalk. The street to the south. Store entrances to bolt into, if the timing was right. Asphalt to run across, if no traffic was coming.

Rutherford was heading east. Not hurrying. Not dawdling. Just drifting along in his own little bubble. Not aimless, Reacher thought. More like preoccupied. Following a familiar route. Comfortable with his surroundings. Not paying attention. Not looking for store entrances. Not checking the traffic.

The west-end guy was around five feet ten. He was wearing a plain black T-shirt and cargo pants. His hair was buzzed short and he had an earpiece like the kind Reacher had seen business people use. The east-end guy was the same kind of size. He had the same clothes. The same hair. The same earpiece. The woman on the other side of the alley was also wearing black but her clothes were more fitted and her hair wasn't buzzed. It was long and red and she had it tied back in a ponytail.

The west-end guy peeled away from his window and started walking. Heading east. Fifteen feet behind Rutherford. Moving with loose, rangy ease. He was clearly having to shorten his stride to avoid overtaking his mark. Ahead of them a woman had stopped at the edge of the sidewalk to tend to a child in a stroller. Beyond her a couple stood, talking. They were dressed for the gym. Just regular folks. Not part of the pattern. Unaware of what was happening.

The envelope was down to a hundred feet.

The east-end guy touched his earpiece. A moment later a car appeared in the mouth of the alley. It had rolled forward from somewhere deep in the shadows. An anonymous sedan. A Toyota. Dark blue. Reacher saw it move rather than heard it. A hybrid in fully electric mode, he thought. A smart choice of vehicle. Too bad the 110th hadn't had them back in the day.

The envelope was down to eighty feet. Reacher stepped on to the sidewalk.

Rutherford approached the woman with the stroller. She stood up as he drew level. Her kid threw his teddy bear on to the ground. Rutherford leaned down and retrieved it. Maybe Rutherford wasn't as clueless as he appeared. It was a perfect manoeuvre to check the sidewalk behind him. Maybe Rutherford knew he was being followed, after all. Then Reacher's optimism evaporated. Rutherford's eyes were only on the kid. He held out the toy. The woman snatched it away, glaring furiously. Rutherford continued walking.

The envelope was down to sixty feet. Reacher changed course. Started heading east. Thirty feet behind the western guy.

The couple in gym clothes moved away from the wall. Their body language had hardened. Their conversation must have turned sour. The man strode forward, leading with his shoulder. He slammed into Rutherford, spilling his coffee. His partner caught up. She grabbed his arm and pulled him away, shaking her head and scowling.

'Hey!' Rutherford said. He didn't get a response.

Turn around, Reacher thought. *Ignore the gym rats. Notice the guy who's pursuing you.*

Rutherford didn't turn around. He carried on walking.

The envelope was down to forty feet. Another twenty feet between Reacher and the western guy.

It was obvious what was going to happen next. Reacher could see it as clearly as if a skywriter had spelled it out with white smoke. The car would roll a little further forward so that its rear door was level with the sidewalk. The eastern guy would open it. The western guy would push Rutherford inside and jump in himself. The woman would get in on the other side. The eastern guy would take the passenger seat. And they'd drive away. Less than five seconds for the whole operation, if they did it right. And it would be silent. No muss, no fuss. No one would see a thing.

The envelope was twenty feet. Ten feet between Reacher and the western guy. Decision time.

It was four against one, now. Maybe five or six against one if they had a mobile backup. Not the kind of odds to bother Reacher. But Reacher was not their target.

The car moved up, right on cue. Rutherford stopped, thinking nothing of it. Just an impatient driver taking a short cut through the alley. He took a sip of coffee, waiting for the car to pull away. It stayed put. The eastern guy opened the back door and held it. The other quickened his pace. He stretched out. His left hand cupped the top of Rutherford's head. His right grabbed Rutherford's elbow. He started to steer him towards the back seat. But he was too slow. All he wound up pushing was empty air.

The envelope was zero feet. Reacher was level with the western guy, on his left-hand side. He took hold of Rutherford's collar. Stuck his right arm across the western guy's chest like a steel barrier. Pivoted clockwise on his right foot. Pushed Rutherford back and to the side. And held him there, out of anyone else's range.

'Let's keep things civil,' Reacher said. 'Show me some ID, or get in the car and drive away.'

'Let him go,' the western guy said.

'If you have a legitimate reason to detain him, you'll have some kind of official ID. If you do, show it to me. If you don't, drive away. This is your last chance.'

31

'Who the hell are you?'

'Given the situation, you should stick to the relevant issues.'

'Who are you?'

'I gave you two options. Asking irrelevant questions was not one of them.'

'Let him go.' The guy went to step around Reacher, his arm stretched out, trying to grab Rutherford. Reacher hit him in the temple and he bounced off the wall and dropped like a puppet with its strings cut.

Reacher turned to the other guy. 'You've had your final chance. Pick up your trash and leave. Or don't, and get added to the pile. Make your choice. Either way's fine with me.'

Reacher caught movement out of the corner of his eye. The Toyota's passenger window was rolling down. The driver was lifting her arm. She was looking directly at him. Raising a gun? Reacher didn't wait to find out. He let go of Rutherford and spun the eastern guy around so that he was facing the car. Grabbed his collar and waistband. And launched him headfirst through the open window, jamming him in tight, his arms pinned and his legs kicking helplessly.

Reacher stepped back to avoid the flailing feet and checked that Rutherford was still there, frozen to the spot. Then he sensed rather than heard a heavy object racing towards them. He grabbed Rutherford and shoved him back and a moment later a black Chevy Suburban lurched on to the sidewalk, stopping right where Reacher had been standing. The driver's door opened and a man jumped out. He was shorter than the others, and wirier. Another man jumped down from the passenger side and joined him. They stood side by side for a moment, both in a version of some strange martial arts stance, then relaxed. They stepped forward. They were comfortable together. They had clearly done this kind of thing before.

'Step aside, mister,' the driver said. 'This isn't your fight. The guy's coming with us.'

Reacher shook his head. 'You're not taking him. That's a given. He walks away. The only question is, will you? Or do you have some strong urge to join your buddies in the hospital?'

The driver didn't reply and Reacher became aware of a scrabbling sound on the far side of the Suburban. The guy he'd thrown through the Toyota's window had wriggled free and along with the woman from the alley was trying to manoeuvre their unconscious comrade into the back seat. A ring of onlookers had formed, starting on the sidewalk and spilling on to the street. It reminded Reacher of the crowds that would gather in the playgrounds on the first day of each new school he attended, growing up. Him and his brother, Joe. Back to back. Fighting them off. He looked at Rutherford. He wasn't trying to run, which was something. But Reacher knew he'd be no help if the mob turned nasty.

The two guys exchanged glances. They were considering their next move. Stealth was out of the window so it was down to a choice between a frontal assault and a tactical withdrawal. Neither option seemed to appeal.

Then a siren started up. The pedestrians scattered. The car pulled away, its gas engine kicking in as the driver buried the accelerator. The wiry guys jumped back into the Suburban and slammed it into reverse, clipping the front corner of the leading police cruiser before racing into the distance. Rutherford stayed still, his eyes wide and his mouth hanging open.

The pair of police cars stopped at the side of the street and killed their sirens and light bars. Four officers jumped out. Three converged immediately on the sidewalk. One lingered to inspect the damage to his car. All had their guns drawn, but not raised. They expected their numbers to give them the advantage, Reacher guessed, but were taking no chances. Which seemed like a sensible attitude to take.

'On the ground,' the lead officer said. 'Face down.'

'You're arresting us?' Reacher said.

'What were you expecting? A lollipop? Get on the ground.'

Reacher didn't move.

The officer stepped closer. 'On the ground. Do it now.'

Cops are the same the world over. Once they commit to a position in public they never back down. Trying to make them is a waste of time. Reacher knew that from personal experience. But still, there are standards to uphold.

'All right,' Reacher said. 'I'll let you arrest us. We'll be released in five minutes, anyway. But we're not getting on the ground.'

THREE

The team's temporary base had been established the week before in a motel eight miles west of town. Traffic was light so theoretically the ground could be covered in twelve minutes without drawing unwelcome attention. But that afternoon the occupants of both vehicles took substantially longer to get back.

The guys from the Suburban made it first. It was easier for them since neither was injured. They started by heading ten miles north. The driver, who went by the name of Vasili, gave it an initial blast to get clear of the arriving police, then slowed to just above the limit until they reached a patch of waste ground behind a dense stand of trees. The place was secluded enough but they knew better than to torch the damaged vehicle. That would be the same as texting a map to the cops and saying *Here's the SUV you're looking for.* And if it could be salvaged the Suburban would still be a valuable asset, so they got to work. Vasili lined up on a concrete post at the end of a fence by the side of the road and slammed back into it. He pulled forward and repeated the manoeuvre then climbed out to check the damage. It was satisfactory, he decided. Deep enough to obscure the dent sustained when they clipped the police car but not so extensive as to give a different cop an excuse to pull them over. He drove around behind the trees and wiped down the interior while his partner, who used the name Anatole, swapped the plates. Then they switched to their secondary vehicle for the final thirteen-mile diagonal stretch.

Natasha was driving the Toyota. She started out going south for six miles. She took it very easy. She had an additional reason to drive slowly. She was worried about two of her companions. The guy Reacher had thrown through the window, *Petya*, had wound up with an injured shoulder. Natasha wasn't sure if the damage had been done going in or wriggling out. He had kept quiet at the time but now his face was pale and he groaned every time they hit a bump or a pothole. *Ilya*, the guy Reacher hit, was still out cold. Natasha was concerned about concussion and didn't want to cause any additional damage. She wanted both of them back in the game as soon as humanly possible. It was hard not to paint what had happened that afternoon as anything but a failure. With failure comes the danger of replacement. That danger grows if the team is left under strength. And that danger had to be avoided at all costs.

After fifteen minutes they pulled into a lot belonging to a chintzy roadside diner. Natasha switched plates while the other woman, *Sonya*, helped Petya into their secondary vehicle. Together the two women transferred the unconscious Ilya and sanitized the Toyota's interior. Then they set out for the motel, looping further west than strictly necessary, which stretched the final leg out to twelve miles.

Natasha had taken her time at each stage of the journey. Partly due to thorough training. Partly due to taking pride in doing the job right. But mainly due to how little she was looking forward to the next step in the process. The report. Making the call presented no major difficulty. There was no particular challenge in describing what had happened. She knew that her contact would listen without interruption. He'd save any questions he might have until she'd finished speaking. He'd hang up. And then there would be the wait. For the verdict. Continue. Or stand down. A fighting chance. Or disaster.

The information would flow up the chain of command until a decision was reached. Who that involved or where they were located, Natasha didn't know. The system was designed that way. For security. Compartmentalization was king in the world she currently inhabited. She suspected there must be a local connection. Someone with their ear to the ground. Who raised the alarm in the first place. Who may or may not still be involved. Who may or may not have a say in the outcome. Identifying him or her would be possible, she supposed. Maybe necessary. Certainly desirable. But that was a problem for the future. Right then all she had to worry about was keeping her team, and therefore herself, in the field.

The lead officer took care of searching Reacher. He was thorough. And slow. Rutherford was in the back of the first car before the officer got as far as Reacher's waist. He was reclaiming a little authority, Reacher guessed. Showing whose timetable they were working to. Reacher stood still and let him finish. Then the officer stepped to the side and made a call on his cell, while another cop guided Reacher into the back of the second car.

Reacher expected the station house to be outside the main part of town, some place where the real estate was cheaper, so he was surprised when the journey ended after two streets. The cop used his lights to blast through the intersection with the broken signals, took the next left, then swung left again into a lot at the side of a wide sandstone building. It was braced with Greek columns and studded with rows of parallel windows. The officer pulled up next to the car that had been hit by the Suburban and climbed out. A framed sign announced the place as the courthouse, and smaller letters underneath added that it was also home to the treasurer's department, the town clerk, and the police department. All it was lacking for full efficiency was the jail.

The officer led the way past the porticoed entrance at the front of the building, which was apparently reserved for members of the public who hadn't been arrested, and continued around to the side. He stopped at a plain metal door, ignored its card reader and unlocked it with a key, then ushered Reacher down a dimly lit flight of cement steps. They emerged at the side of a reception counter. It was glassed in all the way to the ceiling and had a full set of blinds, which were closed. On the opposite side brass handrails lined the stairs that respectable citizens could use on their way to file reports or make enquiries or conduct whatever other kind of legitimate business regular people have.

The officer pressed a buzzer and after a moment a door opened, leading to a booking area. Another cop was waiting at a large wooden table. Behind him there were two desks supporting worn but serviceable computers which were currently switched off, a stack of deep plastic trays in a rainbow of colours, and a pale, droopy potted plant. The walls were covered with posters warning against the dangers of crime and encouraging the public to take responsibility for their own safety. The cop grabbed one of the trays and dropped it on the table near where Reacher was standing.

'Put your possessions in there.' He sounded bored. 'You'll get them back when you're released.'

Reacher produced his roll of cash. His toothbrush. His ATM card. And his passport.

'Is that all?'

'What else do I need?' Reacher said.

The cop shrugged and started to count the cash. When he was done he handed Reacher a receipt then led the way along a corridor to a door marked Interrogation

Room 2. The interior was lined with sound-muffling tiles. Reacher had seen them before. He knew they served no sonic purpose. They were part of a psychological trick designed to give suspects the illusion that they were in a place where it was safe to spill the dirt on their partners. The floor was smooth concrete and the metal table and chairs were bolted to it. The observation window was made to look like a mirror in the usual way and a panic strip ran around the walls at waist level. Reacher guessed they'd brought him there because they only had one cell area. They wouldn't want to take the chance of him talking to the guy he'd rescued. Too much risk of them lining up their stories. And he knew they'd make him wait. An hour, at least. Maybe two. A standard tactic. Isolation breeds the urge to talk. An urge to talk can become an urge to confess. He'd used the technique himself, countless times. And this wasn't the first time it had been used against him.

Both chairs were too close to the table to be comfortable so Reacher sat on the floor in the corner opposite the door. The clock in his head told him that an hour thirty-seven had passed by the time the door opened again. Ninety-seven minutes. The largest two-digit prime number. One of his favourites. He took that as a good sign. A less good sign was the smug grin on the face of the man who'd entered the room. He didn't look a day over thirty and was all curly hair and rounded features. He took the chair with its back to the window and continued to smile.

'I see you've made yourself at home,' the man said.

'Sorry to keep you waiting. Want to grab a seat? Join me? See if we can't get this thing squared away?'

Reacher shrugged as if he didn't care either way then stood, stretched, and wedged himself into the chair on the other side of the table.

'I'm John Goodyear.' The man's grin grew even wider. 'I'm the detective here?'

'Jack Reacher.'

'I know that. But what I don't know is your deal. Why are you in my town?'

'I don't have a deal. I'm in this town by chance.'

'What kind of chance? You get abducted by aliens and they drop you here at random?'

'I hitched a ride. With a guy. This happened to be his destination. I'm not staying here. I'm going to grab some food. Some coffee. Then I'll be gone.'

'You were planning to stay just long enough to rip off a store, in other words?'

'What?'

Goodyear produced Reacher's toothbrush from his pocket and laid it on the table. 'See, I was lying. I do know your deal. You stick this in your pocket and pretend it's a gun. People aren't going to fall for it every time, sure, but plenty won't want to take the chance. Am I right?'

'You're an idiot.'

'I am?' Goodyear smiled. 'Account for this, then.' He placed Reacher's roll of money on the table next to his toothbrush. 'You have an ATM card but you didn't get these notes from any bank. They use fresh, crisp ones. These would get stuck and gum up the machine. So, where did you get them?'

'I earned them.'

'How?'

'A new venture of mine. I recently dipped a toe in the music business.'

Goodyear leaned in and lowered his voice. 'A word to the wise, Reacher. This is the twenty-first century. Police departments have computers now, and those computers are all connected. I'm running your description across Tennessee and nine surrounding states. The results will be in soon. Very soon. In minutes, maybe. The smart thing is to get out ahead of that. Tell me yourself, right now, and I'll help with your statement. Wait until I have a stack of computer printouts to work with and it'll be worse for you. Much worse. Who knows what other charges might come to light? Vagrancy wouldn't be a big surprise, for one.'

'I didn't see any lakes on my way into town,' Reacher said. 'I guess that explains it.'

'Explains what?'

'Why you're trying to go fishing in here. You have no reason to suspect me of any crime. I travel light. So what? I have done for years. Ever since I left the army. And so we're straight, you haven't contacted any other police departments.'

'What makes you think so?'

'If you had, you'd already have an answer. Let's face it, I'm a distinctive-looking guy. There's no one else in Tennessee or anywhere else who matches my description. But that's beside the point for two reasons. First, because I didn't hold anywhere up. And second, you couldn't contact any other departments. Your systems are all down.'

Goodyear's smile faded. 'What do you know about our systems? What did Rutherford tell you?'

'The other guy you wrongly arrested? Nothing. I haven't exchanged a word with him. I didn't need to. I have a system of my own.'

'What system?'

'Eyeball, human, series one. Come on, detective. It's obvious. Your officer called in my arrest on his cell phone. The terminal in his car was inoperative. The computers in the booking area were switched off. The security cameras aren't working. And it's not just the police department. The traffic signals in town are out. Something weird's going on. What is it?'

Goodyear shifted in his seat but didn't respond.

'OK. Let's skip the minor stuff and get to the heart of the matter. Why would someone want to kidnap Rutherford? He seemed like a pretty innocuous kind of guy.'

'Who says anyone tried to kidnap him?'

'I do.'

'What would you know about kidnapping?'

'Enough. I know an ambush when I see one. Rutherford doesn't. The guy needs protection. You should keep him in custody for his own good and call the FBI. Kidnapping's their jurisdiction. It wouldn't create any extra work for you.'

'Let's not get ahead of ourselves.' Goodyear's grin was creeping back. 'There's no need to send up the federal balloon just yet. Maybe those guys you tangled with were trying to grab Rutherford. Are you a mindreader? You don't know what they were planning to do with him. If they were trying to grab him – and I'm not saying they were because we don't know – they probably just wanted to take him someplace private where they could have a full and frank exchange of views. Maybe even dole out a good old-fashioned ass-kicking. If I take my detective hat off I can't say he doesn't deserve one. Hell, if it was an attempt at payback the whole town would be suspects. I'd need a bigger jailhouse. And even if you're right, I say no harm, no foul. So why don't we leave it at that?'

'Why don't I write a statement? You give it to the feds. Do your job. Protect and serve, or whatever you say in this state. You don't need computers to do that.'

'Why don't you keep your whacked-out theories to yourself?'

'Why are you so desperate to sweep this under the rug? What has Rutherford done?'

'Why are you so desperate to keep it in the spotlight? Not the smartest move from your point of view, Reacher. Keep it up and I may have to take a closer look at your role. I hear you knocked one man out cold. Threw another through a car window. Assaults like that, you could be looking at jail time.'

'I didn't assault anyone. The sidewalk was slippery.

That's all. The first guy slid into a wall. The second tripped. He's lucky the car window was open or he could have gotten a nasty bruise.'

'All right. Let's take a step back. You say these guys tried to kidnap Rutherford. Why would they do that?'

'How would I know? No one will tell me what he's done.'

'What's your connection to him?'

'We don't have a connection.'

'Did he give you this cash?' Goodyear gestured to the pile on the table.

'No.'

'Did he hire you as a bodyguard?'

'No.'

'How did he contact you?'

'He didn't.'

'Where did you first meet?'

'We never met. Not before today. I saw him walking into an ambush. I helped him escape. It was a spur of the moment thing.'

'You're just a Good Samaritan?'

'Exactly.'

'Where did Rutherford go before the coffee shop?'

'The moon. He has a secret love nest there. I was thinking of renting it but the mirrors on the ceiling are too small.'

'I advise you to take this process seriously, Mr Reacher.'

'Why? You're not.'

Goodyear didn't answer.

'If you want me to get serious, give me some paper. I'll write a statement for the FBI.'

'I'm not giving you any paper.'

'Then give me a ride to the highway.'

'I'm a detective. I don't give rides.'

'Then unless you're charging me with holding up an imaginary store, it sounds like our business here is done. Or I could bring in a lawyer.'

'There's no need for a lawyer.' Goodyear paused. 'All right. You can go. But take my advice. Don't stick around. Leave town. Right away. And here's the most important thing. Have nothing more to do with Rusty Rutherford.'

FOUR

Goodyear escorted Reacher back to the book-ing area, set his cash and toothbrush down on the table, and went to his office. He needed privacy to make a call. The other cop added Reacher's passport and ATM card like a poker player calling a bet, then followed up with a form and a pen. Reacher signed, stowed his possessions in his pockets, and shook his head when the cop tried to steer him towards the rear exit. He took the public stairs instead and hurried past the bank of framed portraits hanging in the echoey marble foyer. He pushed through the cen-tral door in a row of three, skirted a roughly boxed-in temporary structure where an access ramp was being constructed, and turned to head back to the main street. He wasn't about to hit the road without his coffee. Priorities were priorities. He started across the lawn and as he drew level with the parking lot he heard a voice calling to him. It was Rutherford. He had been waiting by the metal door but now he was scampering forward with one arm raised.

'Excuse me, I'm sorry, I don't know your name. Please wait.'

Reacher slowed and allowed Rutherford to catch up.

'My name's Rusty Rutherford.' He held out his hand.

'Jack Reacher.'

'Mr Reacher, would it be OK if we talk for a moment?'

'If we talk while we walk. There's somewhere I need to be.'

'Please.' Rutherford was out of breath and he was becoming flustered. 'Stop. Just for a moment. I can make this quick.'

Reacher stopped.

'Two things. First, thank you. I guess you saved my ass back there.'

'My pleasure.'

'And second, I need to ask you something. Am I in danger? The detective kept talking about a carjacking, but that's not what happened. I had some time to think in the cell before they questioned me. What happened wasn't random. It was planned. Those guys were waiting. At first I thought they must have been there for you. Nothing like this has ever happened to me before. But then I remembered, one of the men tried to grab me before you intervened. He tried to push me into the car. The detective said I was confused. That I was wrong. But I'm not, am I? I just want to know what's going on.'

'I have no idea what's going on,' Reacher said. 'This isn't my town. I don't know you. I don't know what you may have done to upset people. I don't know what you have that's valuable. But something strange is happening here. That's for sure.'

'So what should I do?'

'That's your call. My philosophy is hope for the best, but prepare for the worst. So given the circumstances I'd say the smart thing would be to leave town. Let whatever's going on blow over on its own. Come back when things have settled down.'

'Leave town?' Rutherford's eyes stretched wide. 'No. I can't do that.'

'Why not?'

'It would make me look guilty.'

'Of what?'

'That's a long story.'

Reacher thought for a moment. It was already late afternoon. He was hungry. He needed to eat, whether there or somewhere else. It would be harder to hitch a ride in the dark. There'd be less to see from the road. And he was intrigued to find out why a mousy little guy in a coffee-stained shirt thought not looking guilty was more important than his own safety. 'Anywhere around here sell good burgers? We could grab a bite and you could tell me about it.'

'You said you had somewhere to be?'

'I do. But I can wait a while to get there. No need to be inflexible. I hear it's bad for your health.'

*

49

The same time Reacher was talking to Rutherford, two people were trying to call Speranski. One on a burner cell. One on the secure phone he'd used earlier. Neither call got through. Not right away. The signal was blocked. Because Speranski had gone down to the generator room. Just for a couple of minutes. He wanted to see the place one last time before his housekeeper cleaned it up. That couldn't wait much longer, he knew. Some of the blood was already more than two weeks old. The subject had held out a long time. She had yielded some critical information. She'd told them about Rutherford. What was in his possession. Which was gold, professionally. And personally, she'd made him feel young again. He didn't get to do much wet work these days. He missed it. He looked at the dark pools on the floor. The droplets sprayed up the walls. The manacles. The tools lined up on the stainless steel trolley. The cleaner patches where the suitcases had been. He relived his favourite moments. And smiled. Normally he didn't know when his next opportunity would arise. Or who it would be with. But this time he knew both.

It would be very soon.

And it would be with the traitor. As soon as she was no longer useful.

The first phone to ring when he got back to ground level was the burner. It was a short call. From a guy a short distance away. A report. First, facts. Then opinions. Brief and concise. The way Speranski liked it. Which meant that when the secure phone rang a few moments later, Speranski already knew what the guy at

50

the end of the line was going to say: 'Rutherford got away.'

'OK,' Speranski replied. 'So we try again.'

'We may not. The Center is concerned. The failed attempt caused a spectacle. And Rutherford had help. We don't know who from, or what size of force is involved. Trying again might draw more attention. It could be counter-productive.'

'So the Center is proposing we do what? Nothing?'

'The final decision has not yet been made. Watch and wait is the current stance. See if the item surfaces on its own. And if it does, see if it's actually dangerous.'

Speranski took the phone away from his ear and fought the urge to smash it into a million pieces. This was the worst part of working in the field. Having to deal with spineless cretins who hid behind their desks all day. Who never put their own necks on the line and then gambled with the lives of the people who did. And then were too timid to take a once-in-a-lifetime opportunity to turn the tables on the enemy even when it was handed to them on a plate.

He lifted the phone to his ear again. 'You need to get back to them. Right now. Convince them that watching and waiting is not an option. The item may never surface. That's true. And if it does, it may not be dangerous. That's also true. But neither of those things matters. If the FBI doesn't find it here, what will they do? Give up? No. They'll keep on hunting. At the source. Until they're successful. Which could be before the mission is complete. Which would be a disaster. And even if it was afterwards, it would be the end of . . . the agent concerned. Which, obviously, I will never allow to happen.'

'I understand. And I agree. But the Center is worried about exposure. About attracting attention. Tipping our hand.'

'Tell them there's no danger of that happening. The interference was a one-off. A fluke. A drifter, some kind of ex-military cop, read the situation and stepped in. He won't do it again. He's been told to leave town.'

'How do you know?'

'I've operated in this town for more than fifty years. I have contacts.'

'Are they reliable?'

'This is coming direct from the police department.'

'OK. That's good. But what if the drifter doesn't leave town?'

'Then I'll take local action.'

'Like you did with the journalist?'

'Exactly like that.'

'All right. I'll talk to them. Try to get them to start surveillance up again, at least.'

'That's not enough. We have to take Rutherford, and fast. They don't understand what it takes to whip up the hysteria. I've used everything. Local press. Whisper campaigns. A whole army of bots on social media. It's holding for now, but it can't last. The bubble will burst. Something else will happen and take the spotlight. Rutherford needs to disappear while everyone in town still hates him.'

*

Rutherford led the way to his favourite diner. It was on the ground floor of an office building on the main street, three blocks from the coffee shop. Reacher wasn't encouraged by the exterior but he had to admit that the designer had done a credible job with the inside. The colour scheme was pure fifties with plenty of chrome, and the booths along both sides of the room all had their own mini jukebox. There was an old-fashioned pay phone on the back wall, and a line of Formica-covered four-tops down the centre. The side walls were covered with giant paintings of cars. They were all convertibles. Cadillacs and Chevys. Turquoise and pink. Speeding down scenic highways or parked by snow-topped mountains and sparkling lakes with happy nuclear families spilling out with picnic sets and footballs.

There were no other customers in the place so they helped themselves to a booth midway along the right-hand wall. It was below a turquoise Chevrolet, where Reacher could keep an eye on the doors to the street and the kitchen. A moment later a waitress emerged. She smiled at Reacher as she approached but her expression cooled when she saw who his dining companion was. Reacher ordered two cheeseburgers and coffee. Rutherford ordered one, then they sat in silence until the waitress delivered their mugs.

'Did you see the way she looked at me?' Rutherford pushed his mug away.

'I've made myself unpopular in certain circles from time to time,' Reacher said. 'But to have a whole town mad at you? That's quite an achievement. What did you do?'

'Nothing.'

'OK.' Reacher took a swig of coffee. 'What didn't you do?'

'I guess my big sin is that I didn't do enough to avoid catching the blame for the mess the town's in.'

Reacher's mind jumped to the traffic signals and the police computers. 'Are you the town treasurer? Some kind of municipal accountant?'

'No.' Rutherford rocked back on his bench. 'Why would you think I was?'

'Nothing in the town is working. Usually that's because bills haven't been paid.'

Rutherford smiled for the first time since Reacher had met him. 'If only that was the problem. That could easily be fixed. The town's situation is much worse. It is kind of connected to money, though. We've been hit by a ransomware attack.'

'I have no idea what that is.'

'Ransomware? It's a malicious program that locks up a computer network. The computers themselves and the data they use. All the records and information from all the different departments. And all the phones and laptops and tablets, if they're connected.'

'OK. So how do you get it all unlocked and working again?'

'You have to buy a key.'

'From where?'

'From whoever attacked you.'

'For real?'

'Oh, yes. More and more towns are getting hit. Sometimes several at once if they share services.'

'What does this town share?'

'Nothing. We do everything for ourselves.'

'So you were targeted specifically? Why?'

'No special reason. We just made it too easy. Our infrastructure is a hacker's wet dream. A hotchpotch of old, out-of-date systems. Vulnerabilities all over the place. No viable defence. And you have to understand, this is a growing phenomenon. Cities are getting hit. Hospitals. Police departments. Corporations, too. But they usually try to hide it and pay up quietly.'

'Corporations pay?'

'Sometimes. Most times? I don't really know.'

'Doesn't paying up encourage more attacks?'

'Probably.' Rutherford shrugged. 'But what choice do they have?'

'The town's not going to pay, is it?'

Rutherford didn't answer.

'Seems to me that this kind of thing needs to be stamped out,' Reacher said. 'Not encouraged. It's one thing to make them think you're going to pay. Set up an exchange: the cash for the key. But the assholes who attacked you shouldn't walk away with a cent. They shouldn't walk away at all. You should check that the key works. Then find their base and burn it down. Identify everyone involved and burn down their houses. Send them a message not to try it again.'

'I kind of wish we could,' Rutherford said. 'But that's not how it works.'

'Why not?'

'We're not talking about cases stuffed full of bank-notes. No physical cash is involved. It's always virtual currency that these people want. Bitcoin, usually. There's not a physical key, either. Just more computer code. It's delivered remotely via the internet from an address that's so scrambled it's impossible to find out who sent it. Sometimes it's from somewhere in the US. Usually it's Russia or Iran or someplace like that.'

'Could you break the code?'

'In theory. There are specialist companies you can hire. I have a friend who founded one, actually. She was an FBI agent. A cyber crimes expert. But all those companies are expensive. And there's no guarantee they'll succeed. Even if they do there's the issue of time. How long can you afford to be without your critical infrastructure? And some ransomware has a built-in time limit. If you don't pay up within x days or weeks or whatever, your data gets permanently wiped.'

A waitress appeared with a coffee pot and topped up Reacher's mug. She was a different woman. Younger, a little taller, and much friendlier. She smiled at Ruther-ford rather than scowling at him then turned to Reacher and tipped her head to the side.

'Do I know you from somewhere?'

'Unlikely. I just arrived in town today.'

'Of course. I knew I recognized you. That's why. I saw you getting out of a car, just across the street. An

Impala, right? Silver? Smart-looking man driving it. A banker, maybe?'

'Insurance.'

'See? I wasn't far off. Is that interesting work, insurance?'

'Why are you asking me?'

'Isn't that man your boss?'

'I don't have a boss.'

'So you're independent?'

'That's the general idea.'

'That must be nice. Anyway, your burgers will be out soon. Holler if you need anything in the meantime.'

Rutherford waited until the waitress was back in the kitchen. 'But anyway. Ransomware. If you don't pay to get the key, you have two choices. Start again from scratch, which is slow and super expensive.' Rutherford hesitated. 'Or wipe everything off all your computers and load a clean copy from your backup.'

'Option B sounds good. Why doesn't the town do that?'

'They'd need two things. A backup with a clean copy of all the data. And an IT manager to re-install it.'

'The town doesn't have an IT manager?'

'Not any more. I was it. They fired me.'

'Because you didn't make a clean backup?'

'Kind of. Only it's a bit more complicated than that. I told my bosses time after time that we needed a system to protect us against an attack, and a backup, just in case. The town was such a soft target. But fixing it was expensive. They wouldn't do it. I should have walked. Many times over. But I like the town. I liked it, anyway.'

'So you let the defence and the backup slide, and that came back and bit you on the ass?'

'No.' Rutherford closed his eyes for a moment. 'I did something even more stupid.'

Twenty-five minutes had passed, and Natasha's phone did not ring.

The motel was a single structure, long and low, clad with brown wood. It was divided into nineteen sections. An office at the east end, with a covered entrance and an alcove for ice and soft drinks. Then eighteen guest rooms, each with a door and a window, starting with room one next to the office and stretching away to the west. Natasha's team had taken rooms fifteen through eighteen. They left fifteen vacant, as a buffer, in case of adjacent occupants and thin walls. Vasili and Anatole, from the Suburban, slept in sixteen. Ilya and Petya in seventeen. And Natasha and Sonya in eighteen. When they got back from swapping cars the two women had carried Ilya to their own room and laid him, unconscious, on the couch. Petya had followed them in, nursing his arm. A moment later the other two men had joined them.

To wait.

Thirty minutes passed. Natasha's phone did not ring.

She checked its signal three times. Three times she

found it was at full strength. Some kind of proverb probably applied, she thought. Watched pots. Something like that. Or maybe something more up to date. She pushed the thought aside and tried to focus on practical matters. Like Petya's shoulder. At first he was reluctant to let her examine it but he eventually relented. She found it was dislocated and eased it back into place. Then she checked on Ilya and found his breathing and pulse were returning to normal.

Thirty-five minutes passed. Her phone didn't ring.

'Should we do something?' Vasili asked.

'Yes,' Natasha said. 'Wait.'

'For how long?'

'For as long as it takes.'

'But why's it taking so long? Something must be wrong.'

'Nothing's wrong.'

'How can you be so certain? What other explanation is there?' Vasili lowered his voice. 'We screwed up. We all know what happens when you screw up. We've all heard the rumours.'

'Cut that kind of talk out right now. You shouldn't listen to rumours.'

'Then why is it taking so long for them to decide what they want us to do?'

'What if they have decided?' Sonya looked up from the table. 'Decided, but not told us?'

'Why wouldn't they tell us?' Vasili said. 'How can we act on our orders if they're not given to us?'

'What if it's not us they're giving orders to?' Sonya said. 'What if they've brought in another team? And don't want any loose ends?'

'Stop it,' Natasha said. 'You're being paranoid.'

'Are we?' Sonya said. 'Think about it. They know where we are. They know we're all together. We're making it easy for them.'

Ilya grunted from the couch and opened his eyes.

Vasili crossed to the window. 'All clear. For now.'

Forty minutes passed. Natasha's phone finally rang.

Reacher bit into his first burger. 'So what did you do that was so stupid?'

Rutherford shook his head. 'I tried to fix it myself. I was working on a system to detect and neutralize cyber attacks. I called it the guard dog. That friend I mentioned? The FBI agent? She was helping me. She wanted to call it Cerberus. If it worked we were going into business together. We were going to industrialize it. And make our fortunes.'

'I'm guessing your system didn't work.'

'Nope. And neither did the backup I tried to build. And yet I get the blame. Which is so unfair. None of these bozos who are on my back have any idea what I was up against. A lot of these attacks are state sponsored. They have giant warehouses full of people. It's their only job. They have endless resources. Then there's me, on my own, cobbling together repurposed parts salvaged from wherever I can find them.'

'Like David and Goliath. Only Goliath won.'

'Right. Which was always the more likely outcome, if you think about it.'

'But however likely or unlikely it was, you still have no job. And everyone hates you. The town is nice, sure, but there's a whole world out there. Why not hit the road for a while?'

'I might do that. Eventually. But first I need to clear my name.'

'How?'

'There are documents on my old laptop that prove I'm innocent. I've hired a lawyer and she's subpoenaed the town to get it. I can show how I warned and warned my boss, and how he ignored me. And there's something else. The asshole is spreading a rumour that it was me who infected the network. He's saying I missed a virus guard update when I was travelling and then opened a contaminated email.' Rutherford rolled his eyes. 'Can you believe it? It was me who introduced the update policy in the first place. I bet it was him who missed one. When I get my laptop back I'll prove it.'

'Rusty, I admire your spirit, but are you sure this is the best path to take? It would be a hollow victory if you can't enjoy it because you've been bundled into the back of some other thug's car.'

'That detective was clear he didn't think it was a serious kidnap attempt. How could it be, really? What would be the point? I'm not rich. I have no famous relatives. I don't know any secrets. I haven't slept with anyone's wife.'

'Well, someone sent those guys after you. And it

wasn't someone wanting to invite you over for milk and cookies.'

'I've been thinking about that. I didn't recognize any of them. So they wouldn't recognize me. It could have been a case of mistaken identity.'

'There are these new things. They're called photographs. I've been told that even cell phones can take them now.'

'Point taken. But hiring a bunch of thugs to drag me somewhere and kick my ass? Why do that? It's a lot of trouble. A lot of expense, probably. And even if everyone in town believes the attack is my fault, who really got hurt? It's all hysteria. The papers, social media, people are talking nonsense. Saying the town's schools are going to close. There'll be no new swings in the park. Half the police department's cars will have to be scrapped. Gas prices will double. House prices will crash. It's all a load of crap. Some of the town's employees are having to work longer hours, sure. And use their own phones. But who doesn't have unlimited minutes these days? The online historical archive is delayed, so the town will lose a little face, but we're not alone. Lots of towns have been disrupted recently. It's not worth committing crimes over. As long as the systems are back up and running by the end of the month for payroll, it's no biggie. Despite the hype.'

'How long have the computers been down?'

'Two weeks.'

'There's a week left to the end of the month. The town has no backup. You said it takes time to start

62

from scratch, and there's no IT manager. Sounds like a biggie to me.'

'But the town's not starting from scratch. We're paying. Didn't I tell you that? The deal must be almost done.'

'If someone's paying, someone's going to be left with a hole in their bank account. They might not be happy about that.'

Rutherford shook his head. 'The insurance company is paying. They've got a guy negotiating, trying to get the price down. Maybe the guy you rode in with. Even if he can't get them to budge and they have to pay full sticker, I don't see a major corporation going after a pound of my flesh.'

The friendly waitress collected their plates.

Reacher took a sip of coffee. 'You said you were working on some kind of new system. To detect these attacks and stop them. It was defeated, I get that. But is there any way it could still help? Think about someone wearing body armour. It's supposed to be impermeable but he gets shot by some new kind of round that is able to penetrate. It sucks for him because he's dead but the forensic guys can still learn a lot. The calibre of the bullet. Was it jacketed? What kind of material? And so on. Then some deductions can be made.'

'I was thinking the same way. That was exactly what I was hoping for. I checked. Multiple times. No luck. And I sent a copy to my ex-FBI friend. She's working on it too. She has more resources but it doesn't look hopeful.'

Reacher put some money down and slid out of the booth. The friendly waitress slipped her phone into her apron pocket and approached. She asked to talk to Rutherford for a moment. There was something she needed help with. Her voice said it had to do with a computer. Her body language said it had to do with something else. Reacher smiled. He found people respond to crises in two ways. Some get to work fixing the problem. Others, proving the problem wasn't their fault. Reacher liked the first kind. Rutherford seemed like the first kind. It was nice to see someone not dumping on him for a change.

Reacher stepped outside. He moved to the side of the window to give Rutherford some privacy. A man stepped out of the shadows. He was around six feet even. He had sunken eyes set into a pale, unshaven face. Shabby work boots with torn leather exposing their steel toecaps. Grubby jeans. A tight black T-shirt under an olive jacket. Army surplus, Reacher thought. Probably Italian, by the shade of green.

The man's hand slid into his jacket pocket and directed something hard and cylindrical towards Reacher's chest. 'Move it,' he said. 'Into the alley.'

FIVE

Speranski was back in his living room, reading his newspaper, when the secure phone rang again.

'Good news,' the voice at the other end of the line said. 'The Center agreed. The team was sent back out. And right away they re-established contact.'

'Excellent,' Speranski said. 'Where?'

'Going into a diner. Opposite Rutherford's building.'

'Can they take him there? What's the plan?'

'Not inside. They're going to wait. Take them when they come out.'

'Them?'

'Correct. Rutherford and the drifter.'

Speranski was silent for a moment. Had his contact in the police department lied to him? Or failed to carry out an adequate interview?

'They showed up together,' the voice said. 'From the direction of the courthouse. Looked like they were getting to know one another, according to the report.

Probably got released at the same time and started talking.'

That sounded like an assumption, Speranski thought. He didn't like assumptions. Maybe it was time to test his contact's loyalty. Or his competence. Or both. Yes. He should definitely do that. But in due course. The current situation had to be resolved first. If it wasn't, nothing else would matter anyway.

'So they'll take them on the street?' Speranski said.

'In an alley,' the voice said. 'There's one right next to the diner, I'm told. You probably know it. They'll lure them in. Block the entrance with the Suburban to avoid any witnesses. And hit them with the tasers.'

Speranski did know the alley. He pictured the scene. It was suitable, he decided. The plan was simple, but sometimes simple is best. And if they got the drifter as well as Rutherford, that could be advantageous. Because he couldn't touch Rutherford. He couldn't afford to leave any marks. Nothing that might raise suspicion at an autopsy. He had to rely on scaring him. But he could do whatever he wanted to the drifter. Which would no doubt help to loosen Rutherford's tongue.

And it would be fun.

He would have to summon his housekeeper. Tell her to prepare the generator room. To clean the instruments, at least. The walls and floor could probably wait.

Reacher looked at the man facing him with the bulging jacket and said nothing.

'Into the alley.' The guy pointed with his free hand. 'Move. Backward. Now. I'll tell you when to turn.'

'What's the rush?' Reacher said. 'This is a serious decision. I'm going to need more information. Let's start with you explaining why I'd want to go into the alley.'

'Because I'm telling you to.'

Reacher shook his head. 'See, that is not a compelling reason. In fact, it's the opposite. A moment ago, before you opened your mouth, there was a possibility I'd wind up in there. Based purely on random chance. It wouldn't have been very likely. If a top mathematician happened to be passing by she could have calculated the probability, tiny though it might have been. Now, on the other hand, even if you invented a whole new branch of mathematics you wouldn't be able to come up with a number small enough.'

The man fidgeted from foot to foot. 'OK. Do the math on this. Go into the alley, right now, or I'll shoot you.'

'Again, not compelling. If you want me in the alley you must have a reason which doesn't involve shooting me on the street or you would have done that already. And on top of that, in order to shoot me you'd need to have a gun.'

'I have a gun.' The guy flapped his jacket. 'I'm pointing it right at you.'

'That's a gun in your pocket? Oh. OK. I didn't realize. What kind is it?'

The guy's mouth opened but no words came out.

'Pistol or revolver?'

The guy didn't answer.

'Thirty-eight or forty-five?'

The guy stayed silent.

'Take it out. Show it to me. You might learn something.'

The guy didn't move.

'You don't have a gun. It's OK. You can admit it. But you do realize that the game's over? Because here's your real problem. You already know you can't make me do anything on your own. That's why you pretended to be armed. Only you're not armed. So here's my decision. I'm going to decline your invitation. And give you a choice. Tell me who sent you and why they want me in the alley, and I'll let you walk away. Otherwise, do you have a phone?'

The guy didn't answer.

'If you do have one, and you choose not to tell me what I want to know, you should take it out. Call 911. Right away. Because I'm going to throw you through that window. You don't want to run the risk of bleeding out on the floor.'

'No one's calling 911.' It was a man's voice, from somewhere behind Reacher's back.

'And if anyone's getting thrown through a window, it'll be you.' A second voice.

Reacher turned and saw two men strutting out of the alley. Both were also around six feet tall. Both were bald with full bushy beards. They were wearing greasy coveralls and were broad with thick ape-like arms curving out in front of them. Reacher pictured them in a truck workshop carrying giant tyres around all day.

'You see, this is why I don't like alleys,' Reacher said. 'They attract rats. Are there any more in there? If so, they'd better slink out now. Because I don't know what you have in mind but whatever it is, two tubs of lard aren't going to get it done.'

'There are three of us.' The original guy now had his hand out of his pocket and he'd bunched it into a fist.

Reacher grabbed him by his ear, spun him around and launched him forward so that he bounced off the other guys' bellies and landed at their feet. 'You're not quite the same weight class, but stay where I can see you all the same.' Reacher waited for the heavier men to help him up. They got him vertical then closed in tight on either side. A subconscious urge to defend the weakest in the group? Or stupidity? Reacher didn't know. But whatever the reason, it was a poor position to adopt. They should have spread out. Formed a triangle. Multiplied the threat they posed. Put the bigger guys on the outside corners. Have them advance together. Attack simultaneously. Then even if Reacher successfully blocked them both he'd temporarily be occupied. The skinny guy would be free. Front and centre. His chance to be a hero.

'I assume there was some kind of message you were planning to deliver,' Reacher said. 'Want to tell me what it was?'

The broad guys swapped glances, then the one who'd been the first to emerge from the alley took a step forward. 'We know what you're doing,' he said. 'Stop it. Go home. And take your boss with you.'

'My boss being?'

'The man you came here with.'

'OK. Now we have a real problem. You know why? If you think that guy's my boss, you must think I'm here to work. If I'm here to work, I'm getting paid. If I stop working and leave, I won't get paid. I'll lose out. So it's like you're trying to take money out of my pocket. Do you know what happens to people who try to do that?'

The guy glanced at his buddy but didn't answer.

'The details vary but the outcome is always the same. A long stay in the hospital. But this is your lucky day. I'm going to give you a chance to forgo the usual penalty. Tell me who sent you and I'll call it even.'

'Can't do that.'

'Are you trying to annoy me?' Reacher said. 'I really dislike the imprecise use of language. You mean you won't tell me. Obviously you can. In fact, you will. You just need the necessary encouragement.'

Reacher grabbed the skinny guy and pulled him forward. Changed their geometry. Cut their options.

'Try again,' Reacher said. 'Tell me who sent you.'

None of the men replied.

Reacher twisted the skinny guy's hand so that his inner arm was facing up, then gripped him by the wrist. 'You know when people say a kid has a broken arm, the bone is often not severed all the way? It's what's called a green-stick fracture. The bone's just

70

bent. Because young people are supple. But as you grow older, your bones become more brittle. They no longer bend. They shatter. Now, this guy's no kid. He's not old, either. I wonder how far his bones will go before they snap?'

Reacher started to bend. The guy started to scream. More in anticipation than pain, Reacher thought, given the limited amount of force he was using. He kept an eye on the broad guys' position. They were running out of time. Their best option now would be for the skinny guy to drop to the ground and the other two rush simultaneously and push Reacher back against the wall, pinning his arms. And if they were lucky, snagging his legs.

They didn't move.

Reacher bent the arm further. The guy screamed louder and rose up on to his tiptoes. Even if he could no longer drop, the other two should still charge. They'd end up in more of a tangle and their guy might get a little squashed but it was still their best bet.

They didn't move.

Reacher bent the arm further. The guy screamed louder. He rose up higher on his tiptoes. The guy on Reacher's right moved forward. Slowly. And alone. Reacher shifted his right hand to grip the skinny guy's neck and rotated so that his head tracked the bigger guy's movement. He waited until the two guys' heads were inches apart. Twisted so that their temples were parallel. Then drove his left fist hard into the side of the skinny guy's skull, using it like a cue ball to sink the

71

bigger guy. Reacher let go and the pair slumped down in a tangled heap of limbs. He spun back, his elbow raised in case the other guy was following in. But he hadn't moved. He was standing still, mouth open and broad ape arms curving uselessly out in front.

'It's just you and me now,' Reacher said. 'What should we talk about?'

The guy didn't answer.

'How about this? Answer my question about who sent you and you can take your friends to the hospital. Otherwise, you'll be joining them there. It's your choice.'

The man stepped back as if retreating but he planted his rear foot way too deliberately. He paused, then sprang forward, arms wide, trying to catch Reacher in a bear hug. It would have been a reasonable move if he'd disguised it more effectively. As it was, Reacher chopped him on both sides of the neck then grabbed the front of his coveralls, pivoted, and launched him into the wall. The man's eyes glazed over, and all the breath was knocked out of him. Reacher jabbed him in the solar plexus, but gently. He wanted to put the guy down but not knock him out. Not until he revealed a name, anyway. The man folded forward, his legs buckled, and he wound up sitting at Reacher's feet. But before he could speak again Reacher heard a siren. Moments later the street was pulsing with red and blue light.

'Stop. Hands where I can see them.' The voice was distorted by the loudspeaker but Reacher recognized it all the same. 'And this time you are getting down on the sidewalk.'

SIX

The same time Reacher was getting processed at the courthouse, Speranski was back down in the generator room. Partly to check on progress. And partly because he was excited at the prospect of a busy night. Maybe many busy nights if the drifter proved as resilient as the journalist had been. While he was underground two calls tried to get through to him. From the same two people as before. One on his burner cell. One on the secure phone. Only this time, when he got back to ground level it was the secure phone that rang first.

'Is it done?' Speranski said.

'That's a negative,' the voice said. 'The team had to abort.'

Speranski resisted the urge to smash the phone. 'Why? What got screwed up this time?'

'Nothing got screwed up. It was the correct decision. The drifter left the diner ahead of Rutherford. He made like he was going to stick around so the team held position, waiting for either Rutherford to catch up or the drifter to move away. Then a wild card got played. The drifter got in a fight. It came out of nothing, right there on the sidewalk. There was no way anyone could have anticipated it.'

'OK. So who did he fight?'

'Three men. Two big, one scrawny. Locals, presumably. No one we've seen before.'

'How badly was he hurt? Is he in the hospital?'

'No. He wasn't hurt. He won. Easily. He demolished all three guys. But just as the fight was winding up a police car responded. They arrested him on the spot.'

'And Rutherford? Did he get hurt?'

'No. He didn't get involved. He avoided the whole thing. He stayed in the diner until the last one went down, then he must have sneaked out through a back door into the alley. He was seen crossing the street and running into his building.'

'Seen? Why was action not taken?'

'The police were still there. The team had to let him pass. There was no alternative.'

'So where's Rutherford now?'

'Still in his building. I don't imagine he'll come out any time soon.'

Speranski took a moment to think. 'So it was only the drifter and the police who were involved? Not any of our people?'

'Correct,' the voice said.

'No attention drawn? No spectacle? Nothing for the Center to get in a wad about?'

74

'Nothing.'

'Good. Where is the team now?'

'Watching Rutherford's building.'

'Excellent. You know, this may work in our favour. It will be easier to deal with them separately. We know their exact locations, and the drifter will be secure until the morning, at least. OK. Here's what I propose. Leave two people to watch Rutherford's building. The remainder of the team should rest. If Rutherford has not appeared by six a.m. they should go to a location I will confirm in due course. They should conceal themselves there and wait. The drifter will be delivered to them. I'll make the arrangements for that myself. They should subdue him using any means necessary and bring him here. Then the whole team can focus on Rutherford. With the drifter out of the way they shouldn't have any further problems.'

The next call came through on the burner. It was short. From a man a short distance away. A report. First, facts. Then opinions. Brief and concise. The way Speranski liked it. Only this time Speranski followed up the information he received with a set of instructions. Which meant that when the burner phone rang again a few moments later, Speranski already knew what the caller was going to say: 'This is Marty. I have something you may be interested in.'

There were four cells in the basement of the courthouse, and no occupants that night aside from Reacher. He didn't know if that kind of ratio was normal. Maybe the crime rate in the town was low. Maybe the police were bad at catching criminals. Or maybe the current situation gave the cops an incentive to avoid filling in forms and filing reports by hand. But whatever the reason, Reacher was happy with the result. He needed a place to sleep, and here was a solution that didn't require him to part with any cash. He took off his jacket and rolled it up to make a pillow. Lay down on the metal bench. Closed his eyes and let Howlin' Wolf loose in his head. Next up was Magic Slim. He gave them a couple of songs each. Then he counted to three and drifted straight off.

Reacher woke himself at 7:00 a.m. so he had been lying awake for an hour weighing his priorities for the day when he heard footsteps approaching. Someone quick and light. Reacher opened his eyes and saw a uniformed cop he didn't recognize. She was about five foot eight and looked like she could run a marathon before breakfast without thinking twice. She had a thick twist of dark shiny hair knotted at the back of her head and a warm, welcoming smile. Her name plate said Rule. Reacher could only imagine the ribbing that had bought her at the academy.

'Rise and shine.' Officer Rule opened the cell door and gestured for Reacher to come out. 'A detective wants to see you.'

'Goodyear?' Reacher didn't move.

'Someone new.' Officer Rule shrugged. 'I don't know who he is. He just got here. Must be from another jurisdiction.'

'Suppose I go see him.' Reacher stood up. 'What then?'

'That's up to him. And Detective Goodyear.'

'Any word on the idiots who jumped me?'

'They— The new detective should have the most up-to-date information.'

'Any idea why they did it?'

'You already said it.' Officer Rule smiled. 'They're idiots.'

'Who are they?'

'Just a bunch of local yahoos. No one for you to worry about.' Officer Rule paused and looked more closely at Reacher. 'Although I'm guessing there aren't too many people you worry about.'

'That's not so.' Reacher picked up his jacket and came out of the cell. 'Just the other day I got into a debate over the well-being of a group of up-and-coming musicians.'

'That's not what I meant.' Officer Rule took Reacher's elbow and guided him towards the corridor. 'And I think you know it.'

The new detective kept Reacher waiting for half an hour exactly. A minute more than one prime number. A minute short of another. Reacher was disappointed.

The guy was wearing a black suit with a white shirt and a narrow burgundy tie. He was older than Goodyear. That was clear. But how much older was hard to tell. Reacher guessed ten years, minimum, but the guy had the kind of podgy face that resisted wrinkles and

77

didn't sag. His head was bald, but freshly shaved so there was no indication of where his hairline would naturally be. He was slim. And he looked fit, in an unassuming, middle-of-the-road kind of way.

The guy sat at the table. He took a black notebook from his jacket pocket, then gestured for Reacher to get up from his spot on the floor and join him. 'My name's Wallwork. It's early and I'm not a morning person so let's get straight to the point. Why did you attack those men last night?'

'Where's Detective Goodyear?' Reacher said.

'He's here somewhere,' Wallwork said. 'But I'm handling this case. So. Tell me. The fight at the diner. What started it?'

'Those cretins did.' Reacher folded his arms. 'They came after me. I gave them a chance to walk away. It's not my fault they were too stupid to take it.'

'Why did they attack you, then?'

'You're the detective. You figure it out.'

'There's no reason you can think of?'

'Aside from stupidity?'

'OK. So I should put this down as a random, unprovoked attack?'

'Unprovoked, yes. Random, no. They thought I was working with some insurance guy. They tried to warn me off.'

'Why would they do that?'

'You're the detective.'

'Fine. Don't help me. But you should certainly help yourself. Listen. I've just been to the hospital. You banged those guys up pretty good. They won't be able to work for quite a while. Won't be able to do much of anything. They're not happy about that. They're looking for some kind of payback. Talking about pressing charges.'

'Let them. Nothing would stick.'

Wallwork shrugged. 'Maybe. Maybe not. But it would lead to a trial. There'd be no way around that. The courts are pretty backed up around here. Could be a while before you appear. We'd have to keep you locked up in the interim. And there's the jury to think about. They'd all be locals. Do you think they'd like the idea of a hooligan blowing into town and beating on their own? And here's another thing. The guys have already had their photos taken. By a professional. Multiple shots. They have all kinds of swellings. Bruises. Cuts. They look bad.'

'They didn't look great to start with.'

'I'm not disputing that. But get a few mothers on the jury? Get them imagining you doing that kind of damage to their sons? You'd be taking a gamble.'

Reacher said nothing.

'Of course, there is another path we could take. These are not the smartest of individuals. I could probably change their minds. Get them to drop all this talk of criminal charges. But if I did that for you, I'd need something in return.'

'Such as?'

'The previous incident. The one involving Rusty Rutherford. Detective Goodyear was left with the sense that you weren't being entirely forthcoming. Level with me, and I'll see you get to walk out of here.'

'Level with you how? Some guys tried to kidnap Rutherford. I stopped them. There's nothing more to tell.'

'You followed Rutherford along the sidewalk for a spell, correct?'

Reacher nodded.

'Did you see him drop anything? In a trash can, maybe, or down a drain?'

'No.'

'After you intervened, before the officers arrived, did he try to hide anything?'

'No.'

'It could have been very small. A key, or a flash drive.'

'He didn't hide anything.'

'Did you see him mail anything?'

'No.'

'At the diner you two must have talked. Did he say anything about having a storage unit? Or a safety deposit box?'

'No.'

'Did he mention having been anywhere recently?'

'No. But he did say he's leaving in a couple of days for a fishing cabin he has in Nova Scotia. But when he pulled out his pocketbook to pay for dinner I saw he had a Mexican passport in there. A plane ticket. And a bunch of pesos.'

Wallwork closed his notebook and set it down. 'Are you messing with me, Mr Reacher?'

'Why shouldn't I be? You're messing with me, detective. Or should I say agent?'

Wallwork didn't respond.

'It's a little bit about the suit,' Reacher said. 'A little bit about your questions. But mainly about your shoes.'

Wallwork instinctively looked down at his feet.

'I bet they set you back three times what Detective Goodyear's cost,' Reacher said. 'And I bet a thousand bucks he wouldn't swap. Not even if they were his size and brand new. Look at them. There's no cushioning in the sole. No room around the toes. No thickness to the leather. No cop in the world would wear them.'

Wallwork let out a long, slow breath. 'I knew this was a mistake. I read your service record. I wanted to be straight with you from the start but my boss wouldn't go for it. She insisted on the subterfuge. I know it's a stretch to ask you to trust me now, but look at it this way. I could just leave. Deny everything. Say this interview never happened. But I'm not going to do that. I'm going to tell you the truth.'

Wallwork took out his wallet, removed a laminated card, and set it on the table next to his notebook. There was a blue and white eagle in the centre. It was clutching a bunch of thirteen arrows in one talon. An olive branch with thirteen leaves and berries in the other. There was a shield with mountains on the left and water on the right. The words *US Department of Homeland Security* were in a ring around the outside. And beneath that, *Jefferson Wallwork, Special Agent, Infrastructure Security Agency.*

81

'This is who I really am,' he said.

'So what do you really want to know?' Reacher said.

'The ransomware attack on the town. You heard about it?'

Reacher nodded.

'There are two ways ransomware can get into a computer network. Over the internet. Or from something that's physically connected. A thumb drive. A disc drive. Something like that.'

'Rutherford didn't do it.'

'You know that for a fact?'

'You've read my service record. I was an investigator. And an investigator develops a sense for people. I've talked to Rutherford. Spent time with him. He didn't do it.'

'Maybe you're right. I kind of hope you are. But without proof it remains a possibility. I have to rule it in. Or rule it out.'

'Then talk to Rutherford. Ask him to his face. Catch him in a lie, or let him clear his name.'

'I wish I could.'

'Why can't you?'

'What if he is involved? We bring him in, he gets word to his buddies, they cut off negotiations with the insurance company. Lock the town's data for ever. And crawl back into their dung heap. We'd have no chance of catching them. Or if his buddies are watching and they see us bring him in, same result.'

'So what are you going to do?'

'The other possibility is online transmission. We're

hunting that down, too. Fingers crossed something breaks. Meantime, I have to ask you not to mention this to Rutherford. Or anyone else. It could have extremely serious consequences if you did.'

'Rutherford lost his job. Everyone in the town hates him. He was almost kidnapped. I'm not going to dump anything else on him.'

'Good. Thank you. Now, before I go I have a message from Detective Goodyear. The thing about the quid pro quo for getting those men to drop the assault charges? That was his idea. I kind of piggybacked on it. And there is something he needs you to do.'

'What?'

'Leave town. This morning. Right now, in fact. He has a car waiting outside to take you to the highway. And he wants your word you won't come back.'

'What if I don't want to leave town?'

'Come on, Reacher. Work with me here. Yesterday you asked him for a ride.'

'That was yesterday. The town has grown on me since then.'

'He's making you a fair offer, Reacher. You've been in town less than twenty-four hours and already you've been in two major brawls.'

Reacher took a moment to weigh Goodyear's offer. There was Rutherford's well-being to think about. And in an ideal world he would root out whoever was behind sending those thugs after him at the diner. It wasn't fair for the foot soldiers to pay the price on their own. But on the other hand the town had no bus station. No sign of much truck traffic, either, which was the best bet when it came to hitching a ride. People were becoming increasingly leery about letting strangers into their cars, these days. Especially strangers who looked like him.

'OK,' Reacher said. 'I will leave. This morning. But I have two conditions.'

'There's no money in this for you. Let's be clear about that.'

'I'm not talking about money. This is about something else. Those idiots attacked me because they thought I worked for an insurance agent. That must be the guy who gave me a ride yesterday. He'll be staying in a hotel somewhere in town. Some New York dude. Young. In his twenties. He can't be hard to find. I need you to make sure that with me gone they don't transfer their attention to him. That means warning them to leave him alone. In language they can understand. You know what I mean?'

Wallwork smiled. 'I think I do.'

'And you need to warn him to watch his back in case whoever sent the chuckle brothers sends someone else. Someone better.'

Wallwork nodded. 'I can do that.'

'And then there's Rutherford. If you need to investigate him, so be it. But you also need to keep him safe. He's certainly not equipped to do it himself.'

The car Goodyear had arranged was waiting in the courthouse lot when Reacher stepped out through the metal door at the top of the steps. It was long and sleek and German, metallic black, and it was shining in the morning sun like it had just been detailed. Technically it was a regular sedan with four doors and a trunk, but to Reacher's eye it looked too low at the back. It seemed to be squatting on the asphalt rather than sitting on its wheels, like it had been squashed before leaving the factory.

The driver saw Reacher emerge. He hit a button to open the trunk, climbed out, and walked stiffly to the rear of the car. He'd be in his mid to late fifties, Reacher thought, with silver hair buzzed short and the tanned, leathery skin of a guy who spent plenty of time out-doors. He wasn't tall – maybe five ten at most – and he was wearing pale chinos and a white shirt. The shirt was tight across his shoulders, and also around his gut. It was like he'd once been in shape but was struggling to stay that way and wasn't ready to admit he might not make it. He looked at Reacher and sneered, making plain his displeasure at the prospect of someone so unkempt being allowed to travel in his pristine vehicle.

'I'm Marty. You're Jack Reacher?'

Reacher nodded. 'You can close the trunk, Marty. No luggage. Just the clothes on my back.'

This revelation didn't make Marty appear any more enthusiastic. He shook his head, prodded a button on the edge of the trunk lid which caused it to slowly close, and stalked around to the passenger side. He opened the rear door and stood back as Reacher folded himself into the cramped space. Then he went to his side of the car and climbed in behind the wheel. He fastened his seat belt, fired up the engine, and pulled out of the lot. He turned past the front of the building, jinked left and right along a couple of streets lined with single family homes that grew larger and further apart as they went until they settled into a straight wide road with fields full of low dark green plants on either side. The position of the sun told Reacher they were heading due south.

'Where are we going, Marty?' Reacher shuffled across towards the centre of the back seat.

'To the highway.' Marty glanced at Reacher's reflection in the mirror before his eyes darted back to the road. 'That's where you want to go, right?'

'I came in on the highway.' Reacher moved further across. 'It's north of town.'

'We're going to a different highway.'

'Which other highway? And why?'

'Listen. Detective Goodyear is a friend. He asked me to give someone a ride to the highway. He didn't specify which one. This way suits me better. It's convenient for some business I have this afternoon. What difference does it make to you, north or south? Beggars can't be choosers. Would you rather get out and walk? In this heat?'

'Actually, yes,' Reacher said. 'I like to walk. The heat doesn't bother me. Let me out right here.'

Marty kept on driving.

'Goodyear wanted to be sure I left town?' Reacher said. 'He made that clear?'

86

'Right.'

'What did he say I'd done to become so undesirable?'

'Getting into fights. General troublemaking. Associating with undesirables. That kind of thing.'

'And any trouble I might make in the future, he wants me to make elsewhere?'

'Right.'

'He didn't figure I might make some trouble right here in your car?'

'He figured you might try. But I was with the police department for twenty years. He knows that if you are dumb enough to try anything, I can handle it.' Marty moved his right thigh to reveal a small pistol and a pair of worn handcuffs tucked against the raised edge of his seat.

The gun was a pointless prop, Reacher thought. There was no way he could use it. He'd need a second guy to have any chance. Someone else in the back seat. To hold the gun on Reacher and keep him penned in behind the empty passenger seat. It was impossible for Marty to do it. Not while he was driving. He couldn't watch the road and aim behind him at the same time. He'd have to twist around. Avoid the head restraints. Fire more or less at random. In which case Reacher would just take the gun from him.

'Think about it,' Marty said. 'The cops are running you out of town for a reason. You think if you were found in a ditch, full of bullets from a gun registered to a punk who died when Reagan was president, anyone would give two shits?'

'I certainly wouldn't be happy about it.'

'Who cares about your happiness?'

Reacher shuffled a little further to the left. 'Seems like we got off on the wrong foot, Marty. Let's start again. Call a truce. How about this? I won't cause any trouble in your car. And you come clean about where you're taking me. And don't say the highway because I know that's not true.'

'OK. Not the highway. You're right.'

'Then where?'

'You'll find out when we get there.'

'You don't know me very well, Marty, so I won't hold it against you, but I'm not the kind of guy who likes vague answers. Precision is important to me. So I'm going to give you another chance. Where are you taking me?'

Marty moved his thigh again and tapped the gun with his right hand. 'What makes you think you're in a position to be giving out chances?'

'During those twenty years you say you spent in the police department, did you ever notice the way squad cars had a plexiglass panel dividing the front and the back?'

'Sure I noticed. And I didn't like it. Those panels are bulletproof. They stopped me from shooting smart-asses when I was driving them places.'

'An understandable attitude in certain situations.' Reacher shuffled the rest of the way across. 'But it's one you might want to reconsider right now.'

Reacher unfastened Marty's seat belt and grabbed

the loose section with his left hand, whipping it back and pinning the tongue against the door with his left knee. He stretched around and laid his left palm over Marty's forehead and pulled back, clamping his head in place. Then he snaked his right arm around the seat and pressed his fist against Marty's throat. The car swerved. Marty struggled with the wheel for a moment. Then he grabbed his gun and flailed around, pointing it backward and trying to bring it to bear on Reacher, who was pressing himself tight against the back of the driver's seat.

Reacher increased the pressure on Marty's throat until he could feel his windpipe begin to collapse. 'Drop the gun.'

Marty continued to flail around for a moment before reality sank in and he let go of the gun. It bounced off the passenger seat and rattled down into the footwell.

Reacher relaxed the pressure a little. 'Good. Now stop the car.'

Marty accelerated.

'Not smart, Marty. If you don't stop the car a number of things will happen. First, I'll compress your neck. There are all kinds of veins and arteries in a person's neck. They'll be squashed flat. That'll cut off the oxygen supply to your brain. Soon you'll black out. If the car's still moving, we'll crash. Which would be fine from my point of view. The back of this seat will protect me. You, on the other hand, would have a problem. A major one. I don't know how strong your grasp of physics is, but one principle in particular would come into play. Inertia. You know what that is?'

Reacher felt a slight shake of Marty's head.

'Inertia is the tendency for an object to maintain its current state. If something is stationary it stays stationary, unless something else moves it. If something is moving it keeps moving, unless something stops it. The same thing applies to the human body. It's why cars have seat belts. Without them, if you crash, the car stops but the occupants keep moving. They burst through the windshield. Impale themselves on sharp objects. All kinds of painful things can happen. Maybe fatal things. And you're not wearing a seat belt, are you, Marty? Not any more.'

The car slowed, but it was still moving.

'And you have an extra problem. Inertia is working against you in another way. You feel how tight I'm holding your head? It won't keep moving if the car hits something. It will stop. But your body won't. There's nothing to arrest its forward motion. The only thing restraining it at all is your neck. Not just veins and arteries in a person's neck. There are nerves, too.'

Marty took his foot off the gas, rolled the car to the side of the road, and finally stopped. Reacher felt Marty's body slacken.

'I was told to take you to a gas station,' Marty said. 'An abandoned one.'

'And?' Reacher said.

'I don't know. I wasn't told and I didn't ask. As I've just demonstrated, I don't have a death wish.'

'Where is the gas station?'

'Ahead, about half a mile. It's on the right. Next to a derelict car showroom. They used to sell Studebakers. When you see the sign, you know you're close.'

'How much is Goodyear paying you?'

Marty tried to shake his head.

'If it's not money, what does he have on you? I hope it's something big.'

'This isn't John's doing,' Marty said. 'He's a straight shooter. He told me he wanted you out of town because you're a troublemaker, and I take that as the gospel truth. He did ask me to drive you to the highway. I did agree as a favour to a friend. The gas station thing is a separate deal. He knows nothing about it.'

'Goodyear's a straight shooter? So straight you could riddle me with bullets from an illegal gun, throw me in a ditch, and he'd turn a blind eye?'

Marty tried to shake his head again.

'No. That's all on me. And it's bogus anyway. I just said those things to keep you under control. The gun's not even loaded. It's something I learned on the job. You make the bad guys believe you're willing to hurt them. Then you don't have to.'

'OK. We'll leave Goodyear aside for a moment. Who did you make this separate arrangement with?'

'This is where things get difficult. I can't tell you. Not because I don't want to. Because I don't know. He's just a voice on the phone.'

'So it's a man, not a woman?'

'Correct.'

'So an unknown man calls you out of the blue and asks you to be an accessory to what? Kidnapping? Murder? And you say, sure, OK?'

'It's not that simple. It goes back to when I was a cop. I tried to do a guy a favour one time when I thought he'd gotten a bad break. I looked the other way on something and that was a mistake because as soon as he was off the hook he demanded more favours so as not to tell what I'd done. It went on for years. That's why I quit the department in the end. I thought I'd be no use to him any more, so he'd leave me alone. But I was wrong. He made me deliver a package here. Collect some money there. Things like that. I thought it would never end. Then one day the guy died. He got run down crossing the street. By a drunk driver. I know it's wrong to be happy about the death of another human being but I couldn't help it. I was over the moon. I thought I was finally free. That I had my life back. It lasted a week. Then one evening the phone rang. A voice I'd never heard before said he'd inherited certain files from the dead guy and that unless I wanted them to be handed over to the police the previous arrangement would continue. He said it would be nothing too heavy. Just a little favour every now and again.'

'And you believed him?'

'Honestly? I didn't know. He did sound kind of serious. But I was tired and I was desperate so I decided to gamble. I told him, no dice. Leave me alone, or go ahead and do your worst. Which I guess he did. The next morning there was a knock on the door. By the time I got there someone had left a pair of packages. Same size. Same shape. They were numbered one and two. I opened number one first. Inside it was a man's . . . private parts. All of them, if you know what I mean. I spent the next two hours in the bathroom. Then I opened the second box. It was empty apart from a piece of paper. There was handwriting on it. Some kind of old-school flowing script. It said if you want your manhood to end up in one of these, do nothing. Otherwise answer the phone at nine p.m. and follow the instructions to the letter.'

'You answered the phone?'

'Hell, yes. Wouldn't you?'

'What did they make you do?'

'A dump job. Four suitcases.'

'The rest of the guy from the box?'

'That would be my guess. But I didn't look inside.'

'OK. So. Back to the present. How did this mystery guy know that Goodyear asked you to run me out of town? Goodyear must be in his pocket, too.'

'No. It was me. The guy put out an order to report any sightings of Rutherford. Or anything to do with him. Goodyear told me Rutherford was involved in these brawls you were in. I figured that connected you. Better err on the side of caution, right? So I called it in.'

'Does he have other people watching out for Rutherford?'

'I don't know for a fact. But this is no small-time guy. I bet he has a whole network working for him.'

'What does he want with Rutherford?'

'You think I'd ask him something like that? Does he sound like the kind of guy it would be a good idea to antagonize?'

'He sounds like exactly the kind.'

'That's probably why you're the one being driven out of town and I'm the one driving.'

'I'll take that as a compliment.'

'Take it however you want. So, what happens next? I guess you want the car. Fine. Take it. Just do one thing for me. I need to make it look like you escaped. If he thinks I let you go, I'm dead meat. Worse than dead meat. So I need you to hurt me. And I need you to make it look convincing. I know you put three men in the hospital last night, so don't hold back.'

'I'm not going to hurt you. And I'm not going to take your car. Not yet anyway. I'm going to recce on foot first and then make a plan.'

'Recce what? The highway's to the north, like you said. Go now. Put your foot down. Get out of the state before they find me.'

'I have no interest in getting to the highway. That was Goodyear's idea. I have unfinished business, and evidently some of it is at the gas station. People have gone to a lot of trouble to catch up with me. It would be rude not to show.'

'Staying here is a bad idea. Remember box number one? That's the kind of thing they're capable of. And the suitcases. I don't want my next job to be scattering parts of you all across the county. And I don't want someone else scattering parts of me. So the best thing would be—'

'Pass me the gun.'

'It's not loaded. I told you.'

'Give it to me anyway.'

Marty retrieved the gun from the floor and passed it back. It was a neat little .22. A Smith & Wesson 2213. Reacher checked it over. It was lacking oil. And the magazine was lacking bullets. Marty had been telling the truth.

'And your phone,' Reacher said.

Marty disconnected his handset from a holder on the dashboard.

'Now your burner phone.'

'I don't have one.'

'Don't waste my time. There's no way you're communicating with a guy who arranges murders using a traceable phone.'

Marty pulled a small folding phone out of his pocket.

'And your keys.'

Marty sighed and passed Reacher a thing the size of a matchbox with four buttons and a logo. A bunch of other keys was attached. Most looked like they were for regular locks. But one was much smaller. Reacher held it up.

'For your handcuffs?'

Marty nodded.

'Lock yourself to the steering wheel. One wrist is fine.'

Marty did as he was told.

'OK.' Reacher opened his door. 'Stay here. Relax. I'll be back in a while.'

SEVEN

Reacher set out walking and after twenty yards he came to the entrance to a field on the right-hand side of the road. There wasn't much growing. He guessed that tobacco had once been cultivated there, but that was more from half-remembered lessons in schools in distant parts of the world than from any familiarity with the stubby brown plants straggling across the surface of the crumbly red soil. He picked his way to the opposite side, which was bordered by a stand of thin trees, squeezed through a gap, and continued parallel to the road.

After a quarter of a mile Reacher saw the rear of a pair of buildings. The nearer one was wider and taller. Foot-square patches of white paint were flaking off its pitted concrete surface. A pillar maybe a yard square sprouted from the far side, more than doubling the height of the roof. A set of large red capital letters was still attached and the backs of the S, T, U, D and E were visible before the rest of the name was obscured by the wall. The second structure was smaller. It was little more than a kiosk at the side of a roofed-in forecourt. There were no gas pumps any more. Reacher guessed they'd been removed and gussied up and sold in arty stores in affluent towns. He'd seen one in a gallery window one time, on sale for more money than a car could cost. A sign of the times, he thought. Like the shuttered gas station itself. Once booming, nurtured by its car-dealer neighbour. Then a lonely fight for survival, clinging on as the flow of people ebbed and weakened and slowed and finally dried up altogether. The road would be a hopeless place to do business now. That was for sure. No vehicles had passed by since Reacher entered the field. There were only two others in sight anywhere. Tucked in behind the larger building. A Suburban and a Toyota. Black and blue. The same as the previous day. The question was, had they carried the same number of people?

Reacher figured they'd put one person on the roof to spot Marty's car approaching and give the word to the others. The car would swing on to the forecourt, and if Reacher was calling the shots he'd have it continue between the buildings and stop when it was halfway out at the other side. One person would break cover, open the rear door on the driver's side, then drop back. Another would follow with a tranquillizer gun and shoot the target before he had a chance to scramble out of the tight space. So three people, minimum. Enough to handle the job easily. But if they were cautious they could use two people to open both rear doors, and have two with dart guns. That would require a higher level of skill and training to ensure that the guys with the guns didn't shoot each other across the back seat of the car, but it would avoid any problems if the target gambled and threw himself at the opening door or managed to grab the gun before it fired. So more likely five people. And if they were more cautious still, they would have someone mobile to sweep up if anything went wrong. Six people. Two pairs, two singles. The same complement as yesterday.

Reacher decided to leave the lookout on the roof until last. They were too physically removed to pose a threat, and even if they were armed they wouldn't risk shooting in case they hit their own people. The pairs were likely to be concealed somewhere near the adjacent rear corners of the buildings. The sweeper was the unknown factor. He or she would be the one to take off the board first.

If one existed.

Reacher settled in to observe. He could wait all day. Meanwhile his opponents would be getting jumpy. They'd no doubt been informed that Marty had left the courthouse. Concern would be creeping in by now. They'd be worrying that something had gone wrong. The longer the delay, the more stress they'd be under. The greater the stress, the greater the chance they'd make a mistake.

Twelve minutes passed. Nothing moved. Nothing made a sound. Then Reacher heard a vehicle. It was approaching from the north. Reacher caught movement on the roof. Near the pillar with the letters. A head appeared, rising slowly. It was a woman. Dressed in black. With red hair. He'd seen her before. Yesterday. On the opposite side of the alley before she helped get her unconscious buddy into the back of the Toyota. She stayed still for five or six seconds then sank back down, raising her hand to her ear as she went. A car appeared. Moving fast. An ink-blue Mustang convertible with its roof down. A man was driving. There was a woman smiling in the passenger seat. It flashed past, engine howling, scattering gravel in its wake.

The next vehicle Reacher heard was heading the wrong way so he stayed still, pressed into the ground, invisible. The engine note was the same so he guessed it was the Mustang coming back. The guy showing off, hoping for action that night. Or hurrying home after an earlier indiscretion. Five more minutes passed. Ten. Then he heard a vehicle coming the right way. Something slower and softer. Reacher pulled up into a crouch, ready to race forward.

There was movement on the roof. The woman's head appeared again. She was rising faster this time. She stood all the way up, touching her ear, and started running towards the centre of the building. She would have been looking right at Reacher if she wasn't so focused on the rooftop beneath her feet. When the southbound vehicle rolled by she didn't even turn her head. Then she was gone. Reacher guessed she'd jumped down through a hatch. He dropped down too, nestling into the ground. Ninety seconds later the woman wriggled out through a gap at the end of a length of plywood hoarding near the midpoint of the rear wall. The guy Reacher had knocked out squeezed through after her and they ran to the Toyota. The two shorter guys Reacher had exchanged words with emerged from the kiosk and sprinted to the Suburban. Then both vehicles fired up and sped away, wheels spinning on the loose surface, heading away from town.

EIGHT

Speranski was in his dining room, eating his breakfast, when the secure phone rang again.

'We have a problem,' the voice at the other end of the line said. 'We've lost Rutherford.'

'How the hell did that happen?' Speranski hurled his newspaper across the room. 'Two people were supposed to be watching his building. Were my instructions not clear?'

'They were clear. Two people were watching. One was the senior agent. She got a text from Rutherford's doorman. Rutherford had asked him to call a cab.'

'So how did that lead to Rutherford disappearing?'

'The agent told the doorman to go ahead. And to order a second cab to arrive at the same time. So they could follow. The two operational vehicles were both in use at the ambush site. She figured that if the doorman didn't get him a cab Rutherford would have just run out and hailed one on his own. Or taken his own car. Either way, just as bad. Maybe worse.'

'So what went wrong?'

'I don't know. Either the doorman screwed up or the cab company did. Only one car came and Rutherford took it.'

'Tell me we at least know its number?'

'We do. Number, description, and photograph.'

'Did Rutherford state his destination?'

'He did. You're not going to like it. Nashville airport.'

'No.' Speranski stood up. 'Rutherford cannot be allowed to board a plane. That would be an absolute disaster. Where are the agents who were watching him?'

'En route to the airport. So is the balance of the team. Given the urgency of the situation I recalled them from the ambush site.'

'Good. Keep me posted. I want to know the moment Rutherford is intercepted.' Speranski paused. 'Wait. What about the drifter? What's his status?'

'That's unclear. There must have been some kind of a delay after he was taken from the courthouse. He hadn't been delivered when the team pulled out. I judged that finding Rutherford was a higher priority.'

'So where is he?'

There was a momentary silence on the line. 'That's another thing we don't know.'

Reacher stayed where he was, silent, and still. He didn't want to reveal himself only to come face to face with another half dozen ambushers who had been lying in wait all along, so he gave it fifteen more minutes before he risked leaving. He crawled back the way he'd come until he reached the trees parallel to the road. Then he stood and started moving faster. He'd covered a quarter of a mile when he felt something vibrating in his pocket. He took out Marty's phones. The burner was buzzing. Reacher opened the phone and held it to his ear.

'Yes,' he said.

'Where the hell are you?' It was a man's voice, broken up and distorted.

The signal must be weak, Reacher guessed. Probably due to the remote location. Probably not great for clarity. But just in case he pulled up his shirt, doubled over the material, and used it to cover the little microphone.

'Two minutes out,' Reacher said.

'What's taking so long?' The other man's words were almost drowned out by the pops and howls on the line.

'That guy you sent me to deliver? He's a piece of work. I had to knock him out.'

'He's unconscious?'

'Pretty much.'

'That's good. There's been a change of plan. The team that was sent to meet you has been reassigned, temporarily. Another situation. More urgent. But that's my concern. Have you got any rope with you? Or plasticuffs?'

'I have a pair of real cuffs. Police department issue.'

'They'll work. Now, do this. When you get to the gas station take the guy inside the building and cuff him to something. Make sure it's secure, and when you leave make sure there's no sign you've been there. And make sure to keep your phone switched on. I may have another job for you later.'

Marty was sitting bolt upright when Reacher got back to the car. He was stiff, proprietorial. Attempting to reclaim a little dignity. Reacher climbed in on the passenger side and gave him his keys and phones and gun.

'Did you find the place?' Marty unlocked the handcuffs.

'I did,' Reacher said. 'Now drive.'

'Where?' Marty fired up the engine. 'Please say the highway.'

'To the gas station. Half a mile, like you said.'

Marty tensed up. 'Is that safe?'

'Completely. There's no one there.'

'Then why are we going?'

'Because I've decided to cut you a break.'

'How? What are you going to do?'

'Cuff you to something solid then borrow your car. I'll leave the keys at the courthouse.'

'You're going to send the police to get me?'

'No. The guy on the phone is sending someone. He thinks they'll be collecting me.'

'I'm not following.'

'The guy called on your burner phone a minute ago. There's some snafu at his end, causing a delay. Tell his guys you tried to cuff me like he told you to, but I must not have been as unconscious as you thought. I got the jump on you, and cuffed you instead.'

'They'll never believe me.'

'I could knock you out if that would help?'

Marty paused like he was seriously considering it.

'How about this?' Reacher said. 'I'll cuff you with your arms so high up behind your back there's no way you could have done it yourself. It'll be uncomfortable, but it should save your ass.'

Marty didn't answer. He just pulled the car on to the old gas station's forecourt and trudged to the kiosk in silence. Reacher followed him inside.

'Why are you helping me?' Marty winced as Reacher tightened the cuffs. 'I tried helping someone once. Look at the trouble it got me in.'

'I've been in trouble before,' Reacher said. 'I survived. And right now I have bigger fish to fry.'

Reacher's general approach to driving was to find someone else to do it. He was capable of operating a vehicle, in a technical sense. The army had provided thorough training. He'd never killed anyone with a car. At least, not by accident. He'd never had any collisions. Not unintentional ones. His problem was mainly one of temperament. Good driving called for a balance of action and reaction, speed and restraint, measurement and control. A middle ground, stable and sustained. Reacher, on the other hand, was built for extremes. His default was to move extremely slowly or extremely fast. One moment he could appear languid, lazy, almost comatose. The next he could erupt into a frenzy of action, furious, relentless, for as long as necessary, then relapse into serene stillness until the next threat presented itself. But that morning, having shackled the only other person in the vicinity to a water pipe, he was out of alternatives. There were no buses passing by. No cars to hitch a ride in. And even if there had been, there was the issue of speed.

Another situation, the guy on the burner phone had said. *More urgent.*

The same guy who had ordered his lackeys to report any sightings of Rutherford.

The same guy whose victims showed up dismembered in suitcases.

Reacher ran back to the car, opened the door, and squeezed in behind the wheel. He hit the button to start the engine, nudged the lever into Drive, and leaned on the gas. He fastened his seat belt with one hand and pulled hard on the wheel with the other. The car slewed around in a tight loop and rejoined the road in a flurry of gravel. He was heading north. Back to town. Moving as fast as he dared. Smooth enough on the straight sections. A little ragged through the curves. Fields and plants and dark green foliage a blur on either side until the road narrowed and the houses began. He jinked right and left through the residential streets. Passed the courthouse. Played chicken with a blood-red Camaro at the intersection with the broken signals. Won. And pulled up outside the coffee shop. His tyres squealed. People stared. He was parked in an illegal spot but Reacher wasn't worried. One way or another he wouldn't be there long.

Reacher yanked open the door and surveyed the inside of the café. The barista was taking her time serving a couple of men in suits. Four more people were waiting in line. Two men. Two women. A pair of teenagers were in the sole booth at the back, pressed together, whispering. Three of the other tables were occupied. One by a man with grey hair, wrinkled and stooped over his cup. One by a woman in her twenties, tapping away at the keys of a slim silver computer. The other by a guy with long straight hair, staring at the wall and moving his hands like he was playing an imaginary set of drums.

No sign of Rutherford.

Reacher took a step into the room. 'Excuse me,' he said.

Silence descended and everyone turned to look at him. Everyone apart from the drummer.

'I'm looking for Rusty Rutherford,' Reacher said. 'Everyone know who that is?'

Heads nodded. Voices muttered and mumbled, all in the affirmative.

'Has he been in today? Or has anyone seen him anywhere else?'

Heads shook. Voices muttered and mumbled, all in the negative.

'Anyone know where he lives?'

Heads shook.

'OK,' Reacher said. 'If you do see Rutherford, I need

you to give him a message. Tell him Jack Reacher says to go home. Or to the police station. Whichever is closer. Without delay. And wait for me to make contact. Can you do that?'

Heads nodded. But not with much enthusiasm.

Reacher drove three blocks and dumped Marty's car outside the diner. Inside, only one booth was occupied. It was beneath a picture of a pink Cadillac. A retired couple, old enough to have owned the real thing, were sitting side by side. They were having a relaxed breakfast. Steak and eggs for him. A short stack with some kind of fruit topping for her. And coffee for both of them. Plenty of it. The waitress had left the whole pot.

There was no one at the centre tables. No one using the pay phone on the wall at the rear of the room. No one visible in the kitchen.

No sign of Rutherford.

Reacher took a step closer to the old couple's booth.

'Sorry to interrupt your morning, folks,' he said. 'Do either of you know Rusty Rutherford?'

'We know him,' the man said, after a moment.

The woman jabbed her elbow into her husband's ribs.

'Well, we know who he is,' the man added. 'It's not like he's a friend or anything. Can't say we've ever even exchanged words, thinking about it.'

'He's an idiot, is what he is,' the woman said. 'Why are you asking about him?'

'I need to find him,' Reacher said.

'To kick his ass?'

'That's not top of my list, no.'

'It should be.' The woman dropped her fork on to her plate. 'You should definitely kick his ass. Kick it good. He deserves it. He's an imbecile.'

'Maybe he deserves it,' Reacher said. 'Maybe he doesn't. Either way I need to find him. And fast. If you see him, will you give him a message from me?'

The man eventually nodded so Reacher told him what he wanted passed on to Rutherford, then turned when he caught movement from the corner of the room. It was a waitress emerging from the kitchen. The first one he'd met the night before.

'You're not here to cause trouble again, are you?' she said.

'Again?' Reacher said. 'I didn't cause trouble before.'

The waitress gave him a hard stare, then collected the coffee pot from the old couple's table. 'All right, then. Table for one? Sit where you like. I'll get you a mug.'

'I'm not staying,' Reacher said. 'I'm looking for Rutherford. The guy I was with last night.'

'I know who Rutherford is. Everyone in town does.'

'Has he been in today?'

'No. Haven't seen him. He never comes in the morning. He's strictly a dinner guy.'

'Do you know where he lives?'

'Not exactly. Somewhere in town, I guess. Not too far away because he always walks. Never seen him get out of a car.'

'Thanks,' Reacher said, and started towards the back of the room.

'Where are you going?' the waitress said.

'To the pay phone.'

'It's not hooked up. Who do you want to call?'

'No one. I want to check the directory. See if Rutherford's address is listed.'

'There's no directory, either. That thing's just a prop. The decorator put it there. Said it added authenticity.'

'Really?' Reacher said. 'OK, then. Guess I'll try something else.' He nodded and turned for the door.

'Why not look it up on your phone?' the waitress said. 'Who uses paper directories these days, anyway?'

Reacher paused. He used them. The same way he'd used military radio and the regular phone network and the United States Postal Service. Things he understood. He'd sent and received telexes and faxes back in the day, too. But he'd never involved himself with cell phones. Not to any major extent. He'd never needed to. Not even when all they did was make and receive calls.

'Could you do that for me?' Reacher pulled out his bundle of cash. 'Look Rutherford's address up on your phone? How much does that sort of thing cost?'

The waitress waved the money away and pulled her phone out of her apron pocket. 'I have unlimited data. I'm grandfathered in to my ex-husband's contract, through his work. Don't knock it. It's the only good thing to come out of our marriage.' She prodded at the front of the phone for a few seconds, then shook her head. 'Sorry. No record. Although that's probably a

110

good thing if you think about it, given how unpopular he is right now.'

Reacher squeezed back into Marty's car, fired it up, and pulled a tight U-turn. He blasted through the intersection. Narrowly missed an ancient Chevy pickup. Took the next two lefts. Parked in a hatched-off area at the end of the courthouse lot. And hurried around to the main entrance.

Officer Rule was on desk duty when Reacher approached the reception area in the basement. He used the public stairs, which she didn't object to. And she didn't seem surprised to see him, which made Reacher happy.

'What can I help you with, Mr Reacher?'

'I need some information.'

'Regarding?'

'Rusty Rutherford. Have any reports been made about him? Since last night? About him going missing, or being dragged into any other vehicles?'

'Mr Reacher, behave yourself. I heard you were an MP. Which means you know that even if we had received any reports . . .' Officer Rule paused for a moment, 'I wouldn't be able to tell you anything about them.'

'Thank you. How about his address, then? Do you know where he lives?'

'I do. But you know I can't share that kind of information.'

'Please. This is important. I'm worried about him.'

'Why are you worried?'

'He's disappeared. I need to find him.'

'I'm sure there's nothing to be concerned about. If Rutherford's not around he probably just left town. He was probably scared after yesterday. He's not exactly the physical type, and almost getting into two fights in one day was probably too much. I bet he went to visit relatives somewhere. That would be the smart move for him to make.'

'I tried to convince him to leave town. He refused. He was adamant about staying.'

'In that case he's probably just holed up again. He went home after he got fired and didn't come out for a week.'

'That's why I need his address. To check he's OK.'

'Why wouldn't he be? Is there something you're not telling me?'

'The guy I spoke to this morning before getting a ride with Detective Goodyear's friend. Is he still around?'

'No. He left right after you did. Why?'

'Did he leave any instructions about watching out for Rutherford?'

'Not that I know of. Should he have?'

'I need that address.' Reacher paused. 'What if I'd received an anonymous tip?'

'Specifically threatening violence? Against Rutherford?'

'Not specifically. Call it an old investigator's hunch.'

'I'd need more than that. And I'd have to go myself.

Make it official. Would he want that, given all the unwelcome attention he's been getting?'

'At least point me in the right direction. You know I'm not trying to hurt him. I'm the one who saved his ass yesterday.'

'You seemed to. That's true. But maybe two groups are after Rutherford and you were just keeping your rivals at bay until reinforcements arrive.'

'Say I did want to snatch a guy like Rutherford. Do I look like I'd need reinforcements?'

'Well, no. But you could be following orders.'

'I used to follow orders. Most of the time. Do I look like someone who does now?'

Officer Rule didn't reply.

'OK,' Reacher said. 'I get it. Don't give me Rutherford's address. Just tell me this. If I was an old friend wanting to pay him a surprise visit, what kind of place should I look for? A cottage in the countryside? A converted loft in the centre of town? A single family home near the place where he worked?'

'You're not credible. Rusty Rutherford's hardly the kind of guy who has truckloads of friends showing up unannounced.'

'Even so. Humour me.'

Officer Rule was silent for a moment. 'There's one thing I don't understand. Why are you going to all this trouble? Why do you care so much about Rusty Rutherford? No one else does. What's he to you?'

Reacher shrugged. 'It seems like he was trying his best to do the right thing and got screwed by the people above him. Something similar happened to me once. It doesn't feel good. And now he's got a bunch of assholes on his tail for some reason he doesn't understand and you people are in no hurry to help him. Someone's got to.'

'And that someone's you?'

'I guess so.'

'Why is that?'

Reacher shrugged again. 'I'm the one who's here.'

'All right. Listen. I can't speak in any kind of official capacity, but personally I would peg Rutherford as the kind of guy who lives in an apartment. And if an old friend happened to eat at the diner you went to yesterday and looked directly across the street, he wouldn't be completely in the wrong part of town.'

NINE

Reacher knew that cell phones could display maps. He'd seen it done. The level of detail was fine for basic navigation, he figured. He'd heard you could factor in real-time traffic information and weather updates, which could be useful if you were driving somewhere. Or hiking. He knew you could call up satellite images, too, if you wanted to see roofs or the tops of trees. But give him the choice and Reacher would always prefer a paper map. The kind he'd trained with at West Point. Large enough and granular enough to reveal the underlying terrain. A critical factor for a soldier. The difference between victory and annihilation. Or between setting a trap and walking into one.

A critical factor for a soldier. Sometimes just as important for a civilian.

Reacher could picture it so clearly. The diner. The apartment building. The coffee shop. A tight triangle. Rutherford's entire area of operations, aside from his brief excursion to the police station. He'd made it so

115

easy for the people who wanted to take him. If Rutherford strayed outside again, Reacher couldn't imagine any way he wouldn't be spotted immediately. And there'd be no one to save him this time.

If Rutherford was holed up in his apartment, he might be OK. For a while, at least. Snatching someone off the street is one thing. By its nature a fluid process. Quick. Easy to disguise. Easy to abort if it goes wrong. Extracting someone from inside a building is a different ball game. Particularly if you want to do it covertly. You can't just smash down the door to someone's apartment. Too noisy. Someone would hear. A neighbour, or someone working in the building. So some kind of ruse is required. That involves additional planning. Greater resources. Maybe props and costumes. And even if you gain entry, there's still the problem of getting the target to the street.

If Rutherford was holed up in his apartment.

Reacher thanked Officer Rule then took the stairs from the courthouse basement three at a time and almost knocked over a guy who was hurrying in through the doors. He was slightly built, wearing chinos and a polo shirt. With a logo. To show he meant business.

Rusty Rutherford himself. Not holed up. Not kidnapped. Not yet.

Reacher grabbed Rutherford by the shoulders, spun him around, and bundled him back outside.

'Let go!' Rutherford tried to squirm free. 'What the . . . what are you doing, Reacher?'

'It would be better to stay away from the police for

a while.' Reacher released him. 'I just told them you're in trouble again. Maybe missing. They might have questions.'

'I almost was in trouble.' Rutherford straightened his shirt.

'What happened?'

'I came downstairs in my building this morning. Heading for the coffee shop. I got as far as the door but one of my neighbours was on his way in. He's an older gentleman so I hung back to let him get past and I saw a face I recognized. Across the street. The woman who was driving the car those assholes tried to push me into yesterday.'

'What did you do?'

'I freaked out. I totally panicked. I ran to the door-man and screamed at him to get me a cab to the airport. Then I went upstairs to grab some things but I couldn't think straight. Couldn't decide what to pack. I knew I had my wallet with my ID and my credit cards so I figured I'd just get away – to anywhere – and buy whatever I needed when I got there. So I went back down and jumped into the cab when it finally came. It took an eternity. Or it felt like it, anyway.'

'So why are you here now?'

'I got halfway to Nashville and then I thought, what am I doing? I don't know how to be on the run. I don't want to be on the run. I want to stay here. Clear my name. And then I thought about you.'

'What about me?'

'You were in jail. For saving my ass. A second time.

I couldn't leave you behind bars so I figured bailing you out was the least I could do.'

'I appreciate the sentiment, Rusty, but the fight outside the diner wasn't about you.'

'Yes it was. Those guys were there to grab me. Holly – the waitress – was sure about that. Which is why she helped me out through the back door into the alley.'

Reacher shook his head. 'Those idiots were there for me. They thought I was working for the insurance guy who's negotiating to get the town's computers back up and running. Holly set it up. Remember the questions she was asking? About who I arrived in town with?'

'I don't understand. They think they can make insurance negotiators work faster by roughing them up?'

'They didn't want me to work faster,' Reacher said. 'They wanted me to back off.'

'That makes even less sense. Everyone in town wants to get back to normal as fast as possible.'

'Someone doesn't. And whatever the reason I think it's separate from the hot water you're in. I think we should find out for sure. And I think we should start by getting something to eat.'

'How will that help?'

'Always eat when you can. Then you won't have to when you can't. And it's an opportunity to kill two birds with one stone. If Holly's there, anyway. It's time for her to spill some beans.'

*

118

Reacher led the way around the side of the courthouse, and when they reached the parking lot he tossed Marty's keys to Rutherford. 'Here,' he said. 'You drive.'

Rutherford stopped dead. 'Wait. Whose car is this? Did you steal it?'

'It belongs to a guy I met this morning. He loaned it to me. He won't be needing it for a while.'

'I don't know.' Rutherford stayed still. 'I have my own car. Why don't we use it?'

'This one's here. Yours isn't.'

Rutherford touched the handle cautiously like he thought it might electrocute him, then opened the driver's door and climbed inside. 'I thought we were going to the diner?' He scrabbled for the button to move the seat forward. 'It's not far. We could walk.'

Reacher shook his head. 'We can't leave the car here. We might need it later. And we're not going directly to the diner. I want you to drive around a little first.'

'Drive around where?'

'Anywhere. Show me your old school. Your first girlfriend's house.'

'Why?'

'Because I'm hoping someone will follow us.'

Rutherford turned right out of the lot and for a few minutes his driving was awkward and jerky, like a nervous teenager trying out for his permit before he was ready. He spent more time looking in the mirror than through the windshield. Twice he clipped the kerb. But

119

after a while he settled and found his way past the house where he'd been born. Then he drove past his grade school. Then the house where an Irish girl named Siobhan had lived, who as a six-year-old he'd hoped to marry until she dumped him for refusing to give up his dream of becoming a race-car driver. Next was the house his family had moved to when he was ten. His high school. And so he continued, threading his way from one neighbourhood to another, some tidy and prosperous, some shabby and depressed, each with some kind of tie to his past. It was like travelling through a bricks and mortar encyclopedia of his life. Each new landmark seemed to relax or rejuvenate him. Each one made Reacher feel more claustrophobic. The idea of spending an entire life in one place made real and solid before his eyes.

The route they took was perfect for Reacher's purpose. Too convoluted for anyone to follow without giving themselves away. Too random for anyone to anticipate and press on ahead. The only disappointment was that no one tried. Reacher wasn't inherently impatient. He wasn't tired of Rutherford's company or irritated by his commentary. But neither did he wish to prolong his time in the town, so after another minute he told Rutherford to cut short his nostalgia tour and head for the alley next to the diner.

'Your building's the one opposite here?' Reacher said as they climbed out of the car.

Rutherford nodded.

'The woman you recognized from yesterday. The one who was watching you. Where was she?'

'I feel stupid now.' Rutherford hung back. 'Maybe I only imagined it was her. Maybe I overreacted to this whole thing. I didn't sleep very well last night and—'

'No.' Reacher turned to face him. 'When your instinct tells you something's wrong, then something's wrong. Always listen to your gut. It's what will save you from getting shoved into the back of some thug's car.'

'The woman was pretending to browse in a store window. Diagonally opposite from the entrance to my building. It's a drug store, basically, but it sells all kinds of fancy things so it calls itself an apothecary. It's full of candles and soft toys and home décor stuff. And it changes its window display every week. It's a jungle now. It was a beach last week. Something to do with giraffes the week before.'

Reacher looked around the corner and identified the store Rutherford had described. No one was near it. He checked the sidewalk in both directions. Neither of the people missing from the gas station was there. None of the people from the aborted ambush were there.

'She's gone,' Reacher said. 'No one from yesterday is in sight. Now you look. Tell me if there's anyone else you've seen before. Anyone who paid you a little too much attention recently. In the coffee shop. At the grocery store. Walking down the street. Even if you're not one hundred per cent sure. Even if it's only a feeling.'

Rutherford peered out of the alley, keeping his body

as far back as possible and stretching his neck like a turtle from its shell. Then he retreated and shook his head. 'No one.'

Reacher took a step towards the entrance to the diner and a synthrock song began to blare from Rutherford's phone.

'I need to take this.' Rutherford checked the number on the screen. 'It's my lawyer.'

He moved ten feet away and talked on the phone for less than a minute.

'Assholes!' he said when he returned. 'Remember I told you I had subpoenaed my work laptop? Obviously my boss knows he's screwed if I get my hands on it because the town is now saying I can have it, sure. But not for eight weeks. And then only if I pay fourteen thousand dollars for them to redact confidential information, now that I'm no longer a town employee.'

'Can they do that?' Reacher said.

'My lawyer says they can. She says they've got me over a barrel.'

'Is there any other way to get the laptop? Any legal-eagle tricks she can pull?'

'Short of breaking in and taking it, no.'

'So what are you going to do?'

'Agree, I guess. I need that computer. I've got the money. I can wait. And they say revenge is a dish best served cold, right?'

The retired couple had left by the time Reacher and Rutherford stepped into the diner and no other customers were in the place. They took the same booth as the previous night, with the turquoise Chevy and the view of both doors, and a couple of minutes later a waitress emerged from the kitchen carrying two mugs and a pot of coffee. It was the woman who'd helped Reacher with the online telephone directory.

'You found him, then,' she said, and nodded at Rutherford as she poured Reacher's drink.

'I did,' Reacher said. 'Now I'm looking for someone else.'

'Who is it this time?'

'Holly. Your co-worker. Does she have a shift today?'

'This is her shift.' The waitress scowled. 'It's supposed to be, anyway. But she's not here. She called in sick. Again. Which is why I'm here covering for her. Again. Instead of going shopping in Nashville with my daughter like I planned.'

'Is Holly out sick often?'

'She's off work often. And she says she's sick.'

'But you don't believe her?'

'I'm not saying that. I guess it depends on your definition of sick. I do believe she's often not in a position to work. Poor girl. Or stupid girl. Take your pick.'

'You think there's something else going on? The bottle, maybe?'

'Not the bottle. Try the fist.'

'She has an abusive husband? Or boyfriend?'

'Not according to her. She says she's single, and I'm not calling her a liar. But the makeup around her eyes?

That surely is. She must put it on with a trowel, some days. And the long-sleeved shirts she wears when it's a hundred degrees plus? They don't back her position. No, sir. She's either hooked up with some kind of an asshole or she's the clumsiest person this side of a circus clown. Now, what can I get for you?'

Reacher ordered a double stack of pancakes with extra bacon, then added two slices of apple pie while Rutherford struggled to choose between waffles and crepes. He finally came down in favour of waffles and as the waitress scribbled on her pad Reacher asked if the place had any newspapers. He saw Rutherford smirk. 'What?' he said when the waitress was out of earshot. 'Don't you like to keep up with the news?'

'I do like the news.' Rutherford pulled out his phone. 'That's the point. News. Not history.'

The waitress sauntered back and dropped a pile of local and national papers on the table.

'She should put them all in the recycling,' Rutherford said. 'There's nothing in any of these you couldn't already have read on here.' He held up his phone. 'In much more detail. Oh. Wait.' He picked up a local paper from the top of the heap. 'I'd missed that detail. Weird.'

'What is?'

'A journalist got murdered. I'd seen it in the headlines online but I hadn't noticed her name. It's there, look.' He put the paper down and pointed to the story just above the fold. 'It jumped out because she had contacted me a couple of times. It feels odd when the

124

victim is someone you knew of. Even if you didn't know them, exactly.' He read more of the story and his face lost all its colour. 'Oh, God. This is gross. It says she was kidnapped and kept alive, probably for days. And she was tortured. Then her body was cut up and dumped in three different places.'

'Let me see.' Reacher took the paper and read the story.

Rutherford picked up his phone, hit some keys, and dragged his finger up and down the screen. 'I can't find any more about it. There's a picture, but only of her before she disappeared.'

'You said she contacted you.' Reacher put the paper down. 'About what?'

Rutherford shrugged. 'The first time was a few weeks ago. She sent me an email. She was researching a story. Something to do with property records, I think. It was around the time the warehouse with all the town's archives in it burned down. All the records and documents going back to the Civil War, everything destroyed. She wanted to know if there were any digital records, so I guess she came to me because I was the IT manager.'

'Could you help her?'

'I remember thinking she might be in luck. The town had just finished a huge project to digitize all its public documents and put them online. It was almost ready to go live but I gave her the email address for the woman running the project anyway in case she could get an early peek. Then a couple of days after the ransomware attack she left me a voicemail message. She wanted to know if there was some other way to view the records now the database was locked. Obviously there wasn't and I had bigger problems on my hands so I didn't follow up.'

The waitress delivered their food but Reacher didn't start to eat right away. He was thinking. A woman who had been in contact with Rutherford had been kidnapped and murdered. A group had tried to kidnap Rutherford. A group with a track record of torture and dismemberment and dumping bodies in suitcases, if the guy Marty was to be believed. Reacher was liking the situation less and less.

'Rusty, I appreciate you coming back to bail me out this morning,' he said, when they had both finished eating. 'Even though I'd already gotten out. I was on my way out of town when some guys tried to ambush me. Four of the guys from yesterday. I think they're the same people who killed the journalist. You need to take this seriously. Very seriously, or the next story in the paper will be about parts of your body being found in a bunch of different places. You should leave town. Right now. Don't even go back to your apartment.'

'Leave town? And go where? And come back when? And do what in the meantime?' Rutherford wiped his face with his napkin. 'If it's true that the people who were after me killed the journalist, that's pretty heavy action for a town this size. They must be from somewhere else. And if they can reach me here, they can reach me anywhere. What if I leave and wind up someplace I don't know my way around, where it's easier for them to catch me? So no. I'm going to stay. And I'm going to fight.'

'Do you know how to fight?' Reacher said.

'No. But you do. You've done OK against these guys so far.'

'Rusty, I've been happy to help. But I'm not going to be here for ever.'

'Don't go just yet. Please. Stay a while. I'll pay you. I have savings.'

'I don't need money. And I wouldn't take your savings anyway.'

'OK then. Forget money. I'll pay by teaching you about computers. Help you get into the twenty-first century. Or the twentieth, anyway. Or at least to use a cell phone.'

Rutherford had a point about there being no guarantee of his safety if he ran. And it wasn't safe for him to stay, either. Not on his own. Not with federal agents who walked away from their promises to protect him. And not with people like Marty on the lookout, under orders to report his whereabouts.

'What if I stay?' Reacher said. 'For a day or two. And in return, you don't teach me anything about computers?'

'It's a deal.' Rutherford held out his hand. 'What do we do now? Stay out of sight? Hope they don't try again?'

'No,' Reacher said. 'We go on the offensive. Tell me, what time does the doorman in your building go off shift?'

'He said he pulled a double today. He'll be there till ten tonight.'

'Good. There are some preparations we need to make. But first there's a visit I want to pay. Grab your phone. Call up the telephone directory. There's an address I need you to find.'

TEN

Reacher had heard stories over the years about people coming home, drunk or stoned, and going into the wrong house. Sometimes they were found there later, asleep in a bed or passed out on the floor. Sometimes they got shot by the home's rightful owner. Sometimes they did the shooting, thinking their own home had been invaded. Reacher had heard plenty of excuses over the course of his career. The idea of a mistaken address was one he'd always found hard to swallow. That changed when he arrived in Holly's neighbourhood.

He could picture it freshly built. Two miles west of town. One squat rectangular house after another. One rectangular lot after another. All on a succession of right-angle streets. All carved out of the surrounding fields by the flood of money flowing around the state in a wave of postwar development. It would have been easy to mistake one for another when they were freshly minted. Approaching the wrong one would still be a straightforward mistake to make despite the minor variations that had crept in over time. There was a newer roof here, less bleached after fewer years in the ferocious Tennessee sun. An extension there, defying the neighbours' uniform contours. Some houses had fresher paint. Some had greener lawns. And others had owners who'd abandoned their attempts at decorating and gardening altogether.

Reacher walked up the path leading to the house next to Holly's, but he wasn't making a mistake. It was a deliberate move. Because of Holly's front door. She had the worst kind, from a cop's perspective. It had no windows so you couldn't see in from the outside. There was a peephole so anyone on the inside could see out. And it was made out of wood panels. They were thin. Useless for security. They could be kicked through in a second. About as far from a boulder rolled across the entrance to a cave as you could get. But that kind of door did have one advantage for anyone defending the premises. Easy as it would be to open, there'd be no need. They could fire right through it. A shotgun would be the best bet. Not that Reacher expected a waitress to be lurking in the hallway with a full load of double aught. But it's what you don't expect that gets you killed.

There was no answer at the neighbour's door. Reacher rang the bell again and waited. He allowed time for the demands of old legs or young babies. Then when he was reasonably certain the house was unoccupied he made his way down the side of the garage. He selected a section of fence which wasn't overlooked and where the wood seemed at its strongest and vaulted over into Holly's back yard.

It looked like someone's hopes for the space had been high. Once. A long time ago. Approximately half the area was given over to a lawn. Its curved edge followed the shape of a sine wave and it was finished with a border of rustic bricks, set end-on. Only now the mortar between them was cracked and the grass was scorched and dead. In the far corner was the wooden skeleton of an arbour. Reacher guessed it had been conceived as a place to relax. Maybe with a bottle of wine in mind. Maybe with a little romance. Only now the vines that had been trained over it were shrivelled and dry. The trellis was smashed in several places. And the chain holding up the swinging love seat was detached on one side.

The part of the yard that wasn't grass had been covered with flagstones. They clearly hadn't seen the business end of a broom for many months. There was also a round metal table, painted green, with an overflowing ashtray and a pair of chairs. They were set near a sliding door. It was made of glass. Much better, Reacher thought.

Reacher stayed close to the wall and moved until he was close enough to look in through the door. He could see one person. A woman. She was wearing a pink robe and sitting at a small table with a mug of coffee in front of her, untouched. She was leaning with her head in her hands and her hair was loose, cascading forward. Reacher tapped on the glass. The woman sat bolt upright. She turned to the door. Reacher got a clear view. It was Holly. Her face was creased with shock. And fear. And she had a giant bruise around her left eye. She tipped her head until her hair covered her face again, then waved Reacher away.

Reacher shook his head.

Holly waved for him go.

Reacher made as if to knock again. He pulled his arm way back. Made it clear that if he did knock, it was going to be loud.

Holly jumped up, hurried to the door, slid it open, pushed Reacher back, and stepped outside. She slid the door shut, trying to be gentle, but made sure it was fully closed.

'What are you doing here?' Her voice was a stern hiss. 'You'll get me in trouble.'

'Looks like you managed that without my help,' Reacher said. 'Who did that to your face?'

Holly tugged at her hair. 'No one. I was in a rush getting ready for work yesterday and it was late when I got home and I was tired so I forgot I left my wardrobe door open and I walked right into it. Anyway, my clumsiness is none of your business. What do you want? And why are you in my yard?'

'I'm here as a representative of the International Fellowship of Luddites. We're having a recruitment drive and after last night it occurred to me that you would be an ideal candidate.'

Holly's good eye narrowed and she took half a step back. 'What's a Luddite?'

'Someone who's opposed to progress. Especially any that comes from new technology. Named after an English guy. Ned Ludd. He broke a bunch of machines back in the eighteenth century.'

'Are you crazy? I don't care about some ancient English guy. And I'm not opposed to progress.'

'Then why don't you want the town's computers working again? What other reason could you have for wanting them to stay locked down?'

Holly shook her head. 'You've got this all wrong. I work at the diner. Our computer's working fine. Why would I care about the town's?'

'The bozos you set on me last night certainly cared. I assumed you shared their feelings.'

'What bozos? Those guys have got nothing to do with me.'

'Sure they do. They're your friends. Or your boyfriend's friends.'

'I don't have a boyfriend.'

'So your friends, then.'

'No.'

'OK, then. Let me ask you this. Before last night do you know how many times I've been mistaken for an insurance guy?'

Holly didn't reply.

'Zero times,' Reacher said. 'In the whole of my life. And then twice in half an hour. First you. Then them. You had a reason. You saw me with the real insurance guy.'

Holly was silent.

'The bozos had a reason too,' Reacher said. 'A different one.'

Holly didn't respond.

'They thought I was an insurance guy because you told them I was,' Reacher said. 'They didn't see me getting out of the real guy's car, and let's face it, they don't have the brains to jump to their own conclusions anyway. Even the wrong conclusions. Can we at least agree on that?'

'I guess,' Holly said.

'Everyone in town knows the insurance company is going to pay the ransom and get the computers working. The bozos wanted the insurance company to back off. That means you want the insurance company to back off. Which means you want the computers to stay locked down. Why?'

Holly didn't answer.

'OK,' Reacher said. 'Let's approach this from a different direction. When did your boyfriend last get himself arrested?'

Holly's good eye widened. 'I told you, I don't have a boyfriend.'

'Yes you do.'

She shook her head and looked at the ground.

'Do you smoke, Holly?'

She glanced at the ashtray on the table. 'Sometimes. After work. When I've had a hard day.'

'You wear makeup at work?'

Holly nodded.

'Then how come none of those cigarette butts have lipstick on them?'

Holly bit her lower lip for a moment. 'Because of when I smoke them. I come home from work and take off my makeup and put on my pyjamas and my robe and I come out for one ciggie right before bed. It relaxes me. Helps me get off to sleep.'

'I don't believe you. I think they're your boyfriend's. I think he sits out here in the fresh air, smoking, while you're working your tail off at the diner to pay for his habit.'

'No. He doesn't.' She shook her head. 'I told you. I don't have a—'

The door slid open and a man stepped out and shoved Holly aside. He was around six feet two, skinny, with pallid skin speckled with uneven patches of ginger stubble. He had greasy hair tied up in a ponytail which dangled between his shoulder blades. He was wearing lounge pants, baggy and shapeless and covered with cartoon superheroes, and a T-shirt that once might have been white.

'Stop asking questions.' The guy stumbled forward. His eyes were barely open as they struggled to adjust to the sunlight. He took another step, picked up one of the metal chairs, and brandished it as if he was trying to tame a lion. 'Shut your mouth. And leave.'

'What's your name?' Reacher said.

The guy didn't respond.

'It's a simple question. Most people get to grips with

135

their name long before they start kindergarten. Some even learn to write it down. But if you need more time, Holly and I could go inside. She could get me a cup of coffee. We could chat.'

'My name's Bob.'

'Good,' Reacher said. 'I'll assume you're lying, but Bob's as good a name as any so we'll go with it. Now, Bob. Do you want to do this out here? I was thinking we could go upstairs. See if any more wardrobe doors have been left open.'

The guy glared at Holly.

'Although it does look like you could use some sunlight so I'll do you a deal. Answer one question, truthfully, and I won't insert any part of that chair into any part of your body.'

The guy didn't reply.

'The last time you got arrested,' Reacher said. 'When was that?'

No reply.

'It's not hard,' Reacher said. 'Start with the day of the week. There are only seven to pick from.'

No reply.

'Are your arms getting tired yet?' Reacher said. 'Feel free to put that thing down any time.'

The chair was not a great choice of weapon. It was too light to use as a club, especially against someone Reacher's size. And it was too unwieldy to stab with. The guy's best option was to throw it, preferably making it spin, and try to exploit Reacher's natural instinct to bat it away. His arms might be out of position, just for a moment. His attention might waver, very slightly. The guy might get one chance to land a blow. If he was fast enough.

The guy didn't throw the chair. He took half a step and jabbed at Reacher's body with it. He took another half step and jabbed at Reacher's body again. Then he raised the chair higher and lunged for Reacher's face. Reacher grabbed the closest leg with his left hand and forced the chair out to the side. The guy clung on. He was pulling as hard as he could, desperate to retrieve it. It was his lance. His shield. His property, and he wasn't about to give it up. He was heaving with both hands. Which left his head and body completely exposed. Reacher could have kept the tug of war going all afternoon but he had a rule when it came to fights. Finish them. And finish them fast. So he launched a huge scything roundhouse punch with his right hand. His fist hit the side of the guy's head like a sledgehammer. His feet left the ground and he flew sideways, landing crumpled in the dirt where the grass should have been and sending up a thin plume of dust.

Holly ran to him, crouched down, and felt his neck for a pulse. 'Is he OK?' she said. 'Is he alive?'

'Probably.' Reacher replaced the chair next to the table. 'Physically, anyway. Now go inside. Get dressed. Grab your purse.'

'Why? Where are you taking me?'

'Nowhere. You're going on your own. You need to stay away from the house for a couple of hours. The police will be here soon. After that you can come back. Or not. It's up to you.'

It took Holly ten minutes to prepare herself to face the world. Reacher used the time to carry the inert guy on to the patio and tie him to the chair he'd just been brandishing. She appeared in the kitchen in a pink flowery sundress, white sneakers, and a denim baseball cap. She glared at Reacher then turned away without saying a word. He looped around the side of the garage and watched her drive away in an old silver Mazda roadster with its roof up. Then he returned to the kitchen and helped himself to the coffee that was left in the pot. He waited another ten minutes in case she doubled back. Then he made his way back to Marty's car and told Rutherford to drive to the police station.

'It's time to level with me, Rusty,' Reacher said as they took the first right-angle bend. 'What are you not telling me?'

'Nothing.' Rutherford glanced across at Reacher. 'I mean, like what?'

'The guys who are after you. We need to figure out what they want. They don't want to kill you – not yet, anyway – or they would have done it already. They don't want retribution or they would have sent a couple of low-rent clowns like the ones from last night. Their operation is too sophisticated for that. And too expensive. So they must want something. Something valuable.'

'I don't have anything valuable.'

'What about information? Something only you know.'

'I don't know anything. Nothing important anyway.'

'Maybe you do. It could be something that seemed trivial when you learned it. Something you came across at work but didn't realize the significance of at the time. You were the town's IT manager, right? So you must have had access to all the town's computers. All its data. Didn't you ever get bored and search through confidential records? Read people's emails?'

'Of course I did. Everyone does that.'

'What kind of secrets did you find?'

'Nothing interesting.'

'Anyone having an affair?'

'No.'

'Anyone being pressured to vote a particular way?'

'Nothing about voting.'

'Anyone taking bribes?'

'No.'

'Any money missing?'

'Nothing like that.' Rutherford blipped the gas and swung around a garbage truck.

'Maybe you picked up some information without realizing. The email from the dead journalist, for example. Could there have been any kind of message hidden in it?'

'No.' Rutherford slowed as a minivan pulled out of a driveway. 'There were no attachments. And her messages were just simple questions about property records. From the 1940s or 50s, I think. Nothing I have any knowledge about, anyway.'

'What about the regular mail? Did you receive anything unusual? At home, or at the office?'

'No. I get hardly any mail. Beside bills. And junk.'

'Have you bought anything recently? An old book? A painting? A piece of furniture? A car? Some vintage clothes? Anything a document or a computer disc could be concealed in?'

'I got some new Blu-rays. But the ones I haven't watched yet are still sealed up in their wrappers.'

'Have there been any other coincidences? Like the journalist contacting you, then winding up dead?'

'I can't think of any. My life really isn't very exciting. All I did was work for the town.'

'I believe you, Rusty. But if I find out you were moonlighting for NASA or the CIA, I'm going to be pissed.'

'I wish. But can you really see a bunch of rocket scientists or spies knocking on my door? Asking for my help? I told you about my only side project. The one I was working on with my friend. And it's worthless. It didn't work. Nobody wants it. Not even me.'

ELEVEN

Reacher left Rutherford in the car like he was a kid. Or a dog.

It wasn't a decision Reacher was entirely happy with. He knew there were risks. He'd heard there were laws against leaving kids in cars. He wasn't sure about dogs. But the risks Reacher was worried about were different ones, anyway. He wasn't concerned about overheating or dehydration or the vehicle getting stolen with Rutherford strapped inside it. He was thinking about the odds of a guy like Marty passing by. Spotting Rutherford. Pulling out a burner phone. Summoning the cavalry. Or of Detective Goodyear recognizing his friend's car and starting in with questions that Reacher wasn't ready to answer. Not yet. Which was the whole point of his being there. Risk versus reward. The opportunity to test a theory. To join some vital dots. Or to find out he was wrong.

Either way, just as valuable.

Either way, better to hurry.

Officer Rule was still behind the counter when Reacher got to the basement. She looked up from a form she was working on and Reacher swore he saw her eyes brighten when she spotted him. Or perhaps he just hoped they did.

'Mr Reacher,' she said. 'Any luck finding Rusty Rutherford?'

'False alarm,' Reacher said. 'Turns out he's fine. I could use your help with something else, though.'

Officer Rule folded her arms. 'Who's missing this time?'

'No one. It's about a recent case. A murder. A journalist who was found cut into pieces. I read about it in the paper. I need to know one thing. When the parts of her body were dumped, were they stuffed into suitcases?'

All traces of good humour disappeared from Officer Rule's face. 'That's an awful case. I can't discuss it. You know that. Detective Goodyear's handling it. You can ask him. But he won't tell you either.'

'Is he here?'

'Not right now.'

'I only have the one question. It's a yes or no answer. Please?'

'You know I can't.'

'Would you if you could?'

'Maybe.'

'Then how about a trade? I scratch your back. You scratch mine.'

Officer Rule paused. 'What have you got?'

'There's a woman who works at the diner opposite Rutherford's building. Holly. She has a boyfriend—'

'Who's an air thief she's so embarrassed about she won't even admit he exists to her co-workers?' Officer Rule shook her head. 'They know anyway, of course. Makeup can only cover so many bruises. But if you're trying to tempt me with a domestic violence beef, you can forget it. I've been down that road with Holly before. It goes nowhere. She won't cooperate.'

'What if you could put an end to the domestic violence without needing Holly's help? And put a major feather in your cap at the same time.'

'How could I do that?'

'How long has the boyfriend been on the scene?'

'A couple of years, at least.' Officer Rule frowned. 'I don't know exactly when he showed up. I'm just going by when I first saw bruises and started asking questions.'

'Did you run the guy's name through the computer?'

'Of course. He came back clean.'

'Are you sure it was his real name?'

Officer Rule shrugged.

'Did you run his prints?' Reacher said.

'No. I couldn't arrest him. Holly wouldn't press charges and there was no other evidence it was him who hit her.'

'Has he been arrested for anything else in the last couple of weeks? Since the computers have been locked down?'

'I don't know. Without the computers it's not as easy

to keep up with who's doing what as it normally is. Why?'

'I think you should check,' Reacher said. 'I think you'll find he was arrested recently. And I think there's another reason Holly keeps him secret.'

'Like what?'

'Could you do some digging and find out if he gave you his real name? And if he has any aliases?'

'Maybe. If I had a good reason to.'

'Do you have any friends you could call in other police departments? Ones with working computers who could run whatever names you find?'

'Maybe. If you tell me why.'

'The guy who gave me a ride into town yesterday is an insurance agent. He's here to negotiate the ransom that needs to be paid so that you can get your computers back up. Holly saw me get out of his car. Then she eavesdropped on my conversation with Rutherford at the diner and got the wrong end of the stick. She thought I worked for the insurance company too, which is why she called in those goons to tell me to back off. The question is, why would she do that? Who could benefit from keeping the computers offline?'

Officer Rule frowned. Then blinked. Then her smile returned brighter than ever. 'Someone who's wanted in another jurisdiction.'

'I'd go one further,' Reacher said. 'I'd guess someone wanted in another jurisdiction for something serious. Something where the statute of limitations is about to time out.'

'Which is why he's been lying low for so long, sponging off poor Holly. He slipped, but at just the right time – for him – because our routine computer checks were impossible. Why is it that assholes have all the luck?'

'Maybe his luck's about to change.'

'I'd happily change it for him. If those phone calls pan out. And if I could find him.'

'Maybe, acting on a hunch, you could take a look in Holly's back yard. Any time in the next ninety minutes should do it.'

'For real?'

Reacher nodded.

'Maybe I will take a look in her yard. Maybe you're right about the suitcases, too. But you didn't hear that from me. It was kept away from the press for fear of copycats. And as a test for anyone claiming to be a witness.'

'Thank you, Officer Rule. And good luck with your phone calls.'

'Reacher, wait. I have a question for you. How did you know?'

'About Holly's boyfriend?'

'No. About the suitcases.'

'It's part of something I'm working on. Maybe. I'm still joining the dots.'

'Be careful where you tread. This is an active investigation. You shouldn't be anywhere near it. If you know something, you have to tell me.'

'Don't worry. I will. When I'm sure.'

*

145

Rutherford was asleep when Reacher got back to the car. Like a kid. Or a dog.

'Get what you need?' Rutherford said, rubbing his eyes as Reacher slid into the passenger seat.

'Another piece of the puzzle,' Reacher said. 'Maybe.'

'So what's next on the list?'

'Accommodation.'

'You could stay at my place.'

'Thanks, but no. And you can't stay there either. You saw the woman from yesterday watching your building. That shows they know where you live. We need to find somewhere else. Somewhere discreet. Anonymous. Where we can come and go without attracting attention. And in a convenient location. A motel outside town, maybe? Or near the highway?'

Rutherford reached for the button to start the engine then pulled his hand back and took out his phone. 'I'll have to Google it. I've lived here my whole life so I've never stayed in a hotel in town.' He pressed and clicked and scrolled for a couple of minutes, then lowered the phone. 'And there's another problem. No offence, Reacher, but are you really the kind of guy who can come and go without attracting attention? Regardless of how anonymous or discreet a motel is?'

Reacher said nothing.

'How about this as an alternative?' Rutherford said. 'I have the key to a neighbour's apartment. It's on the same floor, opposite mine. The guy who owns it is away on a cruise. He hates the heat so he's away most of the year. Except winter. I keep an eye on the place for him.

And water his plants. We could both stay there. My friend wouldn't mind and no one else would know. In fact, it could help us because if anyone saw us going into the building they'd assume we were heading for my apartment so they wouldn't search for us but they'd actually be looking in the wrong place. And if anyone tried to pay us a visit the doorman would call my cell. We could watch them watching us.'

'That might work.' Reacher paused. 'Is there a garage at your building?'

'Yes. In the basement. Access is from the street behind.'

'Is your car there?'

Rutherford nodded. 'Each unit gets one space. You can rent more if you want. And there are visitors' spots if you want to park this car in one.'

'This car can stay on the street,' Reacher said. 'Have you got any duct tape at your place?'

'Why would I have duct tape?'

'How about a sharp knife?'

'I have a couple of kitchen knives. But they're not super sharp. I'm not much of a chef.'

'Where's the nearest hardware store?'

'I'm not sure. But there's a truck stop near the highway that sells those things.'

The truck stop wasn't the biggest Reacher had ever been in, but it was close. More of a small village than a large gas station. It had pizza restaurants and burger joints and fried chicken stands. Two motels. A coffee

147

shop. Even a souvenir shop. The forecourt with the fuel pumps was almost the size of a football field, but it still seemed like an afterthought. The pumps were divided into two groups. Four banks of regular-sized ones for cars and SUVs. And six banks of larger ones, spread wider and further apart for the trucks and their trailers.

They left the car at one of the regular pumps and headed into the main building. Rutherford took a moment to get his bearings, then led Reacher to a cabinet full of knives. Reacher picked out two. A large one and a small one. The large one he didn't particularly like because of its dull, cheap steel but he took it anyway because he figured it looked intimidating, which could be a useful quality. The smaller one was much more satisfactory. Its blade folded so it would fit easily in a pocket. It had a good sharp edge and a mechanism that allowed it to open with a flick of the wrist. Reacher paid for the knives with cash then loaded two rolls of duct tape into his basket, along with a can of pepper spray for Rutherford. He was heading back to the register when he spotted a clothing section. Of sorts. He rooted around until he unearthed a pair of khaki pants and a pale green T-shirt that he thought would fit. He added a denim shirt he figured could double as a light jacket. Then he settled up for his goods and pre-paid for some gas. He handed a bag containing everything but the clothes to Rutherford and went to the restroom to change. He transferred his toothbrush and passport and ATM card and cash into his new pockets, and dumped the old garments in the trash. When he emerged he found Rutherford between two heated cabinets which dispensed the sausages for self-assembly hotdogs.

'I got these for you,' Rutherford said, and held out a different bag.

Reacher took it and looked inside. He saw two brightly coloured boxes. One contained a cell phone. The other a Bluetooth earpiece. He handed the bag back to Rutherford. 'Thanks, Rusty. I appreciate the thought. But I'm not a cell-phone guy.'

'Please take it,' Rutherford said. 'It's really for me. You can't be at my side twenty-four seven and it would make me feel better knowing I could call if I needed you. Even waiting here just now got me so nervous I almost followed you into the bathroom. And look.' Rutherford reached into the bag and took out the phone. 'I got you the oldest-fashioned kind they had. It was the last one left. It doesn't even go online. It can make calls, and it can text. That's all. I'll set it up for you. I'll keep it charged. And when this is all over, if you don't want it any more, give it back. I'm sure there's a museum somewhere that would take it.'

Reacher said nothing.

But he did let Rutherford pass him the bag.

The same time Reacher was changing his clothes, Speranski's burner phone was starting to ring. He picked up right away. It was a very short call. From a man a short distance away. A report. First, a fact. Then an opinion. Brief and concise. Leaving Speranski feeling mightily relieved. He took a sip of iced tea, then dialled a number on his secure phone.

'You can recall the team,' Speranski said when the call was answered. 'Rutherford and the drifter are back in town.'

'You've seen them?' the voice at the end of the line said.

'No. My contact in the police department reported it.'

'He didn't arrest them?'

'He didn't come into contact with them. Not directly. Another officer did. She mentioned it without realizing the significance.'

'Why did they come back?'

'I don't know. Maybe Rutherford got cold feet about flying. Maybe the drifter contacted him and called him back. We'll find out.'

'They give any clue where they're going?'

'Nothing concrete.'

'OK. We'll cover Rutherford's building, the coffee shop, and the diner. He doesn't usually stray far.'

'Good. One other thing. Have the team swing by the ambush site on their way to town. Or a couple of them, at least. My guy was supposed to deliver the drifter. Something obviously happened to him.'

'I'll have them check. We can arrange clean-up if necessary. And if it's not necessary?'

'Make it necessary. The man failed. Or he sold us out. Either way, he's no use now.'

*

Back outside Reacher pumped the gas, then told Rutherford to drive to the street behind his building and stop twenty yards short of the entrance to the garage.

'Is there a camera on the outside?' he asked when they arrived.

'Yes.' Rutherford pointed. 'There's one right above the door. Sometimes if it's late and it's raining and a nice doorman is working you can flash your headlights and he opens it for you remotely. Saves you getting out.'

'How do you open it normally?'

'With a fob. You just hold it up to a sensor. And there's a keypad for backup.'

'Does the code get changed frequently?'

'No.' Rutherford rolled his eyes. 'It's been 1 2 3 4 ever since I moved in.'

'How's the garage laid out?'

'You drive down a ramp, which curves to the left. You're supposed to honk but no one does. Then the main space is just a basic rectangle. There are pillars every three car widths apart. Spaces along each side. And a double row in the centre.'

'Cameras?'

Rutherford thought for a moment. 'Yes. There are those little half globes dotted around on the ceiling. I couldn't say how many.'

'Is there pedestrian access to the building?'

'Yes. There's a door at the far end. It leads to a flight of steps up to the lobby. You need your fob to open it, or there's another keypad you can use.'

151

'Good. We'll risk one drive-by, then I want you to loop around to the front of the building and stop somewhere with a clear view of the main entrance.'

Rutherford drove slowly past the garage entrance then cut through an alley, squeezing past a pair of dumpsters, and rolled the car to the kerb diagonally opposite the diner. He left the engine running, ready to go. Reacher scanned the street ahead, working systematically, projecting a mental grid across the storefronts and the sections of sidewalk. No one was loitering. No one was waiting in any of the parked cars. No vehicle passed them more than once. No one was out walking. Rutherford took the new cell phone out of its box. Reacher repeated his scan, looking behind them this time. Rutherford worked at a credit-card-sized piece of plastic until he'd separated a section which held a little gold chip. He inserted it into a slot in the back of the phone. He slid the battery into place over it and hit the power button. Reacher repeated his scan to the front. Saw no one. The phone lit up and played a tinny electronic tune. Reacher repeated his scan, behind. Saw no one.

'There's a little charge in the battery,' Rutherford said, and passed the phone to Reacher. 'Are we going to be in the car for a while? I could charge it the rest of the way.'

'No,' Reacher said. 'The coast's clear. It's time to move. Here's what I want you to do. Go into your building and tell the doorman you came back from the airport because you forgot something. Tell him you rebooked your flight for this afternoon and you're going to drive to the airport this time but need his advice about when you should leave to get there by a quarter after four. Whatever time he suggests, you should thank him, say you'll see him in a couple of weeks when you get back, then head upstairs. Only don't stay in your own apartment. Go to your neighbour's. Wait for me there. OK?'

'OK.' Rutherford handed the car key to Reacher and opened his door. 'And I'll text you when I get there. You have a phone now. You might as well use it.'

TWELVE

Rutherford's text arrived after five minutes. It contained two words. *In. Safe.* Reacher read it, waited another five minutes, then took the truck-stop bag from the back seat, climbed out of the car, and headed into Rutherford's lobby.

The doorman's booth jutted out from the side wall, opposite the elevators, equally spaced between the front entrance and a door which Reacher assumed led to the stairs to the garage. It had mahogany sides which matched the panels on the walls and its green-veined marble top was the same pattern as the floor. As far as Reacher could tell. At least eighty per cent of its surface was covered. There were ring binders full of directories and procedures and regulations. A computer monitor. A phone, bristling with all kinds of buttons and displays. And a cell phone with a large screen. The space behind the counter was probably the regular size but the doorman seemed to completely fill it. He looked like he was in his late twenties, with a shaved head, a doughy face, small eyes and a heavy build. Very heavy. The kind of guy who had done well on the high-school football team, Reacher figured, but whose life had been all downhill from there.

'Help you?' the guy said.

The years Reacher spent in the military police had taught him that most investigations go with the numbers. A wife turns up dead, it's usually the husband who killed her. Something goes missing from the stores, it's usually a quartermaster who stole it. Someone shares secrets, it's usually for the money. Unless they're being blackmailed, which is less common. Or tricked. Or acting on principle, which is the rarest thing of all.

'Name your price,' Reacher said.

The guy stared back, blankly. 'For what?'

'You just made a call. Or sent a text. Or an email. Name your price to message me instead in future.'

The guy stretched out and covered his phone. It completely disappeared beneath his giant paw. 'I didn't send a text. I don't know what you're talking about.'

'Sure you do,' Reacher said. 'You just had a conversation with Mr Rutherford. Then you told someone what time he's leaving for the airport. Just like you told them he asked for a cab this morning.'

The guy was suddenly on his feet. He was as tall as Reacher. As wide as Reacher. Maybe faster than Reacher. 'You want to hurt Mr Rutherford? Try it. See what happens.'

Reacher paused. Investigations go with the numbers. If the guy wasn't motivated by money, then what?

Blackmail was next in line, statistically, but Reacher couldn't see it. And principle is the rarest thing of all.

'Outstanding.' Reacher held out his hand. 'I knew you'd pass. But we can't be too careful. Not when Mr Rutherford's safety is at stake. I'm glad you're on the team.'

'We're on a team?'

'Of course. Keeping Mr Rutherford safe. You heard he got attacked on the street yesterday?'

The guy nodded.

'I was the one who saved him,' Reacher said.

'That was you?' The guy shook Reacher's hand. 'Thank you. I like Mr Rutherford. He's always nice to the building staff. Not like some of the assholes who live here. I could tell you some stories . . .'

'I bet you could,' Reacher said. 'But after yesterday we have to be extra careful. There might be a leak. That's why they sent me here. To see if anyone changed sides.'

'Not me.'

'Clearly. What about the other doormen? Can we trust them?'

'I think so. The day guys, anyway. The others I don't know so well. But Mr Rutherford doesn't go out much at night anyway. Unless he's working. Then he's out all night, sometimes, if he's upgrading the systems or whatever those computer guys do.'

'OK, good.' Reacher leaned forward and gestured for the guy to move in closer. 'Now here's the thing. I'm going to level with you. We think whoever tried to hurt

156

Mr Rutherford yesterday is going to try again today. I'm here to stop them, but I need your help. I need you to do two things. Are you with me?'

'What two things?'

'First, show me how I can see the pictures from the garage security cameras. Then I need to take your place for a while.'

'You can watch the cameras on here,' the guy said. He pressed the space bar on the computer keyboard and the screen lit up. It was divided into nine rectangles. The one at the top left showed the street outside the garage entrance. Each of the others gave a different view of the inside in clear, crisp colour. 'It records so I don't have to watch all the time, but I do when I'm bored.'

'Sounds good,' Reacher said. 'Now, is there a closet anywhere?'

'Sure.' The guy pointed to a door disguised amongst the panels to the side of the booth. 'Right there. Why?'

'This is the part where I really need you to trust me.' Reacher set the bag from the truck stop down on the countertop. 'I need to make it look like I overpowered you, in case anything goes wrong. We need to safeguard your cover. I need you to lie low in there for a while and I have to warn you, it could be a couple of hours. I don't know exactly what kind of schedule these guys are on. And I have to make it look convincing. These are animals we're dealing with here. So I'm going to use a little tape. Just a bit around your wrists. And your ankles. I better put a piece over your mouth, too. I'm sorry. I know it's not pleasant. But it's the only way to keep Mr Rutherford safe.'

Speranski was poring over a large-scale map, thinking about parking and power supplies for his next project, when his secure phone rang.

'Two things,' the voice at the other end of the line said. 'First, the team found your man. Trussed up with his own handcuffs at the place he was supposed to deliver the drifter. He's no longer on the payroll, as requested.'

Speranski didn't reply.

'Second, Rutherford has been located.'

'Where?' Speranski said.

'At his building.'

'Damn. If he's holed up again he could be in there for weeks.'

'No. He's leaving this afternoon. Going back to the airport. In his own car. Because he's taking something with him.'

'This is via the doorman?'

'Correct. The poor sap thinks he's helping to keep Rutherford safe.'

'Where's the drifter?'

'Unknown.'

'Where's Rutherford's car?'

'In the building's garage. We have the make, model, and licence plate.'

'I know the garage for that building. It's underground. Enclosed. I don't like it.'

'Ambush?'

'That's what I'm thinking.'

'Struck me that way too.'

'Tell the team to be extra careful. We can't afford another spectacle.'

Reacher sat in the doorman's chair for forty minutes, then his eye was drawn to the monitor. To the rectangle at the top left. The one fed by the camera above the garage door. The image was slightly fish-eyed to give a wide field of view, but a black Suburban was still an unmistakable vehicle. It pulled to the side of the street ten yards short of the entrance, close enough for Reacher to make out the blond splashes of the driver's and the passenger's hair. A blue Toyota passed it and pulled up in front of the garage. A mark in the demerit column, Reacher thought. Time had no doubt been tight but they still should have replaced their vehicles.

Reacher watched as a woman got out of the Toyota's rear seat. It was the red-haired woman from the alleyway the day before. Reacher saw her work the keypad. 1, 2, 3, 4. The same code ever since Rutherford moved there. The car pulled forward and the woman got back in. It momentarily disappeared then showed up on the next segment of the screen, emerging from the bottom of the ramp and swinging into the middle of three vacant spaces in the central bank. The driver got out. It was the woman he'd seen behind the wheel the day before. The second woman joined her. Then the guy

Reacher had knocked out. Then the one he'd thrown through the window.

The four fanned out through the space. They checked both regular entrances and looked for alternative ways in or out. Then they located Rutherford's car. An off-white 1970s VW Beetle, parked more or less at the centre of the left-hand wall. There was an empty space on each side of it. Beyond that to the left was a Jeep Grand Cherokee. To the right a Ford F150. A good set-up from an ambusher's point of view. Both were tall vehicles. They offered plenty of concealment. The guy Reacher had knocked out pointed to each of them in turn, then to another empty space perpendicular against the far wall. Reacher could tell what the guy was thinking. The plan practically made itself. The driver could tuck the Toyota into the space by the far wall. One guy could hide behind the Jeep. One could hide behind the Ford. The other woman could conceal herself near the pedestrian door in case Rutherford got spooked and tried to run back into the building. Otherwise they would wait for him to reach his car. Then the Toyota would pull forward. In electric mode, like yesterday, so there'd be no sound. No warning. The two guys would emerge. One would open the door. The other would grab Rutherford and push him inside. A piece of cake.

The garage was a good set-up in a broader sense, too. It was a known location. There was no uncertainty over which route Rutherford might take if they tried to tail him to the airport. No concerns over traffic, or parking. A lower chance of any passers-by becoming involved than if they mounted an operation on the street. And no need to worry about the security cameras, as they had an ally covering the monitoring station. Or so they believed.

The garage was a good set-up, but it wasn't perfect. The chance of members of the public entering the scene was reduced, but not eliminated. That left the possibility of witnesses. And of collateral damage. Too high a possibility, in Reacher's judgement. But he wasn't planning the ambush. The ones who were remained huddled for a minute. Pointing. Waving their arms. Arguing.

Reacher would have liked the image to be bigger, but from what he could make out, the guy he had knocked out was at odds with the driver. The other two had eased back, staying out of the argument. Finally the driver shook her head and pointed towards Rutherford's Beetle. She put her hands on her hips and waited until the knocked-out guy returned to the Toyota. He opened its trunk, took something out, and carried it to the VW. Around to its rear. He knelt down and stuck one hand beneath the car. Reacher's first thought was: Bomb. Then he reconsidered. The box was too small to hold much explosive. It had to be something else. The guy gave up on the underneath and slipped the device into the hollow in the centre of the Beetle's chunky rear fender. The driver pulled out her phone. She checked the screen and nodded. A tracker, Reacher realized. A smart tactic. A mark in the merit column.

Reacher watched the Toyota leave the garage, then turned his attention to the Suburban. It was fifty-fifty in his mind whether it was there as backup, in which case it would leave, or if it would wait and tail Rutherford anyway in case there was a problem with the tracker. Ten minutes passed. There was no sign of movement. Reacher had conceived the exercise as a way to observe his enemies in action. To gauge their competence and decision-making. Now their caution offered him another opportunity. The chance to shake things up a little.

A sign which read *Back in Five Minutes* was peeping out of the heap of clutter next to the monitor. Reacher fished it out, set it on the countertop, then picked up his bag and headed for the main door. He walked down the street, past Marty's car, took the alley Rutherford had cut through, and turned to approach the Suburban head on. He was thirty yards away when the guys inside it spotted him. The driver was the first to notice. He nudged the passenger in the ribs. Reacher saw them both stiffen. He kept on walking. Slow and easy. Arms loose and well away from his sides. He didn't want any misunderstandings. He drew level with the passenger window then stopped and pulled what he hoped was a friendly, non-threatening smile. The passenger looked at him for a long second then lowered the window.

'What do you want?' the guy said.

'First, I want to apologize for yesterday,' Reacher said. 'I stumbled into something I didn't understand. I had no idea what was going on and just acted on instinct. I hope your buddies are OK. Anyway, since then I had a long talk with a very interesting guy. He set me straight on a few things. Like what I need to do if I want to leave this town in one piece. So here's the deal. I know where Rutherford is and I'm willing to hand him to you on a plate. But you'll have to move fast. There's not much time. He set up his doorman to pass on a story about him driving to the airport, but the truth is he's got a guy lined up to smuggle him out of the country. A private plane. False papers. Disguises. The whole nine yards. Meet me in the coffee shop in five minutes and I'll explain everything. Just don't be late. This is a one-time thing. Dawdle and he'll slip through your fingers for good. Only it won't be my fault this time.'

Reacher strolled to the next cross street and as soon as he was out of sight of the Suburban he broke into a run. He looped around towards the main entrance to Rutherford's building and then ducked back into the alley. He eased the pair of dumpsters apart and settled into the gap he had created to wait. He figured the Suburban guys wouldn't tell anyone what they'd heard right away. It was too crazy. They'd want to debate it between themselves first. For at least a minute. They probably wouldn't believe what Reacher had said, but could they afford to ignore it? Probably not. They'd decide they had to follow up. But they'd have to report in first. To whoever was pulling their strings. Then it would be crunch time. If Reacher had oversold the story they

163

might abandon the garage. Drive around and park near the coffee shop. He hoped he hadn't been that convincing. In which case a more sensible response would be for the guys to split up. For one of them to stay on station in the Suburban on the grounds that Reacher's tale was most likely a ploy. And for the second guy to head for the coffee shop on foot just in case Reacher was telling the truth. Time would be tight after all the deliberations. Getting there before the deadline would be tough. So the second guy would take the quickest possible route. Which would be the shortest. Which would be through the alley.

The clock in Reacher's head showed four minutes since he had walked away from the Suburban. No one entered the alley. Four and a half minutes. No one entered. Four and three quarters. Then Reacher heard footsteps. Someone running. Light. Efficient. Purposeful. Coming his way. Reacher waited a beat then stepped out from between the dumpsters. The passenger from the Suburban was in the alley, ten feet away. He stopped himself after another step and dropped into the same kind of weird stance he'd used the day before. Then he had a change of heart. Maybe it was the size difference. Maybe it was the expression on Reacher's face. Maybe it was the recollection of what had happened to his two comrades. But whatever the reason, he straightened up, reached behind his back, and produced a gun. A Beretta M9.

'You're not going to give Rutherford up, are you?' he said.

'I might,' Reacher said. 'On one condition.'

'Which is?'

'Tell me why you're after him.'

The guy paused. 'He has something we want.'

'No shit, Sherlock,' Reacher said. 'Be more specific.'

'I don't think so. And I don't need to. Because very soon you'll be begging to tell us where Rutherford is.'

'Us?' Reacher said. 'Who's us?'

'All will be revealed when the time is right.' The guy made a rotating motion with the gun. 'Now turn around. Hands on the wall. Feet wide apart. I'm sure you're familiar with the routine.'

The guy was standing seven feet away. Reacher was out of his range. But Reacher was almost a foot taller than him.

'You win,' Reacher said. He began to turn. Moving clockwise. Pivoting on his right foot. Bringing his left foot closer to the guy with the gun. Halving the distance between them. He kept rotating until his left shoulder was facing the guy. Then he planted his foot, shot out his hand, and grabbed the underside of the barrel. He twisted the gun viciously away from his body, breaking the guy's finger with the trigger guard and messing up the ligaments in his wrist. The guy howled and pulled back. The Beretta clattered to the ground. He glanced down at his hand. Blood was starting to flow from a break in the skin above his knuckle. He sucked the wound. Then he returned his focus to Reacher. He took half a step back and feinted a kick to the body with his front foot, but instead of following through he used the momentum to rise on his toes and swing a punch around towards Reacher's temple. Reacher leaned back and deflected the blow with his forearm. The force of the block spun the guy around, leaving his left side exposed. Reacher jabbed him in the kidney. He shaped up for a kick but dialled it back at the last moment and more or less pushed the guy's hip with his foot. The guy staggered back and sideways and his legs tangled and he tripped himself, landing in a heap at the base of the far wall.

Reacher stepped closer and waited for the guy to make eye contact. 'What does Rutherford have that you want?'

The guy pulled himself on to all fours then slowly hauled himself to his feet and stood there for a moment, hunched and sagging, like a man thoroughly defeated. Then he exploded forward and threw two quick sharp jabs to try to push Reacher back. He threw two more then spun around, whipping up his right foot and aiming for the side of Reacher's head. It would have been a problem if the kick had landed. It may not have had the weight behind it to knock Reacher out, but it could have slowed him down. Disoriented him. Given the guy a way back into the fight. Only Reacher didn't back off. He did what he always did. Moved closer to the danger. He saw the guy's body begin to twist so stepped in and met his foot when it was only at waist height. He trapped the guy's shin between his arm and his body and slid his hand back to grab the ankle. Then he lifted the guy's foot, leaving him hopping back and forth, fighting for balance with an expression of pure outrage on his face.

'You should save moves like that for gym class,' Reacher said. 'Where there are rules. Out here there are only decisions and consequences. Well, one decision. And you have to make it. Whether to tell me what I want to know. If you decide not to, you'll never walk again. Not without a limp.'

The guy didn't respond.

'Take a moment to think,' Reacher said. 'Have you ever seen an X-ray of a knee? It's not the bones you need to worry about. They heal up easily. It's all the other parts you need to keep in mind. Ligaments. Tendons. Cartilage. But mainly ligaments. If they get damaged, not too severely, and you're a famous sports player with limitless money and immediate access to a hospital, there's a chance of a decent repair. Only you're not a top sports guy. I'm guessing you don't have limitless money. And I can assure you that if my foot crashes down on your knee with all my weight behind it, the damage is going to be way beyond severe. That's for damn sure.'

The guy heaved back, trying to free his foot. He flailed with his left hand, trying to land a blow or gouge Reacher's eyes, but he was stymied by his own locked leg. 'OK,' he said, panting, when he finally gave up. 'Fine. Do what you have to do. I'm not saying a word.'

Reacher didn't move.

'Come on. What are you waiting for? Just do it.'

'This is your last chance,' Reacher said. 'What does Rutherford have that you want?'

'It doesn't matter what you do to me. I'll never tell you anything.'

'If that's the way you want it,' Reacher said. He lifted his right foot, held it still, and looked the guy in the eyes. Then stamped down hard towards the knee of the guy's standing leg. The guy threw his head back and closed his eyes and whimpered, but he didn't say a word. Reacher's shoe was solid and heavy. He stopped his foot with the sole an inch from the guy's knee. He paused, then lowered his foot to the ground. He released the guy's leg and simultaneously punched him just below the ear. The guy went down sideways, his right leg still extended like he'd just kicked a ball, and didn't move again.

Reacher checked that the guy was breathing then retrieved his weapon. It was well maintained and, unlike Marty's, loaded. Reacher searched the guy's clothes. He had a wallet with some cash which Reacher took as spoils of war, but no credit cards or ID or anything indicating a name or an address. Or any kind of temporary accommodation. He had no spare ammunition. And nothing else in his pockets except for a phone. Reacher pressed the button below its screen and a message appeared saying that his print wasn't recognized so to try again or enter a keycode. He held the button against the unconscious guy's thumb and the screen lit up. Reacher touched a picture of a phone and a list of calls appeared. There was nothing since yesterday. There were no voicemails. No text messages. And the picture of an address book only revealed five entries. All were numbers. No names. Reacher put the phone in his pocket, slipped the gun into his waistband, and fetched his bag from the gap between the dumpsters. He took out the duct tape. Fastened the guy's ankles together. Taped his hands behind his back. Stuck a strip over his mouth. Then hoisted the guy over his shoulder and heaved him into one of the dumpsters.

THIRTEEN

The Suburban was still parked in the same spot when Reacher stepped out of the alley. He waved with both arms to attract the driver's attention then gestured for the guy to join him. The driver shook his head and indicated that Reacher should come to him. Reacher threw up his hands as if exasperated and hurried along the sidewalk until he was level with the passenger door. The window whirred down and Reacher could see that the driver was holding a gun. Another Beretta. Presumably also well maintained. Presumably also loaded. He had it in his left hand, low down in his lap, pointing sideways. Not an ideal firing position. But that was compensated for by the size of the target he had to aim at. Reacher's chest.

'Come quick,' Reacher said, ignoring the gun. 'To the alley. Your friend needs help. Bring the car.'

'What are you talking about?' the driver said.

'I waited for you at the coffee shop and when you

didn't show I came back to look for you. I figured I'd cut through the alley to save time and I found your friend. He was on the ground. In bad shape. He was bleeding. He had this big cut on his forehead. He was unconscious. Breathing, but only just. He must have gotten mugged. He had no wallet. No phone.'

'Did you call 911?'

'I couldn't. I don't have a phone. That's why I came to get you. And I figured that with this whole computer situation going on it would be quicker for you to drive him to the hospital anyway.'

The driver paused, then put down the gun. 'All right. Show me.'

'Come on. Follow me. Pull into the alley. Then you'll see him.' Reacher set off at a fast jog, and after a second he heard an engine fire up behind him. Tyres squealed and a moment later the Suburban shot past him. It continued to accelerate then darted into the mouth of the alley without signalling. Reacher caught up and squeezed along the passenger side. The driver climbed out, his gun in his hand, and joined Reacher at the front of the vehicle.

'Where is he?' the driver said. 'I don't see him.'

'I forgot,' Reacher said. 'I put him in the dumpster. The far one. To keep him safe. I didn't know if you'd still be waiting, or how long it would take to find you.'

The driver raised his gun to Reacher's chest. 'You forgot?'

'What?' Reacher said. 'You never forgot anything?'

'All right.' The driver raised the gun to Reacher's

head. 'Back up against the wall. Keep your hands where I can see them.' He waited for Reacher to comply then moved forward to the dumpster. 'Don't move.' He lifted the lid with his free hand and took a glance inside. Reacher waited a moment for him to register the state his buddy was in, then strode forward and pulled the gun from his waistband. He switched it around so he was holding it by the barrel and swung it in a fast sideways arc. The butt smashed into the driver's elbow.

The driver dropped his own gun and the lid of the dumpster and slumped down on one knee. Reacher switched the gun to his left hand, wrapped his right hand around the side of the guy's head and slammed it against the dumpster. Then he grabbed the front of his shirt, half lifted him, and dropped him down in a sitting position with his back against the metal. His body was as slack as a rag doll. Reacher waited a moment to make sure he was conscious, then rammed his gun into the guy's mouth.

'I'm going to ask you a question,' Reacher said. 'I'll give you five seconds to think about it then I'll remove the gun. If you give me the correct answer I'll let you fish your buddy out of the trash and drive away. Give me anything other than the correct answer and I'll put the gun back in your mouth and blow the back of your skull clean off. Are we clear?'

The driver's eyes widened and he did his best to nod his head.

'What does Rutherford have that you want?'

Reacher raised his thumb and each finger on his right hand in turn at one second intervals, then pulled out the gun.

'Go ahead.' The driver raised his chin. 'Shoot me. Don't waste any more time. There's nothing you can say or do that'll make me tell you what it is.'

'You'd rather give up your life than one little piece of information?' Reacher said. 'That seems like a poor choice.'

'It's not just my life. I have a wife. A brother. I know what would happen to them. Come on.' He opened his mouth, leaned forward, and gripped the muzzle with his teeth. 'Do it.'

Reacher pulled the gun away and clubbed the driver on the side of the head with his right hand, knocking him out cold. He retrieved the dropped gun, checked it, tucked both weapons into his waistband, then started to go through the guy's pockets. The contents proved no more satisfying than the passenger's. He had no credit cards. Nothing with a name or an address. No spare ammunition. His phone had been used more recently, but it contained no names or personal information. Reacher took the cash as before, duct-taped his ankles, wrists and mouth, and dropped him in the other dumpster. Then he turned to the Suburban. He checked the glovebox. The sun visors. The door pockets. Under the seats. Under the floor mats. In the trunk. Around the spare and the jack and the little wallet of tools. Under the hood. In the wheel arches. And found nothing. Not even a loose dime or a discarded candy wrapper. Whoever these guys were, they were fastidious. That was for damn sure.

Reacher closed the hood and the tailgate and all the doors apart from the driver's. He was tempted to climb in. Take the vehicle. Partly because it could be useful. And partly to deprive the enemy of a valuable asset. But he had seen one of the same crew stick a tracking device on Rutherford's Beetle. That meant there was a risk they'd use the same technology on their own vehicles. So he made sure the key was in the ignition and left the Suburban to take its chances.

Someone had left a stack of cards advertising a pizza delivery service on the reception counter but otherwise the lobby of Rutherford's building seemed undisturbed when Reacher returned. He was starting to feel hungry again so he tucked a card into his back pocket then approached the closet door. He braced himself in case the doorman had used the time to think. To see through the ruse. Then he worked the lock. And found the guy sitting on the floor with his knees up near his shoulders. He blinked his tiny eyes against the sudden light then recognized Reacher and tried to speak, but his voice was unintelligible through the shiny tape.

'Good news,' Reacher said. He grabbed the doorman's hands and heaved him to his feet, then took out his smaller knife and started to cut him free. 'False alarm. There's no threat against Mr Rutherford. Not today. He's perfectly safe. For now. Although he's not feeling very well. He just called. He's postponed his trip again. He's going to stay in his apartment for a few days until he's feeling better. He doesn't want any visitors, or any other interruptions at all. I'm just going to go up and check if he needs anything, then I'll be heading back to Nashville. It was a pleasure meeting you. Keep up the good work.'

Reacher figured that if Rutherford's neighbour could spend half the year away on cruises he must be an older guy. Retired. With plenty of time on his hands. And many years of accumulating junk behind him. Reacher pictured an apartment crammed with chintzy furniture. Flowery curtains. Pictures of children. Probably grandchildren. But when Rutherford opened the door and stepped back Reacher saw a large, almost empty space. All the dividing walls had been removed. The exterior walls had been painted bright white. The floor was covered with pale grey concrete which was sealed and polished to match the kitchen countertops. Aluminium blinds, angled to allow the afternoon sun to flood in, covered the windows. The coffee table had a lozenge-shaped glass top with a curved wood support rather than regular legs. The rest of the furniture was all chrome and black leather. Reacher had seen pictures of things like it in a magazine about mid-century designers. There were polished walnut units with doors set into them separating the far third of the room. Something that looked like a giant metal egg made out of riveted panels set on a black wood tripod. And a set of blond wood shelves. Each one was an apparently random length, but Reacher figured they were probably carefully calculated to create some kind of effect. They seemed to be floating near the wall rather than being attached with brackets or supports, and they held a sparse selection of random objects. The kind that were no doubt pronounced *objays* by the people who sold them.

'What do you think?' Rutherford said.

'I don't know,' Reacher said. 'Is it a home? Or a showroom?'

'A home. It's been Mitch's for years. Although he does have a couple of other ones too. And it hasn't always looked like this. He had it completely remodelled last year. He has some really cool things now. See this?' Rutherford pointed at the egg. 'It came from a lightbulb factory. In Germany. They used it to test the vacuum seal inside the glass bulbs. Now Mitch uses it for storing his whisky.' Rutherford walked across and opened a door set into the front of the thing. Inside were four crystal decanters full of golden liquid and eight stubby glasses. 'Think twice before helping yourself, though. The cheapest kind costs twenty grand a bottle.'

'I'll stick to coffee,' Reacher said. 'Assuming your friend has anything so pedestrian.'

'Me too,' Rutherford said. He crossed to the kitchen area and opened a wall cupboard containing a vast shiny machine bristling with knobs and gauges and levers. 'If I can figure out how this thing works.'

Reacher moved to the centre of the room. 'I thought

you said you had the keys so you could water your friend's plants?'

'Right.' Rutherford nodded.

'What happened? Did you forget? Have they died?'

'No. Of course not. Mitch would kill me. They're over there on the shelf. Good as new.' Rutherford pointed to a row of three miniature pots on the shelf to the left of the living area window. Each one contained a shrivelled stalk, like the trunk of a tiny decaying tree.

'Those things are alive?' Reacher said.

'The outer pair are over a hundred years old. The other one is younger. Mitch said it's about sixty, I think. They come from a forest in the foothills of Mount Fuji, Japan. It's the only place in the world they grow. The same family has tended to them for generations.'

'Your friend has interesting taste. What does he do?'

'He's in IT, like me.' Rutherford paused and a look of genuine sadness settled over his face. 'Only his million-dollar idea actually worked. Unlike the piece of trash I pinned my hopes on.'

Reacher took a seat on one of the couches and waited for Rutherford to finish his battle of wits with the coffee machine. 'Rusty, we need to talk about something serious now. The people who are coming after you took the bait about you driving to the airport. They showed up in your garage. But they passed on the opportunity to ambush you. That was the correct choice in the circumstances. They planted a tracking device on your car instead.'

'But I'm not going to the airport.' Rutherford placed the mugs on the coffee table and sat on the other couch. 'What will they do when my car doesn't move?'

'I don't know. That depends on how patient they are. And on the urgency of whatever problem they're trying to solve. My guess is that it won't be much longer before they come in and get you. But we could avoid that if we can figure out what they want. I need you to focus all your attention on answering that question.'

Rutherford shook his head. 'I already told you. I don't have anything that anyone could want.'

'There are two possible scenarios here,' Reacher said. 'You have this thing and don't realize it. Or they believe you have it but you don't. Option one we can work with. Option two presents more of a challenge. So here's what I want you to do. Finish your coffee. Then lie back. Close your eyes. And pick a day. Say, the Monday of the week before the ransomware thing began. Tell me everything you did from the moment your eyes opened in the morning until you fell asleep that night. Every single detail. However trivial. You never know what might trigger a connection.'

'OK.' Rutherford took a swig of coffee then slipped off his shoes and swung his feet up on to the cushion. 'I'll try. But I'm not sure it'll help.'

'You need to focus,' Reacher said. 'No distractions, so switch off your phone.'

Rutherford's phone started to ring.

'Ignore it,' Reacher said.

Rutherford was already pulling it out of his pocket.

He checked the screen and held it up for Reacher to see. It read *Doorman*.

'I told him not to disturb you,' Reacher said. 'Ignore it.'

'I can't. What if it's those guys coming up to get me? You said they will. What if he's trying to warn me? I have to check.'

Rutherford hit the speaker button and placed the phone on the table.

'Mr Rutherford? I'm sorry to disturb you, sir. I know you're not feeling well. But I have to give you a heads-up. Someone's here to see you. I told her no but she marched right by me. She's on her way up. And man, she's pissed that I tried to stop her.'

Rutherford hung up then crossed to the door and pressed his eye to the peephole. 'No one's there. Not yet. It must be one of the women from yesterday. The one who was watching the building. She must have found out which is my apartment. She's coming to get me. What are we going to do?'

'We don't have to do anything,' Reacher said. 'No one knows we're here.'

'That's right.' Rutherford took a deep breath. 'We could lie low. Wait for her to go.'

'We could. Avoid a confrontation in a confined public space. And inject some bad intelligence into their decision-making process. Two good outcomes with zero effort on our part.'

'OK. Let's do that.' Rutherford turned away from the door and a moment later his face creased with alarm. 'Wait. What if she breaks in? She could pick the locks.'

'Also good. We could join her. Ask her some questions. And afterwards we'd have the perfect cover. You came back from dropping some trash down the garbage chute and found an intruder in your apartment. She tried to run. She slipped. And she hit her head. Tragic, but the kind of thing that can happen when you choose a life of crime.'

'We couldn't— Shhh. Someone's coming.' Rutherford pressed his eye back to the peephole. 'It's— Oh my goodness.'

He opened the door and stepped out, still in his socks. Reacher saw a woman on the other side of the corridor. She was facing away, ready to ring Rutherford's doorbell. She had the same colour hair as the Toyota driver. It was the same length. She was the same height. But her clothes were different. She was wearing a pale grey suit. And Reacher didn't recognize her face.

'Sarah!' Rutherford held his arms out wide. 'So good to see you. What are you doing here?'

'I was worried about you.' The woman pulled Rutherford into a hug so tight it looked like she was trying to break his back. 'You stopped calling. You didn't answer your phone. I left you all kinds of messages. Then I heard what happened with your job.'

'I didn't get any messages. You must have been calling my work phone. The assholes took it when they fired me. I'm sorry. I should have told you. I should have called.'

'Are you OK?'

'I am. I was down for a while but I'm doing a lot better now.'

'Good. Because there's something we need to talk about. It could be huge.' The woman's giant purse was slipping off her shoulder and as she heaved it back into place her head turned and she spotted Reacher standing in the doorway opposite. 'Oh. Hello. You must be Mitch. I've heard a lot about you.'

'Actually, no,' Rutherford said. 'Mitch is away. This is Jack Reacher. Reacher, this is my friend Sarah Sands. The one I told you about. Sarah was working on Cerberus with me.'

Rutherford made another pot of coffee while Sands fired up her laptop and listened as Reacher ran through a summary of events since he'd arrived in town.

'I don't like this.' Sands took Rutherford's hand when he set her cup on the table and looked up at him. 'I don't like this one little bit. Someone's trying to kidnap you? That's not OK. The Bureau should be all over this. We need to keep you safe.'

'That's what Reacher told the cops yesterday but they weren't too impressed.' Rutherford sat down next to Sands. 'I'm still pretty much *persona non grata* around here.'

'How about you, Sarah?' Reacher said. 'Have you got any contacts from your Bureau days? Anyone who could light a fire under this?'

'Maybe,' Sands said. 'I still know some people. I

could make some calls. Maybe kick up a few sparks, at least. Have you got any idea what Rusty has that they want, whoever they are?'

'We're still trying to figure that out.'

'Maybe I can help. I bet they want the same thing I'm here to get. The system we created. Or part of it, at least.'

'Why would anyone want that piece of junk?' Rutherford slumped back. 'It didn't work.'

'It didn't work the way we hoped. That's true. But that doesn't mean it was a complete failure. Something you said when the attack first happened didn't quite make sense to me, Rusty. It kept on bugging me. So I ran a bunch of simulations and I think I found something.'

'That the whole thing was a giant waste of time?' Rutherford said. 'That we would have been better off creating a crossword puzzle app for people learning Swahili?'

'I can't believe you didn't see this yourself,' Sands said. 'There's a giant clue right there in your backup.'

'No. There's nothing in the backup. Nothing over-wrote what was already there on whatever crappy second-hand servers I used to cobble it together.'

'That's exactly the point.'

'Oh my God.' Rutherford stood up and pressed his palm to his forehead. 'Sarah, I love you.'

'So your system did work?' Reacher took a sip of coffee. 'You said it didn't.'

'Right,' Rutherford said. 'It didn't.'

'So why would anyone want it?' Reacher said.

'It comes down to the way ransomware works,' Sands said. 'Attacks don't happen all in one go. Imagine a computer network is like an enemy fortress. If you want to capture it you don't just lob a grenade over the wall and hope the soldiers are all killed. You start by infiltrating your best guy. You smuggle him past the defences and leave him to sneak around inside for a while. Get the lie of the land. Draw maps for when your main force arrives. Find out where all the good stuff is hidden. And see if there are any traps to avoid. In our case, for traps read backups. Backups are kryptonite to ransomware. There's no point in locking a bunch of data if your intended victim has a clean copy. He'd just laugh in your face. And that's a big problem because some of these groups are in the game for prestige as much as they are for cash. So if they find a backup – which are usually only connected briefly to capture a snapshot of any recent changes and then get taken offline or even off site for safe keeping – they immediately deploy a special kind of program. A particularly sneaky kind. We call it a trident because it does three things all at once. One, it destroys all the data that's already been backed up. It's either wiped clean or replaced with porn or taunting messages, or things like that. Two, it prevents any new backups getting saved. And three, it sends spoof signals to the organization's management system saying that everything is working OK. That way it avoids alerting anyone to

183

what's happening and adds to the blow when the main systems lock up and the ransom demand is posted.'

'But your backups didn't get wiped,' Reacher said. 'Or overwritten with porn. Did they?'

'No,' Rutherford said. 'Something stopped that from happening. But nothing new was saved. And spoof management reports did get sent. That's why I thought we'd be OK after the attack. And why I was so shocked when we weren't.'

'Cerberus interfered,' Sands said. 'It broke one spike off the trident. It's the only explanation. I ran simulations using copies of the most recent ransomware we've come across, and here's where things get interesting for the people who are chasing Rusty. In eight out of nine tests, not only was the existing data untouched, but a fragment of the malicious code was retained on the backup system. It was somehow caught by Cerberus when it stopped the disc from getting wiped.'

'Enough of a fragment to unlock the town's computers?' Reacher said.

'No,' Sands said. 'It doesn't work that way. But it could reveal who's responsible. It's like when a bank robber wears a mask but the security cameras pick up his gang tattoos.'

'That must be why these guys are trying to get their hands on it,' Rutherford said. 'They must have analysed the system maps the ransomware sent back to them. Seen something they didn't recognize – Cerberus. And figured out what it could do. Maybe put that together with the reports in the press about the old data being the only thing that survived. You should have seen the headlines. *Rutherford's Rusty Ransom Response* was my favourite. But we have a different reason to want it. Maybe millions of different reasons. Right, Sarah?'

'That's why I'm here,' Sands said. 'There's life in the guard dog yet. It's not the product we thought it was going to be. It obviously doesn't prevent ransomware attacks happening. But if it bulletproofs any backed-up data, that's the next best thing. A lot of organizations would pay a lot of money for that. All we need is the servers you were using. Bench tests are fine, but we need to make sure it really was our system that saved the old data. Not some random malfunction. So let's go get them.'

'We can't get them.' Rutherford flopped back down. 'When I thought the system had failed I threw everything in the trash.'

FOURTEEN

Speranski was in his study, looking through catalogues from electrical wholesalers, trying to find the closest thing to a World War II anti-aircraft searchlight, when his secure phone rang again.

'We were right,' the voice at the end of the line said. 'It was an ambush.'

'How bad?' Speranski said.

'Could have been worse. The main team, four people, went into the garage. They read the situation, planted a tracker on Rutherford's car, and got out unscathed. The drifter got the two guys who stayed outside.'

'Are they dead?'

'No. But they'll be out of the game for a while. He knocked them around pretty good. And one of them got bitten by a rat before he was found. They were left in a couple of dumpsters.'

'Does the Center know?'

'Yes. But don't worry. The police didn't get involved. No members of the public saw anything. No attention was drawn. They're not pulling the plug. But they are making a change.'

'What kind of change?'

'They're bringing someone in. Denisov. The rest of the team is stood down to surveillance only until he arrives.'

Speranski paused. He had never worked with Denisov. But he had heard of him. Denisov had started out as an interrogator. The human polygraph, he was called. Due to his appearance. And his temper. His ability to loosen tongues. And bowels.

'I thought Denisov wasn't used in the field any more,' Speranski said. 'Too many unfavourable outcomes.'

'No, he is,' the voice said. 'He's been in Chechnya for the last five years. Broadening his repertoire. Working on his self-discipline. He's rehabilitated now. Back in favour with the people who count.'

'And they're letting him loose on Rutherford? Isn't that overkill?'

'On the drifter. The rest of the team can proceed with Rutherford, as before.'

'Wait a minute.' Sands moved over to the window, then turned back to face Rutherford. 'How could you have thrown an entire server array in the trash? How many were you using?'

'Eight.' Rutherford looked at the floor. 'I guess I didn't literally throw them in the trash. But I did kind of trash them.'

'What did you do to them?'

'Well, first off the glass in the cabinet door broke when I slammed it. I did that when I realized the backup hadn't worked. Then I ripped out all the cables. I wanted to fling the whole thing in the dumpster outside but when I tried to drag it to the door the foot of the cabinet got wedged where part of the raised floor had come loose so I left it. Then I went back and stuck on a Post-it note saying it was for the trash.'

'This was before you got fired?'

'Right. On the day of the attack.'

'Was the cabinet still there the day you left?'

Rutherford shrugged. 'No idea. I didn't go back to the equipment room after the first day. There was no point. Nothing was working. I actually thought about checking on my last day but I was only there ten minutes before they gave me the letter.'

'No one's replaced you?'

'Not yet.' Rutherford hung his head. 'The job's hardly a big draw. Nothing works. The title is Head of Department but there's barely a department to head. There are only two other staff. One's part time. And both are furloughed until the network is fixed.'

'So what are the odds that anyone saw the note saying to trash the equipment? And then did anything about it?'

'Probably pretty low.'

'So it might still be there?'

'It might be.'

'Come on then. What are we waiting for? Let's go see.'

'There's no point. We can't get in. They made me leave my key.'

'Rusty. Seriously. Think about this. What did I spend the last decade doing? There's no such thing as a locked door as far as an FBI agent is concerned. And there'll be no one else there. The security system's down. The cabinet may as well be sitting on the sidewalk waiting for us to pick it up.'

'How will we move it?'

'Between us it'll be no problem. There must be dollies in the receiving room. How else did it get brought in when it was first delivered?'

'I mean how will we get it back here? It won't fit in my car.'

'That's why I rented a minivan. But we won't bring it here. Not with people watching the building and doormen reporting your every move. We'll get a storage unit for tonight. Hide it there. And tomorrow we'll rent some office space. Or even a motel room. We'll need power. And space to work. And privacy.'

The plan was straightforward. Sands would leave first and pause in the lobby. She'd apologize to the doorman for her previous abruptness and mention that her friend was feeling much better. So much better that he was about to go out for a drive. Reacher and Rutherford would give him time to send his text. Then they would head to the garage. They'd take Rutherford's Beetle. Reacher would drive. He'd cut through the alley with the dumpsters, moving slowly enough for Rutherford to hop out, hide, and wait for Sands to collect him. Then Reacher would continue to drive around in the Beetle, towing the Toyota behind him as if on an invisible rope, and give Rutherford and Sands a clear shot to and from the town's IT building.

No plan survives first contact with the enemy.

Or in this case, Reacher's desire for contact.

He started out aimlessly crisscrossing the town's streets the way a person might if he didn't realize there was a tracking device attached to his fender and was trying to spot anyone tailing him. He was uncomfortable, even with the seat racked all the way back. The pedals sticking up out of the floor were stiff and awkward. There wasn't enough room for his feet. The manual box was cranky and the frequent corners called for what seemed like constant gear changes. But most of all Reacher didn't like having to take it on trust that he was actually being followed at all. He liked being able to sense his pursuers. To see them in his head like moving dots on a map. He felt cast adrift. Less like the tow rope was invisible. More like it never existed.

Reacher checked the VW's fuel gauge. It was almost dry. He was always surprised at the way civilians so often failed to refill their vehicles after driving them. What's the point in equipment that isn't maintained and ready for use? He shook his head and changed course for the truck stop he had visited earlier with Rutherford. He chose the pump nearest to the main building and approached from its right side so that no one watching from the road would get a clear view of the passenger seat. Then he locked the car and went inside.

Reacher started with the clothing section. He didn't usually change twice in a day but conditions were fluid. Operating in the dark was now on the cards so conceal-ment was a priority. He picked out a pair of black pants and a black hoodie, paid, and went to the restroom to change. Then he returned to the clothing area and grabbed a pack of three T-shirts off the shelf. He took a map, a flashlight, and an emergency gas can from the auto section. A twelve-pack of bottled water from the refreshment area. Filled a twenty-ounce cup with the kind of extra-caffeinated coffee truckers drink when they have to drive all night. And at the register he added two cigarette lighters and prepaid for plenty of gas.

Back outside, Reacher stowed his new items. Every-thing other than the coffee and the gas can went on the floor on the passenger's side of the car, along with the larger knife and the duct tape he'd bought earlier. He put the smaller knife and the lighters in his pocket and tucked the guns he'd captured into his waistband. He filled the Beetle's tank and topped off the can. Stowed the can in the trunk. Checked the map to see if there was a way to join the route Marty had taken that morn-ing without driving through the town again. Found one which looped around to the west. Then he folded him-self back into the little car and pulled out on to the road.

On the map the road was represented by a thick black line. It suggested something wide. Substantial.

Broadly equivalent to the one Reacher had taken on his way to the truck stop. It proved to be a poor example of the cartographer's art. On the ground the road was little more than a track. Reacher imagined agricultural workers getting it started with horses and carts, then solidifying it with tractors and trailers, until finally the county adopted it. Widened it a little. Straightened it. Added a meagre layer of blacktop. Maybe sent an occasional maintenance crew to tend to the rough, pitted ribbon of scorched asphalt that twisted around sudden bends and snaked through fields and the occasional stand of trees. Reacher took it easy. He wanted to keep gear changes to a minimum. And he didn't want to end the night in a ditch.

Eventually the track dumped him out on to the route Marty had used, south of the town. The light was fading fast and the traffic, which had been thin earlier in the day, was now non-existent. Reacher checked his mirror every few seconds. There was no sign of a car behind him. No glinting of the setting sun on a windshield. No trace of headlights. Reacher came to a long, straight section so he pushed the gas pedal all the way down to the floor. The engine rattled and growled behind him. The steering wheel twitched and throbbed. He kept his speed up for as long as he dared and hit the brakes going into the next bend. He was a fraction late. The car pitched and squirmed. Its narrow tyres squealed. He emerged into the next straight half on the wrong side of the road, corrected course, and slowed to walking speed. He checked his mirror. There was no sign of a car behind him. He passed the spot where Marty had stopped. Checked his mirror. There was no sign of a car. He saw the entrance to the field he had cut across. There was no sign of a car. He accelerated under a bridge that had once been used to carry water for the crops. No sign of a car. Then the Beetle's feeble beams picked out the tall shape of the Studebaker sign. Reacher eased off the gas. He wanted his pursuers to be clear what he was doing. Assuming anyone was pursuing him at all.

Reacher steered the Beetle through the gap between the old showroom and the abandoned gas-station kiosk. He stopped the car at a careless angle and climbed out, leaving his door open. He checked the kiosk to make sure Marty wasn't still shackled to the water pipe then fetched the gas can from the trunk and took the water bottles, the T-shirts, and the flashlight from the passenger's footwell. He left the passenger door open and made his way to the section of hoarding at the back of the showroom where he had seen the woman and one of the guys emerge when they fled. He tugged at the plywood. It was loose at one side so he enlarged the gap and squeezed through. He stepped into a large space with an arc of tall windows in place of a front wall. They were all boarded up. A range of tall display cases covered one side. The glass was broken and the shelves were bare. Reacher swept the flashlight beam around slowly and picked up a line of footprints in the dust on the floor. He followed them to a door at the far side of the showroom. It led to a flight of wooden steps. They'd seen better days. That was for sure. Their paint had long since worn away. There were cracks in their surface. The hand-rail sagged when Reacher touched it. He thought twice about going up. What he had in mind could be accomplished from the ground, given sufficient cover. But he was in the mood for something theatrical, not functional.

Reacher kept to the edge nearer the wall, where the steps should be at their strongest. He took them slowly, testing each one carefully before committing his weight. He crept his way to the top, which gave access to a hatch leading to the roof. He heaved the water bottles up and through. Then the gas can. Then he climbed out after them. The surface was flat. It had once been covered with some kind of silver coating. To make it waterproof, and to protect the building from the worst of the sun's heat. Now the surface was dull and peeling. It was covered with leaves and twigs and assorted pieces of trash that the wind had somehow deposited there. Much of it had blown against the base of the wall that enclosed the whole space. It was three feet tall. Like the rampart on a miniature castle, Reacher thought. Which was just how he was planning to use it.

He crossed to the rear corner at the side of the building next to the kiosk and separated six bottles of water from the pack. He emptied them, then half filled them with gas. He cut two of the T-shirts into strips and fed them into the bottles, leaving plenty hanging over their necks. Then he lined the bottles up at the base of the wall and took one of the lighters out of his pocket.

*

Reacher's plan was only missing one component. A target. He sat and waited and no car appeared in the gap below. He began to worry that he was on a wild goose chase. And that he was the goose. He crossed to the stem of the vertical sign and looked for movement on the road. There was none. Then he caught a glimmer of light, a quarter of a mile away. He thought. But he wasn't sure. He kept watching, willing it to reappear, and he picked up the sound of a vehicle. It was coming from the other direction. A panel van. It was bouncing and swaying along the road. Moving fast. Maybe a plumber, anxious to get home after a long day. Or an electrician. Or a drunk.

The van slowed a little and its lights picked out a familiar shape hunkered down beneath the water bridge. The blue Toyota. It had followed him. But it wasn't looking to engage. Just to observe. To note where he went. Close enough to see if he switched cars or got a ride with someone else. Too far away for Reacher to incinerate. He kept watching, willing it to change tack. To approach. Another five minutes passed. There was no movement. Then Reacher's phone buzzed. It was another text. Also from Rutherford. It said the same thing as the first. *In. Safe.* That meant Reacher could head back, too. He could let the Toyota follow. Creeping along behind him on its electronic tether. The guys in it could file an innocuous report. Inform their bosses about every detail of Reacher's evening. But he didn't like that idea. When he sent a message he liked it to be clear and unambiguous. Someone had sent six guys

195

after him. It would be wrong to let the day end with only two of them in the hospital.

Reacher put the lighter back in his pocket and emptied the gas out of the bottles. He eased his way back down the steps to the showroom and crossed to a door in the centre of the back wall. It led to a corridor with another door at the far end, one door on the left, and two evenly spaced on the right. The one on the left opened into a double office. Based on the age of the building Reacher guessed the outer part would have been for a secretary and the larger, inner room for a manager. Or the owner of the franchise. Both offices were empty. The first door on the right led to a small kitchen. There were no appliances or utensils. Just a Formica countertop with enough space for preparing drinks or light snacks.

Next up was a pair of bathrooms. There was a cleaning closet tucked in between them. A broom had been left behind. And a mop. And a bucket. A roll of towels. A bottle of bleach. And some floor polish. Reacher moved on to the door at the end of the corridor. It led to the final section of the building. A car-sized space with a roll-up door to the side, drain holes in the floor, but no vehicle lift and no room for serious tools. Some kind of valet bay, Reacher thought. Where cars had been detailed before going on display. Or got ready for collection. There was a metal cabinet against the far wall. Reacher wrestled it open and found a tub of hand cleaner, long dried up. A tin of wax. Some chalky paste for brightening up whitewall tyres. A bottle of detergent. A tube of tar remover. And a bottle of glass cleaner. Reacher opened it. Sniffed the contents. Nodded to himself. And doubled back to the cleaning closet to collect the bleach. He figured it was time to find out how well he remembered his high school chemistry.

Reacher squeezed out through the gap in the plywood hoarding and made his way back to the Beetle. To the rear. He felt around the inside of the fender until he found the tracking device. He detached it and placed it on the ground directly below the car. He took a last swig of coffee. Removed the lid. Emptied the dregs. Tied the one remaining T-shirt around his head so that it covered his mouth and nose. Then, working at arm's length, which was further for Reacher than for most people, he poured bleach into the coffee cup until it was half full. He topped it off with glass cleaner. Replaced the lid. Closed the passenger door. Wound down the driver's window then climbed into the car and started the engine. He held the cup in his left hand so that he could shift and set off slowly back to the road. He drove with no lights, as smoothly as he could manage, in the direction of the town.

The Toyota was still under the bridge. It was tucked in with its passenger side close to the thick brick pillars that must have supported the structure for the last hundred years. Reacher pulled across so the Beetle was tight up against its driver's side, making it the meat in a sandwich. He pulled the T-shirt away from his face. The driver stared at him. She looked surprised for a moment. Then suspicious. Reacher gestured for her to roll down her window.

'How are you guys doing?' Reacher flashed what he hoped was a friendly smile. 'Surveillance duty can be pretty dull, can't it? That's why I've brought you something. Should liven things up.'

Reacher removed the lid, stretched his arm across the driver's lap, and tipped the contents of the cup all over the Toyota's centre console. Then he wound up his own window and sat for a moment and watched as curly fingers of thin green smoke began to rise and twist inside the other car. High school chemistry. He'd remembered it pretty well. The four occupants squealed and clawed at their eyes then scrabbled for their door handles. The doors on the opposite side slammed into the brick pillars leaving a gap too narrow to escape through. The doors on Reacher's side were snagged against the Beetle's running board. Reacher held his position for another moment then pulled away. In his mirror he saw the first pair tumble out. Then the second pair followed, stumbling around with their arms stretched out like horror movie zombies.

Reacher felt like he was getting a peek into the future when he arrived back at Mitch's apartment. Rutherford was stooped. Hunched. He dragged his feet along the floor as he walked. His eyes seemed dim and unfocused, as if he'd aged fifty years in the course of the evening.

'Have you been drinking?' Reacher said.

Rutherford didn't reply.

'Where's Sarah?' Reacher said.

'Bathroom.' Rutherford made it as far as the couch and slumped down.

'How did you do?'

'We have some good news,' Rutherford said. 'Some OK news. And some absolutely catastrophic news. Which do you want first?'

'Start with the good.'

Rutherford gestured towards the kitchen. A large grey laptop was sitting on the countertop, connected to an outlet by a twisted grubby wire. 'We got that.'

'A computer?' Reacher said.

'Not just any computer.' A hint of defiance crept into Rutherford's voice. 'The computer the asshole town lawyers wanted me to pay fourteen thousand dollars to see. Which leads to the OK news. I at least have a future as a cat burglar ahead of me if I can't get my job back. We got in. We got out. No one had a clue we were ever there.'

'And the server things?'

'That's the bad news. They're gone. We looked everywhere. Not even the broken glass from the cabinet door was left.'

'But we're not giving up, are we, Rusty?' Sarah emerged from a door to the side of the kitchen. Her hair was wrapped in a towel and she was wearing a black satin robe that was several sizes too big for her. 'We're going to find those damn things. Starting

199

tomorrow. We'll search the whole state. The whole country, if we have to. They must be somewhere.'

'What do they look like?' Reacher said. 'Could you describe them to me?'

'I can get you pictures, if you like,' Rutherford said. 'Model numbers. Serial numbers. Why?'

'You should let me find them. You and Sarah should leave town.'

'No way.' Rutherford crossed his arms. 'We've been over this before.'

'We should find the servers, then leave.' Sands sat on the couch next to Rutherford. 'They're portable. We can work on them anywhere. There's nothing to be gained by staying in harm's way longer than we have to.'

'You should leave now,' Reacher said. 'Someone wants these things badly enough to send six guys after you. Those six failed. Do you think they'll give up? No. They'll send twelve guys. Eighteen. Who knows how many? And if they get their hands on you, how far do you think *I don't know where the servers are* will get you?'

Sands adjusted the towel on her head. Rutherford said nothing.

'You should leave,' Reacher said. 'If I can find the servers I'll get them to the FBI. They can do whatever they need to with this digital fingerprint you think is in one of them. Then when it's safe, if you want to, you can come back.'

'No.' Rutherford shook his head. 'I don't care how

many people they send. I'm not being driven out of my home. And I'm not handing the servers over to anyone. Not yet. Not if there's a chance we could develop Cerberus into something that's worth serious money. I don't want to sound shallow or greedy, but look at this place. Mitch is ten years younger than me. He had one good idea. I've worked my ass off all my life. I deserve my shot.'

'That's fair.' Sands tucked a loose strand of hair back under the towel. 'You do deserve a shot. You should benefit if Cerberus turns into a success. We both should. But you can't benefit if you're dead. So don't look at it as being driven away. Think of it as a sabbatical. If Reacher finds the servers we could give a copy to the FBI. Have them sign some kind of agreement not to develop any products out of what they find. That's not what they do anyway. And in the meantime we could do more work with the models. At my place. It's safe there, and imagine what it would be like driving back here in a brand new Rolls-Royce. Your old boss pleading with you to go back. You telling him to stick his job.'

An electronic chime sounded in the kitchen and Rutherford stood up. 'That's my computer. It's finished its updates. Finally. Let's see—' His phone rang. He checked the screen. 'It's a local number. I don't recognize it. Should I answer?'

'It's your phone,' Reacher said.

Rutherford pressed a key and held the phone to his ear. 'Hello.' He listened for a moment, then passed the phone to Reacher. 'It's Officer Rule. She wants to talk to you.'

'This is Reacher.' He stood and walked to the window.

'We need to talk,' Officer Rule said. 'I'll give you an address. Come alone. The garage will open. Drive in and stay in your car.'

Reacher found the address Officer Rule gave him without any problem. It was a small single family home with a neat but plain yard on a neat but plain street in a sleepy neighbourhood half a mile from the courthouse. The blacktop had been resurfaced within the last year judging by the colour and the lack of severe cracking, but Reacher thought it was strange that there were no sidewalks. The street butted right up to people's properties. To their lawns or driveways or beds full of medium-size shrubs. Reacher wondered if that was down to the heat. Or the humidity. Or if people in that town were particularly averse to any form of exercise that involved leaving their own yards.

The correct house was easy to spot because it had a police cruiser parked outside along with a late model Honda Civic. Reacher guessed that would be Officer Rule's personal vehicle. He slowed as he approached, checked his mirrors a final time to be sure no one was following, then turned on to the driveway. The garage door immediately began to clang and clank its way up and when it was all the way open Reacher rolled inside. He killed his engine and the door began its descent.

There was an aluminium ladder fixed on the wall on one side and a bicycle suspended by its front wheel from the other. There was a stout shelf covered with gardening fertilizers and weedkillers and tools of various kinds. Reacher had no idea what any of them were for.

Once the door to the driveway was all the way down a personnel door opened on Reacher's left and Officer Rule stepped through. She was wearing navy sweatpants with a matching T-shirt. Her hair was held back by a gold clip. And she was holding a slim envelope. Reacher opened his door and started to get out but she shook her head and gestured for him to stay put.

'We've got to be quick. My neighbour will be home any minute and I don't want her to see you leaving.'

'You think she's spying on you?'

'You've never lived in a small town, have you?' A smile spread briefly across her face. 'Of course she's spying. Everyone is. Maybe not the way you were thinking but I still want nothing to do with it. Here.' She passed the envelope to Reacher. 'This is for you.'

'What is it?' he said. There was nothing written on it. Nothing printed. No label.

'A file. A copy, anyway. For the journalist you were asking about.'

'Why are you giving it to me?'

'Because I'm sick and tired of it. What happened to her is horrible and no one in the department is doing anything about it. You were a military cop. You showed good instincts with Holly's scumbag boyfriend. Maybe you can shake something loose. Get some justice for this woman. Her name was Toni Garza. I've never even heard Detective Goodyear say it out loud.'

The photographs of the dead journalist were safely tucked inside the envelope, and the envelope was safely tucked beneath the floor mat on the passenger side of Marty's car. There was always the chance of a random traffic stop and Reacher didn't want to fall foul of a cop with prying eyes if he got pulled over. But even though the pictures were hidden the images continued to cycle through Reacher's head as he drove. His having seen them made no difference to Toni Garza. She was still dead. It did make a difference to Reacher, though. He had to assume that whoever had killed Garza was the person chasing Rutherford. Or part of the same organization, at least. And now that he'd seen the level of brutality involved, there was no way he could leave Rutherford alone.

Sands opened the door to Mitch's apartment when Reacher knocked. She'd dried her hair and styled it and had changed into yoga pants and a loose, pale blue silk shirt. 'Everything OK?' she asked. 'What did this Officer Rule person want with you?'

'She had some information for me. On the QT. A kind of cop to ex-cop thing. Related to a case I'd asked her about at the station house earlier.'

'Is it helpful, this information?'

'Helpful's not the word I'd use. But it does add perspective.'

Rutherford was in the kitchen, tethered to his computer. Apparently it was showing its age by refusing to operate unless it was attached to an outlet.

'Is that thing working?' Reacher said. 'I need you to find the email Toni Garza sent you. The journalist.'

Rutherford rattled some keys and prodded a square pad and after a minute he gestured for Reacher to come closer.

'Here it is.' Rutherford pointed at the screen. 'Like I said, she was enquiring about property records. For a particular address. No mention of an owner's name.'

'What about her second message?' Reacher said.

Rutherford shook his head. 'That was a voicemail. I deleted it as soon as I listened to it.'

'Do you have the address of the property?' Reacher said. 'Is it still standing? If someone lives there I want to pay him a visit. Or her. First thing in the morning.'

'We have to track down the servers in the morning,' Sands said.

'Let's see what I can find,' Rutherford said. 'Give me two minutes.' He pressed and prodded and called up maps and databases, then nodded. 'Oh, yes. It's still standing. It's actually famous. Or notorious. I've never seen the street address before. I only know it by its local name. The Spy House. Two Soviet secret agents lived there. Back in the 1950s. Now it's owned by a businessman. Henry Klostermann.'

FIFTEEN

There were two bedrooms in Mitch's apartment, and two other occupants that night alongside Reacher. Although Reacher felt that describing the sleeping areas as bedrooms was going a little far. They had no doors. No windows. No walls to speak of. The only things separating them from the rest of the apartment were the wooden dividers, and they only came up to Reacher's chin. He knew without looking that the beds would be too short so he figured his best bet was to let Sands and Rutherford use them. He could sleep on the couch. He'd have to forgo his usual practice of pressing his clothes under the mattress. But it would be better from a security perspective. It meant that if anyone found out where they were billeted he would be the first one they came to if they got through the door.

Reacher woke himself at 7:00 a.m. He could hear slow peaceful breathing plus the occasional grunt and snort from the other side of the dividers so he lay still

206

for another half hour and ran a few of his favourite guitar riffs through his head. Then he got up, coaxed Mitch's complicated coffee machine into action, and while it gurgled and hissed he took a shower. He emerged from the bathroom fourteen minutes later, still unshaved and with his hair still damp, and found Sands perched on a stool at the kitchen counter. She was wrapped in the same robe as the day before and was sipping coffee from a plain white mug. She stood when she saw Reacher and poured a mug for him, and then poured another as Rutherford stumbled out from behind the dividers, rubbing his eyes.

Sands was in favour of calling ahead to set up an appointment at the Spy House. She felt it was the polite thing to do. And also the practical thing. They could make sure someone was home. Avoid the risk of a wasted journey. And the risk that the sight of Reacher arriving unannounced could lead a panicked homeowner to call the police. Reacher didn't agree. Experience told him that surprise was his friend. He'd prefer to be knocking on the door at 4:00 a.m., the way the KGB had done back in the day. And if no one was home, all would not be lost. It's easier to search a house when the owners aren't there.

Rutherford was still too dopey to voice a coherent argument either way so they decided that Reacher would go unannounced and Sands would stay at the apartment and find out what the town did with its discarded computer equipment. She was clinging to the hope that they could find the servers Rutherford

207

had trashed and keep the dream of making their fortune alive. Reacher drained one more mug of coffee then stood up to leave.

'Wait.' Rutherford slid down from his stool. 'I'll come with you. Give me two minutes to get dressed.'

'You don't want to stay and help Sarah?' Reacher said.

Rutherford shook his head. 'There's no point. No one would talk to me. Sarah's far more persuasive, anyway. And I always wanted to see inside the Spy House.'

'Why? It's not going to be full of spies in disguises practising secret codes with invisible ink. It'll just be a normal house.'

'I know. I still want to see it.'

Reacher sat back down and drank another mug of coffee while Rutherford rustled and rummaged behind the divider. He returned wearing the same pants as the day before and the same kind of polo shirt, only in a different colour. Reacher stood and picked up the key to Marty's car.

'You know what?' Rutherford said. 'Why don't we take my car?'

Reacher smiled to himself. 'I get it now. You don't want to see the Spy House at all. You just want to find out if I brought your Beetle back in one piece.'

'Can you blame me?' Rutherford said. 'I love that car. It's irreplaceable.'

In the garage Reacher waited for Rutherford to walk around the VW and inspect every inch of paintwork.

Then he got down on his knees on the passenger side and peered underneath.

'What are you doing?' Rutherford said. 'Did you drive over something? Tell me you didn't hit a deer.'

'I'm looking for tracking devices,' Reacher said. 'You do your side. Underneath the car. Along the running boards. Inside the fenders. Anywhere a magnet could stick.'

'But you checked yesterday. You found a tracker. You said you ditched it.'

'I was in the army for thirteen years, Rusty. We check. And then we check again. It's what we do.'

Rutherford shrugged and then worked his way from the front to the back. He came up empty-handed. 'Nothing on my side. You find anything?'

Reacher leaned across the hood and held out his hand. 'Another tracker. The same kind. In the same place. And there was this.' He showed Rutherford a scrap of paper. 'It was held in place by the magnet.'

Rutherford took the paper and read it out loud. 'Romeo, Juliet. A bunch of numbers. Eight bells. What does it mean?'

'Romeo Juliet is R J in the NATO phonetic alphabet. My initials, military style. Reacher, Jack.'

'I get it,' Rutherford said. 'And the numbers? They could be a grid reference. What about eight bells?'

'That's noon in Navy time.'

'Maybe someone wants you to go to this place at noon? But why write it like that?'

'To show they know my background? To gain my trust? Or intrigue me, perhaps.'

'What if it's a trap? You shouldn't go.'

'Have you got your phone? Can you figure out where this place is?'

Rutherford tapped his screen then made some swiping and pinching movements. 'Reacher? Don't go.'

'Why not?'

'I know about this place. It's an old factory. Just outside town. It's been abandoned for years. Growing up, there were all kinds of rumours. No one who went in was ever seen again. I never dared go.'

The Spy House was hidden behind a wall. The wall was built of stone, eight feet high, and topped with broken glass. The driveway was blocked by a gate. Made of iron. Also eight feet high. The kind that slides to the side so there are no hinges. No join in the centre, either. No weak spots at all. This particular one was plain. No nonsense. No ornamentation. Just thick vertical bars. It reminded Reacher of a grate covering a giant drain or a sewer. You'd need a tank to knock it down. The bars were too close together for anyone but a child to squeeze through. Not a welcoming proposition. And there was a sign mounted at eye level to complete the effect. It read *No Photographs. No Trespassing. No Interviews without an Appointment.*

Rutherford pointed to the sign. 'Maybe Sarah was right. Maybe we should have called ahead.' Then he wound down his window and pressed a call button on a keypad set on a pole.

'Yes?' A woman's voice answered after half a minute. It was quiet and cold like a whisper from a tomb.

'Good morning. My name's Rusty Rutherford. Is Mr Klostermann available?'

'Can you read, Mr Rutherford?'

'Yes.'

'Do you have an appointment?'

'No.'

'Then you should already know that Mr Klostermann is not available.'

Reacher leaned towards the open window. 'Actually we don't know that. Your sign says you need an appointment for an interview. We're not here for an interview. So we don't need an appointment.'

There was a pause. 'Then what are you here for? There are no maintenance visits scheduled for today.'

'We're following up on something that will be of interest to Mr Klostermann. Considerable interest. To do with some correspondence from a journalist. About property records for his house.'

'Please wait.' A faint electronic buzz told them they hadn't been disconnected, then after three minutes the woman's voice returned. 'Mr Klostermann will see you. When the gate opens drive directly to the front of the house.'

Beyond the gate the site was divided by a line of mature trees. Cypresses and sycamores. The area to the left of them was rough. Unfinished. There were no structures, and no plants taller than stalks of coarse, scrubby grass. The house was to the right. It had an attached two-car garage. Next to that was a covered porch. It was raised up on a stone base and plain white pillars stretched up to support its roof. The rest of the building was finished with wood siding. Long horizontal strips. Painted olive green. There were four windows on the ground floor. Four on the first. Each had shutters. All were open, pinned back against the wall, finished in a darker shade of green. The roof was covered in cream-coloured shingles. A chimney extended six feet above the ridge on the far left.

Rutherford followed the driveway towards the garage, then pulled into a parking area in front of the house and killed the engine. Reacher climbed out. Rutherford followed him and together they climbed the three steps and crossed the porch. Reacher rapped on the door. A woman answered. She was in her late twenties, wearing a knee-length black dress with a white apron. Her blonde hair was tied up in a bun. She was thin, almost malnourished, but she moved with effortless grace, like a ballerina.

'Please come in,' she said. Hers was the voice they'd heard on the intercom. Quiet and cold. There was no question about that. 'Can I offer you gentlemen some refreshment? Iced tea?'

They declined and the woman led the way along a narrow hallway. There was tile on the floor. Family portraits on the walls. Four doors. A pair on each side. Plain, pale wood. No panels. Narrow architraves. The woman paused outside the second door on the right, knocked, then opened it and stood aside to let Rutherford and Reacher enter. She didn't follow.

There was one person already in the room. A man, slim, rangy, with a mane of white hair. Like Einstein if he'd worked in a bank, Reacher thought. He looked around seventy. Probably born around the time the house was built. Maybe born right there in the house. The man put down his newspaper, hauled himself out of his armchair, and offered his hand.

'Mr Rutherford, I'm Henry Klostermann. It's a pleasure to meet you. I know you by reputation, of course. And I don't envy the position you're in. I've done work for the town in the past. I'm essentially retired now but I make sure my company doesn't even bid for municipal contracts any more. The penny-pinching. The endless finger-pointing. It drove me up the wall. Made it impossible to do a job properly. I can only imagine what it was like to work there permanently. And your friend?'

'Reacher.' Reacher didn't offer his hand. 'Jack. I'm Mr Rutherford's life coach.'

'Really?' Klostermann said. 'How interesting. Now please. Gentlemen. Take a seat.'

Klostermann lowered himself into his chair. Rutherford perched on the edge of a couch with thin tweed cushions and a slender wood frame. Reacher joined him, hoping it would take his weight.

'Now that you're here, how can we help each other?' Klostermann said.

'Well,' Rutherford said. 'As you can imagine, I have some time on my hands right now. I'm trying to put it to good use, following up on things that fell by the wayside when I was working around the clock after the computer system was attacked. One of them is an email. Actually an email and a voicemail. I received them from a journalist. She was asking about property records to do with your home.'

Klostermann steepled his fingers. 'The journalist. That would be Toni Garza, I presume. You heard she was killed? Such a tragedy.'

'We heard.' Rutherford paused. 'It sounds awful, what happened.'

'It was. Toni was such a lovely girl. She had so much talent. So much integrity.'

'You knew her?'

'Of course I knew her. She was working for me. In fact, it was me who suggested she should contact you. I was hoping you could help with some research she was doing.'

'To do with your home?' Reacher said. 'Its unusual history?'

'Goodness, no.' Klostermann frowned. 'There's no need. What little there is of that stupid story has been done to death.'

'Living in a nest of Cold War spies? That sounds like a great story. If the problem is you're tired of telling it, why not have someone write a book about it? A journalist would be an obvious choice. Specially one with talent and integrity.'

'It wouldn't be a book. More like a haiku. There's not enough material. And this place was hardly a nest. There were only two of them. They were brothers. They only owned the place for eighteen months. And they didn't even do any spying while they lived here. They wrote a textbook. On math. I wish that was the angle the public latched on to. Imagine if this place was known as the Math House. Then I wouldn't be swamped with tourists every time a new Bond movie comes out.'

'If not your house, what was she researching?'

'Parts of my family history. My father fled to the States from Germany in the 1930s. He could see the way things were going politically, and somehow of all the places in the world he settled here in Tennessee. He founded a business. Started a family. Did all kinds of things. But the details of his early years in the States are sketchy. I felt it was time to find out as much as I could and record it before it was too late. Where he lived before he moved here. When exactly he bought this house. I think someone else owned it between him and the spies, but I'd like to be sure. I want as much detail as I can get. Including the human aspect, you know? There's a story that when he bought his first house he had no money and credit was hard to come by so he used a painting he brought with him from Germany to back the purchase. These are the little quirks that are so easily lost. I want to know all of them. I want my son to know. And his son, if he ever has one.'

'That sounds like a wholesome family project,' Reacher said. 'But it's not the kind of thing anyone should get killed over. Are you sure there's not more to it? Buried treasure? The location of the Lost Ark?'

Klostermann's face was blank. 'Someone was killed over my project? Who?'

'Toni Garza.'

'No. That's crazy. Why would her death have anything to do with my project? Toni was a hard worker. She was driven. She wasn't working for me exclusively. She had a dozen projects on the go. Some she got paid for, like mine. Others she was doing off her own bat. She was digging into all sorts of unsavoury things. She dreamed of becoming an investigative reporter for one of the big papers, although that was always unrealistic. There are so few of those left now.'

'What kind of unsavoury things? Did she tell you?'

'Not chapter and verse. But Toni did confide some things. She wanted to root out crime and corruption. I think she saw me as a kind of father figure. She looked to me for advice from time to time. I warned her to be careful. More than once.'

'This seems like a nice town. Is crime and corruption a big problem here?'

'No. But she was based out of Nashville. She did most of her work there.'

'How did you find her if she's not local?'

'I came across her name online. She was recommended by someone on an ancestry forum.'

'Are you going to replace her? Or had she finished her work?'

'I guess I will have to replace her. I haven't had the stomach for it yet. Toni had completed the broad outline but there's plenty left to do. The biggest problem is confirming all the dates. That's why she wanted access to the town's records. And why she contacted you, Mr Rutherford.'

'I can see why you would want access,' Rutherford said. 'But not why Toni reached out to me. Why did she think I could get my hands on the papers you need? I was the IT manager. Not the archivist.'

'As far as I understand, it worked like this,' Klostermann said. 'Toni was in touch with the archivist. There was a project running to digitize all the records. The archivist told Toni there'd been a kind of false start. The computer memory thing they tried to use was too small so halfway through the process they raised some extra money and got a bigger one. They copied everything, then you as the IT manager took the old one into storage until it was needed for something else. So it's possible the records I want are still on it.'

Rutherford thought for a moment. 'I know the equipment you're talking about. I did take it. I thought it might be useful for . . . something else.'

'Do you know where it is now?'

'Not exactly. But I'm trying to find it. I need it for . . . something.'

'If you do find it, would you let me see if my father's records are there?'

217

'I'm not sure if I could,' Rutherford said. 'It's town property. I'm not sure if—'

'We're talking about seventy-year-old documents,' Klostermann said. 'Maybe older. Whose confidence could possibly get betrayed? And it's all theoretically public domain stuff anyway. It was in the physical archive before the fire. So come on. What do you say?'

Rutherford didn't reply.

'I can make it worth your while if compensation is an issue?' Klostermann said. 'Very much worth your while if I can get the first look. Patience is not a virtue of mine. And I'm not getting any younger.'

Rutherford squirmed on the edge of the cushion. 'It's not about—'

'Time is the issue,' Reacher said. 'Rusty has a lot to do to prepare for the next chapter in his life and as I'm sure you know, an IT manager's time is expensive.'

'How expensive?' Klostermann said.

'Ten thousand dollars should cover it. Cash.'

Klostermann struggled to his feet and held out his hand. 'You're a life coach, you say, Mr Reacher? I'm beginning to think I might need one of those myself. How long to find the records?'

'That's hard to predict. We're working on it. I'll let you know.'

Reacher walked back to the car in silence. His gut was telling him that he'd met Klostermann before. In barracks rooms. Bars. Jail cells. Offices. Back streets. All kinds of places. All over the world. Or that he'd met guys just like Klostermann, anyway. Guys with something to hide but who imagine they're smart enough to think on their feet. To cover their trails. Reacher didn't think every word Klostermann had spoken was a lie. His father's immigration, for example. His businesses. There were too many things that would be easy to check on, and only a fool would be dishonest about details that could be disproved in a matter of seconds. It was the family history aspect that didn't pass the smell test. Writing it for his son. Tying it up in a pretty bow. No. It was more likely that there was some kind of skeleton in the family closet. Something illegal. Something embarrassing. Something Klostermann wanted to bury. Or spin. Something worth ten thousand dollars just to see a record of. But a sack of cash was one thing. Was it also worth Toni Garza's life? Was it worth Rutherford's?

SIXTEEN

There were two people at the kitchen counter in Mitch's apartment alongside Reacher, and they were both mad at him.

'I can't believe you offered to sell the server.' Both of Rutherford's hands were clenched into fists. 'You had no right. It's not yours. We don't know where it is. And ten measly grand? Cerberus will be worth a hundred times that much. A thousand times.'

'I can't believe you would even think of going.' Sands threw the slip of paper on to the countertop. 'It's a trap. It's obvious. How can it not be?'

Reacher took a mouthful of coffee. 'OK. First of all, Rusty. Don't worry. I have no intention of selling your computer thing. And Sarah, yes. It's almost certainly a trap. But sometimes the only way to know if the stove is hot is to touch it.'

Sands glared at him.

'Someone smart told me that once,' he said.

220

'You're obviously not smart if you're even considering walking into a trap.'

'I never said I was smart. Stubborn, maybe. Obstinate even, on occasion.'

'Why offer to sell if you had no intention?' Rutherford said. 'Are you going to rip Klostermann off? We can't do that. I have to live here. My reputation's tattered enough already.'

'We're not ripping anyone off,' Reacher said. 'It was a test. To get a sense of how important these records are to him. Or sensitive. Or embarrassing. I named a big number and he didn't turn a hair. That tells us something. And here's another reason. Say Klostermann isn't what he seems to be. Say he's somehow behind Garza's murder and the attempt to kidnap you. Do you want him thinking you're not willing to play ball? This way his incentive is to keep us alive.'

'If you care so much about being free and healthy why would you knowingly walk into an ambush?' Sands said. 'Are you crazy?'

'Not in the slightest,' Reacher said. 'And I'm not going to walk into anything. The best way to defeat an ambush is to be there first. Which I will be. But logistics aren't the most important thing. You're focusing in the wrong place. Look at the note.'

Sands picked up the scrap of paper. She re-read it slowly, and checked the other side. 'What? I don't see anything.'

'The first two words. What do they mean?'

'Romeo, Juliet. R J. Reacher, Jack. Your name.'

'Exactly. Someone made it personal. I'm not some faceless guy who got in the way any more. They're coming after me specifically. They need to understand that's the wrong thing to do.'

Reacher parked Marty's car half a mile south of the factory and covered the rest of the ground on foot. He moved slowly. He stopped frequently, but never at the same interval. He never continued until he was certain no one was following. And no one was watching. The clock in his head said 10:45. Seventy-five minutes before he was due at the rendezvous. More time would have been better but experience told him seventy-five minutes would be enough. Nine times out of ten.

The moment the abandoned building came into view Reacher knew that no kind of ghost story could have kept him away when he was growing up. Or his brother Joe. There were too many iron girders to climb. Too many nooks and alcoves to hide in. Too many frontal assaults and insane last stands and against-the-odds escapes to stage. And too much prime real estate to fight over with the other kids.

Plus ça change . . . as his mother used to say. *The more things change* . . .

The moment Reacher stepped through the gap where the tall wooden door used to be he knew seventy-five minutes weren't enough. Not this time. He'd hit the one in ten. The ambushers were already there. He couldn't see them. Yet. Or hear them. Or smell them.

But he knew. Eyes were on him. He could feel them. He could feel a chill on his neck. Some kind of primal response to being watched. A warning mechanism hardwired into his lizard brain, as finely tuned as his ancestors' had been millions of years ago. Then, forests. Now, a factory. Either way, evading predators. Not getting eaten. Not getting shot. Living to fight another day.

Plus ça change . . .

Reacher kept moving. Same speed. Same direction. He didn't want whoever was watching to know he was aware of their presence. Not until he knew exactly where they were. And how many there were. He strained his ears. Heard nothing. Scanned the rubble and the weeds covering the ground. Checked the long line of smashed windows. The gaping holes in the roof. Looking for movement. Shadow. Shape. Shine.

He saw nothing.

Reacher took another step. Something made a sound behind him. Metal shifting against stone. But not someone looking to shoot him. They could have done that already. A decoy? Reacher scanned the ground in front. Behind. Both sides. He increased the radius. Looking for signs of disturbance. A place for someone to hide. To spring out of when his attention was drawn away. To get in close, quickly, and neutralize his advantage in strength and size.

He saw nothing.

'It's just you and me, Major.' It was a woman's voice. Behind him. Calm and confident. 'And there's no need to worry. No need to do anything either of us will regret in the morning. I just want to talk.'

Reacher turned around. The woman he'd last seen driving the Toyota was standing next to a sheet of corrugated iron against the wall. She must have eased her way out from behind it. She was dressed all in black, with a small tactical backpack slung over one shoulder and her hair tied back in a ponytail. There was a gun in her hand. A Glock 19. Reacher approved of her choice. It was compact. Easy to conceal. And reliable. The chances of a misfire were slim to none. Her hand seemed steady. He was a sizeable target. They were fifteen feet apart. If he rushed her she would have fifteen chances to hit him, assuming the magazine was full. Sixteen if she had one already in the chamber. More than one chance per foot. Not odds Reacher liked.

'I've never been much of a conversationalist,' he said.

'Then just listen. I know a lot about you. Enough to believe I can trust you. I need to even those scales. And I need to do it quickly. So I'm going to tell you one story from my past. My father was a Stanford man. He wanted me to follow in his footsteps but I had other ideas. I wanted to study in England so I applied to college there. One of the old ones. It doesn't matter which. But because I was foreign I had to jump through a couple extra hoops. One was writing a special essay. There was no word limit. No time limit. And no choice of subject. The title they gave me was *What is a risk?* You know what I wrote?'

Reacher said nothing.

'Four words. *This is a risk*. It worked. I got in. And I wasn't lying. It was a risk. The biggest one I'd taken at that time. Now I'm going to take a bigger one. The biggest I've ever taken.'

She slipped the backpack off her shoulder and lobbed it underarm, straight at Reacher. It landed at his feet and kicked a small cloud of dust up over his shoes.

'Pick it up,' she said. 'Open it.'

The pack was made of black ballistic nylon. It wasn't new. One of the shoulder straps was starting to fray and the bottom corners were scuffed. A tried and tested piece of equipment. The best kind. It had a small pocket on the right-hand side. An identical pocket on the left. Both were empty. There was a triple row of MOLLE webbing across the front, with nothing attached. And one internal compartment. Reacher unzipped it and looked inside. There were three spare magazines for the Glock. A set of car keys. For the Toyota, Reacher assumed. A hairbrush with two elastic ponytail holders wrapped around the handle. And a book.

'See the Bible?' she said. 'Take it out.'

Reacher set the pack down and fished out the book. It was a King James hardcover edition. It had a dark red cardboard front. A dark red cardboard back. Gold printing on the front. Gold printing on the spine. It was scuffed and worn as if she carried it everywhere. The leaves were yellow and dark as if the victim of some spillage, long ago. Maybe some kind of fruit drink. Certainly something sticky, because the pages were gummed up solid.

'Go ahead,' she said. 'Dig your fingernails in. Pull. It will open.'

'I don't need to.' Reacher slipped the book back into the pack. 'I've seen one just like it before. You're with the FBI?'

'Special Agent Fisher,' she said. 'Margaret. You can call me Mags. If you help me.'

'What kind of help do you need? The same kind Toni Garza gave you? Did you know enough to trust her, too? And did she trust you in return?'

'Who's Toni Garza?'

Reacher said nothing.

'I'm serious,' Fisher said. 'I don't know who Toni Garza is. I have an entirely different problem.'

'Toni Garza was a journalist. She's dead. Murdered by the people you're working for. In a very nasty way.'

'I can believe that,' Fisher said, after a moment. 'I'm working for some very nasty people. But I didn't kill her. My cell didn't kill her. I don't know anything about her. But I do know this. If you don't help me, more people like her will get hurt. Maybe murdered. Also in a very nasty way.'

Reacher said nothing.

'The cell I've infiltrated was sent here to bag someone named Rusty Rutherford. But I guess you know that since you stumbled into the op and royally screwed it up.'

'I'm not helping you capture Rutherford. Even if you convince me about Garza.'

Fisher held up her hand. 'I'm not asking you to. All

I need from you is information. Rutherford was to be taken because he has something a certain foreign power is desperate to get its hands on. He either has this thing in his possession or he knows where it is. If I can get to it first, before they go after Rutherford again, that's the best way to keep him out of further danger.'

'Which foreign power are we talking about?'

'I can't say.'

'If you want my help you're going to have to turn your cards all the way up.'

Fisher sighed. 'Russia.'

'OK. And what is the thing they want?'

'I don't know. Not exactly. All the cell was told is that it's an item. An object. Something physical. It contains data or records of some kind so it could be a paper file or a photograph. But I think it's most likely to be computer related, given the job Rutherford just lost.'

'What kind of records?'

'I don't know exactly. Something that reveals a name or an identity. Or that would enable us to deduce one.'

'Of an agent?'

Fisher nodded.

'Theirs or ours?'

'Theirs.'

'An active agent?'

'Very active. And that's a situation that needs to be corrected.'

'Why is there an agent in a sleepy town like this?'

Fisher shook her head. 'The information is here. Not the agent. He's somewhere else. Or she.'

'Where?'

'Repeat a word of this and I'll kill you. I'll probably have to kill myself, too. Have you heard of the Oak Ridge National Laboratory?'

'Near Knoxville. Where they develop the supercomputers?'

'They do many things there. Supercomputing is one of them. Another is cyber security. The United States is facing a lot of threats. We have a lot of defensive programs running. And the Russians have an agent in place who's attempting to steal a copy of the most critical one. Its official name is project C02WW06BHH21.'

'Snappy name.'

'Only the geeks call it that. Everyone else calls it The Sentinel.'

'What does it do?'

'It protects the integrity of the election system software in forty-eight states. It's the only thing that does.'

'Why not all fifty?'

'Politics. I haven't got time to go into it.'

'And the Russians are trying to steal a copy. So what? If they succeed what could they do with it? Change the result of an election? Aren't there fail-safes? Paper backups?'

'In some places. But changing the result is not their goal. That's too direct. This is the Russians we're talking about. You've got to understand just how long a game these people play. Their philosophy is if you hit a man with a fire hose he goes down, but he can get up again. If you gather enough raindrops and use them in the right way you wind up with the Grand Canyon. They're trying to carve gaps in society that are too big to bridge. It's all part of a bigger campaign. To sow discord and division. It's been running for years. On social media. Conspiracy theories. Attempts to undermine the mainstream media.'

'Fake news? I've heard about that.'

'This time they're specifically trying to erode faith in the election system itself. We know they're serious. They already had a dry run four years ago, in Kentucky. What happened was, on election day, they sent out a phishing email. You know what that is?'

'No idea,' Reacher said.

'It's an email that looks legitimate, like it's from some official trusted source. Like a bank or an insurance company.'

'People trust banks and insurance companies?'

'Some do. Anyway, the messages look genuine and they generally have a subject that sounds tempting in some way. Or urgent. Like half-price car insurance if you apply within twelve hours.'

'So gullible people open these messages and something bad happens? Like an old-school letter bomb.'

'Right. Opening the message or following a link or downloading an attachment, one way or another it infects the computer. A malicious program gets in and gains access to your files and passwords, and if you're on a network it gets into that too. In the Kentucky case the Russians sent an email to all the election officials purporting to be from the VP of technical support at the company that supplied the election software. The subject line said it contained a critical update to the operating instructions.'

'I can see how people could fall for that.'

'They shouldn't. They're specifically trained not to. But trained or not, the email went to two hundred people. Six of them opened it.'

'So the Russians got access?'

'Yes.'

'What did they do?'

'Nothing. That time. They were proving the concept. Laying the foundations. Building up to a wider-scale attack this year. Imagine the scenes on election day if every person who shows up to vote at the correct precinct is told they've been re-registered without their knowledge at some other precinct on the other side of town. Or that their registration's been cancelled altogether. Or when the results are announced it turns out that in some marginal districts Mickey Mouse and Daffy Duck are registered. Or that a bunch of people are registered in multiple precincts, even if they didn't know it at the time or act on it.'

'There'd be chaos.'

'Total chaos. Only The Sentinel can stop it.'

'It didn't stop their dry run.'

'It didn't exist then. That's why it was developed.'

'Are you sure it works? This is the Russians we're talking about. Maybe they've already penetrated some local elections and are just pretending they want to steal it to make you think they're frightened of it.'

Fisher shook her head. 'No. We know The Sentinel works. It's already stopped twelve attempts in six different states. Plus we have a source who's confirmed the Russians don't believe they can defeat it. They weren't too worried because they have an agent in place to steal it. Then panic set in because a record of some kind surfaced here that could lead to his exposure.'

'I heard the town archive burned down.'

'It did. The Russians did that. They're also behind the ransomware attack that cost Rutherford his job. Evidently they wanted to shut down the new digital archive before it could go online.'

'The town's going to pay to get it unlocked. It had insurance. Why not wait until it's up and running again, and go through it with a fine-tooth comb?'

'The town might pay, but that archive is never going to see the light of day. I guarantee you that. Not all of it, anyway. Not the part we need.'

'Rutherford figured out that some system he built might have captured the identity of whoever ran the ransomware attack. He thought that's what someone wanted to get from him.'

'Not possible. We know it was the Russians. The Russians know we know. And they want us to know, frankly. Every successful attack is them giving us the finger.'

'I spoke to a guy yesterday at the courthouse. He said he was an agent with Homeland Security. Infrastructure Protection. He had a theory that Rutherford had colluded with the attacker.'

'Agent Wallwork? He's my partner. Sorry for the deception. We were hoping Rutherford might have somehow revealed what the item is. Or where it is. No. The panic's about whatever can unmask their agent. That's definite.'

'In that case, how much do you know about a guy named Henry Klostermann?'

'Who lives at the so-called Spy House? Don't even think of going there. It's such an obvious coincidence but we checked it out anyway. Those original guys from the fifties weren't KGB agents. Just misguided citizens giving secrets to people they thought were their friends. They did some serious damage when they were in Los Alamos but nothing at all while they were here. They moved on after two years and defected soon after because they felt the noose beginning to close. They're both dead now. They never married. They had no illegitimate offspring. No cousins. No other family that we know of. And they weren't members of any parties or groups that might be looking to carry on their work.'

'So there's no connection to Klostermann other than the address?'

'No. None. Why?'

'I met him this morning. I think he's looking for the same thing you are.'

'You know what the thing is?'

'Possibly. A computer thing. A server. It has a preliminary copy of part of the town archive on it.'

'Jesus Christ. Why didn't you say so before?'

'I didn't know about the agent and The Sentinel

before. Klostermann said he wanted it for a different reason.'

'What reason?'

'Some family tree project, he claimed. It didn't quite ring true. I think he's trying to hide something.'

'How does he know about this server?'

'He said he hired Toni Garza, the journalist who was murdered, to dig up some property records going back to when his father immigrated. She found out that when the town started putting the archive on the computer they were using this server. It turned out to be too small so they switched it for a larger one, and Rutherford as IT manager took it back into stock for some future use.'

'When did Garza start working for Klostermann?'

'I don't know exactly.'

'But before the archive burned down?'

'Yes. She started searching the paper records, then was going to use the online archive, then contacted Rutherford as some kind of Hail Mary, hoping he still had the server.'

'This is finally starting to make sense. She must have found something in the records. Realized the significance and tried to report it. Or just mentioned it to the wrong person without even knowing its importance.'

'Or the Russians could have had some kind of trip-wire in place. Something to alert them if anyone was close to finding whatever they wanted to keep hidden. They're not reckless. They'd know that one document sitting unnoticed amongst how many – thousands?

millions? – in a dusty old archive would attract less attention than a fire.'

'Either way, Rutherford needs to hand over that server. Like, yesterday.'

'That's a logical request. But it's impossible.'

'Why?'

'Rutherford doesn't know where the server is.'

Fisher turned and slammed her palm against the wall. 'Damn. Are you sure?'

Reacher nodded. 'He already tried to get it back.'

'How did Klostermann account for his project getting someone killed?'

'He claimed Garza wasn't working for him exclusively. Said she had a bunch of projects on the go. Blamed her death on some hoodlums from Nashville that she'd been sniffing around.'

'But you didn't believe him.'

'I'm not saying he killed her. I'm not saying he's working for the Russians. But I know when someone's hiding something.'

'I'll have my people take another look at him. The organization is so compartmentalized you could be married to the local Russian contact and not know it.'

'I get that.'

'And Rutherford? Not knowing where the server is? Are you sure he's telling the truth?'

'I am. It turns out he used the server for some other project and—'

'Tell me he didn't wipe it.'

'No. He didn't. Don't worry. Before the ransomware

attack he pressed the town to buy a backup system for all the computers. They wouldn't come up with the cash so he tried to build one of his own out of spare parts. It was supposed to overwrite whatever was on the server, but that didn't happen. That's how he knew it had failed. He was so mad about it he threw all the equipment in the trash.'

'He's got to get it back.'

'He's trying.'

'Why? To give it to Klostermann?'

'No. He thinks the server can help with another thing he's working on. He wants it back for himself.'

'Can you help him find it?'

'Can't you? With all the resources of the Bureau?'

'No.' Fisher shook her head. 'If the Russians latch on to a bunch of federal agents searching the local trash heaps they'll know where to look. We have to keep this under the radar. Give it another couple of days. Please.'

'What difference will a couple of days make? The election is weeks away. Rutherford can find the server on his own and figure out a way to get a copy to you. He's a smart guy.'

'It's not that simple. For a start, the election. Yes, it's a while away. But for thirty days leading up to it there's what's called a systems freeze. Nothing computer related can be changed in any way. It's the same kind of thing the credit card companies and online retailers do heading into Black Friday and Christmas. It makes sure no one loads new software which turns out not to work

235

properly and screws everything up at their most critical time. So, if we can't positively confirm that The Sentinel hasn't been compromised before then, we have a real problem. And if – when – we get our hands on Rutherford's server we don't even know what we're looking for. There could be thousands of documents on there, and I very much doubt one of them will be labelled *Identity of Russian Spy*. All kinds of cross-referencing will be needed. Lateral thinking. Reading tea leaves and casting chicken bones, probably. So the bottom line, like I said, is we need that thing yesterday.'

'I'll tell Rutherford to search quickly. And anyway, how many trash heaps can there be in a town this size?'

'Finding the server's not the only problem. You said you care about keeping Rutherford safe.'

'And?'

'The original plan was for us to snatch Rutherford. He'd give up the item – the server, as we now believe – or its location and then, overcome by shame and depression after losing his job and bearing the blame for the ransomware attack, he would kill himself. I'm the senior operative so it would have been me who staged it. Obviously I'd have made sure Rutherford walked away. Only before that could happen you arrived and put half the team on the disabled list. The rest of us have been switched to surveillance only. A new guy is being brought in to finish the job. A specialist, from Moscow. He'll outrank me. So if you leave and he gets his hands on Rutherford, there may be nothing I can do about it.'

SEVENTEEN

Reacher drove the six miles from the factory to the town with six words on his mind.

Forty eight hours. And *Need to know.*

The issue of timing was the more straightforward, in a conceptual sense. They had a two-day window to operate with relatively little interference while Fisher's cell was restricted to surveillance. After that things would get more difficult. The offensive would resume. Reinforcements would arrive. A specialist. From Moscow. Outranking Fisher. With unknown capabilities. But certainly unsympathetic to Rutherford. Which meant that if they were going to retrieve the server and turn it over to the FBI it would be advantageous to do so before the new guy got his feet on the street.

The issue of secrecy was more difficult to resolve. It brought practical considerations into play. Back when Reacher had run the 110th MP Special Investigation Unit he had tended to be open with his people. Sometimes more open than he should have been. More open than his superior officers would have liked, anyway. If they'd known. But Reacher trusted his team. He had hand-picked each of them. He had worked with them. He could predict how each of them would respond in any given situation. And besides, when you were dealing with the likes of Frances Neagley, trying to keep anything hidden was a fool's errand. Reacher liked Rutherford. He had no wish to keep him in the dark. Not just for the sake of it. But he didn't know him in the same way. Rutherford had already expressed a reluctance to let the authorities have the server. His eye was on the prize he thought his Cerberus system could win for him. Reacher was fairly certain he would change his mind if he understood the full implications. The Sentinel. The integrity of the election. The Russians. Discord and division. But there was no way to bring him into the picture without revealing that there was an agent in place in one of the Russian cells. Or at least implying it. And if something went wrong and Rutherford fell into the Russians' hands there would be no way he could avoid spilling that information. Either now, or later if they came back to run some kind of post-mortem into what went wrong with their operation. When Reacher wouldn't be around to watch out for him.

When Reacher got back to Mitch's apartment he realized that he needn't have worried about instilling any sense of urgency into the other two. The lure of the almighty dollar had taken care of that for him. Sands had started digging first thing that morning but she'd turned up nothing useful, so Rutherford had taken up the baton. He had started trawling through the files on his laptop the moment Reacher left for the factory. He found the minutes of a Heads of Department meeting he must have dozed through the previous month. One of the agenda items had been the town's refuse contract, and a follow-up note confirmed it had been renewed for another year with a local company. Warhurst's Waste-Away Express. He googled their contact information and Sands called their office. She said she was writing a story about responsible refuse management for *The Tennessean*. She had to try four different people before she found someone who believed her. But she did finally manage to finesse the information they needed. The town's surplus or obsolete electronic equipment was separated from the regular trash. Then it was sent for recycling at a facility eleven miles west of town. She and Rutherford were on the verge of leaving to investigate the place when Reacher arrived at the door.

Reacher didn't like the sound of a recycling plant. It conjured visions of equipment being dismantled and harvested for parts. Or melted down. Or crushed. Or pulped. Or otherwise rendered useless. He sensed the prospect of retrieving the server in serviceable condition receding into the distance, which at least made his second decision easier. He figured there was no need to mention what he had learned about its contents, or who needed to see it. Not at this stage. Not until they found out for sure whether the thing still existed.

'There's dirt on your shoes,' Sands said when Reacher

joined her and Rutherford in the elevator. 'And on your pants legs. So you must have showed up at the factory. But it's not noon yet. So you didn't wait. What happened? What brought you to your senses?'

'Nothing happened,' Reacher said. 'I got there early, as planned. The opposition showed up, as expected. But only one of them this time. And she didn't hang around very long.'

'Why only one of them?' Sands said. 'And why didn't she wait? At least until the appointed time, to see if you even took the bait. It makes no sense.'

'Maybe she got a message calling her away,' Rutherford said. 'Like yesterday. Maybe the doorman thought he saw me leaving and texted in a wrong report.'

'Sounds plausible,' Reacher said. 'But who really knows why anything happens?'

Reduce. Reuse. Recycle. That was a mantra Reacher was familiar with. The first two parts he was personally acquainted with. Because of his mother. She was a kid during World War II and grew up in France during the occupation. Food was in short supply. All kinds of essentials were. Clothes. Shoes. Fuel. If something ran out or wore out or was lost or broken or stolen it may never have gotten replaced. Recycling was a different story, though. There hadn't been much of a role for it at the military bases that Reacher grew up on all around the world. As far as he knew. It may have gone on behind the scenes at West Point during his four years there, but if so he hadn't been aware of it. He'd had other things on his mind. So his concept of it was very much a product of his imagination. He pictured it as something new and high tech, involving shiny modern plants with advanced equipment and lots of automation. Maybe even robots.

The reality was very different. At least at the facility the town used. It was surrounded by a ten-foot-high fence made of metal strips, divided and sharpened at the top, and draped in razor wire. Very old school. Inside the gate the operation was ingenious rather than advanced. The blacktop gave over to compacted dirt, rising and turning to form a broad, elevated half doughnut before dropping back down towards the exit. Within the semicircle there were six dumpsters, extra large, with no lids. They were arranged end-on, meeting in the centre like the spokes of a wheel. Each one was dedicated to a different material. Giant signs specified which kinds. Paper and cardboard went in the first. Then glass. Ferrous metal. Non-ferrous metal. Plastic. And finally a catch-all for any other kinds of trash that had been brought there by mistake. Reacher assumed the recycling trucks would drive up, swing around to the appropriate dumpster, and unload. The height and width and incline and turn radius had probably been calculated specially. There was only one snag that he could see. There was no place designated for electronic equipment.

Sands stopped the minivan between the third and fourth dumpsters and Reacher climbed out to investigate. He discounted paper and glass and was wondering whether computers could be classed as plastic due to their outer cases, or metal due to their inner workings, when he heard a voice. A man's. Yelling at him.

'Hey!' the guy said. 'The hell are you doing? You can't be here. Where's your permit?'

The guy had emerged from a Portakabin that was hidden from the entrance to the site by the earth mound. It was presumably some kind of an office. Or a place to hide from the sun. He looked to be in his mid-sixties. His face was burned and wrinkled like a walnut. His hands were shrivelled and the veins and tendons stood out like cords under his skin. His hair was thin and grey and tangled and it hung down past his shoulders. Technically he was wearing faded blue coveralls with some kind of corporate logo on the chest, but he was so skinny and the material was so stiff from the laundry it looked like the clothes had swallowed him.

'Computers,' Reacher said. 'Which dumpster would they be in?'

'Get back in your car,' the guy said. 'Leave. Right now. Or I'm calling 911.'

'It's no good calling 911. The police department's phones are down. Haven't you heard? And there's no need. We'll be happy to leave. Just as soon as we pick up something that got sent here by mistake. Something that belongs to us.'

'If it's here, it belongs to us. It says so in the contract with the town. You take something, you're stealing it. Can't have that.' The guy ducked back into the cabin and reappeared a moment later holding a shotgun. A Benelli M1 Tactical. A nice weapon. Shipped in all the way from Italy. Capable of holding six 12-gauge cartridges. It looked brand new. 'That's why the company gives us these. And trains us how to use them.'

Reacher wasn't entirely convinced that a recycling company would hand out military-grade weaponry to its employees. And he was certain that this particular employee had not gone through any kind of training. Not in the last thirty years, anyway. Given the state he was in, if the guy pulled the trigger the recoil would knock him on his ass. Break his collarbone, for sure. Maybe his whole shoulder. But if he pulled the trigger from that range, any damage the guy did to himself would be the least of Reacher's worries. He was conscious of the captured Beretta in his waistband. The old guy's movements had been pretty slow up to that point. Putting him out of action before he could bring the Benelli to bear would be pretty straightforward. But maybe a little premature at that stage. It was a little early to abandon diplomacy altogether.

Reacher started to move away from the minivan. Very slowly. Just in case negotiations failed.

'Hold it,' the guy said. He raised the shotgun to his shoulder. 'I told you to get in the car. Not move away from it.'

The driver's door opened and Sands climbed out. She had a black leather wallet in her hand. She held it out in front of her, at shoulder height, like a tiny shield. 'Federal agents,' she said. 'Put the gun down.'

Diplomacy, Reacher thought. *Or lying*. It could be hard to tell them apart.

The old guy lowered the gun, but he didn't let go of it.

'What's your name?' Sands said.

The guy hesitated for a moment. 'You can call me Polk.'

'OK then, *General*. Here's what we're going to do. First, you're going to answer a question. The electronic equipment that gets brought here from the town. What happens to it?'

'It gets stored. Along with the 'tronics from our other clients. Then it gets taken away.'

'Who by?'

The guy shrugged. 'Whoever buys it, I guess. One year it's one guy. The next year, someone else. I don't get to pick.'

'When do they take it? How often?'

'Once a month. First Monday, usually. Unless they're late. Which they sometimes are.'

'So everything that came in the last three weeks is still here?'

'Right. Why wouldn't it be?'

'Where?'

The guy gestured over his shoulder, to the cabin. 'In there. Locked up.'

'Show me.' Sands started down the slope.

'Hold it,' the guy said. 'You got a warrant? You can't come in demanding to see stuff without one. I know my rights. We've had training.'

Sands continued until she was standing right in front

of him. Reacher tracked her movement, keeping six feet to the right.

'You want paperwork, huh?' Sands tipped her head to the side. 'I'm surprised. You don't look much like a paperwork kind of guy. But that's no problem. Not for me, anyway. Got a fax machine in there? I can get warrants. Subpoenas. Criminal records. Whatever I want. Assuming that's a path you want to go down?'

The guy didn't respond.

'Anything in the system your bosses don't know about?' Sands said. 'Yet?'

'Assholes,' the guy said. He ducked back into the cabin and replaced the Benelli in its rack, then led the way to the far end of the structure. He worked a lock. Pushed down on a handle, which took all his weight. Heaved open a pair of doors. Leaned inside. Hit a switch, which brought four pairs of fluorescent tubes flickering into life. Then stood to the side.

'See for yourself,' he said. 'It's all there.'

The space accounted for half the footprint of the cabin. There were grey metal shelves, floor to ceiling, lined up around all three walls. Some smaller items were scattered on the shelves nearest the entrance. Reacher could see cell phones and cameras and DVD players and a couple of laptops. But the main action was on the floor in the centre of the room. There were dozens of computers and keyboards and monitors and printers and widescreen TVs along with a bunch of other devices Reacher didn't recognize. All heaped up together. All tangled in a chaotic jumble of cables

245

and wires like a giant electronic spider had been absorbing it into its web.

'Which ones are they?' Reacher moved to let Sands get a better view. 'Can you tell?'

'I don't know,' Sands said. 'There's no sign of the cabinet they were in. But that did have a broken door. They probably took the servers out and threw the rest of it in one of those dumpsters. Better get Rusty down here. I'll need help finding them in all this junk.'

'I'm here.' Rutherford appeared from around the corner of the cabin. He looked into the room and nodded his head. 'All right. They must be buried in the middle of all this. Come on. Let's get to work. I want all eight of them, just in case.'

Rutherford scrambled through the mess to the far side on the basis that each new delivery was apparently shoved in on top of the last and the servers could have been there for a couple of weeks. Sands handed her purse to Reacher and went in after him. It was hot inside. The roof was made of metal. So were the walls. There was an air conditioner but it only cooled the office area. Not the storage side. It was as if their prize was hidden in an oven. Reacher stayed outside. It wasn't a great deal cooler in the direct sun. But he wanted to keep an eye on the guy with the grey hair. He knew the man pulling Marty's strings had put out an order to watch for Rutherford. The man with a liking for suitcases and bone saws. There was no reason to believe the grey-haired guy was involved. Or that Fisher's cell would be put back on active duty if anyone called in a sighting. But plans change. Opportunities present themselves. Sometimes they're too good to resist. They were in a remote location. Two of them were in an enclosed space. And the guy had a shotgun.

Rutherford and Sands continued to sift through the mound of discarded equipment. The grey-haired guy leaned one shoulder against the cabin wall and watched them. He made no move for his phone. Or a panic button. Or an alarm. The sun continued to beat down. Reacher continued to watch all three people. Until finally Rutherford and Sands emerged into the open air. They were blinking against the light. Their clothes were clinging with sweat. Their skin was smeared with dust. And their hands were empty.

Sands took back her purse.

Rutherford approached the grey-haired guy. 'Where's everything else?'

The guy straightened up. 'Like what? This is everything.'

'It can't be. Some things are missing. Eight things, at least. From the town IT department.'

The guy shrugged.

'Where else could they be?'

'You accusing me of something?'

'What? No. Is there another site somewhere, is what I mean. Like an overflow?'

'No. Everything comes here.'

'Who else works here?' Reacher said.

'No one. Just me.'

'What if you're out sick? Or on vacation?'

'My boss would send someone. To fill in for me.'

'When was the last time that happened?'

The guy chewed on his lower lip for a moment. 'Let's see. Last time I was sick was 1986. In the summer. I had my appendix taken out. At Vanderbilt. Nice place. And my last vacation? It was at the millennium. I went to Canada to see my brother. Used to go every New Year's. But now he's dead.'

'I don't get it,' Rutherford said. 'These things. What could have happened to them? They can't have disappeared into thin air.'

The guy shrugged again. 'If they're not here, whatever they are, then they never came. Or they've already been taken away again.'

'What about site logs?' Sands moved across and stood next to Rutherford. 'You must keep records of what comes in and out?'

'Deliveries and collections,' the guy said. 'Sure.'

'Show me.'

The guy sighed, then led the way to the entrance to the office. He indicated that everyone should remain outside and ducked through the door, reappearing a moment later with a clipboard in each hand. He passed the first one to Sands. Reacher read it over her shoulder. It was for collections. There were eight entries for the current month. But only one for electronics. It was dated the second. Before the ransomware attack. Before Rutherford had trashed the servers. So before they could have arrived at the facility, let alone been removed.

Sands swapped clipboards. The second one listed the deliveries. There had been thirty-two so far that month. The most frequent kinds were glass and non-ferrous metal. Bottles and cans from the local bars and restaurants, Reacher guessed. Then paper. Probably a surge due to the municipal computers being down. Electronics was all the way at the bottom. There had only been two consignments. Both had come from the town's IT department. And both were after Rutherford had discovered his backup had failed.

'The electronics deliveries, here and here,' Sands said, pointing at the entries. 'Show me the itemization for those.'

The guy looked at her blankly for a moment. 'What itemization? We don't list all the things that come in. How could we? There are too many. And what would be the point? *Computer mouse, beige, not working. Computer mouse, beige, not working. Computer mouse, beige, not working.* How would you tell one from the other?'

'OK.' Sands pointed to another entry on the sheet, next to the column for the delivery vehicle's licence plate. 'Driver ID. It's the same both times. #083. Whose number is that?'

The guy looked at the signature line. 'Dave. Dave Thomassino.'

'Where can we find him?' Sands said.

'How would I know? He's a delivery guy. He drives in, drops off a bunch of stuff, and drives away again. It's not like we hang out.'

'What's his route today?'

'How would I know? I'm not his boss.'

'When's his next delivery scheduled?'

'No idea. The guys just show up when their trucks are full and they need to unload.'

'Where does he live?'

'No idea. Like I said, we're not buddies.'

'What about his truck?' Reacher said. 'Does he take it home at night?'

'No.' The guy shook his head. 'They're not allowed to. They leave the trucks at the depot. Drive home in their own vehicles.'

'Do they work on their own?' Reacher said. 'Or in pairs? Or teams?'

'For the bigger stuff it's two men to a truck,' the guy said. 'Thomassino's is smaller. He works alone. You don't need two men to toss in a bunch of iPhones or whatever.'

'Where's the depot?' Sands said.

'Next to the office,' the guy said.

'Where's the office? And don't say *next to the depot* or we're going to have a problem.'

'I'll write the address for you.'

'Write Thomassino's cell number as well.'

'I can't. I don't know it.'

'Good,' Sands said. 'Make sure it stays that way. Because if Thomassino doesn't show up at the depot for any reason, I'll be coming back. And you'll be spending whatever time you have left on this earth in a federal penitentiary.'

EIGHTEEN

Reacher, Rutherford and Sands left the guy with his clipboards and trudged back up the slope. They climbed into the minivan. Sands fired up the engine. She cranked the air all the way up and set off slowly, following the curve around and down and off the dirt and through the exit gate and back out on to the blacktop. No one spoke. Reacher sprawled out in the back. He was thinking about the servers. About what might have happened to them. He had two plausible theories. Option A was that they'd been trashed. He pictured the guy, Thomassino, going to collect them. Thomassino worked alone. Which was probably fine when he was picking up small things like cell phones. But there were eight servers. They were housed in a cabinet. It was six feet tall. Heavy. Hard to manoeuvre. Stuck on some kind of irregularity in the floor. And its door was broken. Glass shards would be sticking out. Making it dangerous to handle, as well as difficult. The log showed that Thomassino arrived at the recycling centre after 5:00 p.m. on each occasion. Probably his last job on both days. Would he have bothered to wrestle with the cabinet on his own, so close to the end of his shift? Or would he have slipped the guys on the regular garbage duty a couple of crisp twenties to take care of the problem for him?

Option B assumed Thomassino would have made the effort to remove the cabinet. Or at least its contents. It was only Rutherford's experimental software that had failed. The servers themselves were in working order. Maybe Thomassino kept an eye out for such things. Maybe he had a regular buyer on standby. Reacher had no idea what second-hand computer equipment was worth. Maybe a lot. Maybe not very much. The reward may not have been high. But the risk was virtually non-existent. How would the theft ever come to light, under normal circumstances? The town guys would be happy because their unwanted items had been removed. The recycling guys would never know to expect them, because nothing was itemized.

So, laziness or greed? Even money in Reacher's experience. Impossible to pick between them without knowing more about Thomassino. And most likely irrelevant, anyway. The servers could have been crushed or incinerated or sent to a landfill. They could have been wiped and restored to factory settings and sold. Either way the data would be lost. The identity of the Russian spy would remain a secret. And Rutherford would still be in danger. Reacher would have to decide what to do about that. Staying in town to babysit him indefinitely was out of the question. So was leaving him alone and vulnerable. The best option would be to persuade him to get out of town, but Reacher had tried that. He saw little hope of getting Rutherford to change his mind. Not without divulging dangerous information. Maybe Sands could help, he thought. She was ex-Bureau. He could talk to her. Hint at the source of the problem. Obliquely enough to avoid compromising Fisher. Directly enough to stress the urgency. That might work. Unless Thomassino rendered the problem moot. Maybe he would serve up a miracle. Maybe the servers were sitting safely at his house, untouched, contents intact.

Hope for the best.

Given a free hand Reacher would have proceeded directly to the depot. The site log showed Thomassino working past 5:00 p.m. on the days he delivered electronics to the recycling facility but there was no guarantee those were his regular hours. The safest course would be to locate the truck drivers' personal vehicles as quickly as possible and wait. An hour. Two hours. Five. As long as necessary. It was all the same to Reacher. He could wait all day. But he could see it wasn't the same for Sands and Rutherford. They were cranky after failing to find their equipment. Probably worried about their prospects of ever recovering it. And definitely uncomfortable after rooting around inside the hot metal cabin. He was going to have to cut them some slack. Unless he went to find Thomassino on his own. Which was a possibility. The risk should be

253

minimal. Fisher's cell was stood down to surveillance only.

Reacher decided they should stick together. There was another factor to take into account. Suppose their luck changed and Thomassino came clean immediately. Admitted to stealing all the serviceable equipment he came across and took Reacher to his stash. Reacher didn't know what a server looked like. He needed Rutherford with him to handle the identification. And Sands had proved herself more than valuable, finding the location of the recycling plant and then duping the guy with the shotgun. A little downtime wouldn't kill them, Reacher figured. As long as they were at the depot by 4:00 p.m.

Sands leaned across and hit some buttons on the minivan's GPS screen which caused it to display the locations of the five nearest gas stations. The closest was the truck stop Reacher had visited twice before. They continued in silence, and when they arrived Sands pulled up at the pump Reacher had used the previous night. Rutherford stayed in the car. Sands climbed out and pumped the gas. She used her credit card to avoid having to go inside the main building. Reacher went in anyway. He was hungry. He rounded up the ingredients for four hot dogs, assembled them, loaded them with extra cheese and onions, then grabbed a bunch of newspapers. A disposable razor. A can of shaving cream. And a pack of bottled water, figuring the others could probably use some hydration.

Sands dropped Reacher and Rutherford two blocks

from the apartment building and went to find a random spot to leave the minivan. She got back to Mitch's place ten minutes after the others, fired up the coffee machine, then went to take a shower. Rutherford stayed in the kitchen, hunched over his computer. Reacher stretched out on the couch and made a start on the newspapers. Neither of them moved for half an hour. Neither said a word. Then Sands came out of the bathroom and Rutherford went in. She poured two mugs of coffee, carried them to the living room, and took a seat opposite Reacher.

'Can I ask you something?' Sands said. 'You were in the army. You were an MP. You investigated things. And people. Yes?'

'That was the general idea,' Reacher said.

'You must have had resources. Records. Databases. Other soldiers who could make calls. Verify information. Find out if people had been telling the truth?'

'All of the above.'

'Do you miss that, now that you're on your own?'

'Life in the army was pretty good, overall,' Reacher said. 'I worked with some outstanding people. Aside from the time I wasted dealing with bullshit from senior officers. Other than that I left with very few regrets.'

'No,' Sands said. 'I mean the support you had. The ability to get facts checked. If you found yourself in a particular situation, for example, and you were given a plausible account for it. Then you realized there might be an alternative explanation. A much less favourable

255

one, from a certain individual's point of view. What would you do now?'

'I'd listen to my gut. If I had any doubt, I'd walk away.'

'Even if that meant leaving a friend in danger?'

'OK, Sarah. Enough beating around the bush. What's your real question?'

'Well, when I was in the shower just now I started thinking, what if I wanted to get something from Rusty? Something critically important. And I wanted to do it without anyone realizing. I wouldn't steal it, because he'd notice and report it missing. I wouldn't try to buy it from him or trick him into handing it over, because he might see through me. He might play along and then report the attempt. Or run. I could kidnap him, of course, and force him to give it to me. But then I'd have to kill him to preserve the secret. So maybe I'd do this instead. I'd stage a kidnapping attempt. Make it look very professional. Very convincing. The kind of thing that would certainly have succeeded if someone hadn't intervened. Someone with all the right skills and experience who just happened to be walking by. Someone who would instantly gain Rusty's trust, and then offer to stick around and help him.'

'That someone being me?' Reacher said.

'I'm not trying to be an asshole here. But you have to admit it's a possibility.'

'It's absolutely a possibility. It wouldn't be the first time something like it happened.'

'Is that supposed to make me feel better? Because

it's not just the kidnap attempt that could be fishy. Every other time you've had contact with whoever we're up against you've been on your own. A series of coincidences? Or clandestine meetings?'

Reacher smiled and looked away.

'What?' Sands said. 'Is this funny to you?'

'No. It's just this town. There must be something in the water. First I get mistaken for an insurance guy. And now you think, what? Follow it through. If I'm working with these kidnappers, I must be some kind of mercenary. Someone good, because this operation wasn't thrown together on a budget. Therefore someone expensive. So I must be secretly rich. What's your theory? This whole image is a sham? I really live in some Manhattan mansion with closets full of silk suits and a garage crammed with Ferraris?'

'Is that any less likely than a retired major being homeless?'

'I'm not homeless.'

'So that's one lie you told.'

'When?'

'You told Rusty you don't own a house. You just drift around. A night here. Two nights there. No fixed abode.'

'That's true.'

'So you are homeless.'

'No. My situation is not the same at all. It's like the difference between being alone and being lonely. Two separate, distinct things.'

'OK, then. Back up. Say you have earned a fortune

257

as a mercenary. It doesn't follow that you spent the money on a house and clothes and cars. That's faulty reasoning. You might not have spent the money at all. You could have stashed it all in a bank in the Cayman Islands. Or hidden it inside a hollow tree. Or given it to a cat shelter.'

'True. I could have. But I didn't.'

'Can you back that up?'

'How? I can't prove a negative. No one can.'

Sands slumped back on the couch.

'Try this,' Reacher said. 'Flip it around. I have the means and the opportunity, sure. But what's my motive?'

'Money,' Sands said.

'I'm not interested in money. I have enough already. Why would I want more?'

'Have you met the human race?'

'You're on the wrong track, Sarah. The point is, I do have a motive. To keep Rusty out of danger. You're equally capable of that. So why don't you take over? If you move him somewhere safe, today, I'll walk away. I'll never come near him again.'

'Or with us out of the way you'll go straight to the depot and lean on Thomassino.'

'Look, if you really don't trust me, talk to your friends at the Bureau. Have them run my background.'

'I already did. Five minutes after I met you. They didn't find anything. But what does that mean? You're telling the truth? Or you're good at covering your tracks?'

'I guess it boils down to this,' Reacher said. 'I could be helping Rusty. I could be setting him up. Only time will tell. So right now it just depends on what you believe. And you obviously don't believe I'm in league with the devil.'

'What makes you so sure?'

'You're a smart woman. That's clear. So if you really thought I was a hired killer you wouldn't say so to my face. You'd drug my coffee and slip away while you had the chance. Or shoot me before I could hurt your friend.'

'That's an interesting theory. Which begs another question. Who just made your coffee?'

Reacher picked up his mug. It was a decent size. Maybe eight fluid ounces. It had started out full. Now only a quarter was left. Was six ounces enough for an effective dose of tranquillizer? For a man his size? He didn't feel dizzy. Or nauseous. Or tired. He sniffed the remaining liquid. There was no unusual odour. It had tasted fine. But then he wasn't the world's greatest connoisseur when it came to flavour. He was mainly a fan of strength.

'Here,' Sands said. 'Pass it to me.'

Reacher put the mug back on the table and slid it across. Sands picked it up and took a mouthful.

'I was joking about the coffee,' she said, then revealed why her robe was gaping a little that day. There was something in the pocket. Something heavy. Sands reached inside and pulled it out. It was a gun. A Colt Government Model .380. Small. Light. Reliable.

She flicked the safety down with her right thumb. 'I'm not joking about this. And remember, you may be bigger. But I'm faster. So look me in the eye and tell me you're on the level.'

'I'm on the level.'

Sands rested the Colt on her lap. The tips of her fingers were touching its grip.

'So,' Reacher said after a long minute had ticked past. 'What are you going to do?'

'What choice do I have? Do what you said. Go with my gut.' Sands flicked the safety up and slipped the gun back into her pocket. 'And pray you don't make me regret it.'

NINETEEN

Rutherford emerged from the bathroom with a towel wrapped around his waist and scurried to his sleeping area behind the wooden divider. Sands got up and followed around to hers. Reacher stayed on the couch. He could hear the others rustling and rubbing and fidgeting, then two hairdryers started up almost simultaneously. They ran for almost the same length of time. There was more rustling. Then Sands reappeared. She was wearing loose linen pants and a pale blue T-shirt. She was using her sunglasses to hold back her hair, and her purse was slung over her left shoulder. Positioned to ensure easy access for her right hand, Reacher thought. No doubt with the Colt at the top. Maybe in a special built-in holster, so that it wouldn't get buried or snagged.

Rutherford rejoined them. He had on a fresh pair of chinos and a clean polo shirt. Another sombre colour. Another logo. To show he still meant business.

*

Sands left the apartment first, alone, to avoid being seen with the others. She retrieved the minivan, rendezvoused with Rutherford and Reacher in the alley with the dumpsters, and entered the waste company's address into the GPS. The machine predicted a ten-minute drive, which turned out to be accurate. It led them to a compound at the end of a long straight road with squat, shabby warehouses on either side. The site was surrounded by a chain-link fence made of heavy-gauge steel. Eight feet tall. The only entrance they could see was blocked by a red and white striped barrier. Sands drove up close and stopped next to a tall metal post. There were two keypads attached to it. One high, for trucks. One low, for cars. Sands wound down her window and hit the intercom button on the lower one. There was no response. She hit it again. The box didn't make a sound. Not even a buzz of static. She stretched up to give the other one a try but stopped before her finger made contact. There was movement from inside the compound. A shiny black pickup was approaching. It looked like a regular F150. No light bar on the roof. No security company logo on the door. Sands took her fake federal ID out of her purse, just in case.

The Ford slowed as it drew nearer, almost to a walking pace. The barrier twitched like it was waking from a deep sleep, then jerked its way up through ninety degrees. The pickup accelerated and sped away. The driver didn't give them a second glance. The barrier stayed up. It was swaying slightly from its recent movement. But it wasn't descending. Yet. The timing had probably been calculated with trucks in mind. Long. Heavy. Slow to get moving. Sands glanced around. No one else was watching so she hit the gas and they were inside the compound long before the pole lurched back down on to its supports.

There were two buildings on the site, set at four and eight o'clock when viewed from the gate. The eight o'clock unit was the smaller of the two. The office, Reacher assumed. It was a single storey, built of rough brick, with a flat roof, six square windows, and a crude concrete slab sticking out to shelter its doorway. It had parking for thirty cars. Half the spaces were occupied. There were two silver German sedans sitting alone in the row nearest the building's entrance. The rest were middle spec, medium-sized domestic models in varying pale colours, scattered at random throughout the rest of the lot. Belonging to the office workers, most likely.

Not the cars they were looking for.

The four o'clock building must have been what the guy with the shotgun had called the depot. It was a simple rectangular shape, built out of cinderblocks, painted white, with a pitched metal roof and a line of four roll-up vehicle doors along one side. All were tall enough for a full-size garbage truck to fit through. All were wide enough. All were closed. There was a single line of parking spots outside to the left of them, near a personnel door. Four were taken. All by pickups. Three Fords and a Dodge Ram. Not new but clean and well maintained. Belonging to the mechanics, Reacher figured.

Not the cars they were looking for.

There was an empty area on the right of the depot building. It stretched across to the fence. Where the trucks parked at night. There was room for at least half a dozen. And beyond that, where the fence turned back towards the entrance and the space narrowed, there was another line of vehicles. Seven of them. An old, open-top Jeep with most of its paint missing. A Chrysler 300 sedan in black with chrome wheels and heavy tints on the windows. A Porsche 911, dark blue and gleaming in the afternoon sun. A 1980s Cadillac, originally burgundy, now chalky and dull. A mustard-coloured Volvo station wagon. A tiny, sky blue Fiat. And a white Hyundai SUV.

Possibly the cars they were looking for.

A sign mounted to the fence said *Unauthorized Vehicles Will Be Towed At Owner's Expense.* Sands swung the minivan around and reversed right up to it, at the side of the Hyundai. She kept the engine running and adjusted the air. Outside the heat shimmered off the cracked concrete slabs. The flat surfaces in the distance wobbled and danced. Sands unfastened her seat belt and leaned back, relaxed but alert. Rutherford was beside her in the passenger seat, anxious and fidgety. Reacher stretched out behind them, so still he could have been asleep.

Thirty minutes passed. No trucks appeared. Fifteen more minutes passed with no arrivals. Then after another five minutes they heard a vehicle engine. A big diesel. Coming their way. Sands and Reacher simultaneously snapped upright. A garbage truck came into view at the far end of the road. It was full size. So not Thomassino's. They watched it creep along the road, negotiate the gate, lumber across to the parking area, then settle to a halt with a long hiss of its air brakes. Two men jumped down. They were wearing blue coveralls like the guy at the recycling plant. They made their way to the line of cars. The first guy climbed into the Jeep. The second, the Chrysler. They set off together, driving side by side until they were close to the gate. Then the Jeep took the lead. They made it through while the barrier was still up from their entrance, accelerated hard, and soon disappeared from view.

Another truck appeared seven minutes later. Also full size. So not Thomassino's. It followed the same routine. Its occupants took the Cadillac and the Volvo. That left three cars. The Hyundai. The Fiat. And the Porsche.

The next truck to arrive was smaller. They had to wait until it passed them to read the licence plate on the rear. It matched the entry on the recycling site log next to Thomassino's ID number. It parked alongside the two larger trucks, but it pulled further in, vanishing from sight. A man appeared after thirty seconds. He was around five ten. He had blond hair, buzzed short. Mirrored aviator sunglasses. Shiny black boots. And the same blue coveralls, only darker and crisper, like in his mind he was wearing a flight suit. He walked towards them. Heading for the Porsche. Sands reached for her door handle, then paused. The guy was on the wrong side of the car. He went up to the Porsche's passenger window. Leaned in close. Cupped his hand against the sun. Gazed inside for ten seconds. Then straightened up, shook his head, continued past the Fiat, and made his way between the Hyundai and the minivan. Sands jumped out and hurried around, holding her black wallet out in front.

'David Thomassino?' she said.

'That's me.' The guy paused. 'Who's asking?'

'Federal agents. We need to talk.'

'About what?'

'Get in the van for a second. I'll explain everything.'

Rutherford twisted around in his seat and hit a button which caused the side door to slide open, revealing Reacher crammed inside like a caged gorilla.

'I don't think so.' Thomassino stepped back. 'I'm not getting in there with him. I'll talk to you. But at the police station. I'll drive. You can follow.'

'Let me put it another way.' Reacher leaned out, grabbed the front of Thomassino's coveralls, and pulled him inside. Sands climbed in after Thomassino and guided him through to the bench seat at the very back. She pulled a lever that made her middle row seat swivel around so she was facing him, then hit the button to close the door. Reacher rotated his seat as well. Rutherford peered through the gap between the front seats.

'Before we start it's very important that you understand something,' Sands said. 'We're not here for you. We're not looking to jam you up or cause you trouble

266

of any kind. We don't care about you at all. All we
want is one piece of information. Give it to us and you
can go about your business. You'll never see us again.
And no one will ever know you helped us. Is that
clear?'

Thomassino swallowed hard, then nodded.

'Good,' Sands said. 'Now, your job is to collect
unwanted electronic equipment and take it to the recycling facility outside town, correct?'

'It's just a sorting facility. The actual recycling's
done somewhere else.'

'But you take the electronic things there?'

'Right.'

'This month you've made two collections from the
town's IT department.'

'If you say so.'

'That's what the site log says.'

'Then I'm sure it's right.'

'On one of those occasions you picked up eight network servers.'

'I don't know what they are.'

'Boring-looking black boxes,' Rutherford said. 'But
they were in a cabinet. In the equipment room. Right
in the middle. With a broken glass door.'

'Do you know how many things I move in a week?'
Thomassino said. 'I can't remember all of them.'

'I see you're wearing a wedding ring, Dave,' Reacher
said. 'Do you have any kids? Or is it just you and your
wife?'

'One kid. On the way,' Thomassino said. 'Why?'

'Boy or girl?'

'A girl. Why?'

'Because I can picture the scene,' Reacher said. 'Her first day of kindergarten. Your wife goes to bring her home and she says, "Mommy, how come I don't have a daddy? All the other children do." And your wife says, "You do have a daddy, sweetheart. Only he's in federal prison. Because he was too stupid to help himself when he had the chance."'

'All right.' Thomassino closed his eyes for a moment. 'I collected them. On my second visit. They were there the first time too but I pretended I hadn't seen them. They were a pain in the ass to move so I was hoping one of the regular garbage crews would take them.'

'What did you do with them?' Sands said.

'Put them in the truck. Then later that day I emptied the truck at the sorting plant.'

'Let's try that again.'

'What? It's the truth.'

'I believe you put them in the truck. But they never made it to the sorting plant. What happened to them?'

'I didn't steal them, if that's what you're implying,' Thomassino said. 'I didn't sell them. I didn't pitch them on the way. Everything that was in the truck, I unloaded at the plant.'

'But they weren't at the plant,' Sands said. 'We checked. So what happened to them?'

'I have no idea. Search my house if you don't believe me. Talk to my wife. My friends. Check my bank account. I'll take a lie detector test. But I didn't steal them. I didn't sell them. And I don't know where they are.'

Reacher looked at Sands. She replied with the slightest shrug of her shoulders. It wasn't the answer they wanted. It didn't help them. But Reacher was inclined to believe it. He had questioned a lot of suspects over the years. He had a good sense of when someone was lying and Thomassino seemed sincere in what he said.

'OK, then.' Sands took a piece of paper and a pen from her purse. 'I'm going to give you a number, and if you—'

'I have a question,' Rutherford said. 'Sarah, at the recycling place, did anything strike you as strange?'

'No. It was just a heap of junk.'

'Exactly. And the old weird guy? When you asked him about itemization, he said what would be the point? *Computer mouse, beige, not working.* Over and over.'

'Yes. So?'

'What are the odds of every single electronic device discarded by people in the town being broken? Surely some things would still work, even if they were old and slow. Like the servers. There was nothing wrong with them. It's like everything with life left in it had been syphoned off, somehow.'

Thomassino looked at the floor. His first tell.

'Dave?' Reacher said. 'Anything to add?'

Thomassino didn't answer.

'I wonder if your daughter will get married, Dave. I bet she will. Most people do, in the end. The question

269

is, who will walk her down the aisle? Who will be there when she has a kid of her own?'

Thomassino leaned forward and held his head in his hands. 'It started in my second week on the job. My boss asked me to lunch. Said there were a couple of things he needed to bring me up to speed with. So I went to meet him. At a diner. Fat Freddie's.'

'I know the place,' Rutherford said. 'It's supposed to have the best milkshakes in town.'

'I got there first,' Thomassino continued. 'So I sat down and waited. I got a text from the boss. He said he was running late so I should go ahead and order. I did, and after my food came I got another text. He said he couldn't make it after all. I finished eating and asked for my check and the waitress told me my meal was on the house. I asked why, and she said I should hang on a minute. Someone would come and explain. Then a big fat guy appeared and sat opposite me. I think he's the owner. I thanked him, and he said it was no problem. He said I could always eat there for free. I just had to do one thing in return. Always stop in on my way to the sorting plant. And make sure my truck wasn't locked.'

'What did you do?' Sands said.

'Tried to talk my way out of it. Said my routes varied, it wouldn't always be practical, sometimes I ran late, that kind of thing.'

'But he wouldn't take no for an answer.'

'He handed me a photograph. Of my wife. Taken through a windshield. She was crossing the street out-side her work. The car was real close to her. Only a couple of feet away. She'd turned towards it. I'll never forget the look on her face. Pure terror. Like she was certain she was getting run down.'

'Did he say anything else?'

'He didn't have to. The message was clear.'

'So you always stop there on the way to the plant,' Reacher said. 'Can you just show up? Or do you have to call ahead? Give notice?'

'Just show up. And stay at least thirty minutes. And always leave the truck in one particular spot.'

'Which one?'

'Around the back, to the side of the staff parking lot, there's a brick outhouse. Where the dumpsters are. And where they keep the used cooking oil. There's a patch of ground marked off in yellow. I have to leave the truck there.'

'How many doors does the outhouse have?'

'One. Right by where I have to park.'

'Any windows?'

'None.'

'Is the door locked?'

Thomassino thought for a moment. 'I guess. It has a padlock. A big one.'

'So while you're inside eating your free food someone rifles through your truck, takes everything that looks valuable, and locks it in this outhouse?'

Thomassino shrugged.

'What?' Reacher said. 'Is there more to the story?'

'I honestly don't know. I'm in a crappy situation here. Am I really going to put my wife's life in danger over some worn-out electronics? Stuff that people have already thrown in the trash? Which is part of a racket that even my boss is in on? No. I'm not. So I see no evil and I hear no evil. I go in. I eat. I go back out. I empty the truck at the plant. If someone helped themselves to some stuff when I wasn't looking, I don't know anything about it.'

'Plausible deniability,' Rutherford said. 'I get it.'

'Semi-plausible,' Sands said.

'Plausible or not, you went to the diner the day you picked up the servers?' Reacher said.

Thomassino nodded.

'And the servers were gone when you got to the plant?'

'I guess,' Thomassino said. 'I mean, it's not like we keep records. But I remember the cabinet thing. It was a pain in the ass getting it into the truck. I don't remember getting it back out.'

'All right,' Reacher said. 'One more question. The guy at the diner. The owner. Who had the picture of your wife. What's his name?'

'I heard someone call him Bud,' Thomassino said. 'But I think his real name is Budnick. Bill Budnick. There was a story about Fat Freddie's in the paper one time and he was mentioned. About a year ago. Right after he bought the place.'

'Good,' Reacher said. 'Now did this guy Budnick ever talk to you about what to do if anyone came around asking questions about him?'

'No. Nothing like that came up. I only spoke to him that one time.'

'So if we happen to visit Fat Freddie's to, say, check out their reputation for milkshakes, Budnick wouldn't be expecting us?'

'Would I tip him off, do you mean? Look, that asshole threatened my wife. I wouldn't piss in his mouth if his teeth were on fire. I'd love for you to pay him a visit. I'd love for you to bust him and throw his ass in jail. Just please, keep my name out of it.'

'How could we bring your name into it?' Reacher said. 'We've never met.'

Sands hit the door button, climbed out, and beckoned Thomassino to follow her. He got halfway out of his seat then sank back down.

'There's one other thing,' he said. 'Something I want you to know. The food I eat at Fat Freddie's. I always pay for it. Apart from that first time when they caught me by surprise. I do what I do for my wife. To keep her safe. Not to get something for nothing. As far as I'm concerned, maybe they rob my truck. Maybe they don't. But I am not one of them.'

TWENTY

So, it wasn't laziness. It was greed. Only not on Thomassino's part. He was just a pawn. He could have made a stand, Reacher supposed. In which case the servers would already be back in their hands. But he couldn't blame the guy for looking the other way while his work truck got looted. Not with his wife's life on the line. And not over a bunch of junk that people had already thrown away. Reacher would have been happier if they were driving away with the servers stacked safely in the back of the minivan. But having another breadcrumb to follow was better than nothing.

The GPS predicted a twenty-two-minute drive to Fat Freddie's, but that turned into forty-six minutes because Reacher asked Sands to make a detour via the truck stop. He wanted to get his hands on two more things. A bolt cutter. The biggest they had. And a padlock. The strongest he could find. Sands took the opportunity to top off the gas while Reacher was inside

274

and she was waiting when he returned with the engine running and the next leg of the route highlighted on the screen. She drove faster than before. Buoyed up with the prospect of retrieving the servers, Reacher figured. She pushed the minivan hard, swaying and drifting through the curves until a robotic voice from the dashboard announced that their destination was on their left. They were still north of town. A few houses were dotted around amongst the fields and the trees but the concentrated development was still at least a mile away. There was a pre-war flatbed parked on either side of the driveway, like a rusty automotive equivalent of the statues Reacher had seen at the entrance to grand estates. The diner itself was set back from the road. It was a wide rectangular building made to look like it was constructed from logs. It had a green metal roof and a full-width porch and a neon sign mounted in the centre of the front wall. It spelled out *Fat Freddie's* in flashing red letters and below the script an animated cartoon cowboy repeatedly lifted a colossal cheeseburger from his plate to his mouth.

The parking lot was out front. It was packed. The dinner rush was still in full swing. Sands threaded her way around the cars and trucks that had been left at the ends of rows and half up on the kerbs and looped around to the back of the building. There was another line of spaces marked *Staff Only*, again all taken. Beyond them was the outhouse, just where Thomassino had said it would be. It was low and square, built of pale brick, with a flat roof and a fenced-off area attached at the front to contain the garbage cans. Sands pulled up at the side, next to its door. Reacher climbed out. He was holding the bolt cutter low down, tight against his leg. He checked that no one was watching. Raised the tool. Closed its jaws over the top of the padlock. And squeezed. Hard. The metal loop severed. He swung the body of the lock aside, pulled it clear, and stowed its remains in his pocket. Sands jumped down and joined him. Rutherford scurried around from the far side of the van.

'Ready?' Reacher said.

Sands and Rutherford looked at each other and nodded.

Reacher pulled the door. Its hinges squealed. Daylight flooded in almost to the far wall. Inside, the floor was covered with heaps of equipment. A similar mix to the junk at the recycling plant. Only here it was neatly sorted into categories. Computers in one area. Monitors next to them. Then keyboards. And mice. And printers. And TVs. And DVD players. Presumably everything was serviceable, although Reacher didn't know how to tell for sure. Everything was certainly ordered and organized. And there was only one thing that wasn't electronic. A cabinet. It was six feet tall, standing on its own at the back of the space, half hidden in the shadows. Its solid right side was facing them, and the remains of its glass door was hanging open.

'There it is!' Rutherford pushed past Reacher and rushed forward, pulling out his phone as he went. He switched on its flashlight. Dodged around to the front of the cabinet. Looked inside. Then slumped sideways, ending up with his right shoulder propped against the wall.

'What's wrong?' Sands said.

Rutherford couldn't speak. He just gestured vaguely with his left hand.

Sands crossed the room, looked into the cabinet, and turned back to Reacher. He knew what she was going to say before she opened her mouth. 'It's empty. They're gone.'

Reacher had a vision of the servers receding even further into the distance. And the new guy from Moscow heading in the opposite direction. On a plane. Growing ever closer.

'Any chance they're in one of these piles?' Reacher said.

Rutherford struggled back upright and shook his head. 'No. There's only one lot of computers, and they're all desktops. The servers aren't here. We're too late.'

'That's the wrong way to look at it,' Reacher said. 'We're not too late. We're a step closer. We know for sure they were here. Which means we're on the right track.'

'That's true,' Sands said. She took Rutherford's arm and led him to the door. 'Come on. We're not giving up.'

'What can we do?' Rutherford said. 'It's a dead end.'

'No, it isn't,' Sands said. 'The servers were here. Someone knows what happened to them.'

'I guess,' Rutherford said. 'But who?'

'We already know who,' Sands said. 'Bill Budnick. The man who threatened Thomassino. Who owns this place. We'll talk to him. Make him tell us who he sold them to.'

'Think he's still here?' Rutherford said. 'What if he doesn't work evenings?'

'We'll go inside,' Sands said. 'It should be easy to see if he's around. And if he's not, someone will know how to contact him.'

'No need to go looking for him,' Reacher said. 'Give it five minutes. Maybe less. He'll come to us.'

Reacher leaned into the van and slid the bolt cutter under his seat then turned and shoved the outhouse door closed.

'Right,' Sands said. 'The half-hour thing.'

'I don't follow,' Rutherford said.

'Thomassino said he could show up here any time the place is open.' Reacher slid the new lock into place and clicked it shut. 'No need to call ahead. He just had to stay for half an hour.'

'Meaning that whoever searches his truck is always here,' Sands said. 'He needs time to look through all the stuff. Figure out what's valuable. Move it to the outhouse. And get clear before Thomassino comes back out. Thirty minutes is already tight. Anything else, like relying on another person to notice Thomassino had showed up, taking their call, driving here from wherever he's based – that would add too much overhead.'

278

'Maybe,' Rutherford said. 'But it doesn't follow that Budnick does that himself.'

'True.' Reacher leaned against the wall. 'But professional criminals generally want two things. As much reward as possible. And as little risk as possible. If Budnick doesn't deal with the trucks himself he has to bring in someone else to do it. At least one person. Maybe two, to cover all the week's shifts. These people would need to be paid. Which dilutes the profit. They might drop a dime on him. And they would have to keep sneaking away from the kitchen or the dishwasher or whatever their cover job is, which would be suspicious. Which would increase the risk.' He pointed to a fire door at the back of the main building. 'A dime gets a dollar that the next guy who comes out of there is Budnick. Meantime, Rusty, you better get back in the van. Keep your head down. You're local. You've been in the paper. He might recognize you.'

The fire door opened after three minutes and a man stepped out. He was dressed in a pale grey suit with a white shirt and a flowery tie. His hair was neatly parted. And he was enormous. Six two and at least four hundred pounds. The perils of being surrounded by free food all day, every day, Reacher thought. The guy stood still for a moment, head tipped slightly to one side. Assessing the situation.

The guy came to a conclusion and started towards the outhouse. He was light on his feet. He moved fast. Reacher updated his appraisal. The guy was not a slob, after all. Maybe a former wrestler. Or a lineman.

279

Not that his background was going to make any difference. Not unless he had a heart attack before giving Reacher what he wanted.

'I'm sorry, folks,' the guy said. 'You can't park there. I'm going to have to ask you to move.'

'That's not right, is it, Mr Budnick?' Reacher said. 'We can park here. Clearly. Because we have. And you don't have to ask us to move. You want to.'

'Who the hell are you?' Budnick said. 'And how do you know my name?'

'I know a lot about you,' Reacher said. 'I know you own this restaurant. And I know that owning a restaurant isn't enough for you, because you do a little business on the side. So I'm here to make you an offer. Something very simple. We both get what we want. We go our separate ways. Sound good?'

'Firstly, I have no idea what you're talking about. I run my diner. That's it. Period, full stop. I have nothing else going on the side. And second, even if I did, what have you got that I could possibly want?'

'Nothing. I'm not selling. I'm buying. Or more accurately, bartering, as no money is going to change hands. You're going to give me something. And I'm going to do something for you in return.'

'You're very sure of yourself.'

Reacher said nothing.

'All right,' Budnick said. 'I'll bite. What do you want?'

'A piece of information.'

'Such as?'

'Some electronic equipment was brought here. Now it's gone. The problem is, it belongs to us. And we want it back. So you're going to tell me who you sold it to.'

Budnick didn't reply.

'And in return I won't break your legs,' Reacher said.

'Screw you.' Budnick took a step back, pulled a phone out of his jacket pocket, and started poking at its screen.

Reacher took it from him and tossed it to Sands.

'You obviously weren't dialling 911 since we're talking about stolen goods,' Reacher said. 'Which means you were calling whoever you pay for protection. To do what? Send over three or four guys? Now, normally I'd be in favour of that. I've spent a lot of today sitting on my ass, waiting and talking. A little light exercise would be welcome. But unfortunately I'm short of time. Which means that either you tell me what I want to know, or I take my frustration out on you.'

'Oh yeah?' Budnick raised his chin. 'Come on then. Try it. See how it works out for you.'

A wrestler, Reacher thought. Or a lineman. Which meant he'd probably try some kind of grappling manoeuvre. Or he'd charge, hoping to knock Reacher down. He'd have to do something like that. There was very little chance of his landing a punch. Or a kick. Reacher was confident about that. Budnick was three inches shorter, to start with. And Reacher had abnormally long arms. The simplest thing would be to wait for Budnick to make his move then punch him in the face the moment he was in range. But not too hard. Reacher didn't want to knock him out. Not until he'd given up a name.

Budnick shuffled to the side, moving clockwise, closer to the outhouse. Trying to get a straight shot towards the parking lot. Meaning he was going to charge. Not grapple. He was a big guy. Hauling a body that size around would take a lot of energy. Reacher changed his plan. He had space to his left and right. He could dodge out of Budnick's way. Run the guy around. Wear him out. Let him defeat himself.

Budnick moved another six inches. Braced himself for launch. Then Sands stepped up. She drove the side of her foot hard into his knee and he went down sideways like a felled tree, squealing, then rolled on to his back and clutched his injured leg.

'What?' Sands turned to Reacher. 'Why should I let you boys have all the fun?'

Budnick scrabbled into a sitting position, his hurt leg still bent.

'That kick?' Sands stepped in front of him. 'Half power. The next kick? Full power. And forget your legs. I'm going right for your balls. And I never miss.'

Budnick whimpered and tried to scramble away backwards.

'Unless you give us the name,' Sands said. 'Who you sold the electronics to. Right now.'

'I can't,' Budnick said. 'I didn't sell it.'

'Go ahead,' Reacher said. 'Kick him.'

'No,' Budnick said. 'Please. You don't understand. I

282

don't sell the stuff. It's not my operation. I just rent out the space where it gets stored.'

'Who do you rent it to?' Reacher said.

'The guy I pay for protection.'

'OK. What's his name? Where do we find him?'

'No. Please. I can't. Look, the guy doesn't even pay me. He regards it as a favour. A courtesy.'

Reacher and Sands looked at each other.

'It's true.' Budnick held up his hands. 'I swear. Look, this is the hospitality business. I knew protection would be a thing. I even put it in the budget. Under a fake heading, obviously. I had cash set aside, ready to go. The guy showed up the night I reopened. Like clockwork. Told me how much I had to pay. It was a lot, but what could I do? I agreed. Then he told me about this other thing, with the electronics. A sideline of his. It had been going on for years, apparently. The guy I bought the place from must have forgotten to mention it. The asshole. Anyway, the protection guy said he was happy with the arrangement. He suggested I might like to keep it going. For the sake of my health. What was I going to say? I'm not stupid.'

'Maybe you are stupid,' Reacher said. 'Maybe you're not. But here's the thing. Who told you what, and when? What you get paid for, and what you give away? I don't care. I only want to hear two things from you. The name of this guy. And where we can find him.'

'I can't tell you. He'll kill me.'

'And if you don't tell me, my friend is going to kick a field goal with your testicles. I can't imagine that would feel good. So you're going to have to do all kinds of thinking. About your priorities. About current certainties versus future possibilities. And you're going to have to do it fast, because I'm running out of patience.'

Budnick was silent for a minute, then he struggled to his feet. 'You mentioned priorities. Well, what are yours? Getting your stuff back? Or getting the guy who's got it? Because the way I see it, for your stuff to end up here, it must have gotten thrown in the trash at some point. Maybe that was a mistake. Maybe someone did it to mess with you. But however it got there, it wasn't my guy's fault. So what if I could help you get your stuff back, but without involving him?'

Reacher took a moment to think. A protection racket suggested organized crime. Organized crime suggested prostitution. Drugs. Gambling. Loan sharking. All things he had no time for. All things, in an ideal world, he would tear down. But he wasn't living in an ideal world. And he wasn't dealing in the hypothetical. He had more tangible concerns. The identity of the spy who was trying to steal a copy of The Sentinel, for one thing. And Rutherford's safety, for another.

Priorities, indeed.

'All right,' Reacher said. 'Suppose I forget about your guy. Suppose I only care about getting my stuff back. How could that happen?'

'I know where he keeps it,' Budnick said. 'The good stuff. I'm assuming your stuff is good?'

Reacher nodded.

'One of his guys let it slip once. Where he was taking it. The guy didn't realize what he was saying. He was just running his mouth. And it was months ago. He wouldn't remember, anyway. So you could go there. Make it look like a random robbery. And no one could ever tie it back to me. Everyone could walk away happy. Except for the protection guy. But, hey, screw him.'

Reacher looked at Sands. She nodded.

'OK,' Reacher said. 'Where is the place?'

'It's called Norm's Self Storage. He has unit E4. You can Google the address. I can tell you the code for the gate. I know it because I started renting a unit for myself during the renovations. It's the unit number – mine is A6 – and the last seven digits of my cell.' He rattled off a string of numbers.

'Good,' Reacher said. 'But you know, before we go racing across town, maybe we should make absolutely certain our stuff isn't here? The door is padlocked and it was hard to get a good look through the crack. Can you open it for us?'

'You didn't check inside?'

'How could we?'

Budnick shrugged then took a Titans fob out of his pocket. It had a single key attached. He handed it to Reacher. 'Makes sense, I guess. Here. You open it.'

Reacher stepped into the space between the building and the minivan. He switched keys while his back was turned. Worked the new padlock. And pulled open the door.

'Why didn't we think of this before?' Reacher

pretended to hit himself in the forehead with his palm. 'It was inside all along. Budnick, come here. I need your help moving it.'

Budnick limped forward. 'Which thing is yours?'

'It's all the way at the back,' Reacher said. 'See that tall cabinet with the broken door? That's it.'

'No way.' Budnick shook his head. 'I remember dragging that thing in. It weighs a damn ton. Look, take it if you want. But you're on your own.'

'OK,' Reacher said. 'Your choice.' He braced one foot against the side of the minivan and slammed into Budnick's back, hard, right between the shoulder blades.

Budnick staggered through the doorway. His arms flapped like the wings of a giant flightless bird. He stumbled forward. Steered around one pile of equipment. Two. Then he stepped in the heap of computer mice. His feet got tangled in the wires and he pitched forward, landing next to the widescreen TVs.

Reacher tossed the Titans key ring in after him. 'Don't worry. Someone will come by and let you out. Unless you were lying about the storage unit. Or it's a trap. In which case it won't be the protection guy who's screwed. It'll be you.'

Sands gestured to Reacher to hold his position then darted around to the other side of the minivan. She returned a moment later with two bottles of water from the pack he had bought earlier. Set them down just over the threshold. Waited for him to close the door and work the lock. Then she took hold of his arm. 'You are going to come back and let Budnick out, right?'

'If we need to have another conversation,' Reacher said.

'And if you don't need to? If we get the servers? You can't just leave him locked in there.'

'I won't leave him. Not for long. I'll call Officer Rule. Tell her where to find him. Let her put another feather in her cap.'

'Isn't that a bit hard on Budnick? It's not his operation. He's not profiting from it. Just like Thomassino isn't, which is why we let him go. Shouldn't we stick the police on the protection guy instead? He's the one who made Budnick do it.'

'The protection guy will go down too, I'm sure. But all he did was make Budnick let him use the outhouse. It was Budnick who chose to threaten Thomassino's family. He took that step by himself. And that's a line he should not have crossed.'

TWENTY-ONE

The GPS directed them back to the same side of town as the waste company depot. It took another twenty-four minutes. And brought them to another compound at the end of another long straight road with another line of fenced-in lots on either side. Only Norm's Self Storage wasn't like the other units. It didn't have a regular fence. The whole exterior was designed to look like an old-time fort. It had wooden palisades. Watch towers. A line of cannons. A pole flying Old Glory. Another with the Volunteer State flag. And a third with some weird garish banner covered with images of muskets and sabres and shields. Maybe something of Norm's own design, Reacher thought. Maybe Norm was a history buff. Or maybe he thought the whole military vibe would give his place a sense of safety and security. Some kind of subliminal reassurance for his clients. Could be a valuable thing in his line of work.

Sands stopped in front of the gate. There was a rustic

wooden post next to the driveway, but no sign of an intercom or a keypad or a card reader. The only thing attached to it was a reproduction Pony Express mailbox. Sands glanced at the others then rolled down her window and prodded it. The front swung open. Inside was a digital screen. It was blank. Sands touched it and a grid of letters and numbers appeared. She took a deep breath and entered the code Budnick had given them.

Nothing happened.

'Am I cursed?' she said. 'Or do all entry systems just hate me?'

She tried the code again.

Nothing happened.

'Maybe they changed the system?' Rutherford said.

'Or Budnick bullshitted us,' Reacher said.

'Maybe he just misspoke,' Sands said. 'Let's check, before we go jumping to conclusions.' She reached for her purse, rummaged around inside for a moment, and pulled out Budnick's phone. 'He said the digits were the last seven of his cell number. Let's get that from the horse's mouth.'

Sands touched the screen four times and the phone came to life.

'Wait a minute,' Rutherford said. 'How did you do that? Do you have some kind of FBI master code? I thought that was a myth.'

'Of course the Bureau has a code. They can get into any phone, any time. Remotely, too. Via satellites. You didn't know?'

'Really?'

'Of course not. I was looking over Budnick's shoulder when he tried to call his protection guy. I saw what he keyed in. Now let's take a look. Here's his number. Damn. It matches what he told us.'

'I bet they changed the system,' Rutherford said.

'I bet Budnick was bullshitting,' Reacher said.

'Hold on,' Sands said. 'The phone number is only part of it. Maybe he got the unit number wrong. He was under a lot of stress.'

'How can we check that?' Rutherford said. 'We'll have to go back and ask him.'

'There's one other thing we could try,' Reacher said. He pointed to a 24-hour helpline number posted above the screen. 'Pass me Budnick's phone.'

Sands entered the digits, hit *call*, then *speaker*, then handed the phone to Reacher.

A man answered after seven rings. He said his name was Steve. He sounded sleepy.

'Steve, this is Bill Budnick,' Reacher said. 'Listen, this is a little embarrassing, but I'm at the gate of the storage place and I can't get it to open. I haven't been by for a while and I'm thinking maybe I'm mis-remembering my unit number. Could you confirm it for me?'

'Sorry, Mr Budnick. Can't do that. It's against the rules.'

'Oh, come on. Help me out here. I'm not much of a numbers guy. And I'm too busy down at Fat Freddie's to come by very often, which is why it's slipped my mind. I'm the owner there.'

'I know. Your picture was in the paper.'

'When I bought the place. Right. Anyway, I tell you what. How about this? You confirm my unit number, just this once, and I'll make a note. I'll write it down, right now, so this will never happen again. And then, any time you want, you can come down to the diner and have anything on the menu, on the house. What do you say?'

'I don't know. I shouldn't.'

'OK. Dinner for two. Bring your significant other. Or come twice on your own. You won't regret it.'

'I shouldn't.'

'We have the best milkshakes in town, Steve. The best everything, if you ask me. I might be biased, but that doesn't mean I'm wrong.'

'I don't know. Can you at least tell me which block you're in?'

Budnick had said A6. *Hope for the best.* 'Sure. Block A.'

'OK. Wait one.'

Reacher heard the sound of papers rustling, then Steve came back on the line. 'Anything I want on the menu, right? And I can come twice?'

'You got it.'

'You're in A4, Mr Budnick. Just don't let anyone know I told you.'

Sands turned back to her window. She hit the A and

291

the 4 on the screen, then the last seven digits of Budnick's phone number.

Nothing happened. For a long moment. Then the gate swung open.

Once inside the fake stockade they saw there was no further pretence of antiquity. Just six solid, utilitarian structures. The smallest was the office, tucked immediately inside the gate. Its neon sign was switched off, and there were no lights showing inside. The other five buildings were set further back, lined up side by side. They were finished with corrugated metal, painted battleship grey. Each was forty feet wide. A hundred feet long. The shorter sides faced the gate. Each one had a heavy-duty air-conditioning unit sitting next to it. And each had a red letter stencilled on the end wall high up in the angle of the roof. *A* was level with the office. *E* was all the way to the left. For a moment the order bothered Reacher. He would have preferred *A* to *E*. Not *E* to *A*. Then he figured they must have started out with one unit, at the right-hand side of the lot to correspond with the access to the road, then worked their way left as they expanded.

Reacher asked Sands to head for Budnick's unit first. He figured that the guy on the phone, Steve, might be monitoring the site from some remote position. It would be suspicious if they immediately turned the wrong way. And he wanted to get a sense of the security measures they were up against. He had been worried about guards being present. Roving patrols. Dogs.

People brought in by the protection guy to keep an eye on his interests.

It quickly became obvious that the site was unmanned. There were only two kinds of precaution in play. Locks. And cameras. The locks varied from unit to unit so Reacher figured it must be down to the individual clients to provide their own. The cameras were a different story. There were identical ones mounted at the corners of each block. Fifteen feet from the ground, where they couldn't be accidentally knocked. Or easily sabotaged. They were aimed along the front of the buildings, meaning that the door to every unit in the outer rows was covered by two separate cameras. And all the others by at least two. Possibly four, depending on their field of focus.

There were ten units on each side of each building. The odd numbers were on the right. The even numbers on the left. The protection guy's unit was E4. So it was on the left. In an outer row. Only covered by two cameras. Sands pulled away from Budnick's unit and drove to the near side of the E block. She turned and reversed, parallel to the wall, staying as close to the building as she could. She continued until the back of the minivan was just under the outer camera. Reacher cut an eight-inch length of duct tape from the roll. He scrambled on to the roof of the van. Took a step towards the rear. The paint was slippery. The van pitched and yawed on its suspension. Reacher braced himself with one hand against the wall. Crept further back. Stretched up. And covered the lens with the tape.

293

Sands looped around the perimeter of the site and they repeated the procedure with the camera at the far end of the E block. That meant they could have been recorded approaching Budnick's unit. And leaving it. And passing the odd-numbered A units. Not ideal. Not disastrous. But more importantly it meant that no one would be able to see them on the even side of the E block. And if no one could see them, no one could report them. To the police. Or to anyone else.

Sands made straight for the protection guy's unit. She reversed up to it and stayed in the van with the engine running. Reacher got out, carrying the bolt cutter. Rutherford joined him. They checked the number stencilled on both sides of the door frame, then Reacher closed the cutter's jaws around the stem of the lock. It was surprisingly slim. Reacher broke it open with barely any effort. He removed it. Took hold of the handle low down at the centre of the door. Pulled it up. And saw – furniture. A dining table. Eight matching dining chairs. A couch. Two armchairs. A sideboard. A drinks cabinet. A bureau. And a floor lamp. Nothing electronic. Nothing that had been made in the last fifty years. Maybe seventy-five. Reacher guessed that someone's relative had died. A parent or a grandparent. Leaving a house to be cleared. Everything else sold or given away or taken into service. The remnants too unfashionable to be used. But too valuable or too sentimental to be disposed of. So they were banished here. A practical solution for someone. But absolutely no help to them.

Sands read their body language and climbed out to join them.

'Budnick's an asshole,' Rutherford said. 'Reacher was right. He was lying.'

'Not necessarily,' Sands said. 'He got his own unit number wrong. Maybe he got this one wrong too. We should start trying the others.'

'Is there time?' Rutherford said. 'There are a hundred units. Someone might come and see what we're doing. And what about the cameras? We can't disable all of them. Even with two down we could have a problem. If someone's monitoring them. They're bound to investigate if they notice a whole row's gone dark.'

'We wouldn't have to check all the units,' Reacher said. 'Budnick's story might be bullshit. But if it's not and the protection guy does keep his contraband here, he will use one of the end rows. They're the only ones with units you can't see into from the opposite side. And it's more likely to be this one than the A block because it's further from the entrance. Fewer people to see his trucks coming and going.'

'So nine more to try,' Sands said. 'Nineteen, worst case.'

'Maybe only one more,' Reacher said. 'Budnick told us his unit was A6 and the protection guy's was E4. His was actually A4. So maybe he transposed the digits. Maybe the protection guy's is E6.'

Reacher moved one unit to the left. Its lock was also slender and unobtrusive but it must have been made with some kind of specially hardened steel. Reacher had to put some serious effort into breaking it. He wrestled with the cutter for maybe half a minute before the stem finally gave way. Then he flipped the body aside. Pulled it clear. Dropped it into his pocket with the other two defeated locks. Took hold of the door handle. And froze. A sound reached him. They were too far from the gate to have heard it open but there was no mistaking the purr of a large motor. The thrum of tyres on concrete. It was a vehicle. Coming their way.

Reacher nodded towards the minivan. Sands and Rutherford jumped inside. Reacher heaved the door to the furniture unit back into place and followed them. A pickup appeared from around the corner of the building. A Toyota. Some kind of metallic bronze colour. Very shiny. No light bar on the roof. No security company logo. No wannabe gangsters with guns. Just the driver. He looked to be in his fifties. And he was in no hurry. He trundled by, gave a friendly wave, and continued towards the far end of the block. Stopped at the last but one door. E18. Climbed out, unlocked the unit, took a box from his load bed, and carried it inside. He was back in his truck within a minute. He waved again. Then fired up the engine and continued around the far corner.

'Come on,' Sands said. 'I have a bad feeling about this. Let's get it over with before anyone else shows up.'

They climbed out together and Reacher hauled up the door to E6. Only it didn't open on to a space the size they'd seen before. This time four units had been knocked together. Two on the even side. Two on the odd side.

Rutherford hit a switch on the wall which caused a dozen fluorescent tubes to flicker into life. 'Holy mother of God.'

Shelves had been installed throughout in rows about two yards apart. They held pretty much every kind of electronic gadget Reacher had ever heard of. Domestic. Commercial. Industrial. Even some low-grade military. But whether the servers were part of the cache, he had no idea.

'I could live here for the rest of my life.' Rutherford stepped inside and made his way slowly along the first shelf, scanning each item and muttering quietly to himself. Then something caught his eye a little further ahead. He raced forward six feet, dropped to his knees, and threw his arms around a stack of black boxes on the lowest level. 'I don't believe it. They're here. We've found them.'

'Do they work?' Reacher said. 'Have they been wiped? Can we test them?'

'Not here,' Rutherford said. 'They're not like laptops. You can't just turn them on and see. You have to connect them to a network. Then you can use a computer to check what's on them. Think of them as giant external hard drives.'

'We'll show you how, later,' Sands said. 'Networking them's easy. Right now we need to get them in the van. Take them somewhere safe. Work on them there.'

Rutherford and Sands carried two servers each.

Reacher carried four. They loaded them into the narrow cargo area behind the rear bench seat. Sands took another minute to make sure they were secure. Then she made for the driver's seat.

'Hold on,' Reacher said. 'If you want to copy what's on a server, what do you need? Another server?'

Rutherford nodded. 'And a network and some software. But basically, yes.'

'Are there any other servers here? That would be the right kind?'

'Sure. There's a whole bunch.'

'You used eight servers altogether. But only one from the archive project?'

'Correct. The rest I scrounged from other places.'

'OK. Let's grab a couple we could copy on to. No. Let's make it four.'

'Why? What are we going to copy?'

'Maybe nothing. I'll explain once we're out of here.'

TWENTY-TWO

There were five words on Reacher's mind as they headed back to town.

Need to know. And *Forty hours.*

Five words rather than six. Because eight hours were gone. But the same two concepts remained. Along with a single question. Which begged a one-word answer. Had the servers been wiped? Yes, or no? Either way Reacher would have two things to do. If the data was intact he would have to persuade Rutherford to duplicate it, and get a copy to the FBI. If the data was gone, he would have to break the news to Agent Fisher and persuade Rutherford to leave town. He knew which was preferable. But he had no idea which would be easier.

Reacher looked at Sands and Rutherford in the front seats. They were different people from the ones who had entered the storage unit. Their fatigue was gone. And their worry. He could feel their excitement now. Their enthusiasm. Their certainty that with the servers successfully recovered, everything else was bound to

fall into place. Reacher himself was feeling less confident. He was the only one who knew what was at stake.
And he was the only one who had no experience with
computers. He had no idea how to extract their secrets.
Or how to find out if they even held any secrets. He
would rather be dealing with humans, any day of the
week.

Their first port of call was the apartment building so
that Rutherford and Sands could pick up some clothes
and toiletries and grab their laptops and all the cables
and connectors they would need to hook the servers
together. Next they collected Marty's car, which
Reacher drove. Then they headed north again, in
tandem, back to the truck stop. Not for fuel or supplies
this time. But because of its two motels. One in particular had caught Reacher's eye. He figured it was the
oldest part of the whole complex. The design was very
traditional. He had seen similar places all across the
country. It had a blue and red neon sign out front
depicting some kind of mythical bird. The building
was a single storey high. It was clad with strips of dark
wood. It started at its south-west corner with an office,
which had a covered entryway and machines outside
for soft drinks and ice. Then it continued around three
sides of a square with a regular pattern of window and
door, window and door. Thirty-six pairs altogether.
Each with a parking space outside. Leaving no distance to walk from your vehicle to your room. Making
it easy to carry your luggage inside. And reducing the
chances of anyone seeing what you had brought.

However unusual it might be. Or incongruous. Such as three mismatched suitcases and a dozen sleek black boxes.

The layout suited Reacher very well. As did the fact that of the thirty-six parking spaces only four were occupied. Three were taken by ancient sedans, their paint bleached and blistered by years of sun. The other by a bright yellow Toyota SUV with red mud sprayed right up to its roof. Two of the sedans were on the office side of the courtyard. The third sedan and the Toyota were on the opposite side. Leaving one section completely vacant.

Sands pulled up next to the vending machines, climbed out, and headed into the office. Reacher parked next to the minivan and went inside with her. The space was long and narrow. The reception counter was immediately to the right, followed by a tall freezer with double glass doors and a table with a microwave and a drip coffee machine. Three white plastic tables were lined up along the left-hand wall. Each had four white plastic chairs. And a vase with a red plastic flower.

Reacher rapped on the counter and after a moment a door opened and a guy came through. He looked about nineteen. His hair was shoulder length, he had round glasses, and he was wearing a baggy white T-shirt and a pair of faded, baggy jeans. He plonked himself down in the receptionist's chair and peered at Reacher.

'We need to talk about the price of your rooms,' Reacher said.

301

The guy pointed to a sign on the wall behind him: *Rooms $95+ / night.*

'Those are your standard rates, I guess,' Reacher said. 'I'm not interested in those.'

'No discounts,' the guy said. 'Ninety-five plus tax. Take it or leave it.'

'I'm not looking for a discount. I need something else. A special arrangement.'

'No special arrangements, either. Whatever they are.'

'Don't be hasty. You haven't heard what I have in mind. Do you want to miss out on a good thing?'

The guy paused. 'Go on.'

'Two rooms,' Reacher said. 'A week in advance. One at ninety-five a night, on a credit card, as normal. The other at one fifty a night, in cash, directly into your pocket.'

'Go on,' the guy said.

'Three conditions. First, the rooms must be together in the centre of the vacant block facing out across the courtyard, and they must have a connecting door.'

'Can do.'

'Second, we register for one of the rooms as normal. The other you enter in your system as not available for occupancy.'

'I don't know what that is. I don't think we have it here.'

'Sure you do. All hotels have it. Or some version of it. For when a customer dies and you have to wait for the coroner to sign off. Or someone gets busted for drugs and you have to wait for the police to clear the scene. Or even if the plumbing breaks down and you have to wait to get it fixed. Look in your employee handbook. It'll be there.'

'Handbook? What century are you from?' The guy woke his computer and called up a help screen. 'Oh. OK. We do have it. No problem. What else?'

'This arrangement is completely confidential. You don't mention it to anyone. Not your boss. Not your co-workers. Not the people who clean the rooms. Not your friends. Not your mom or dad. Not even your cat or dog.'

'I don't have a cat or a dog. But I get your point. Can do. And just to clarify, you said a week for both rooms? As in seven nights?'

'Seven nights. A thousand and fifty bucks, if that's what you're thinking about.'

'All right then. We have a deal.'

'Outstanding. My friend here will take care of the credit card and the forms. I'll take care of the cash. Half now. Half when we leave. Assuming you've kept your mouth shut.'

Reacher and Sands walked out of the office with the keys to rooms eighteen and nineteen. Eighteen was above board. Nineteen was off the books. Invisible to anyone who might come looking for them.

Reacher parked Marty's car outside room eighteen. Sands reversed the minivan close to the door to room nineteen. They carried the servers inside. Then the suitcases. Then the bolt cutter and the duct tape and the remains of the other supplies Reacher had bought. Four minutes' exposure. An acceptable risk. Then Reacher took the minivan and dumped it way on the far side of the site. Sands would be able to return it to the rental office at the airport once everything was resolved. But for the time being it was too hot to use. Thomassino had seen it. Budnick had seen it. The random customer at Norm's Self Storage had seen it. And it had most likely been recorded by half a dozen of Norm's security cameras.

Reacher picked up three pizzas and three Cokes at the first restaurant he passed and took them back to the motel. He let himself into room eighteen and switched on the light. It was the kind of place that was probably considered luxurious at one time. Now most people would call it adequate. Or economical. There was a pair of queen beds with flowery covers and a scattering of cushions. An armchair. A TV. A fridge. A desk. A bathroom. And a closet. The floors were fake wood. The walls were painted in pale, neutral tones. Finishes selected for durability rather than comfort, Reacher figured. Even the wattage of the lightbulb was designed to save on the electric bills rather than to provide a cosy atmosphere. But none of that bothered him. There was a bed. A place to wash. And access to coffee.

Reacher opened his half of the connecting door and knocked. Sands opened the other side and he stepped through to room nineteen. It was a mirror image of eighteen. Identical, except for the modifications Sands and Rutherford had made. They'd taken the duvet from one of the beds and taped it over the window to prevent any light from spilling out. They'd taped all around the door frame, for the same reason. They'd set up one of the eight original servers on every flat surface they could find. And they'd created a rat's nest of power cables and thick yellow wires to connect everything together. Except for Rutherford's laptop. It was on the edge of the stripped bed, tethered to the other equipment with a thick blue wire. Rutherford was sitting in front of it, cross-legged, concentrating so hard on the screen he didn't notice that Reacher had returned.

'How's it looking?' Reacher handed a pizza and a drink to Sands, and dropped another on the bed next to Rutherford.

'Good, I think,' Sands said. 'Rusty?'

'What's that?' Rutherford said. 'Oh. Thanks.'

'How is it looking?' Reacher said. 'With the servers. The data. Is it still there?'

'Oh. Yes. Seems to be. Cerberus is pretty messed up, though. Looks like the ransomware tried to rewrite parts of it. Might take a while to figure out what and how. And why. And how to build some protection into our final product. But I've got to say, this is better than I'd dared hope for. End of the day, Cerberus got bent, but it didn't get broken. And that's a result, in my book.'

'That's good,' Reacher said. 'But the records from the archive project. Are they still there? All of them?'

305

'The disk is full. Nothing seems corrupted. So I guess so.'

'Can you find out for sure?'

'I could, but—'

'Then do it now, please.'

'But I need to figure out how Cerberus—'

'Rusty, this is important. Check now. Please.'

Rutherford sighed then spent a couple of minutes tapping on his keyboard and prodding at his touchpad. 'OK. Look. I haven't opened every one of the thousands and thousands of scanned images – basically photographs of documents – but to the best of my belief, the archive records are all intact and undamaged.'

'In that case I need you to make a copy,' Reacher said. 'No. Two copies.'

'No way. Forget it. I already told you, I'm not letting anyone have a copy of anything. Not until Cerberus is perfected. My future depends on it. Sarah's too.'

'I understand. But here's the thing. When I got back to Mitch's apartment this morning, I told you the truth about what happened to me. But I didn't tell you the whole truth.'

TWENTY-THREE

'What do you guys know about a thing called The Sentinel?' Reacher said.

'Zip,' Rutherford said. 'Never heard of it.'

'I've heard a little about it,' Sands said. 'Mostly gossip. From some people at the Bureau. Word is, about four years ago there was a major brain drain out of cyber crimes. A bunch of the top guns all upped and left, out of the blue. At first people thought one of the big Silicon Valley corporations was on a recruitment rampage. Then there was a theory that some start-up was throwing crazy money around. But finally someone found out the government was behind it. An emergency response. To the Russians having a new weapon that could totally shred our election systems. Everywhere in the country was vulnerable. No results could be trusted. The guys at Quantico did some modelling. They figured the fallout from even one compromised general election could be anything from civil disobedience to full-scale rioting to possible insurrection. Imagine some of these foil-hat militia guys if they had evidence someone stole an election. Some of them have serious firepower and are already a hair's breadth from using it.'

'You're about on the money,' Reacher said. 'The Sentinel is the only thing that can stop this weapon. The Russians can't defeat it. So they're trying to steal it.'

'How?' Rutherford said.

'They have a spy inside Oak Ridge Laboratory. Where The Sentinel was designed.'

'Why don't they arrest him?'

'Because they only know a spy exists. They don't know who it is. The Bureau thinks it's a sleeper. With some kind of connection to this area. Which is where things start cutting close to the bone. A document surfaced in the town archive which could have revealed the spy's ID.'

'The archive burned down.'

'Not a coincidence.'

'The online archive had the same documents. It got locked by the ransomware attack.'

'Also not a coincidence.'

'And my server has some of those documents on it. Because Cerberus protected them.'

'Which is why you almost got kidnapped. The Russians want those records. To destroy whichever one could incriminate their guy.'

'How do you know all this, Reacher?' Sands said.

'You thought the rendezvous at the old factory was a set-up. It was. Only not in the way you expected. The

308

woman who showed up? She's an FBI agent. Undercover. She's infiltrated the Russian cell that's tasked with recovering the server. She has two jobs. To get a copy of it for the Bureau so they can ID the spy. And to protect Rusty. She lured me there to ask for our help.'

'And you're only telling us now?'

Reacher shrugged. 'There was no point telling you before we had the server. What if it had been destroyed? I'd have revealed the agent's existence for nothing. And the fewer people who know about her the better.'

'Fair, I guess,' Sands said.

'One other thing,' Reacher said. 'Full disclosure. Because I messed up their attempt to grab Rusty on Monday the Russians are bringing in a new guy. From Moscow. To try again. So the bottom line is this. If we want to avoid all the bad things that would follow a compromised election, and if we want to stop this new Russian going after Rusty, we have one option. Give a copy of the server to the Bureau.'

Rutherford jumped off the bed and picked up a pair of the extra servers they had brought from the protection guy's unit at Norm's. 'Sarah, what are you waiting for? Help me. We need two more power outlets over here.'

It took Rutherford ten minutes to get the extra servers fixed up the way he wanted them. Reacher used the time to call a number Agent Fisher had given him for Wallwork in case of emergencies or breakthroughs. He figured this qualified. Wallwork answered on the first ring and Reacher cut straight to the chase: the server had been found; the data was intact. Wallwork was all business in return. No thanks. No congratulations. Just a pair of rapid-fire questions: where are you, and how soon can we meet. Reacher told Wallwork to be in the vicinity of the truck stop in one hour, and that he would call back shortly with a precise location.

Reacher excused himself and hurried to the office. He rapped on the counter. The long-haired kid appeared. This time he looked surprised and worried. He no doubt had visions of the balance of his thousand in cash evaporating before it ever saw the inside of his pocket.

'Let's talk about your room rates again,' Reacher said. 'Your standard is ninety-five dollars a day. Which works out to about four bucks an hour. So if I wanted another room for two hours, no questions asked, no records kept, how much would that cost me?'

'Fifty bucks. Cash. Up front.'

'What's your name, son?'

'Carmichael.'

'Well, Carmichael, I believe in the illustrative power of stories. Do you?'

'I guess.'

'Take the man who killed the golden goose as an example. Have you heard that one?'

'Forty bucks. I can't go any lower. I'll have to split the dough with the housekeeper, remember.'

'That won't be necessary. I won't make any mess. I won't even sit on the bed.'

310

'What do you even want the room for, then?'

Reacher said nothing.

'Thirty bucks,' Carmichael offered.

Reacher said nothing.

'Twenty.'

'That's better.' Reacher took two tens out of his pocket. 'Pass me a key. And make sure it's in the same section as the other two. Near them. But not adjacent.'

Reacher stepped outside and called Wallwork back. He gave him the motel's name and address and specified room fourteen for their meeting. Then he returned to room eighteen. Sands was sitting in the armchair. Reacher smiled at her and lay down on one of the beds.

'Your pizza will be cold,' Sands said after a few moments of silence. 'Want me to go to the office? Heat it up for you?'

'No thanks,' Reacher said. 'Cold pizza doesn't bother me. Unless you want to heat yours?'

'Cold pizza doesn't bother me, either. And anyway, I ate while you were gone.'

Reacher took a bite. Sands smiled.

'Cold pizza,' she said. 'Cheap motel. It's like I'm back at the Bureau.'

'Do you miss it?'

'I don't miss the backache from all the crappy mattresses I had to sleep on when I was on the road. That's for sure. But hearing you talk about the agent you met. What she's doing. Protecting our elections.

311

Stopping the Russians' sabotage. Things like that, they make you think.'

'Did you work undercover much?'

'No. A few sting ops when they needed someone who could talk the talk. Other than that I was too specialized. Spent most of my time getting loaned out to different field offices. Wherever they had a cyber crime problem. Same shit, different desk. Staring at a screen.'

'Is that why you left?'

'No. It wasn't the work. I actually enjoyed that. But as the years rolled by I came to realize, as much as I liked it there, the FBI was never going to give me what I want in life.'

'Which is what? Your own corporation?'

She shook her head. 'No. That's just a means to an end. A way to generate more cash. Which is why Cerberus is so important. If it pays off big enough, I'll be one and done. See you. And goodbye.'

'What do you need the cash for?'

'I can't tell you. You'll laugh at me.'

'Try me.'

Sands closed her eyes and took a deep breath. 'I want to have enough in the bank that I can quit working. Sell my home. And most of my stuff. And buy a houseboat.' She opened her eyes. 'You think I'm crazy, right?'

'That depends,' Reacher said. 'This houseboat. Would you keep it moored in one place?'

'Of course not. That would defeat the whole purpose. I'd go where I want. When I want.'

312

'I'm the last person in the world who would think the freedom to move around is crazy. I'd say it was essential.'

Reacher was about to add that he was less enthusiastic about the idea of swapping a home on dry land for one floating in the water. He had never been personally involved with a boat, but it struck him that owning one could be even more problematic than a regular house. Aside from being able to move, it would have all the same disadvantages. There would be repairs to make. Maintenance schedules to follow. All kinds of expenses to meet. And on top of those it might sink. It might get run into by a bigger boat. It might grow barnacles. Who knew what other pitfalls there could be. But before he could speak again the connecting door opened and Rutherford appeared.

'All right,' Rutherford said. 'All done. Two copies, as requested.'

Rutherford had stacked the pair of cloned servers on the bed, next to his laptop. Reacher picked them up and carried them back to room eighteen. He put one in the closet. And took the other one outside. He held it flat against his chest with his right hand, kept his left arm slightly forward, and angled his body away from the courtyard. It wouldn't have fooled anyone up close, but no one behind him or at a distance would have realized he was carrying anything. He had plenty of time before Wallwork was due to arrive but he wanted to be already set up in room fourteen when the agent

313

got there. He wanted to give the impression he had driven to the motel specially from some undisclosed distant location. Not that he was staying four rooms away. He didn't have any reason to distrust Wallwork. But he had learned years ago that caution is the key to a long and healthy life.

Reacher set the server down on the desk and sat in the armchair. He had the drapes open and the light off. He waited, and he watched the courtyard. Ten minutes passed. No vehicles arrived. No vehicles left. No one moved between rooms. Another five minutes ticked away. Then the courtyard was filled with light. A car pulled in. It slowed in the centre of the space as if the driver was getting to grips with the layout. Then it speeded up and headed directly for room fourteen. It swung to the left when it was a couple of car lengths short, reversed, and stopped with its trunk three feet from the wall.

Reacher opened the door before Wallwork had the chance to knock. He stood aside to let the agent enter, then pulled the drapes and turned on the light.

'Is that it?' Wallwork stepped over to the desk and leaned down to look at the server.

Reacher nodded.

'Thank you, Major,' Wallwork said. 'You've done us a solid and we appreciate it. You have my number. If there's ever a way I can return the favour, don't hesitate. Also, apologies for yesterday. Hiding my identity. I didn't want to mislead you. But in the circumstances I didn't have a choice. I hope you understand.'

'No apology necessary,' Reacher said. 'Your partner is in the field. Protecting her comes first, second, and third. But your thanks should go to Rusty Rutherford. It's down to him that the records exist at all.'

'That's good to know.' Wallwork picked up the server and started to move. 'Please pass on our gratitude if you see him. Me, I need to get back on the road. Time's not on our side with this thing.'

Reacher stepped between Wallwork and the door. 'Two questions before you go.'

'OK. Make them quick.'

'Klostermann. The guy I met at the Spy House this morning. Agent Fisher said she'd have him checked out again. Is there any word on that?'

'She told me. We're on it. Nothing yet. What else?'

'The server. I guess you're going to take it to a field office. Probably Nashville. Where a bunch of pointy heads will descend on it, looking for whatever secret it holds.'

'You guess right.'

'How long will that take?'

'To get to Nashville?'

'To find the secret.'

'How long's a piece of string? It's impossible to say. There could be thousands of documents to search through. It'll be like looking for a needle in a haystack. Only not a needle. Looking for something, but not knowing what. Just hoping we recognize it when we see it.'

'So you're not likely to get it done in, say, thirty-seven hours or so?'

'I don't know. It could take two seconds. It could take two months. We won't know till we try. That's not your problem, Major. But it is why I have to get going.'

'It's not Major. It's just Reacher. And it is my problem. A little bit. But mostly it's Rutherford's problem.'

'How do you figure?'

'Agent Fisher told me her cell was restricted to surveillance until roughly lunchtime the day after tomorrow. Then they're expecting reinforcements. A big hitter from Moscow. Now, if you haven't figured out who their agent inside Oak Ridge is by then, you won't have been able to arrest him. The Russians won't know you have the server, either, so they'll think they still have a chance to get it themselves and protect their guy. So they'll come after Rutherford again. And Fisher might not be able to keep him safe because of the new arrival.'

Wallwork shrugged. 'All true, I guess. Tough break for Rutherford. Specially after he helped us. Any chance you could convince him to leave town?'

'I doubt it. I already tried. He refused. And I can't blame him. He's done nothing wrong. In fact, he's done everything right. He shouldn't be driven out of his home.'

'I agree. But we have limited options here. Could you stay awhile? Keep an eye on him?'

'For a while. Not for ever.'

'It won't take us for ever to figure out who the agent is.'

'You said it could take two months. I rarely stay in one place two days.'

'I'm sorry, Reacher. We're dealing with the unknown here. The unknowable, in fact. I'd like to help Rutherford. I really would. But I've got to think about the bigger picture. I don't know what else we can do.'

'I know what I can do.'

'What?'

'Klostermann offered me ten grand for the server. I'm going to accept.'

'Absolutely not. I can't authorize—'

'I'm not asking permission, Wallwork. I'm giving you a heads-up. As a courtesy. There's something off about Klostermann. I could feel it when I met him. The Russians have some kind of permanent presence here. I'm going to find out if it's him.'

'No.'

'This is happening. Embrace it. There's no danger. There's no downside. If I'm wrong, an old geezer gets to see some files that used to be public anyway. If I'm right the Russians will think their mission is accomplished. They'll think their agent inside Oak Ridge is safe, so they'll leave him in place, giving you time to figure out his identity. They'll pull Fisher's team out of the field, taking her out of the firing line. And Rutherford will be in the clear too.'

'It's out of the question.'

'Listen. You wouldn't know about the server without me. You wouldn't have a copy of the server without me. You'd still be chasing your tails wondering what you're looking for. So you can damn well cut me some slack.'

Wallwork didn't respond.

'If you have any sense you'll watch how this plays out. And if it works, take the credit. No one will hear any different from me.'

Wallwork was silent for another minute. Then he squeezed around Reacher, to the door. 'I have to get this thing to Nashville. People are waiting. And I have to tell you. Officially I cannot condone what you're proposing.'

'And unofficially?'

'Call me when it's done. But this stays between you and me.'

TWENTY-FOUR

Reacher woke himself the next morning at half past seven. He showered and dressed, and fetched coffee and cinnamon rolls from the office while Sands got herself ready. Rutherford was in room nineteen, still hunched over his laptop, too focused on his work for conversation, so Reacher left him his breakfast and went back through the connecting door. He took a bed. Sands took the armchair. He sprawled. She perched. They ate, and Reacher filled her in on his meeting with Wallwork.

'So this could all be over by tonight?' she said, when he finished. 'If you're right about Klostermann. If he's working for the Russians and gets the server back for them, they won't need to come after Rusty for it.'

'If I'm right about Klostermann,' Reacher said.

Sands frowned. 'I think you're missing something. If you're right about Klostermann, he must have killed the journalist. Or had her killed. What if he sees you and Rusty as loose ends, after getting the server? And decides to kill you both, too?'

'The journalist's situation was different. She wasn't a loose end. She knew something. From her work at the archive. She found out whatever it is that can identify the Russian agent. That's why she was killed. To keep her quiet. We, on the other hand, are just greedy fools as far as Klostermann is concerned. He thinks we bought the bullshit about researching his family history. He'll take the fact that we're happy to sell him the server as proof we don't realize what's on it. Meaning killing us would be unnecessary. And more than that. It would be dangerous. Because it would risk attracting unwanted attention. And if there's one thing the Russians don't take, it's unnecessary risks.'

'What about leaving Rusty with a copy of the server? So he could stumble across their secret at any moment, just like the journalist did? Wouldn't Klostermann call that an unnecessary risk?'

'He might. If he knew Rusty had a copy.'

'He won't suspect you're lying if you tell him otherwise?'

'I won't lie. I'll let him reach that conclusion on his own.'

'How?'

'Can you get his number for me?'

Sands picked up her phone and clicked and swiped for a few moments.

'Here it is,' she said. 'Want me to dial it for you?'

'No thanks,' Reacher said. He took out the phone Rutherford had bought him. 'Read it out to me.'

'Why not use mine? It's already up on the screen.'

'Then Klostermann would know your number. Phones can be tracked.'

'If he's not a danger to you or Rusty, how can he be a threat to me?'

'He probably isn't. But the Russians aren't the only ones who don't take unnecessary risks.'

Klostermann's icy housekeeper answered on the first ring. She claimed her boss was unavailable, but Reacher dangled a hint about a valuable item, recently recovered, and two minutes later Klostermann was on the line.

'This is excellent news,' Klostermann said. 'You worked fast. When did you find it?'

'About five minutes ago,' Reacher said. 'We started looking the moment we left your house. Followed the trail all night.'

'Where was it?'

'In a storage unit. Waiting to be sold.'

'Is it in one piece?'

'It seems to be. I'm no expert, but Mr Rutherford is and he's confident it's in full working order.'

'That's music to my ears. Where should I come to collect it?'

'I'll bring it to you.'

'Oh. OK. When? How soon can you be here?'

'How soon can you get our money?'

'It's already here. I have it in my safe.'

'Then I'd say tomorrow? Or possibly Saturday. Sunday at the latest.'

'What's wrong with today? This morning? Right now?'

'Can't do today. That's too soon. We still need to figure out how to make a copy. You need special equipment. Servers aren't like laptops, you know. You can't just turn them on. They're more like giant external hard drives. You need computers and networks and software. And now that Mr Rutherford is no longer working for the town he doesn't have access to the same facilities. He'll have to beg a favour from a friend. There's someone in Nashville who might be able to do it. If not we'll have to go to Knoxville.'

'Why do you need to make a copy?'

'Well, I guess we don't need to. More like want to. You said there are some of the town's records on there. They could be interesting. And if there are any problems getting the digital archive back online after the ransomware thing is resolved, Mr Rutherford was thinking he could donate it to the town. To show there are no hard feelings.'

'That's very generous of him. But here's the thing, Mr Reacher. As I told you yesterday, I'm not a patient man. I hate having to wait for anything. So how about this? Bring the server to me right away. Or let me come and collect it. I don't mind which. And if there is any problem with the digital archive further down the line,

I'll donate the thing to the town in Mr Rutherford's name. What do you say?'

'I don't know. Mr Rutherford was kind of looking forward to seeing what's on it. Finding out more about the history of the town. Now he has time on his hands.'

'Have you ever seen these kinds of records?'

'No, I can't say I have.'

'They're dull as ditchwater. Believe me. Unless you have a vested interest, as I do because of my father, they're deadly boring. Blow-by-blow accounts of arguments over how many chickens people should be allowed to keep in their yards. Whether people were permitted to sell wet fish from their houses. Things like that. So Mr Rutherford really wouldn't be missing out on anything if you brought it straight over. And I'd be very grateful.'

'How grateful?'

'Say, an extra thousand dollars?'

Reacher said nothing.

'An extra two thousand?' Klostermann said.

'Make it an extra five thousand,' Reacher said, 'and it'll be yours inside thirty minutes.'

Reacher pulled the second cloned server out of the closet, loaded it into the trunk of Marty's car, and set out on his own towards Klostermann's house. He felt the way he imagined a baseball player would in the bottom of the ninth. At bat, score tied, two outs, two strikes against. One chance left to win the game

323

without going to extra innings. At which point the other side would bring out a pinch hitter. A new guy, signed from another league. Not in the stadium in time to make the starting lineup. Unknown. Untested. But with a big reputation.

Reacher arrived at the mouth of the driveway. He hit the intercom button, announced himself, waited for the gate to roll aside, then drove through and parked in the spot he'd used the day before. He climbed the steps and crossed the porch. The housekeeper was waiting for him at the front door. She was wearing the same style of black dress. The same apron. Her hair was up in the same kind of bun. She greeted him in her quiet, cold voice and led the way down the corridor, gliding effortlessly past the portraits, across the tile, to the door at the end on the right. She knocked, opened it, and stood aside to let Reacher enter. Klostermann was already inside, in his armchair. He was wearing a black suit with a white shirt and a narrow black tie. His hair was under a little more control that day. He looked like he was ready for a funeral.

Klostermann put his newspaper down and got to his feet. 'Is that it?' He nodded towards the black box under Reacher's arm.

'As promised,' Reacher said.

'Excellent. Put it on the table.'

Reacher set the server down next to a bowl of small white flowers. He'd seen some like them before, but not in real life. In a book he'd read. In history class. Years ago.

Klostermann retrieved a package from the side of his chair. It was made of brown paper and its top was folded over like a carry-out bag from a restaurant. He handed it to Reacher. 'Your fee. It's all there. Including your bonus.'

Reacher looked inside. The bag held three bundles of banknotes. Each was about an inch thick. Made up of crisp new twenties. Two hundred and fifty in each one. Making each bundle worth five thousand dollars. And weighing about the same as a decent burger. Reacher took out the cash, put each bundle in a different pocket, and handed the bag back to Klostermann.

'Remember your promise,' Reacher said. 'Any problems with the digital archive getting back online, you donate the server to the town. In Rutherford's name.'

'You have my word,' Klostermann said. 'Now, if you'll excuse me, I have an important meeting to prepare for.' He took a small grey box from his pocket. It looked like a garage door opener. He pressed its button. Waited. And nothing happened.

Klostermann looked annoyed. He pressed the button again. He waited. Nothing happened.

'I apologize,' Klostermann said. 'Anya must be occupied in some way. Please. Allow me.'

Klostermann crossed to the door and led the way back along the corridor. As they approached the far end Reacher heard the housekeeper talking. He figured she was on the phone. Her voice was louder than before, and her tone was even colder.

'No,' she said. 'You cannot. You're an hour early. You

are to leave and come back at the correct time. I don't care. I'm not interested. That's not Mr Klostermann's problem. If you cannot follow simple instructions perhaps he doesn't need your services at all.'

Klostermann continued, apparently oblivious of the one-sided conversation, until he arrived at the front door. He opened it, waited for Reacher to step through, and closed it again without saying another word.

Reacher knew he had to be out of the house for the plan to move forward, but he still wanted to know what Klostermann was doing. Communicating, he hoped. Sending a message up his chain of command: *Server recovered. Verification in progress.* Followed by an order for the team in the field: *Mission Accomplished. Stand down.* And a final instruction to the specialist from Moscow: *Presence no longer required. Return to base.*

Reacher drove up to the gate and while he waited for it to open he pulled out his phone. He dialled Wallwork's number. Told him the server had been delivered and asked for an update on Klostermann. Wallwork had no new information. He promised to let Reacher know the moment he heard anything. Or, more importantly, received word from Fisher that her cell was being pulled out. Reacher drove on. The ball had been slow and over the plate, he thought. He had taken his swing. Made good contact. Now it was in the air and there was nothing to do but wait and see if it cleared the fence.

Or maybe there was one thing he could do. Klostermann had mentioned a meeting. He hadn't stated that it would be at the house, but that was the implication Reacher had taken. He had said *prepare for*. Not *go to*. And someone had showed up an hour early for something. Which might be completely unconnected. Or mean a bunch of Klostermann's contacts were about to arrive. Maybe to talk about flower arranging at the local church. Maybe to talk about something else. Not the server, though, Reacher figured. The person who had shown up early was dispensable. The housekeeper had made that clear. And the Russians would only allow members of their trusted inner circle to be involved with something so valuable. But whatever the subject, Reacher figured it would be worth an hour of his time to see if anyone showed up. And if so, who. Wallwork was struggling to come up with fresh intel on Klostermann. Maybe it was time for Reacher to gather his own.

There was nowhere Reacher could reasonably conceal himself and the car, so he pulled over to the side of the road and turned on his blinkers. He judged the location carefully. Humans have a subconscious tendency to infer associations based on physical proximity. You see a guy standing at a crosswalk, you assume he wants to cross the street. Reacher didn't want to be so close to Klostermann's house that it looked like he was waiting outside it. He wanted to appear unconnected, beyond the intangible boundary linking him to the place. But neither did he want to be too far away. It wouldn't help his cause if he was unable to get a clear look at Klostermann's guests.

If he had any.

Reacher felt under the dashboard to make sure he could locate the hood release lever. He called Sands to let her know what was happening. Then he leaned his head against the rest.

Nothing stirred for half an hour. Then a mail truck trundled past. A minute later a woman went by in a silver SUV. Neither driver paid Reacher any attention. Nothing else moved. Reacher sat tight until he figured he had five minutes until people would start arriving for Klostermann's meeting. If it was happening at all. Then he climbed out, lifted the hood, and pretended to examine the engine. His face and head were hidden. And he had a clear view of Klostermann's driveway along the passenger side of the car.

Nothing moved for seven minutes. Then a Mercedes rolled up. A sedan. It was long and black and shiny. Reacher made a note of the licence plate and watched it approach Klostermann's house. It stopped at the gate. An arm in a white shirt sleeve stretched out of the driver's window. Aiming for the intercom, Reacher thought. But the guy hit four keys, not one. He was entering a code. The gate slid aside and the car moved forward and headed for the parking area in front of the house. The next vehicle to arrive was a Dodge Ram. It was blood red, and even shinier. The driver used the intercom, waited for the gate, and drove inside. After that an F150 showed up. Then a white panel van with *Gerrard's Generators – Power 2 U* painted on the side in jagged letters. Both their drivers used the intercom, too. Finally a motorcycle rattled into sight. It was some kind of customized machine with flames painted on the fuel tank, tall wide handlebars, and pegs for the rider's feet set way out in front. The guy sitting on it had black boots. Black leather pants. A black leather vest with a picture of a giant spider stitched into the back. A pair of round, mirrored sunglasses. And a Stars and Stripes bandana in place of a helmet. He pulled up short of the gate and took a phone out of his vest pocket. This was the guy who had been early, Reacher thought. Now he was late. The guy hit a button then raised the phone to his ear. Held it there for thirty seconds. Then lowered it, jabbed a button, and jammed it back into his pocket. He pulled the bike into the tightest turn he could manage. Revved the engine a few times. Then released the clutch and screeched away. Smoke poured from his back wheel and the tyre left a long wide strip of rubber on the asphalt.

He was dispensable. The housekeeper had made that clear.

Reacher waited another five minutes to see if anyone else tried to get in, then dropped the hood into place and climbed back inside the car. He started the engine to get the air going and Wallwork called him before he could shift into Drive.

'News?' Reacher said.

'Some,' Wallwork said. 'But nothing from Fisher. This is about Klostermann. Some background on his family. On his father. Henry senior. Or Heinrich, as he was originally called. He did immigrate from Germany. That's confirmed. We have him getting processed through the Port of Entry in New York in 1946, then showing up in Tennessee. He got married in fifty, and little Henry was born the same year. Heinrich bought the Spy House in fifty-two, directly from the spies, and lived there until his death in 1960. Not very exciting, all told. Nothing that sounds like it could be worth ten grand.'

'He went to fifteen in the end.'

'What did you do? Threaten to break his legs?'

'Told him there was a supplement if he wanted the only copy.'

'Nice move, Reacher. If he really wanted it for family history research, why would he care if there were copies? Let alone pay through the nose to stop any getting made.'

'Right. It only makes sense if he thinks there's something secret hidden on it. Something he never wants to see the light of day.'

'Meaning he's working for the Russians. Please God.'

'Indeed,' Reacher said. 'But listen. After I left Klostermann's place a bunch of guys showed up there for a meeting. Could you run their licence plates? They could be connected.'

'I shouldn't,' Wallwork said. 'But I will. I'll call you back when I've got something.'

TWENTY-FIVE

Reacher was feeling pretty good when he hung up the phone and started back to the motel. He figured the server was where it needed to be. The Russian technicians would get to work on it and everything would fall into place from there. The beginning of the end was surely under way. But the further he drove, the more unsettled he became. He could feel a scratch at the back of his brain. It was nagging at him. Telling him something was wrong. Two things, in fact. The first he couldn't put his finger on. Yet. It had to do with something he'd seen at Klostermann's house. Wallwork had triggered a connection when they spoke. It was there, but not in focus yet. Like a photograph from an old Polaroid camera. Vague and indistinct at first, but definitely something. All Reacher could do was wait. The image would sharpen up. His brain just needed time to join all the dots.

The second thing was already clear. It reminded him of a French legend his mother used to tell. About an ancient soothsayer who could catch a person's words and scatter them on the surface of a magic lake. At first the words would all look the same. They would all float and bob around. Then the true ones would soak up the water and sink, leaving only the lies at the top for all to see. In this case the false words belonged to Klostermann. He'd spoken them the first time they'd met and they were still there, afloat in Reacher's memory. *My father fled to the States from Germany in the 1930s.* But Wallwork had checked the immigration records. Heinrich Klostermann arrived in the United States in 1946. After World War II. Not before. Not the kind of detail a person would forget. So either Henry Klostermann misspoke or misremembered. Or he had something entirely different to hide.

Reacher was almost at the truck stop when his phone rang. It was Wallwork again.

'News?' Reacher said.

'Nothing from Fisher,' Wallwork said. 'I'm calling back about those licence plates. That was an inter-esting group Klostermann met with. The guy in the S-Class is a neighbour. He owns a bunch of buildings in town, plus a heap of land outside it. One of the other guys is a lighting designer. One does sound systems. And the generator guy speaks for himself. If you ask me, Klostermann is putting together some kind of out-door concert. Maybe it's a new venture for him. Maybe it's a hobby. Or a one-off thing, to celebrate some kind of event or anniversary.'

'What about the guy on the bike?'

'He's an all-round disaster zone. His jacket's two inches thick. I can't imagine him doing anything useful. Directing traffic at the event, maybe? Or sticking up posters?'

Reacher was quiet for a moment. 'Have you got an address for him?'

'Sure. Why?'

'It looked like they kicked him to the kerb. He'll likely have the loosest lips of the bunch. I have nothing to do until we hear from Fisher. I was thinking I could have a conversation with the guy. See what comes out if we look at Klostermann from a different angle.'

'Could be useful, I guess. Obviously I shouldn't tell you. So you didn't hear it from me.'

Reacher thanked him then hung up, called Sands back, and told her what he was planning to do. She didn't respond right away.

'Everything OK?' he said.

'Yes,' Sands said. 'It's just Rusty.'

'What's he done?'

'Gone down with a migraine. I knew he would. This always happens when he works too hard. He won't take breaks. He won't eat. Won't drink. And then, bang. He's face down on the floor.'

'I'll be there in five minutes.'

'No. Go and lean on this guy. One thing I learned in the Bureau – never leave a lead unfollowed. Those are the ones that bite you in the ass.'

*

333

The address Wallwork gave Reacher for the guy on the bike was in the same subdivision as Holly's place. Reacher cut roughly southwest from the truck stop to avoid driving back through town and threaded his way through the rows of rectangular houses on their rectangular lots until he arrived outside the final one on the final street. The last one to be built, Reacher figured. Maybe a couple of years younger than the first. Which could be an advantage, if all the kinks in the design had been ironed out. Or a disadvantage if the contractor's enthusiasm had worn off by then and the pick of the crew had left for fresh projects. But whichever way the scale had leaned originally, the point was no longer relevant. It looked like the house had been beamed in from a scrapyard. Shingles were slipping off the roof. The windows were opaque with dirt. Paint was peeling off every flat surface. The yard seemed to be filled with spoil from a chemical plant. And in the centre, shiny and incongruous, sat a bike. Flames on the fuel tank. Tall wide handlebars. Foot pegs way out in front.

Like Holly's, the house had a front door with no window. Reacher was even less inclined to knock on this one so he drove past and stopped in the fishtail. Made his way down the far side where there were no neighbours to worry about. And found he wouldn't have to climb over the fence. He wouldn't be able to. Because it had already fallen down. Reacher stepped over the remains and surveyed the yard. If any attempt at horticulture had ever been made, the signs were long

334

gone. Nothing was growing. The soil was dull brown. It looked utterly desolate. Reacher wouldn't have been surprised to find scientists there in hazmat suits collecting samples. He cut across to the rear of the house. It also had a sliding glass door. This one had a diagonal crack running across it. Some kind of clear tape had been applied. It was yellow with age and the peeling edges were encrusted with ancient bugs. Reacher looked inside, into the kitchen. The cupboard doors were shabby. Several weren't lined up straight and a couple weren't closed. There were pots on the stove. The sink was stacked high with dirty plates and mugs and glasses. Cans and bottles were overflowing from the trash. There was a full ashtray on the small round table. But no sign of the biker. Or anyone else.

Reacher knocked on the glass. He heard a scraping sound above him. A window opening. He moved closer to the wall.

'Whoever you are, they're not here.' It was a woman's voice, raspy from cigarette smoke. 'Now get out of my yard.'

'I need to talk to Zach,' Reacher said.

'I told you, he's not here.'

'His bike's out front.'

'So talk to the bike. Zach's not here. None of them are. Come in and look if you don't believe me. If your shots are up to date.'

'So where are they?'

'At the workshop, obviously. Trying to fix up that dumb-ass car.'

'Got an address on the workshop?'

'If you don't know that, you don't know Zach. What do you want him for?'

'To talk about a job.'

The woman let out a little shriek. 'You really don't know Zach if you think he wants a job.'

'He wants this one. Trust me.'

The woman paused. 'Is there money involved? As in actual cash you can spend at the store?'

'There's plenty.'

'OK. Here's the deal. I'll tell you where Zach's at. You tell Zach half of what he earns comes to me. Or I'll kick his ass out. Again.'

Reacher followed the woman's directions. They took him due west on a straight road, wide in places, narrow in others, flanked by telephone poles, with fields on either side. Some had drainage ditches, some a hazy covering of green. None had any sign of purpose. Maybe they'd once been cultivated. Maybe they'd been earmarked for development into more houses. But whatever had been planned was long forgotten and they'd descended into a state of permanent disuse.

Reacher continued for nineteen miles, until he came to a crossroads. The woman had said twenty, but he figured that was close enough. Most people work in round numbers. He saw a single building on the far side of the intersection, on the right. The workshop. Positioned to be convenient for traffic approaching from the east or north. Maybe a random choice. Maybe the result of some in-depth study of traffic patterns and emerging demographics. Either way, not enough to guarantee a long-term future.

The structure was about as simple as you could get. There were columns at the corners and in the centre of each wall. Steel, presumably, encased in concrete. The sides and back were solid. The roof was flat. And the front had two vehicle-width doors, both rolled up. Originally they would have led to two bays. The right-hand one was still in commission. It had a lift, banks of tools, pneumatic lines, the whole nine yards. A car was raised up with its wheels at head height. A two-door coupé with a long hood, maybe from the late sixties or early seventies. It was bright orange. A guy was standing under it, fiddling with something. Four others were next to it, giving advice. To the side of them the other bay had been converted into some kind of clubhouse. There were three leather couches. None of them matched. A fridge. A table made out of three tyres stacked on their sides with a circle of glass on top. And there were posters on the walls. Some of cars. Some of women. Some of cars and women.

Outside, five trucks were lined up on the forecourt. They were all American brands. All were black with chrome wheels and knobbly tyres. And all had versions of orange flames painted down the sides. Reacher pulled up at the end of the row. He got out and looked at the guys in the vehicle bay. Their ages ranged from late twenties to early forties, he guessed. Two were wearing black leather pants and vests. Two, jeans and

T-shirts. One – the guy under the car – was wearing black coveralls. All were pale. All were blond. All were broad and stocky. Reacher could imagine them working out together. Maybe with some kind of improvised equipment. Maybe at one time in a prison yard. Maybe more than one time.

Another thing they had in common was that none of them was Zach.

'Problem with your car, friend?' The coveralls guy took a step forward. 'Can't help you here. Sorry. Private club. Not a commercial operation.'

'I'm here for Zach,' Reacher said.

The guy glanced at his buddies. 'Don't know any Zach. Sorry.'

A door opened at the back of the clubhouse area. Maybe from a storeroom. Maybe from a bathroom. Zach stepped out. He was still wearing his bandana and shades.

'You don't?' Reacher said. 'Here he is now. Want me to introduce you?'

'Funny guy,' Zach said. He made his way to the threshold. 'What do you want?'

'To talk.'

'About what?'

'Henry Klostermann.'

'Don't know any Henry Klostermann, do we, boys?'

The others shook their heads and grunted.

'Sure you do,' Reacher said. 'He has some business up for grabs. There was a misunderstanding. You wound up on the back foot, I get that. But Mr

338

Klostermann doesn't like quitters. You should give it another shot. And here's the good news. I can help you. If you help me first.'

'Bullshit,' Zach said.

'No. It's the truth. But I guess if you don't want to work with Mr Klostermann . . .'

'If you know Mr Klostermann you must be in the Brotherhood. So why haven't I seen you at any meetings?'

Reacher shrugged. 'I spend a lot of time on the road.'

'So you are in the Brotherhood? Prove it.'

'I don't need to prove anything. I'm Mr Klostermann's business associate. We just closed a deal today, as a matter of fact. At his house. I've been there more than once. That's where I saw you. I overheard what happened. Just confirm a couple of details for me, and I can get you back on the books in no time.'

'You can take your business deals and stick them in your ass. The Brotherhood. Are you a member? Yes or no? Because we all are. Show him, boys.'

As one, the guys with T-shirts lifted them. The guys with vests opened them. And the guy with the coveralls undid the tunic buttons. They all had the same tattoo. On the left side of their chests. A bald eagle. Holding arrows in both talons, not just one. And across the centre of the bird's body, in place of the Stars and Stripes, there was a round shield containing a black swastika on a red background.

The blurry image that had been in Reacher's head since talking to Wallwork snapped into focus. The white flowers in Klostermann's living room. They were edelweiss. Adolf Hitler's favourite. Which told him what Klostermann was hiding. His father had arrived from Germany in 1946. With at least one valuable painting to use as collateral to start a new life. He was a war criminal. A Nazi. And Henry was carrying on the family business.

'Well, that simplifies things,' Reacher said. 'I had thought there were two ways this could go. Now I see there's only one.'

'Lift your shirt,' Zach said. 'Show us yours.'

Reacher didn't move.

Zach closed his vest and turned to his buddies. 'He must be Antifa. Mr Klostermann said they'd be on our trail. That's why he needed our help.'

'Help with what?' Reacher said. 'Tying his shoe-laces? I guess if you all worked together you might be able to do it. If you had a couple of days. And a dark room to lie down in afterwards.'

The six guys stepped forward as one, drawn by the insult.

'Fellers, slow down,' Reacher said. 'You're failing to use the resources available to you. Look around. There are wrenches. Hammers. Tyre irons. All kinds of sharp heavy things.'

The guys looked at each other. They were confused. Why was their enemy helping them? Then frustration took over. Now that Reacher had suggested using the tools as weapons that was the last thing they could do. They would lose too much face.

Reacher looked at them. They were lined up, bubbling with aggression. Gripped by ideological fury. The pack versus the infidel. He was the infidel. And he'd found out what he needed to know. The core of it, anyway. He had a car. He could drive away. That would be the smart thing to do. But – Nazis. He thought of his mother. A child during World War II. In occupied France. Often hungry. Often cold. Sometimes in danger. This was no time to walk away.

The six guys were standing in a line about a foot apart, ten feet away from Reacher, advancing slowly. It was a straightforward problem. The goal was to reduce their numbers as quickly as possible. Reacher's usual tactic was to goad his opponents when he was outnumbered. Make them come at him fast. He would wait until they were five feet away then burst forward and smash through the centre of the line, elbowing the guy to his right as he went. The enemy force would instantly be depleted. And turned around. Literally. Reacher would be behind them. Out of sight. So they'd process the surprise, and turn. Only Reacher would already have turned. He would have launched himself back the other way. Elbow still up. Still swinging. Flattening the guy who had been on his left, but was now on his right. If Reacher timed it right, the guy would rush into the blow like a drunk heading the wrong direction on the highway. Timing came with expérience. Reacher had plenty of experience. But on this occasion, he also had a problem. Zach was in the spot to the right of centre. And he didn't want Zach to go down first. He wanted to save him for last.

Reacher waited and watched. The guy at the end to his left was creeping wide. Moving away on a diagonal. Aiming to sneak around him while he was occupied with the others. Which gave Reacher an idea. He pretended to look to his right, to encourage the flanking guy. Waited until the line was seven feet away. Six. Then he took a half step to his right. But he didn't follow through. He planted his foot and used it to propel himself left, aiming for the gap between the end two guys. He found it. Raised both elbows as he moved. Swung them forward. Caught one guy below the chin. The other full in the face. Both went down like planks. Reacher spun back clockwise, leading with his right elbow. The blow missed the next guy in line, but its momentum fuelled the roundhouse punch Reacher was aiming with his left. His fist connected with the side of the guy's head. Three down.

Half his opponents were out of the game. And the remainder were no longer facing him broadside, where their numbers could be brought to bear. They were lined up single file, as if asking to be knocked down one at a time. A single solid punch to the first guy's face might even account for all of them. More than likely two of them. Reacher was tempted to try it. But there was a problem. The next guy in line was Zach, so a different approach was called for. Reacher feinted a jab towards Zach's face, and when his guard was raised kicked him in the knee. Zach flopped down and

Reacher kicked him again, in the solar plexus, driving the air out of his body and leaving him curled up on the ground, gasping.

The last two guys pulled back and fanned out. Reacher could practically see the cogs spinning in their heads. What had just happened? What should they do now? Run? Fight? How? He used the momentary respite to stamp on Zach's hands, in case he had a hidden gun or blade, then stepped forward.

'I've got to tell you this, even though I'll hate myself for it,' he said. 'The fight is over, guys. You lost. You should walk away. Spare yourselves the pain.'

The guys glanced at each other. Neither spoke. Then they spread wider, forming a triangle with Reacher at the tip. Reacher was calculating the angles. Assessing the geometry. Concluding that the next shape would be a straight line. With him in the centre. So that the guys could rush him simultaneously. Present two targets. Two threats. Making it hard to defend. If he allowed it to happen it was likely he would at least get hit. And Reacher was opposed to getting hit. Not out of vanity. Not out of an aversion to pain. But because it reduced efficiency. His normal response was to let a pair of attackers close in. Gain pace. Then he would lunge to his left. One would be driven back in surprise. The other would be pulled forward, a hunter pursuing its prey. Then Reacher would reverse. And reverse again, catching each attacker by surprise. But this time there was a problem. The guys were moving too slowly. They were creeping cautiously forward.

Reacher's plan required pace. Momentum. So he changed it. He sprang to the side and grabbed the larger guy by his right arm. He continued to turn, dragging the guy with him, then pivoted into a full 360-degree spin. Reacher planted his feet and used his weight like a hammer thrower so that when he was three quarters of the way around the other guy's feet were off the ground. And when he was all the way around the guy's feet were waist high. They slammed into his buddy like a double roundhouse kick, sending him sprawling. Reacher set his guy down. Waited a moment to make sure he was steady on his feet. Then punched him full in the face. It was a massive, savage blow, landing like a sledgehammer, smashing all kinds of bones and cartilage and teeth. The other guy was trying to crawl away so Reacher went after him and kicked him in the head. Normally he would have used his left foot in a situation like that, where the guy was already down. His weaker foot. But this guy was a Nazi. So he used his right. And he didn't hold back.

Reacher crossed to where Zach was rolling and whimpering. He grabbed him by the hair, dragged him to the nearest truck, and propped him up against its wheel.

'Man, you broke my leg.' Zach's voice was an octave higher than before. 'You broke my hands.'

'That's possible,' Reacher said. 'A few of the smaller bones, anyway. But there are plenty left. So the question is, do you want me to break those too? Or are you ready to share a little information?'

'I'll tell you anything you want to know.'

'The event Klostermann is organizing. What is it?'

'Some kind of rally. Honestly, it's stupid. I'm glad I got disinvited. He doesn't even have a real venue. Just some half-assed idea to point a bunch of lights up in the air, like they would make pretend walls. It's dumb.'

'I don't know. A little Austrian guy used to do that. I heard it was quite effective.'

'Huh?'

'Don't worry about it. Where will this rally be?'

'Some field. A friend of his owns a bunch. I don't know which one.'

'When?'

'Not till next year. April twentieth. Ages away. But he was definite about the date. I don't know why.'

'You really are a moron, aren't you, Zach?'

'Huh?'

'How do you get tickets for the rally?'

'It's invitation only. Two people from each state, plus a bunch of locals.'

'How does Klostermann decide who to invite?'

'I don't know. But I heard each year it's going to get bigger. Two from each state the first time. Then four. Then eight. Like that.'

'OK. And what was your role going to be?'

'Security. I was going to pick a team. Be on duty at all times, in case Antifa found out and tried to shut us down.'

'I have some news for you, Zach. You're getting shut down anyway. You can count on it. Only not by Antifa.

345

I know some other people who will be happy to do it. People who work for Uncle Sam.'

Reacher left Zach for a moment and went to drag the unconscious bodies into a pile near the road. He picked up Zach and put him on top of the heap, writhing and screaming. He checked the trucks. The key was in each one so he moved them over to the building and parked them as close to the walls as possible. Then he went back to talk to Zach.

'Have you got a phone?'

'Yes.'

'Does it record video?'

'Yes. Why? What are you going to do?'

Reacher tore the T-shirt off the nearest guy's inert body.

'Go ahead,' he said. 'Start filming. Because you're officially resigning from your *Brotherhood*. Any time you think about rejoining, watch the movie. And remember. Next time it'll be your house. With you in it. Tell your friends when they wake up. The same goes for them. And everyone else you know.'

Reacher went back to the workshop. He poked the T-shirt into the orange car's fuel pipe. Pushed it further in with a screwdriver. Waited for some gas to be soaked up. Lit it. And walked away.

TWENTY-SIX

Reacher put a couple of fast miles between him and the blazing workshop, then pulled over and dialled Wallwork's number.

'Nothing from Fisher, right?' Reacher said when his call was picked up.

'Not yet,' Wallwork said.

'There won't be.'

'Don't give up hope, Reacher. It's only been a few hours. You know how cautious the Russians are.'

'Klostermann isn't a Russian. He's a Nazi.'

'There's something wrong with the line. It sounded like you said Klostermann's a Nazi.'

'I did. Talk about the ultimate bait and switch.'

'Run it for me.'

'I just talked to the biker. Seems Klostermann's father was a war criminal. That's why Klostermann wanted the server. There must be some kind of incriminating record on there. And the event he's organizing? With the guys he met this morning? Are you ready for

347

this? Because you're going to make some serious headlines when you stop it. He's re-enacting the Nuremberg Rallies. Complete with his own Cathedral of Light.'

'If you're joking, Reacher, stop now.'

'This is no joke.'

'Where does the biker fit in?'

'Klostermann sold him on providing security. *Just in case* Antifa shows up.'

'OK. So Klostermann's organizing a little off-piste violence.'

'That's my guess. You know how those guys love violence. Especially when it has an us versus them flavour to it. They need their demons.'

'Thanks, Reacher. I'll get some people on to it.'

'The biker and his asshole buddies had tattoos on their chests. Eagles with swastikas. They said they were part of a brotherhood. That might help track the rest of them down. But there's no immediate rush. The rally's not until April twentieth. Hitler's birthday.'

'They love their symbolism, too.'

'The Sentinel is much more urgent right now. Klostermann's not Russian, so the Russians don't have a copy of the server. They'll still come after Rutherford. And they could still panic and pull their agent out of Oak Ridge.'

'We have the server, at least.'

'Have the pointy heads got anywhere with it yet?'

'No.'

'Then we need a new Plan B. Their new guy from Moscow is due here in under twenty-four hours.'

'I know. Leave it with me. I'll think of something. And if inspiration strikes you, don't be shy.'

'I won't be. And in the meantime I'll get Rutherford to try to find whatever Klostermann could be embarrassed about in the town records.'

'That reminds me. We have a name for Klostermann's mother. Natalia Matusak. We're thin on detail. She may have been married once before. We're still checking. Not that it probably matters now.'

Sands was asleep when Reacher got back to the motel. She was lying on top of the duvet on the bed Reacher hadn't used. Reacher could see her eyes moving behind her lids. She was dreaming. About boats, he hoped. He crept outside and went to the office to fetch coffee and cinnamon rolls. Sands didn't wake up when he came back into the room. But she did a minute after he placed a cup and a plate on the nightstand.

They ate and drank and Reacher brought Sands up to speed on what he'd found out. She had a tough time processing it. With her ex-FBI hat on she was thrilled at the prospect of smashing a neo-Nazi network. Particularly one that was trying to recreate Hitler's Cathedral of Light in rural Tennessee. But she was also worried about the implications of losing The Sentinel to the Russians. And scared for Rutherford. And Fisher. She'd developed some kind of bond with the agent even though they'd never met. In the end she slid off the bed and made for the connecting door.

'Come on,' she said. 'We can't change anything by

349

sitting around. Let's get to work on the server. See if we can find old man Klostermann's smoking gun.'

Rutherford was still out for the count in room nineteen. He was curled up at the top of his bed, under the covers. His laptop was sitting at the other end, tethered to the other pieces of equipment. Sands sat cross-legged and fired it up. He didn't stir. There was no sign he knew she was there even when she started hammering on the keyboard. Reacher stood and looked over her shoulder. One by one a series of images appeared. Some were mildly interesting. Most held no appeal at all. None had any relevance to Klostermann's father. And none gave any clue about Russian spies, however laterally Reacher tried to think about what he saw.

'OK,' Sands said after a few minutes. 'I'm starting to get an idea of how they put this together. The scans were done in loose chronological order. There are a few outliers, ones that were misfiled or found later or whatever. And they kind of branch into rough categories. Property records. Meeting minutes. That kind of thing. They do seem to cover the right period. 1946 to 1952, correct? When the father arrived, to when he bought the Spy House.'

'That should do it,' Reacher said.

'I'll keep looking. There are hundreds of files, though. Don't feel like you have to stay. I'm weird. I like this kind of thing.'

Reacher stuck it out for another ten minutes then made his excuses and went back to room eighteen. He took a long shower. Then he put his shirt and pants under his mattress and got into bed. He listened to a few of his favourite songs in his head. Counted to three. And didn't drop right off to sleep. Something was bothering him. It was the damn flowers, he realized. The edelweiss. Something about his memory of them still wasn't right.

Reacher did finally get to sleep. He woke up again at half past two in the morning. Or more accurately, something woke him up. Like a switch being thrown. From sound asleep to completely conscious in an instant. An instinctive response. Something had triggered a warning. A sound. He heard it again. Something metallic. It was coming from the door. To the courtyard. Not the next room. Someone was picking the lock. Trying to get in. Reacher took one of the captured Berettas from under his pillow and moved it beneath the duvet. Then he lay completely still.

The door opened a quarter of the way. A slim figure darted inside. The door eased back into place. Only one person had come through. Small. Wearing black. With a tactical backpack.

'Reacher?' It was a woman's voice, and she was whispering. 'Reacher, are you in here? Please say you are or I'm going to be mighty embarrassed.'

'Fisher?' Reacher said.

'Thank God. Your crappy old phone is hard to track. Wallwork couldn't say for sure if you were here or next door.'

'I'm here.' Reacher sat up and switched on the bedside light. 'I'm supposed to be. It's my room. The question is, what are you doing here?'

'There's a problem. I have new orders. The guy from Moscow is in the country already. He's ramping things up. Going after the server even harder than before.'

'That's not much of a surprise.'

'No. But maybe this is. Going after the server means going after Rutherford. And since none of the Russians know where Rutherford is, the new guy wants to flush him out. By going after his mother.'

Reacher said nothing.

'You see the issue here,' Fisher said. 'We can't do anything to protect her. If we did the Russians would know there's a leak. And aside from what that would mean for me personally – as in a slow and agonizing death, which I'd rather avoid – they would pull their agent out of Oak Ridge. We would never find out if they got a copy of The Sentinel. It would be a disaster all around.'

'You have to do something,' Reacher said.

'That's why I'm here. I'm assuming you know where Rutherford is?'

'Let's say I do.'

'Good. Then I need you to do two things. First, get Rutherford to make another copy of the server. Second, bring him to the diner opposite his building. I need him there at six a.m., with the server in a car parked outside. Any questions?'

'You're resurrecting the original ambush idea?'

'I'm adapting it. I know what the objective is now. And where it will be. But I have to truncate the time-scale. I need it done and dusted, including Rutherford's apparent suicide, before noon. That's still the Moscow guy's ETA in town.'

'It won't work.'

'It has to. Time will be tight. And it's not without risk. Mainly for me. I have to go against orders. Try to pass it off as initiative, combined with the desire to redeem myself in the eyes of my superiors. The fact that I will get the server this time ought to be enough to save my bacon. It better be. All Rutherford has to do is play along. He'll be fine. And it's better than the alternative.'

'No. It's not possible. Rutherford's down with a migraine. He couldn't copy a shopping list, let alone a server. And he can't move.'

'That's not funny, Reacher. Tell me you're joking.'

'It's no joke.'

'Then we're screwed. The whole operation's shot to hell. There's no way to save it.'

'Don't panic. The fat lady's not singing yet. Let's say I have another way to get the copying done.'

'How?'

'Doesn't matter. There's no security risk. That's all you need to know.'

'How will I get my hands on it? And make that look convincing?'

'I'll give it to you. In place of Rutherford.'

'Reacher. You already stopped a kidnapping by me

and five other people. I couldn't grab you now with the three I have left. It wouldn't be believable.'

'You're right. You couldn't take it from me. But you could buy it.'

'How would you come to be selling it?'

'Here's the story. It all began with the journalist. Convince your people I was working with her. She told me about the server. Not what was on it, specifically. Just that it was valuable. I came to town to get it from Rutherford because I'm greedy. I saved him from getting kidnapped. Buddied up to him until he let slip where it was. I stole it, thinking I could sell it to the newspaper. Only they hit me with a load of bull about being public-spirited and giving it to them for free. So I put it on the market. Via the dark web. Which you were monitoring because you're so thorough. We set up a meet at the diner, because I insisted on a public place. At, say, 0800. Four hours before the new guy shows his face. You're the hero, and he's on the next plane back to Moscow.'

'I don't see it. Aside from foiling the last kidnap attempt you left two of my men unconscious in a dumpster and attacked the rest of us with improvised chemical weapons. No one's going to believe you're a journalist's assistant.'

'So sprinkle in some of the truth. Say I'm a former soldier, now working as an occasional bodyguard. Say the journalist hired me to look after her in Nashville. Where she was investigating those mob guys. The ones Klostermann warned her to stay away from.'

'That could work. I guess. I might need to embellish it a little more. But it's the best we've got so let's try to make it happen. You get to work on the copying. Wallwork will call you at 0600 with a go / no go.'

'Sounds good. See you at the diner. I hope.'

'I hope so too. Oh, and Reacher? One other thing. Before 0600 – charge your damn phone.'

Fisher let herself out, then Reacher switched off the light and lay back down. He was annoyed with himself. He had just broken the soldier's most basic rule. Never volunteer. He should have known better. But on the other hand, what choice did he have? It was either go himself, or leave Rutherford's mother in the firing line. He didn't know anything about her. Maybe she could handle herself. Maybe she was a former Marine, ready to teach this Moscow guy what happened to anyone who messed with her son. It was possible. But he didn't know. So the safest thing was to take care of business himself.

Reacher turned the light back on, slid out of bed, and let himself into room nineteen to search for the bag with the phone charger in it. He tried to be quiet but Sands woke up anyway. He talked her through the developments and she agreed to take care of copying the server. She made a start right away. Reacher figured that since he and Sands were both awake he might as well make his way to the diner as soon as the server was ready. Then he changed his mind. Getting there ahead of time would be pointless. He had to go through with the exchange, come what may. Even if the Russians had replaced the entire wait staff with paratroopers and locked all the customers in the basement, he still had to make sure they got the server. Otherwise their attention would turn back to Rutherford's mother. The path he'd already ruled out. And there was another reason for playing it dumb. Fisher knew who he was. But the rest of her cell didn't. They needed to see a not-very-bright part-time bodyguard chasing an easy payday. Any hint that he was something different and the whole house of cards could collapse. So he went back to bed. Plugged in the phone. Took three deep breaths. And fell back to sleep.

Reacher opened his eyes thirty seconds before his phone rang. It was Wallwork, checking in as agreed.

'We're good to go,' he said. 'Fisher sold them on it. Should be a piece of cake. Better than the ambush, in the end. Less complicated. No need for the fake suicide.'

'OK. Let's keep radio silence from here on in, except for emergencies. I'll call you when it's done.'

Reacher hung up and swung his legs over the side of the bed just as Sands came through the connecting door.

'How's Rusty?' Reacher said.

'No change,' she said. 'He's totally out of it. But the good news is the copying went without a hitch. The clone is on the bed, next to Rusty's laptop.'

'Thanks, Sarah. I appreciate it.'

'Don't thank me. Just be careful. Come back in one piece.'

Reacher paid a quick visit to the truck stop's main building after he left the motel. He wanted something to carry the server in for the last part of his journey, when he would be on foot. The best he could find was a giant tote bag. It was made of coarse, brightly striped nylon with fluorescent yellow handles. The luggage equivalent of hiding in plain sight, Reacher thought. He picked up a cup of the extra-strong truckers' coffee on his way out, continued to town, and parked four blocks behind Rutherford's building.

Reacher timed his walk so that he arrived at the diner at 0802. He spotted one of the Russians on the street, acting like he was looking in a store window on the far side of the alley. Reacher pretended not to notice him and went inside. Four of the booths were occupied. Agent Fisher was in Reacher's favourite. The one midway along the right-hand wall, beneath the turquoise Chevrolet. Then there was the other female Russian agent, evidently recovered from her exposure to the chlorine, alone, reading a magazine. A man in a suit, tucking into a mound of scrambled eggs and bacon. And a group of three women. They looked very similar, with maybe twenty-five years between each one. Three generations of the same family, Reacher thought. Maybe in town for a reunion. Or a wedding.

Reacher waited for Fisher to beckon to him then took the seat opposite her in the booth.

'Reacher?' she said.

Reacher nodded. 'Dragon Tattoo 99?'

'My screen name,' Fisher said. 'Is that it?' She pointed at Reacher's bag.

'As promised,' Reacher said. 'All I need from you is the money.'

'No problem. The money's in my car. Out back. Come with me.' Fisher started to pull a ten-dollar bill from her purse. She paused when it was a quarter of the way out, making sure to keep her body between it and the Russian woman in the next booth. Three words were printed in the margin, in pencil. *AMBUSH. PLAY ALONG.* She pulled the bill the rest of the way out and went to leave it on the table, but ended up dropping it in her water glass instead. 'Damn it! I'm so clumsy today. Give me one second.' She grabbed a wad of napkins from the dispenser by the wall, fished out the bill, and dabbed at it until it was almost dry. And completely free of handwriting.

Fisher led the way to the door that opened on to the alley. She pulled the handle then stood aside to let Reacher go through. A vehicle was waiting, three yards away. A black Lincoln Town Car. The old, square model. A retired limousine, Reacher thought. Or a stolen one. A guy climbed out of the passenger seat. The specialist from Moscow, no doubt. Arrived early. A huge slab of a man crammed into a black suit and tie. Like an unfinished waxwork. He must have been six five. Easily three hundred pounds. His head was square, with sharp angles that were emphasized by his complete lack of hair. His ears were small, and they jutted out from his skull like they'd been stuck on as an afterthought. He had no eyebrows. Bright blue eyes. A nose that had been broken a couple of times. A mouth that gaped open in a cruel smile, revealing several uneven brown teeth. Huge arms that hung straight down from his massive shoulders. And thighs that were wider than some people's waists.

The primitive part of Reacher's brain took in all the subliminal cues. It assimilated them in an instant. And flashed a warning in return. Amber. Not red. The guy would present a challenge, it said. Significant, but not insurmountable. Normally Reacher would be reassured by that kind of assessment. But he wasn't that day. Due to a twenty-first century reality that his ancient cortex was not wired to appreciate. This wasn't a fight to the death. It was a ploy. And it would only work if Reacher didn't blow his cover. Which meant he couldn't kill anyone. Or even seriously hurt them. Which turned the situation into a very big problem indeed. Particularly if he was to avoid getting killed himself.

The Russian Reacher had knocked out appeared in the mouth of the alley, to his left. The guy he'd thrown through the Toyota's window appeared to his right. Fisher was behind him. He felt another presence join her. The other Russian woman. And straight ahead the Moscow guy took a step closer. Reacher was surrounded. The Moscow guy took a key fob out of his pocket and clicked a button on its remote. The

Lincoln's trunk lid slowly rose until it was vertical. The inside of the trunk was shiny. Someone had taped black trash bags over every surface. The guy put the key fob away and took a pistol out of his jacket pocket. A SOCOM Mark 23. Developed from the Heckler & Koch USP for the US Special Operations Command. Presumably sourced locally, rather than brought from Russia. A status symbol, in its way. Then the guy took out a suppressor and screwed it on to the end of the barrel. Unnecessary showboating, Reacher thought. He should have had his weapon ready ahead of time. Then Reacher realized the show wasn't for his benefit. It was for the agents'. The new guy was making his mark. He was saying *The problem you couldn't solve? It's easy to fix. It's done like this.*

It would have been a good demonstration if it wasn't for the one mistake the guy made. He hadn't forced Reacher to put down the bag. With the server in it. Their big prize. That gave Reacher options. He could fling the bag high in the air and simply walk away while they scrambled to catch it and protect its contents. He could hold it in front of his chest as a shield. Or threaten to smash it if they didn't back off and let him go. He could have done any of those things on a normal day. But not that day. Because his need to get the server safely into their hands was at least as great as their own.

The guys in the alley moved closer. The women pressed in tighter behind. The Moscow guy gestured with his gun for Reacher to step forward. Reacher was running out of options. His brain was running through scenarios like slides in a magic lantern. He could see ways to escape. He could see ways to give them the server. But not a way to do both. And he was almost out of time.

A second set of fingers closed around the bag's shiny handles. Much smaller than Reacher's. Fisher stepped past him and ripped the bag out of his grip. She handed it to the Moscow guy. Took his gun. And pointed it at Reacher's chest.

'Into the trunk, numb nuts,' she said. 'Or die right here in the alley.'

Reacher didn't move. His mind was racing. Had she played him all along? Or was she saving his life? Then the primitive part of his brain kicked back in. Assessed the cues. And flashed its verdict. Green. No threat. Reacher stepped forward. And stopped. There was another twenty-first century factor that his ancient cortex could not take into account. The trunk itself. The Lincoln was not a small car. Its trunk was a reasonable size. But Reacher wasn't. And he hated enclosed spaces. He always had. Some primeval aversion to being trapped. There was nothing he could do about it.

So he moved to his right. Along the side of the car. To the passenger door. Opened it. And slid inside.

TWENTY-SEVEN

Reacher had spent plenty of time in places he didn't want to be. Mostly during his army service. Places that were too hot. Or too cold. Where everything that moved wanted to bite him. Or where everyone he met wanted to kill him. But in those days he didn't have a choice about where he went. He was following orders. And at least he was getting paid.

Reacher didn't want to be in the Lincoln. He wasn't getting paid. And he did have a choice. The Moscow guy had secured Reacher's wrists with plasticuffs before firing up the engine but that was no kind of an obstacle. It would be the easiest thing in the world for Reacher to wait until the car slowed at the mouth of the alley. Open the door. Step out. And walk away. It would be more satisfying to elbow the Moscow guy in the side of the head and then get out. But given the role he was supposed to be playing – a not-very-bright part-time bodyguard – a more prudent option would be to leap out and add a little drama to his performance. Act panicked. Zigzag down the sidewalk and dive into the nearest store, or dash headlong into the traffic. Reacher knew he could make it look convincing. He wasn't worried about that. He settled back in his seat. The car started to move. A few more seconds. A few more yards, and the game would be won.

Reacher wasn't worried. Not until Fisher leaned forward and jammed the tip of the SOCOM's suppressor into the base of his skull.

'I know what you're thinking,' she said.

Fisher's hand seemed to twitch slightly. Not enough to pull the gun away from Reacher's skin. Nothing that the other woman would notice from the other side of the back seat. Nothing that would catch the Moscow guy's attention. But enough for Reacher to feel the variation in pressure. Three short jabs.

A slight twitch.

Or an *S* in Morse code.

'You're wondering if you could escape,' she said.

Her hand twitched again. One long push. A *T*.

'Well, you can't,' she said.

A jab, and a push. An *A*.

'That would be a mistake,' she said.

A push, a jab, and two more pushes. A *Y*.

'You could get hurt,' she said.

Four jabs. An *H*.

'And there's no need, anyway,' she said.

One jab. An *E*.

'We just need to check that the server's the real deal,' she said.

363

A jab, a push, and two more jabs. An *L*.

'That won't take long. Then we'll give you your money,' she said.

A jab, two pushes, and another jab. A *P*.

'And then, and this is the truth, you can go,' she said.

Reacher put the letters together. *STAY HELP*. 'Me?' Reacher said. 'I'm not going anywhere. Not without my money.'

The Moscow guy drove west for eight miles, not too fast, not too slow, and twelve minutes later he pulled up outside the room furthest from the office at a motel that Reacher thought must be a similar vintage to his own. It had a similar mythical bird on its sign, lit up with neon. Similar wood cladding. The same selection of vending machines. A familiar rhythm of window and door, window and door. Only this place was built in a straight line, not around a courtyard. It had half the number of rooms. And when the Moscow guy led him into number eighteen, Reacher saw there was already someone inside. A woman, in her late thirties. She was wearing a pale, knee-length skirt. A peach-coloured polo shirt, with a logo. Her hair was cut in a neat bob. Her face was plain but earnest. She was sitting at a large wooden table with a laptop computer. A thick blue wire led to a three-foot-high equipment cabinet with reinforced edges and heavy-duty castors, parked next to her chair. She was the Russians' version of Rusty Rutherford, Reacher figured. There to assess the server. And she was already in place. Reacher appreciated the efficiency.

Beyond the woman at the table with her computer Reacher could see that the space was much larger than his motel room. It was more like a suite. There were doors leading to a pair of bedrooms. A small kitchen. And a sitting area with a couch and a TV. The Moscow guy pushed Reacher a couple of yards further forward. The other woman on the crew followed them in and continued into one of the bedrooms. Fisher came in last. She put the stripy bag containing the server on the table and pulled out another chair. Then she took Reacher by the arm and guided him to it.

'Sit,' she said. 'And be careful. Don't break it.'

Reacher lowered himself down and Fisher took a length of paracord from the thigh pocket at the side of her pants. It was blue with red flecks. And narrow. Its diameter wasn't much greater than a decent bootlace. But Reacher knew the size was deceptive. It would be strong enough to take a regular person's weight, in an emergency. He would have no chance of snapping it. Fisher used it to tie Reacher's right ankle to the leg of the chair. She bound it tight. There was no slack. No room to wriggle free. No way it could come undone. Fisher pulled out another piece of cord and tied Reacher's left ankle. Then she grabbed hold of the little finger on his right hand. Pulled it to the side, as far as it would go. Took a folding knife out of her pocket. And extended its blade.

'I'm going to cut this tie,' she said, sliding the knife blade between Reacher's wrists and the plasticuff. 'Do anything stupid and I'll break your finger.'

'I've already done something stupid,' Reacher said. 'I've come here with you.'

Fisher freed his wrists and tied them one by one low down to the chair's back legs. When she was done she moved aside. The Moscow guy took her place. He checked the knots. Each one in turn. Carefully. And when he was satisfied he turned to the woman at the table. The server was lined up next to her laptop, and another pair of cables snaked down from the back of it and into the portable cabinet.

'How does it look?' he said.

The woman nodded. 'Genuine. No doubt about that.'

'Good. Call me the second you find the document. Or when you're certain it's not there.' Then he turned to Fisher. 'And you – watch Mr Reacher. Carefully. He and I will need to have a conversation. Whatever the outcome.'

Fisher waited for the door to close behind the Moscow guy then sat down next to the woman at the table. Reacher could see the laptop screen between their heads. It was like when Sands had searched the original server at their motel. A succession of images, presumably documents and records of various kinds. Reacher could see official-looking scrolls and seals on some but others looked more like handwritten letters and notes. Most of the words were impossible to make out. They were too small. Too spidery and intricate. And he was too far away. Though he doubted they would be any more interesting if they were legible. To him, anyway. The Russians clearly had a different reason for reading them. They didn't just want to confirm that the server was genuine. They wanted to know if the incriminating detail was there. If it wasn't they were free and clear. There would be nothing that could help the FBI expose the spy. And they'd have no further use for Reacher. If it was there, though, that would be a different story. There would be a chance for Fisher to save The Sentinel. And then the question of copies would come into play. As in, had Reacher kept any. Which was presumably the reason the Moscow guy had changed the plan. Why he had wanted to bring Reacher to the motel. That, and his desire to stamp his authority on the team. Neither of which amounted to an attractive proposition, from Reacher's point of view.

Fisher kept up a constant stream of conversation. She talked about TV shows. Movies. Celebrity gossip. She was trying to bond with the computer woman, Reacher guessed. To appear friendly. Non-threatening. Not the kind of person who needed to be kept in the dark. Not the kind who would steal a vital secret. The woman paid her no attention. She was too focused on her screen and her mouse. She had fallen into a steady rhythm. She clicked an entry on a list. An image opened. She studied it for about a second, then she closed it. She clicked on the next entry. Studied the image for a second. Closed it. Clicked. Studied. Closed. On and on. Over and over. The whole thing made Reacher simultaneously tense and bored.

The other woman appeared in her bedroom doorway. She fetched a bottle of water from the fridge, crossed to the table, watched the images flicker across the screen for a couple of minutes, then went back to her room. The computer woman kept going like a robot. Click. Study. Close. Click. Study. Close. She went on for another ten minutes. More than five hundred documents. Fisher was still chatting away. Then the woman's pattern changed. She held one image open for three seconds. Then she checked five more, reverting to a one-second interval for each.

'Time for a bathroom break.' The computer woman closed the laptop, stood up, and headed for the second bedroom. 'Back in a minute.'

Fisher rested her head on the table and looked for all the world like she was about to fall asleep. But the moment the bedroom door closed she sat back up, fully alert. She opened the laptop. A picture appeared on the screen. A church, all bright colours and twisty onion-shaped domes. It was clearly Russian. Reacher recognized it. The Church of the Saviour on the Spilled Blood. In St Petersburg. Reacher had visited the city on a trip after the Soviet Union fell. He remembered it because it was the first major church to be designed from the outset for use with electric light.

A box popped up in the centre of the screen. There was a line of Cyrillic characters in a bar at the top. Reacher assumed it was asking for a password. Fisher typed something. Reacher couldn't tell what because each keystroke was represented by an asterisk. But whatever she entered, it worked. The church gave way to the list of files. Fisher used the mouse to select the entry five places above the one that was highlighted. An image appeared. Fisher pulled a small folding cell phone out of her pocket. She opened it and took two photographs of the screen. She closed the phone. Closed the image. Opened the entry that had been highlighted. Closed it. Closed the computer. Then stepped across to Reacher. She pushed the phone into his pocket, followed it with a car key, and leaned in close to his ear.

'Found it,' she whispered. 'There was a third brother. You have to get the picture to Wallwork. Wait till the tech comes back. Break free. Should be easy; I removed most of the screws. You'll have to knock us both out. Me first, so she sees. Sonya too, if she comes out. The car's parked out front. Chevy Malibu. White.'

Fisher gripped Reacher quickly on the shoulder and rushed back to the table. She rested her head on the surface. The technician came back from the bedroom. Sat down. Opened the laptop. Entered her password. And resumed her routine. Open. Study. Close. Open. Study. Close. Reacher gave it two minutes. More than a hundred extra documents. Then he leaned forward, lifting the chair legs and pivoting on the balls of his feet. He slammed back down. The chair disintegrated. Reacher wound up on the floor surrounded by fragments of wood. Some were smashed and shattered. Others were virtually intact. The upright sections of the legs were still attached to his wrists and ankles by the paracord. He ignored them and started for the door.

Fisher blocked his path. The SOCOM was in her hand. The suppressor was still attached. 'Stop. Hands behind your head. Right now.'

Reacher glanced at the technician. She was still sitting, frozen, no sign of a weapon. He looked at the bedroom door. It was still closed. That simplified the geometry. He kicked the gun out of Fisher's hand then moved half a step to his right so that his body was in a straight line between the two women. That way the technician could see him pull his arm back. Wind up for a punch. Launch his fist towards Fisher. But she couldn't see what kind of connection he made. All she saw was Fisher crash down to the side, hit the floor, and lie there totally inert.

Reacher checked the bedroom door. It was still closed. He looked at the technician. Her training had finally kicked in. She was scrambling for her purse. Trying to pull out her Glock. Reacher stepped across and hit her on the side of the head, left-handed. Not too hard. Enough to put her lights out. But not to cause lasting amnesia.

Reacher retrieved the SOCOM from the floor. He looked at the bedroom door. The handle was turning. It was beginning to open. The muzzle of a Glock appeared in the gap. Held in two hands. Moving slowly forward. The woman was clearly cautious. Which was fortunate. It kept her out of danger when Reacher fired two quick rounds into the door frame. She ducked back inside the room and slammed the door. Reacher made for the exit. The shots hadn't made an excessive noise, thanks to the suppressor. Like someone whacking a table with a rolled-up magazine. But it was possible the sound had carried to the next room. Maybe occupied by other members of the Russian crew. Maybe by civilians. Either way, Reacher figured that the charade had gone on long enough. He went outside. Identified the car. Climbed in. Started the engine. Nudged the lever into Drive. And pushed the gas pedal all the way to the floor.

Reacher drove fast for half a mile then pulled over to the side of the road. He slid the SOCOM under his seat and took out the phone Fisher had given him. He needed to call up the pictures she had taken and then send them to Wallwork. He hit the *menu* button. Then closed the phone.

Something was bothering him. Something about the situation was not right. He put the phone back in his pocket. Pulled back on to the road. And continued, as fast as he dared, to the truck-stop motel where he'd left Sands and Rutherford.

The same time Reacher was approaching the truck stop, Speranski's secure phone was starting to ring.

'The bait has been taken,' the voice at the end of the line said.

Speranski smiled to himself. 'How soon will they bring her?'

'I said the bait's been taken. Not swallowed. She

gave the phone to the drifter. He left with it. But he hasn't sent the message.'

'Why not?'

'I don't know. Maybe he's holding out for more money. Maybe he doesn't know how to work the phone. Maybe he got cold feet. We'll find out. And we're monitoring around the clock. The moment he sends it, you'll know.'

Reacher parked the Chevy outside room eighteen and hurried inside. Sands was there. She was standing at the end of the second bed. Eyes wide. Feet shoulder-width apart. Arms straight. Holding her Colt in both hands. A classic shooter's stance. The isosceles. Named for the triangle shape made by the back and the arms. A good stance for accuracy. Which could have been a problem for Reacher, given that Sands was aiming directly at his chest.

'Reacher!' Sands lowered the gun and hurried towards him. 'Where have you been? I was worried sick. I kept calling and you didn't pick up.'

'Long story,' Reacher said. 'Major developments. I'll explain everything, but right now I need your help.' He pulled Fisher's phone out of his pocket. 'There's a picture on here. Of a document. From the server I gave the Russians. Fisher thinks it's the one with the spy's ID. She wants me to send it to Wallwork.'

'That's easy. Give me the phone. I'll do it now.'

'No. I think there's something wrong. I think Fisher is being set up.'

'Why?'

'A few reasons. Starting with the flowers. Klostermann's edelweiss. They weren't there when Rusty and I went to his house. Then they were the next day. When he was meeting with the Nazis. Seems a little coincidental.'

'Not necessarily. Could be lots of reasons for not having flowers every day.'

'There's also the money. Why pay fifteen thousand dollars for the server when Klostermann could just wait a week for the ransom to be paid and the digital archive to open up again? That's what a normal person would do. And why pay Toni Garza to go looking for the server the moment the ransomware attack happened? It's like he knows the archive won't be unlocked.'

'It won't be unlocked, according to Agent Fisher.'

'That's my point. How could Klostermann know that? Only the Russians know, because they're behind the attack.'

'But Klostermann is part of the Nazi group. You met them. Saw their tattoos. They're organizing a rally. That's all for real.'

'The group's for real. The rally's for real. That doesn't mean Klostermann is. Those Nazis believe he's one of them. But that doesn't prove anything. They weren't the sharpest knives in the drawer. Klostermann could easily be a Russian. Discord and division. The core of their strategy. Boost rival groups and set them against each other. Breed violence and hate.'

'But if Klostermann is a Russian, why was Fisher's team not pulled out when he got the server?'

'Here's the favourable explanation. They didn't believe me when I said it was the original. They were waiting to see if any other copies came to light. So they could mop them all up.'

'That makes sense. And what's the unfavourable version?'

'Long story short, I wound up at the Russians' motel after I was at the diner. They had a computer expert there, ready to go. She homed in on this file right away. Even though the FBI guys haven't found it in what? Almost forty-eight hours.'

'She knew what she was looking for. The FBI guys didn't.'

'Maybe. But this expert, she practically signalled to Fisher that she found it. Then she left the room, making it mighty easy to get a copy. And as for my escape, I just strolled out of there. So here's what I'm worried about. They left her team in the field specifically so that Fisher would see the document.'

'They planted it? Why?'

'To misdirect the FBI. To protect their agent by setting up a second, disposable asset to take the fall.'

'You know what that means. They know Fisher's a mole. They're playing her. Reacher, the Bureau has to pull her out.'

'If I'm right, yes. But we need to be sure. Can we see if the document Fisher found is on our server? If it

374

isn't, we know it's a fake. And if it is, we can compare the two.'

'Theoretically. But there are thousands of documents. It could take weeks to find it. We need something to narrow it down.'

'Like what?'

'A filename would be great.'

'Where would we get that?'

'It would be in a bar at the top of the image, probably. Like a title. Here – give me the phone.' Sands looked at the screen then shook her head. 'The image is too small. And the phone's too basic to have email. I'll text the image to my phone, then send it to the computer.'

Sands hit some keys on Fisher's phone, then some more keys on her own phone, then led the way through the connecting door to room nineteen. They found Rutherford standing next to his bed. He looked pale. His hair was a disaster. But he was upright, and that had to count as progress.

'What's happening?' he said.

Reacher brought Rutherford up to speed while Sands woke the laptop and retrieved the email she'd sent herself. The screen filled with the image of a form displayed on another computer screen. The picture was a little fuzzy but it looked like the paper had originally been a very pale green. With some kind of large watermark at the centre. A Greek key border in black around the edge. The official headings and boxes and instructions were also printed in black. So was a stamp saying *DRAFT*. Then back in 1949 someone had completed the necessary sections by hand, in flowing cursive, with royal blue ink. They had stated the address, which was familiar. And the names of the three owners. Artur Klich and Kamil Klich, the spy brothers. And Krystian Klich, who must have been the third brother. Whose identity had been kept secret. Who Fisher thought was the link to the spy at Oak Ridge.

'There, look,' Sands said. She pointed to a strip of white text at the centre of a blue band at the top of the image. Scan00001968.jpg. 'That's what we need.' She typed on the keypad and clicked on the trackpad and entered the filename into a box that appeared. She hit the *enter* key, and a second later the screen filled with a clearer version of the same form.

'Wait,' Sands said. She pointed at the section of the form that listed the property owners. It looked like the same handwriting. It was the same colour ink. It also gave three names. Artur Klich. Kamil Klich. And Natalia Matusak. 'It isn't the same. And who's Natalia Matusak?'

'Natalia Matusak is Henry Klostermann's mother,' Reacher said. 'Heinrich Klostermann was her second husband. A dime gets a dollar her original name was Klich. The third agent wasn't another brother. It was her. Artur and Kamil's sister.'

'This document was a draft,' Sands said. 'They destroyed it to keep Natalia's existence a secret. Or thought they had. But this is the original version. The one Fisher saw had been altered.'

'How could they do that?' Rutherford said. 'The server was never out of your sight. Except when it was in the trunk.'

'They must have gotten a copy of the document from the server we sold Klostermann. That would give them plenty of time to doctor it. Their expert loaded it while Fisher was tying me up. Then she made sure Fisher saw it, knowing she would pass it to the FBI. Who would miss the connection to Klostermann. And jump to the wrong conclusion about the identity of the spy at Oak Ridge.'

'How would that help them? If the third brother is made up, there can't be a trail leading to anyone.'

'There absolutely can. The Russians will have planned for this. There'll be a perfect trail. Complex enough to seem real. Not so convoluted that the average agent couldn't follow it. It'll lead to a patsy. Someone sitting in Knoxville right now. Probably with a copy of The Sentinel hidden in their shoe. Waiting to run. And to get caught. And to confess.'

'Why would anyone do that?'

'They could think they're making a noble sacrifice for a worthwhile cause. Or to get a big payday for their family back home. Or to stay out of the gulag. Who knows?'

'But if the evidence is fake, how can the Bureau figure out the right identity?' Rutherford said. 'They're back at square one.'

'They're not,' Reacher said. 'They can start with Klostermann. He mentioned having a son. He might have grandkids by now. The angle was never followed up because no one knew his mother was a spy.'

'That makes sense,' Sands said. 'The Bureau wanted the server because the Russians knew it could reveal the spy's identity. The link in that document is to Klostermann. So Klostermann must be linked to the spy.'

'Not using the Klostermann name, obviously,' Reacher said. 'Or someone would have noticed. Maybe Matusak, since that's the name they were trying to hide.'

'OK,' Rutherford said. 'I see that. But take a step back. The journalist found the document in the archives. The document showed there was an extra branch to the spy brothers' family tree. The Russians didn't want anyone to know about that because it would lead to Klostermann. And his son. And maybe grandchildren. So they destroy the physical archive. Lock up the digital one. And get hold of the server. The wild card. Why not leave it at that? All their tracks were covered. Why set up Agent Fisher with this red-herring ID?'

'The FBI knew the Russians had a spy at Oak Ridge,' Reacher said. 'If the Russians had destroyed the records and left it at that, the FBI would have kept on digging. Maybe found some other clue. If the Russians' plan had worked the FBI would have thought they'd caught the spy. And stopped digging. There's no need to search for something you already have.'

*

378

Speranski was pacing around his living room when his secure phone rang again.

'The bait has been swallowed,' the voice at the end of the line said. 'The message has been sent. But not to the Bureau itself. To a former agent who is now a cyber security expert. The Americans must believe it's genuine.'

'So, Natasha?'

'She's outlived her usefulness. The Center says you may do with her as you please.'

Reacher left Sands and Rutherford looking through other random records on the server and went next door to call Wallwork. He told him Fisher's cover was blown. And about the two possible leads to Oak Ridge. One likely fake. One likely real. Wallwork wasn't too worried about the difference.

'We'll find them both,' he said. 'Even if one's only a decoy. And we'll nail them both. Then pull Fisher out. Make sure she's safe.'

'No, Wallwork,' Reacher said. 'You've got to pull her out right now.'

'We can't do that. If Fisher disappears right after seeing the records on the server, the Russians will be suspicious. They'll pull their agent out of Oak Ridge. We'll never know if The Sentinel is compromised. What we have to do is coordinate her exfiltration exactly with the arrests.'

'You're wrong. You're still looking at the mission from your original position – that Fisher's identity was unknown to the Russians. But they do know about her. They're using her as a conduit for misinformation. So they're not going to let her live until their patsy is arrested. Right now Fisher believes what she sent is genuine. She was focused on finding it for months, so when it was dangled in front of her she bit. It was a reflex. But when the heat of the moment has passed? And all the coincidences line up in her head? They won't run that risk. They'll kill her as soon as they're confident you've received her information. In other words, now. So you've got to act. Immediately.'

Wallwork didn't reply right away. Reacher could hear him fiddling with a pen. He pictured the guy. The pieces falling into place in his head. Him not liking the picture that was produced.

'OK,' Wallwork said after another minute. 'You're probably right. We have a small window. But we're lucky, in a way. How things worked out, with her giving you the phone.'

'How's that lucky?' Reacher said.

'I think you're right that they'll kill her as soon as they know her information has been sent. But how will they know it's been sent? By monitoring her phone.'

'Fisher wouldn't use a Russian-issue phone.'

'Of course not. She procured a clean one, specially for the purpose. They'll have cloned it. That's what I would do, in their shoes. It's easy, and it will tell them the moment a message is sent. Or a call is made. But we don't have that problem. You didn't send me the picture, and you called me from your own phone.'

'But a message was sent from her phone. Just now.'

'Why? Who to?'

'We needed a filename to trace the original document. To compare. The picture was too small to read on the phone. We needed to see it on the computer.'

There was another pause. Reacher heard Wallwork fiddling with his pen again. Then there was the sound of breaking glass.

'Well, congratulations, Reacher,' Wallwork said. 'You just killed Margaret Fisher.'

Sands drove Reacher to the Russians' motel. Wallwork had warned him not to go. He promised to send in the cavalry himself. But then he mentioned procedures. Levels of classification. Clearance protocols. Reacher knew what words like those added up to. Delays. So he figured it was an outside chance, but if Fisher was still there, and still alive, maybe he could do something more direct. Something that didn't involve warrants. Or sign-offs. Or permissions of any kind.

All the cars had gone from the end section of the building. When they swung by they could see the drapes in room eighteen were open. No one was visible. So Sands stopped the Chevy right by the office door and went inside with Reacher. They went straight to the counter. A guy was sitting behind it, maybe thirty years old, with a plain baseball cap and a grey shirt with red piping and the name *Chuck* embroidered in an oval on his chest.

Sands pulled out her worn black wallet. 'Federal

agents,' she said. 'We're looking for the people who are renting room eighteen. Are they here?'

'They were,' Chuck said. 'The same group had fifteen, sixteen and seventeen as well. The four rooms all the way at the end. Anyway, they're gone now. They checked out a few minutes ago.'

'Did they say where they were going?'

'No, ma'am. And one of them didn't seem well. One of the women. I think she was sick. Or drunk.'

Fisher, Reacher thought. Drugged so that she would be easier to manipulate.

'OK,' Sands said. 'Never mind. We'll need to see inside the rooms.'

'No problem.' Chuck took four keys from a pegboard on the wall and set them on the counter. 'Just bring these back when you're done.'

They started in eighteen, as that had been Fisher's room. Then they moved on to the others. The rooms were pristine. Reacher had checked into places that weren't as clean. Even the bullet holes he'd made in the bedroom door frame had been spackled over. There was no trash. Nothing of any kind had been left behind. Not by accident. Not hidden by Fisher. Reacher looked under the mattresses and between the folded towels and inside the toilet rolls and in the cupboards and drawers and wardrobes. He tried everywhere he'd ever heard of anything being found in all his years in the military police. He even ran hot water in the basins in the bathrooms in case Fisher had left a message on any of the mirrors. He didn't find as much as a hair.

'Nada,' Sands said as they finished up in fifteen. 'What now?'

'Call Wallwork back,' Reacher said. 'See if he has anything to add.'

They ducked into the office to drop the room keys on the way to the car, and Chuck beckoned them closer.

'I was thinking, ma'am,' he said. 'I don't know where those people went. But I know what they went to do. Would that help you at all?'

'It might,' Sands said. 'What?'

'They went golfing.'

Sands crossed her arms. 'Golfing? Are you sure?'

'Pretty sure. I heard two of them talking. They were speaking Russian. I know a little because my grandparents were from St Petersburg. Anyway, one of the people used the word бункерный. It means *bunker*. Where do you get bunkers? Golf courses. There are a few around here. The second guy said something about it having been there for ever, so it must be an old one.'

'Golf?' Reacher said, when they were back in the car. 'What an idiot.'

'He was wrong about the golf,' Sands said. 'That's for sure. But I think he just told us where the Russians took Fisher.'

'He did? Where?'

'When you were on the phone with Wallwork, Rusty and I pulled up some of the old records. We found a few for the lot next to the Spy House. The Klich brothers bought it about the same time they bought the land for the house. They filed a bunch of construction permits. Some more than once. And there were file notes about neighbours complaining about noise. From excavators and cement trucks. Rusty thought that was weird, because the Spy House is pretty much on its own. He said there was nothing built next to it. Not above ground, anyway. So I'm thinking, what kind of thing do you need excavators and lots of cement to make?'

'A bunker,' Reacher said.

'Right,' Sands said. 'Only a Cold War bunker. Not one that's full of sand and golf balls.'

'Fisher thought the spy brothers did nothing while they were in Tennessee,' Reacher said. 'She was wrong. They supervised the building work.'

'And when they left their sister took over,' Sands said. 'Klostermann's mom. They took her off the records so no one would make the connection. She married Heinrich Klostermann and the house went in his name. Like money laundering, almost. Only with real estate.'

'Then their son Henry took over when they died.'

'Which is why he still lives there. You can't sell a house with a Cold War bunker in the back yard without raising a few eyebrows. Not that the bunker can be much use these days.'

'Until now. Come on. We need to head over there and recce the place.'

'We can make a start from here.' Sands picked up her phone and prodded and pinched at the screen until a satellite image of the Spy House's yard was displayed. She zoomed in as close as she could but there still wasn't much to see. Just an expanse of flat, scorched grass on the far side of a row of trees. The kind of field you might keep a donkey in if you didn't like it very much. There was only one other feature. A set of concrete steps. They were at the end of a dirt driveway, and appeared to descend directly into the raw earth. 'There's not much to it. I thought there'd be hatchways and ventilation pipes and water tanks. Things we could use to get in.'

Reacher shook his head. 'It was built for people to shelter in after a nuclear war. Everything will be self-contained. The water, the air, it will all be treated and recirculated. By machines. Deep underground. There could be some kind of umbilical connection to the house, I guess. For power. Maybe water. To keep things ticking over during peacetime. Or for maintenance. But probably no other contact with the outside world at all.'

'We should let Wallwork know. He'll need explosives. Digging equipment. Tunnelling machines.'

'He will. If the place is locked down. I'll call him from the car. But then I want to see this bunker for myself. There's one thing that's on our side.'

'What?'

'They don't know we're coming.'

TWENTY-EIGHT

S ands stopped the car in front of Klostermann's
gate. She looked at Reacher, crossed her fingers,
then stretched out and hit the intercom button.

There was no reply.

Hope for the best.

She tried again.

Nothing happened.

The gate was made of iron. It was eight feet high.
And it was the kind that slides to the side so there are
no hinges. No join in the centre. No weak spots at all.
So there was no chance of breaking it down. Or forcing
it open. If no one operated it for them, the only way
through was to enter the correct access code.

A four-digit code has ten thousand permutations.
They needed to narrow the odds, so Reacher climbed
out and scooped up some dirt from the base of the wall.
He ground it into fine powder between his finger and
thumb. Blew it very gently across the keypad. Blew
again to remove the excess. And saw that a tiny trace of

386

dust had stuck to three of the keys. The zero, the two, and the four.

Now there were eighty-one permutations.

In Reacher's experience people often used dates as code numbers. They're easy to remember. And they often have some kind of sentimental significance. In which case the first digit would have to be zero. The second would have to be two or four. And the final pair could not both be zero. Now he was down to ten possibilities. Or possibly only one. Reacher remembered the black Mercedes. The neighbour, whose land was earmarked for the rally. Who believed that Klostermann was a fellow Nazi. Reacher entered 0420. Hitler's birthday.

The gate started to move.

Reacher jumped back into the car and Sands drove through. She headed away from the house. Into the scrubby field. To the top of the steps they'd seen on the satellite image. Two cars were already parked there. A black Lincoln Town Car. The one the Moscow guy had been driving. And another Chevy Malibu. This one was red. Sands stopped right next to it.

Reacher got out and headed down the steps. There were twenty-six. Made of concrete. Pale and flaky and pitted from age and the weather. A vertical drop of maybe twenty feet. Leading to a metal door. Painted grey. It was dull. Featureless. Solid. Reacher pushed it with both hands. It didn't move. He leaned his shoulder against it, braced his feet on the bottom step, and shoved again. Harder. The door didn't give even a fraction of an inch.

Reacher climbed back up and got into the car. Sands drove across and parked in front of the house. They crossed the porch, approached the door, and Reacher knocked. There was no response. He figured there was no point looking for a hidden key so he landed a solid kick right below the handle. The door swung open, scattering pieces of frame across the tiled floor. Reacher crunched over them and turned to his right, alongside the staircase. Sands followed. There was a door at the far end. It led to a flight of stairs, heading down. They descended and came out into a basement. Reacher found the light switch. There were wooden shelves along the left-hand wall, stacked high with suitcases and cleaning supplies and all kinds of cardboard boxes and plastic tubs. There was a furnace on the right along with a bunch of other air handling equipment, all feeding into rectangular metal ducts that disappeared into the ceiling. And a little further along, set into the wall, was a pair of grey metal breaker boxes.

Reacher ducked down to avoid the joists and made his way across to them. He opened the first one. A printed label inside said *HOUSE*. The label in the second one said simply *PANEL 2*.

'A house this size doesn't need two panels,' Reacher said. 'The second one must feed the bunker. When it's not running its own generator.' He pointed to the master switch. 'Give me three minutes, then throw that. It should cut them off. Then they'll send someone to investigate.'

'What if they don't?' Sands said. 'What if their generator is working, or they have a battery backup? Or the panel is for something else altogether?'

'Then we wait for Wallwork's people. But we have nothing to lose by trying. Throw the switch, then wait for my text. After that, get clear. Find somewhere safe to wait.'

Reacher went back outside and walked across to the bunker. He stayed at ground level, looped around the stairwell, and stopped in a spot above the vertical threshold of the door where he would be invisible to anyone who came out. He took the SOCOM from his waistband. Screwed the suppressor back into place. And waited.

The clock in his head told him the three minutes were up. Nothing happened. Another minute passed. And another. Then Reacher heard the screech of metal on metal, followed by the slap of heavy footsteps on concrete. The back of a head appeared. It was bald. With little ears stuck on the sides like an afterthought.

The guy from Moscow. Who had tried to force Reacher into the trunk of the Town Car.

Reacher waited until the guy got to the top of the steps, then raised his gun.

'Hey,' Reacher called out.

The guy stopped and turned around. Reacher

moved closer, skirting the stairwell, keeping the gun levelled on his chest.

'The woman you call Natasha,' Reacher said. 'You brought her here?'

The guy didn't reply.

'Describe the layout of the bunker.'

The guy stared back at Reacher, but didn't speak.

'Who is down there? How many?'

The guy was silent.

'You're out of time.' Reacher nodded towards the Town Car. 'Open the trunk.'

The guy's mouth twisted into a smile, revealing more of his crooked, stained teeth.

'Think your vest will save you?' Reacher raised his aim to the bridge of the guy's nose. 'Think again. Open the trunk.'

'You're not going to shoot me,' the guy said. His words were clear, but heavy with a Russian accent. 'The FBI has rules.'

'True,' Reacher said. He lowered the gun. About a foot. 'But I don't work for the FBI.' Then he pulled the trigger.

The bullet hit the Moscow guy dead in the centre of his chest. It tore through the fabric of his shirt and slammed into a layer of Kevlar. The guy staggered back. Just one step. At that range most people would have been knocked down. Maybe with broken ribs. Maybe with damaged organs. The mesh of polymer strands is too strong and too tight for the slug to tear through. But all its dissipated energy has to go somewhere.

Reacher returned the gun to eye level. 'Last chance.'

The guy held up his hands. Nodded. Then slowly took his keys from his pants pocket. He fumbled, one-handed, trying to get his thumb lined up with the correct button on the remote. The key ring slipped through his fingers. It landed on the ground in front of him. He leaned down to retrieve it. Grabbed a handful of dirt. Whipped his arm up and hurled the dust and grit at Reacher's face. Reacher stepped back, avoiding the cloud. The guy flung another handful then sprang forward. He was surprisingly fast for someone his size. And agile. His knee came up. His foot flicked out. It came around in a tight crescent. Caught the extended barrel of the suppressor. Tore the gun out of Reacher's hand. And sent it spinning away in a slow, looping, lazy arc. Reacher heard it rattle and clatter down the concrete steps.

The guy glanced down at the hole in his shirt. At the pancaked remains of the bullet. He smiled. Then launched a giant scything roundhouse punch towards Reacher's head. Reacher sidestepped and ducked and crashed his elbow into the guy's side as he spun under his flailing arm. It was a pointless blow. No way was it going to bother the guy through his Kevlar vest. Pure muscle memory on Reacher's part. The guy whipped around and tried the same move again. Reacher stepped and spun and kept his elbow tucked in by his side this time. The guy locked his knees and bounced back and aimed a jab at Reacher's head. Reacher ducked and felt the breeze in his hair as the guy's giant fist zipped over his head.

The vest denied Reacher a number of targets so he focused on the guy's face. His nose was crushed and bent. It had obviously been broken in the past. Maybe more than once. Which revealed a vulnerability. Reacher darted forward. He feigned the wind-up for a round-house punch with his left arm. And jabbed his right fist square into the guy's face. It was a beautiful blow. Powerful. Accurate. It rocked the guy's head way back, bending his neck and straining his ligaments. It would have put a regular person on his back. Maybe kept him there. The Moscow guy just shook his head and straightened up. There was no sign of blood. No ragged breath sounds. So Reacher hit him twice more. With the same fist. In the same place. With every ounce of power he could muster. Then he pulled back to assess the damage he'd caused.

There was no sign of damage. The Moscow guy was bouncing on the soles of his feet, grinning like he was having the time of his life. Then he sprang forward and launched punches with both fists at once. Reacher blocked one blow. He started to counter. Muscle memory again. A reaction to seeing the other guy's face and body completely unguarded. Then he recognized the danger. Adjusted. Went to parry the second blow. But was late. By a fraction of a second. The guy's fist flashed past Reacher's raised forearm and piled into his chest, just inside his left shoulder. The force spun him around and knocked him sideways. He went down on one knee and only just recovered before the guy followed up with a kick aimed at his gut. Reacher arched around it and crashed his right fist into the guy's temple. The guy staggered to his left. Regained his balance. Took four more steps. Then reversed direction and came at Reacher. Fast. Aiming to charge into him. To knock him down. A schoolyard manoeuvre. Brutally effective against the unwary. But not against someone with Reacher's experience.

The guy was leading with his right shoulder. Reacher stepped to his left. To place himself behind the guy as he passed. Away from the danger of a right jab. Or a left hook. Or a forearm smash. Only the guy didn't pass. He jammed his right foot into the ground. Locked his knee. Pushed back. Spun around counterclockwise. And slammed his left elbow flat across Reacher's chest.

The force lifted Reacher off his feet and this time he went down on his back. His head hit the ground. The air left his lungs. The Moscow guy loomed over him. Lifted his right foot. Held it high, ready to stamp down on Reacher's head. Or throat. Or gut. Or groin. Whichever he picked, that would be the end. Or the beginning of the end. Only the guy hesitated. Maybe he was spoilt for options. Maybe he wanted to make his victim sweat. But whatever the reason, it gave Reacher time to flip over on to his front. Push down with his hands. Pull his knees forward. Plant his feet flat on the ground. And spring up, locking his legs and driving the top of his head into the base of the guy's jaw just where it narrowed under his chin.

The guy went up and back and down and wound up sprawling and winded in the dirt. With Reacher looming over him. And Reacher did not hesitate. He was a

393

street fighter at heart. A brawler. He knew the first rule. When you get your guy down, you finish him. Right there. Right then. So he kicked the guy in the head as hard as he could. Then he kicked him again. And again. And then he knelt on his chest and punched him in the throat with all his weight and strength.

Reacher stood back to survey the damage. He took a moment to get his breath back. Then he dragged the guy's body over to the Town Car. He searched his pockets for spare ammunition for the SOCOM. He didn't find any, so he used the remote to pop the trunk. Heaved the guy up. And folded him inside. Then he opened the driver's door. Leaned in and wrenched the rear-view mirror off the windshield. Texted Sands: *Switch on.* And started back towards the steps. He was on the third one down when his phone rang.

It was Wallwork.

'News,' he said. 'From Oak Ridge. You were right about Klostermann having a kid who works there. But not a son. A daughter. Diane. And she doesn't go by Matusak. She's married. She uses her husband's name. Smith. The most common last name in America. Useful thing for a spy, right? Anyway, we're watching her now. First clear chance, we'll grab her. She could be a useful bargaining chip.'

Reacher ended the call and continued down the steps. He retrieved the SOCOM, paused at the bottom, pushed the heavy door. And went through.

*

The space was tiny. And low. Like a cubicle in a clothing store fitting room. Maybe adequate for normal-size people. But very tight for Reacher. The floor and walls were made of concrete. The ceiling was lined with massive steel joists. Ahead was another door. Also grey. With a giant wheel in the centre in place of a lock. Reacher pulled and the door opened. He went through into another space, slightly larger but still uncomfortable. Steel joists continued to support the ceiling. The walls were plain concrete. And there was a hatch set into the floor. Reacher had expected something like this. Some kind of vertical shaft. If someone was waiting at the bottom with a weapon, it would be game over. But there was no way around it. If he was going to find Fisher, he would have to go down.

Reacher held the SOCOM in his right hand and lifted the hatch with his left. He swung it all the way open, then took out the mirror he'd removed from the Town Car. He held it over the opening and angled it so he could look down. The shaft was cylindrical. It was lined with curved concrete sections. Precisely lined up. No gaps. No cracks. The drop was twenty feet deep. There were D-shaped metal staples set into the wall to act as rungs. Four dim lights in wire cages. And no sign of anyone lurking at the base. Reacher put the mirror back in his pocket and tucked the SOCOM into his waistband. He figured the space lower down would be limited. Likely with solid walls. A bad environment for ricochets.

The area at the bottom of the shaft was twice the

width as at the top. There was another hatch set into the floor to the right, presumably leading to a lower level. And a grey metal door in the wall ahead of him. He opened it a crack and used his mirror to look through. It led to a corridor. There were more grey surfaces. Lots of precise right angles. But no people. Reacher opened the door the rest of the way and stepped through.

Fisher was struggling to focus. Her head felt like it was filled with sand. She was suddenly cold. Wet. Conscious of being upright, but not exactly standing. Her arms were above her head. She tried to bring them down. Couldn't. Realized she was hanging from them. Her shoulders started to protest. There was pain in her wrists. Something was biting into them. Something metal. And her feet were bare. Only her toes were on the floor. The surface felt rough beneath them.

She shook her head and a guy swam into her view. He was old. He had white hair. Masses of it, all curly and wild. He put something down. A bucket. He reached to his side. To a metal table. There were things lined up on it. Tools. With blades. And jaws. He picked one up. Like scissors, only larger. Maybe sharper. He held it up in his right hand, in front of her face, and pulled the hem of her shirt towards him with his left.

'Now then, my dear,' he said. 'Let's get you out of these damp clothes.'

Reacher could see another door straight ahead at the far end of the corridor. Three doors on the left. And two on the right. He opened the first door on the left. It led to a bedroom. It was small. Utilitarian. There was a metal cupboard against one wall. And a metal-framed cot. No other furniture. No home comforts of any kind. The first door on the right opened on to a bathroom. It was communal, with urinals and stalls and sinks. Stainless steel and plain white porcelain. White tile on the floor. The second door on the left led to another bedroom. It was identical to the first. A metal cupboard. A metal cot. No other furniture. The second door on the right was for a dormitory. There were three double bunk beds. They had metal frames and thin striped mattresses, and a row of cheap wooden footlockers was lined up next to them. The last door on the left opened on to the kitchen. There were refrigerators and freezers. Cabinets and countertops. Tables and chairs. Two sinks. And a painting on the wall of a window with billowing drapes and a view of trees and flowers and grass. The final door led to a square room. It was as big as all the others combined. There was a dining area to the right, with a pale wooden table and eight chairs. A sitting area to the left with two couches and two armchairs. Bookcases lined the walls. Some full. Some empty. Some holding stacks of board games. Some with stacks of magazines. But there were no people. And no sign of Fisher. Which is what Reacher had been afraid of. It meant he would have to go down to the lower level.

Fisher's mental fog was starting to lift. Her head still ached but she was able to make better sense of her surroundings. She only had on underwear, she realized. She was starting to shiver. Her arms were above her head because her wrists were manacled and attached to a chain which ran through a metal ring in the centre of the ceiling. The room she was in was about ten feet by fifteen. There was one door, which was ajar. The walls were made of cinderblock, which had been painted. Originally white but now yellowing, except for lots of patches that were covered with brownish splatters and stains. The floor was concrete. There were the stubs of thick bolts sticking up from apparently random spots. Fisher guessed that some kind of heavy machinery had once been anchored there.

Aside from her there were five people in the room. The old guy with the white hair, holding the pair of shears he'd used to cut off her clothes. The three remaining members of her crew. And a woman she didn't recognize. She was exceptionally thin, wearing a black dress with a white apron like some kind of uniform, and her blonde hair was knotted on top of her head.

Fisher's shredded clothes were on the floor at her feet. There was a bucket, which she guessed the guy had used to bring the water he'd thrown on her. And now she saw the metal table had two levels. Her eyes were drawn to a device on the lower shelf. It was made of polished wood with an angled front and a dial, like an old-fashioned radio. A cable snaked from its back to an outlet on the wall. And it had two other wires. They were coiled up. One ended with a wad of some kind of fuzzy metal. The other had an insulated handle with two sharp brass spikes sticking out of its far end.

'I see you're admiring my device,' the old guy said. 'It's vintage. From Moscow. It belonged to my mother. She was an expert operator, by all accounts. Maybe we'll use it today. These guys have probably never seen anything like it in action. High voltage, low current. That's the secret. So it can cause more pain. For longer. The steel wool goes up inside . . . well, you can probably guess. And the probe goes wherever I like.'

Reacher went back through the door leading to the foyer. He raised the hatch in the floor and used his mirror to look inside. The shaft went down another twenty feet. Reacher didn't like that. He was too far below ground already. The skin on the back of his neck started to prickle. There was a reason his ancestors told tales of trolls lurking beneath bridges, and dragons living in caves. Those places were dark. Cramped. Unnatural. People shouldn't go in them.

There were five rooms on the lower level. Two on the left. Two on the right. And one at the end of the corridor. There were signs on the doors. *Air Purification* and *HVAC* on the left. *Switchboard* and *Generator* on the right. And *Water Purification* on its own. Reacher didn't need to search these rooms one by one. The doors to four of them were closed. Only one was open. The generator room. Just a crack. But enough for Reacher to hear a voice. Someone he recognized.

*

Klostermann was sliding his shears up between Fisher's breasts. He caught the thin strip of her bra between the blades. Centred them on the little decorative bow. And started to squeeze the handles.

'This is mainly for my amusement, as I already know all about you, Natasha. Or should I call you Margaret?' he said. 'But I do have one question. The drifter. How do I find him?'

'Just turn around,' Reacher said from the doorway.

Five people turned. Two backed away towards the far wall. Klostermann and his housekeeper. Three drew their weapons. The Russian agents. They were to Reacher's right, about halfway into the room. In a straight line. Shoulders almost touching. The men on the outside. The woman sandwiched between them. Reacher stepped towards them. They raised their guns. Reacher raised his hands. Slowly, until they were at face height, palms out, fingers spread.

'Here's how I see things,' Reacher said. 'You're all professionals. Here to do a job. Nothing personal. So if you put your guns down, lie on the floor, and put your hands behind your heads, I won't kill you. I'll hand you over to the authorities. They'll ask you a bunch of dumb questions. Give you crappy food for a few months. And then trade you for the next Americans who get caught in your country. You'll likely be home by the end of the year. What do you say?'

None of the Russians responded.

'This is a limited time offer,' Reacher said. 'It expires in three seconds. Ready? Three. Two . . .'

Reacher shot both hands forward, his fingers closing into fists as they moved, and punched both the men in their throats. They dropped their guns and fell down backwards, clutching their necks and desperately trying to suck air in through their crushed larynxes. Then he drove his right knee up into the woman's abdomen. She folded forward, gasping, and he smashed his right elbow down into her neck where her spine joined her skull. She collapsed like a switch had been thrown and landed at Reacher's feet.

Not bad, Reacher thought. Quick. Effective. Though not quite symmetrical. No points for style.

The housekeeper zipped forward. Reacher hardly saw her leg move, but he felt the side of her foot when it hit his cheek. He lunged for her but she danced back towards the corner, twisting and weaving, too fast for him to grab. He moved towards her, crowding her, aiming to trap her in the corner and nullify her speed. She dodged to the side, pulling something from her hair as she moved. A pin. More like a blade. Six inches long. Slender. Razor sharp. She slashed at Reacher as she passed. Caught him on the chest. Sliced his shirt. And his skin. Not too deep, but enough to draw blood. She slashed the opposite way. Missed. And ran for the door. Reacher followed. Looked down the corridor. Saw she was already halfway to the end. He took the SOCOM from his waistband, aimed and fired three shots. Going for her centre mass. But hitting the end wall, high and left. The suppressor must have gotten bent when the gun tumbled down the steps. His instinctive side screamed: *Chase her!* His rational side said: *She's too fast. Forget her. She's gone.*

Reacher went back into the room and found Klostermann just inside the door. He kicked him in the balls. Klostermann doubled over and went down on all fours, puking and gasping and moaning. Reacher crossed to Fisher. He stretched up and unfastened her manacles. Fisher steadied herself for a moment with a hand on Reacher's chest. Then she wrapped her arms around herself.

'I'm freezing,' she said. 'I'm dizzy.'

Reacher stepped back over to the Russian woman's body, hauled it into a sitting position, and wrestled her shirt over her head. He handed it to Fisher then went to work removing the dead woman's boots, socks, and trousers. He left Fisher to finish getting dressed, walked across to Klostermann, and helped him into a sitting position against the wall.

'I want you to tell me two things,' Reacher said. 'I've seen how you get information from people. Do I need to get busy with your tool kit? Hang you from the ceiling? Fire up your electric toy?'

'No.' Klostermann's voice was barely louder than a whisper.

'Good. Now, these are things I already know, but I want to hear you say them. First, Toni Garza. The journalist. You killed her?'

'Yes.'

'And tortured her?'

402

Klostermann nodded.

'And Marty? The guy who drove me?'

'He's dead.'

'You killed him, too?'

'No. I had them do it.' Klostermann gestured towards the Russians' bodies.

'OK. Thank you for being honest. And while the spirit of sharing is upon us, I have a couple of things to tell you. For a start, your plan to use Fisher to feed false information to the FBI? It failed.'

'I don't know what you're talking about.'

'All it did was alert them to the real agent.'

Klostermann stiffened.

'They're going to arrest her real soon.'

'I don't believe you.'

'It's true. Otherwise, how would I know her name? Diane Smith. Diane Klostermann, before she got married.'

Klostermann didn't react. He sat perfectly still. For ten seconds. Fifteen. Then he lunged for his ankle. His fingers closed around the grip of a little pearl-handled .22. But he never got it out of its holster. Because Reacher grabbed a handful of his wild hair. Pulled his head forward. And smashed it back into the wall.

Just once.

That was all it took.

Reacher took two phones from Klostermann's pockets. A plain vanilla burner, and one with all kinds of extra buttons and icons. He figured someone at the

FBI would be interested in that one, so he handed it to Fisher. Then he led the way out of the room, down the corridor, and through the door to the lobby. Fisher took a step towards the ladder, then sank down into a crouch.

'I'm not feeling good,' she said. 'Whatever that drug was they used, it's messed me up. I don't think I can climb.'

'I'm not leaving you down here,' Reacher said. 'That's for damn sure.' He hoisted her over his shoulder, climbed to the next level, and squeezed through the hatch. 'See, no problem. One more flight and we're home free.'

Reacher climbed the next five rungs. And stopped. Something was wrong up at the top of the shaft. It was too dark. He continued to the space at the top, gently lowered Fisher down and rested her against the wall. Closed his eyes. And tried the door.

It didn't move. Not even a fraction of an inch.

Reacher was trapped. Underground. In a small space. The only thing since childhood that could give him nightmares. His worst fear. The only thing he couldn't fight.

'I don't get it,' Fisher said. 'Why is there no handle?'

'It's on the other side,' Reacher said. He was focused on continuing to breathe. 'It's a kind of airlock. With two doors.' He paused. 'They should never be open at once. So the handles are on the same side. Then one guy can control them both.'

'So someone locked it from the other side? Who?'

'My money's on Klostermann's housekeeper.' Reacher pressed his back against the door and slid down until he was sitting on the ground. The skin between his shoulder blades was beginning to prickle. He was starting to sweat.

'The skinny woman? Who ran? But you shot her. I heard it. No. Wait.' Fisher shook her head, trying to clear the lingering fog. She pressed her fingers against her temples. 'Her body wasn't in the corridor. She got away?'

Reacher shrugged.

'The way she fought?' Fisher said. 'The way they let her take part in the torture? She's not just a house-keeper. She's one of them. She'll report what happened. The Russians will pull their agent. We've got to warn Wallwork.'

'He's on his way,' Reacher said. 'He should be. I told him you were here.'

'We can't wait. We have to warn him now.'

Reacher took out his phone. It had no signal. They were near the surface, but behind too much concrete. Too much steel. The same things that were keeping them in were keeping the radio waves out. Reacher tried Klostermann's phones. Neither of those could connect, either.

'OK,' Fisher said. 'Then we have to stop her.'

'How?' Reacher said. 'This door is the only way out. It's impossible to open.'

'There must be another way. Where the utilities come in? Some kind of pipe? Or duct?'

405

Reacher shook his head. 'These places are self-contained. The water is processed and recirculated. Same with the air.'

'What about power? The generator. It's gone now, but there must have been one. This place was built, when? The 1950s?'

Reacher nodded.

'What kind of generators did they have back then?' Fisher said.

'Diesel, probably,' Reacher said.

'And diesel engines require air to run. Which would have to come from outside. Come on.' Fisher struggled to her feet. 'Back to the generator room. We'll start looking in there.'

Reacher looked at the mouth of the shaft. It was the last place in the world he wanted to go. But where he was, trapped behind that massive door, was the last place in the world he wanted to stay. And he had the Russian agent to think about. Klostermann's daughter. Maybe with her hands already on The Sentinel. Maybe already ordered to disappear. Reacher knew Sands would raise the alarm when she didn't hear from him. Wallwork should be on his way, too. But how long would help take to arrive?

'I'll go.' Reacher handed the SOCOM to Fisher. 'Someone might come. They might open the door. If they do, make sure they don't close it again.'

Reacher climbed down the first ladder. One rung at a time. Nice and slow and calm. Then the second ladder.

Then he walked down the corridor to the generator room. Went in. Glanced at the bodies on the floor. And turned his attention to the ceiling. He surveyed every inch. There was nothing that looked like it could have been a vent or an air supply. He moved down to the walls. There were two filled-in circles that could have been pipes. In which case they were doomed. They were only nine inches across. Which left two square panels set into the opposite wall. Reacher walked over and knocked on one. It sounded solid. He tried the second.

It was hollow.

He tried to tear it off but couldn't get any kind of purchase. It had been painted around, sealing up any gap, not even leaving enough space to jam his fingernails into. He went to the metal table. Scanned the top level. The line of ghastly tools. Found a chisel. And a hammer. Tried not to think about why Klostermann had wanted them. Or what he'd used them for. Reacher took them back to the panel. He started at the top left corner and hammered the tip of the chisel between the wood and the wall. He worked his way all around the perimeter, then knocked the chisel in further. Three inches. Four. And started to lever the handle away from the wall. He felt the panel move. He kept heaving until the gap grew larger and finally he was able to wrench the wood away altogether. It had covered a square hole in the wall, three feet by three. The space also went back three feet, forming a cube. Reacher felt inside. The floor was solid. So were the walls. But the top wasn't. A circular shaft rose out of it, three feet in diameter. He tried to look up inside it, but it was pitch dark.

Reacher crawled into the space then stretched his arms above his head, hunched his shoulders and clawed his way upright. Nothing obstructed him. He felt the sides of the shaft. They were cold and smooth. Stainless steel, he thought. He moved his hands down and found a rib. An inch deep. The join between sections of steel liner. Not much. But something. He stretched up and found another, three feet above the first. Like tiny ladder rungs. Leading into a tight, dark space. Maybe to the surface. Maybe to oblivion.

Only one way to find out.

Reacher started to climb. He pulled himself up to the next rib. Found the one below with his feet. Pressed his back into the metal surface behind him. Took a breath. Pulled up to the next rib. Took another breath. He was still sweating. He pulled himself up. His skin was still prickling. Then the shaft started to get narrower. It was squeezing in. Gripping him. He was going to get jammed. It was like the black holes in space he'd read about. Matter got sucked in. Crushed. And it never got back out.

No. That wasn't true. His mind was playing tricks. He forced himself to keep going. He made it to the eighteenth rib. The nineteenth. He stretched up. And his fingertips touched something. It was solid. Rough. Wood, he thought. He was at the top, but something was covering the exit.

Reacher pressed his hands against it. Tucked his head into his chest, and shifted his feet up one more rib. Uncurled his back until his neck and shoulders were in contact. Started to push. And his left foot slipped. He fell sideways. His head hit the metal lining of the shaft, disorienting him in the dark. He scrabbled with his hands. Pushed sideways. Stabilized himself. Got his bearings. Caught his breath. And tried again. He hunched over. Pressed up with his shoulders and neck. Slowly built the pressure. And felt the thing above him move. Very slightly. He pushed harder. It gave a little more. He wriggled and twisted and pushed and managed to slide it to the side. An inch. Two inches. Enough to see light. To breathe fresh air. He pushed harder. Twisted further. Kept going until he'd made a space wide enough to climb through. Then he hauled himself out and collapsed on the rough scrubby grass, covered in sweat, staring up at the sky.

Reacher sat and pulled his phone out of his pocket. It vibrated in his hand and two words appeared on its screen: New Message. He hit the button to make the message play and lifted the phone to his ear. It was from Wallwork. With news from Oak Ridge. As terse as ever. He said Klostermann's daughter had tried to run. The FBI had stopped her. But she wasn't talking. Not yet.

Reacher put the phone away and hauled himself to his feet. He took a quick look at the top of the shaft. A neat, square concrete collar had been built around it. The stubs of sturdy bolts were sticking out, so he figured there had originally been some kind of baffle fixed over the entrance to guard against whatever kind of nuclear debris the Cold Warriors were worried about. That had probably been removed when the generator was taken out of service. Dismantled parts may even have been hauled up the shaft. It would have been easier than carrying them up the ladders. That was for sure. And when the project was done, someone just tossed a board over the hole. Over time the board got covered with soil. And the soil grew scrappy grass like the rest of the field. Which is why nothing showed up on the satellite photo.

Reacher hustled across to the steps. He got all the way down and saw someone beyond the first door, hunched over, with her ear to the second. It was Klostermann's housekeeper. Back from raising the alarm. No doubt wondering about the fate of her comrades.

'You're wasting your time.' Reacher stepped through the doorway. 'They're all dead. Your agent's been caught. So do the smart thing. Give up.'

The housekeeper turned around. Her mouth gaped open. Her eyes stretched wide. She pressed herself back and at the same time she pulled the pin from her hair. Reacher moved closer and she jabbed at him, slashing back and forth. He swotted her arm aside, knocking the pin from her grip. Then he grabbed her by the neck with his left hand, turned the wheel with his right, and opened the door. He waited for Fisher to come out and get to the top of the steps. Then he shoved the housekeeper through the doorway.

Maybe she fell down the shaft. Maybe she didn't. Reacher didn't feel the need to check. He just closed the door and spun the wheel.

Reacher and Fisher sat on the hood of the red Chevy and waited for Sands to arrive. She appeared after three minutes, pulling up in the same spot she'd used earlier. She got out. Hugged Fisher. Helped her into the passenger seat. Then came back to talk to Reacher.

'I should take Agent Fisher to the hospital,' she said. 'You coming?'

'No,' Reacher said. 'There's something I have to do here.'

'And after that? Will I see you again?'

Reacher said nothing.

'If our paths don't cross I wish you luck, Reacher.'

'Good luck to you, too,' Reacher said. 'I hope Cerberus pays off for you. I hope you get your boat.'

'Thanks. I hope you get whatever it is you need, too.' Sands came closer. She stood on tiptoe and kissed Reacher's cheek. Then she turned towards the car.

'Sarah?' Reacher took his phone out of his pocket and handed it to her. 'Give this to Rusty for me? I don't need it any more.'

TWENTY-NINE

It was the calm before the storm, Reacher thought. The gate had clanked shut behind Sands and Fisher, leaving the place quiet and peaceful. But it wouldn't stay that way for long. Swarms of FBI agents would soon race in to tear the house apart. And another crew would be sent underground. To the bunker. To bring up the bodies. And with them would come questions. The kind Reacher didn't want to be around to answer. So he knew he would have to hurry.

Reacher took out Klostermann's burner phone. It was a basic model. An old design. Presumably cheap. Which made sense, given it had been bought with no long-term future in mind. It meant there was no fingerprint ID. No facial recognition. Just an old-school PIN. Four digits. Ten thousand permutations. No time to try them all. So Reacher scooped up some dirt. Ground it into dust. Sprinkled a little over the keys. Blew the excess away. Held the phone sideways to the light. And found that none had stuck. He tried again with a little more dirt. None stuck. The technique gave him no help this time. But it had told him something at the gate. Klostermann had used 0420. Adolf Hitler's birthday. A subtle reinforcement for the people he wanted to convince he was a Nazi. Which he wasn't. But his choice did reveal a possible affinity with dates. So what would Klostermann pick? The opposite of a Nazi? Reacher tried 0505, for Karl Marx. The phone buzzed angrily and refused to unlock. He tried 0422, for Lenin. The phone refused to unlock. He tried 1107, for Trotsky. The phone refused. Then Reacher refined his thinking. Klostermann had been born in 1950. He grew up during the height of the Cold War. His parents were Soviet agents. His uncles were Soviet agents. Who, from that era, could inspire lifelong loyalty? Reacher entered 1218. Joseph Stalin's birthday.

The phone unlocked.

Reacher worked his way through the phone's menus until he found a list of received calls. There were four different numbers. Three of them each appeared only once. The other, four times. Reacher started with it. He highlighted it, and hit *call*. It was answered after three rings.

'Yes?' It was a man's voice. Reacher was fairly sure he recognized it. He thought he heard a door close in the background, as well.

'A word to the wise,' Reacher said. 'Henry Klostermann is dead. FBI agents are on their way to search his house. ETA, twenty minutes.'

Reacher hung up and started walking towards the

house. He crossed the porch. Went inside. Crunched over the pieces of shattered door frame. Made his way down the corridor. Past the photographs. And continued all the way to the end. He knew the last door on the right was the living room, which gave him three to pick from. He tried the last on the left. And found what he was looking for straight away. Klostermann's study.

The room was square with windows on two sides. There was a desk in front of the one to the right, facing into the room. It was big and oppressive, made of polished mahogany, with a green leather inlay on top. Behind it was a green leather captain's chair with a row of heavy brass studs around its edge. There was a bookcase next to the door. And a line of waist-high filing cabinets against the fourth wall. Hanging above them was a framed portrait, in oils. It was of Stalin. He was wearing his World War II military uniform. Reacher took it down. There was a different image on its other side. Adolf Hitler. Reacher replaced the picture with the Nazi leader facing out.

Reacher checked the drawers in the desk and the cabinets. All were locked. He considered breaking in, but decided against it. He would have been interested in any historical artefacts unique to Klostermann's life and times, but the FBI was welcome to the job of sifting through papers and documents. He looked behind the books on the shelf out of pure habit, found nothing, then settled in next to the bookcase to wait.

Five minutes passed in silence, then Reacher heard footsteps in the corridor. Someone medium weight, he thought. Wearing sturdy shoes. Trying to be discreet, but also in a hurry. The sound came closer. It paused outside the door. The handle turned. The door began to swing. Slowly. Its leading edge moved about a foot, then stopped. The muzzle of a gun appeared in the gap. A whole barrel came into view. It belonged to a revolver. A Smith & Wesson Model 60. The first stainless steel revolver made anywhere in the world. Designed to avoid the danger of corrosion when carried close to the body. Not police issue. The hand holding it became visible. Followed by a wrist. Protruding from the cuff of a white shirt beneath a grey suit sleeve.

Reacher kicked the door. It slammed shut, crushing the wrist. The guy screamed. He dropped the gun, pulled his hand free, and jumped back. Reacher jerked the door all the way open. And saw Detective Goodyear cowering against the far wall, clutching his forearm. Reacher stepped into the corridor. Grabbed Goodyear by the lapels. Dragged him into the study. And flung him head first into the wall beneath the window. Then he leaned on the edge of the desk and waited for the guy to roll over and pull himself into a half-sitting position.

'I guess you've answered one question,' Reacher said. 'The one I asked you at the courthouse when we first met. About why you were so desperate to sweep Rutherford's attempted kidnapping under the rug.'

Goodyear didn't respond.

'That means there's one question left,' Reacher said. 'Why were you helping Klostermann? Money? Blackmail? What?'

'Principle,' Goodyear spat back. 'Mr Klostermann was working to save our country. Our race. I was proud to help him.'

'Stand up.'

Goodyear didn't move.

Reacher pushed away from the desk.

Goodyear hauled himself to his feet.

'Take off your jacket,' Reacher said.

Goodyear slipped his arms out of his sleeves and dropped the coat.

'Open your shirt.'

Goodyear undid his buttons, one by one, starting at the top, working down to his waist.

'All the way,' Reacher said.

Goodyear slowly pulled the sides of the shirt apart. Reacher looked at his chest. At the left side. Where there was a tattoo. Of an eagle. With a swastika.

'You might have heard that I met some of your so-called brothers the other night,' Reacher said. 'They all resigned from your little band. With orders to explain that anyone who didn't would get their house burned down. With them inside.'

'No,' Goodyear said. 'Don't do that. Please. I'll resign.'

'You will. But not just yet. Your buddies told me Klostermann was planning to recreate Hitler's Cathedral of Light. They were too stupid to understand what that was. I'm hoping you have a better grasp of history.'

'You're damn right I do. I helped Mr Klostermann with every stage of the planning.'

'So you know about bringing people in from all the other states.'

'Damn right.'

'So you have contacts. With similar sad-ass groups in other places.'

'You can stop right there. I'll go to jail before I betray my brothers.'

'Refuse, and jail will be the least of your worries. But let me ask you one thing about your cause. You shared it with Klostermann?'

'Correct.'

'Henry Klostermann was your brother?'

Goodyear nodded.

'He wasn't your brother,' Reacher said. 'He was a Russian agent. He was playing you for a fool. Using you every step of the way. I bet he laughed himself to sleep every night, thinking about how dumb you are.'

'Nice try, Reacher. But I'll never believe that.'

'That picture.' Reacher pointed at the wall above the filing cabinets. 'Was it always up when you came here?'

Goodyear stood and threw out a sharp salute. He winced as he tried to straighten his hand. 'Always.'

'Take it down. See what's on the other side.'

Goodyear stayed where he was. 'Touching it would be sacrilege.'

'I'll do it then.' Reacher stepped forward, but Goodyear darted in front of him.

'No,' Goodyear said. 'If anyone's going to, it should be me.'

Goodyear paused in front of the picture as if saying

417

a prayer. Then he stretched out and took hold of it. He used both hands. One on each side of the frame. Lifted it down. Paused again. And turned it over.

'You know who that is, right?' Reacher said. 'Klostermann's true idol. Henry Klostermann dedicated his entire life to destroying everything you believe in. And he tricked you into helping him. The journalist who was murdered? Toni Garza? Klostermann killed her. Because she was going to expose him. Only you buried the investigation. Because he told you to. You helped him get away with it.'

Goodyear shook his head. 'I don't believe you.'

'Doesn't matter if you believe me or not,' Reacher said. 'The FBI will explain it to you. I wasn't lying when I told you the agents are on their way. You can stay and help them round up the other groups. Which would be doing your brothers a favour, honestly. It would stop anyone with a double-digit IQ being able to exploit them. Or if you don't like that idea we can go to your house.' Reacher pulled a cigarette lighter out of his pocket. 'We can pick up some gas on the way.'

Goodyear sank back down on to the floor. 'No. I'll stay.'

'Take out your cuffs,' Reacher said.

Goodyear pulled them from a leather pouch on his belt.

'Secure yourself to a filing cabinet. To the drawer handle.'

Goodyear did what he was told.

'OK,' Reacher said. 'Two last things before I go.' First he took the painting and smashed it over Goodyear's head, leaving the frame hanging like a necklace. Then Reacher punched Goodyear in the face. Normally he would have used his left hand. Maybe dialled back the power a little too. But making an exception seemed the right thing to do.

Reacher left Klostermann's burner phone on his desk. There were four numbers in its call log. Goodyear's, which was accounted for. Marty's, which was a dead end. Literally. But that still left two for the FBI to track down. Two more crooked cops, maybe. Or two more suitcase carriers. Whatever they turned out to be, they needed to be stopped.

He checked that Goodyear was breathing. Then made his way out of the house and across to the red Chevy. He figured he would drive to the truck stop. Leave the car in a parking lot. Walk over to the gas station. To the truck side. And go wherever the first driver willing to take him was heading.

He pulled up to the gate. Waited for it to slide to the side. Drove through. And stopped dead. A car had pulled in front of him. From out of nowhere, it seemed. Certainly not the road ahead. It must have been up on the grass verge, parallel to the wall.

Reacher waited for the car to move. It was small. A late model Honda Civic. A woman was driving. She was wearing plain clothes. Which was why it took Reacher a moment to recognize her. It was Officer Rule.

Rule recognized Reacher at the same moment. She climbed out of the Honda and walked around to Reacher's door. He rolled down his window.

'Reacher?' Rule said. 'What are you doing here?'

'Leaving,' Reacher said. 'In fact, I was never here. You?'

Rule was silent for a moment, as if she was trying to decide whether to answer. 'I followed someone here.'

'Detective Goodyear?'

Rule nodded.

'Why?' Reacher said.

'I figured something weird was going on. Something wrong.'

'There was. How did you know?'

Rule shrugged. 'Call it a cop's instinct. I saw Goodyear take a call on a cell phone, then hurry into his office. Only it wasn't his regular phone. We've all had to use our own while the department phones have been down, and I know he has an iPhone. The latest kind. But several times now he's used this other one. It's old. And he's often seemed kind of furtive. I've always ignored it before. Then I thought, this is it. I have to know what his deal is.'

'This was at the courthouse, where he took the call?'

'Right.'

'So why aren't you in uniform? And how come you're using your personal vehicle?'

'I was at the courthouse to hand in my notice. I quit. I'm sick of the place. I mean, think about it. You're a stranger. Drifting through town. And you cared more about stopping crime here than our detective. You've already helped me more than anyone in the department ever did. I've had enough. It's time for a fresh start somewhere else.'

'Your letter. Will anyone have read it yet?'

'I doubt it. Why?'

'You might want to get it back.'

'Why would I want to do that?'

'The town has a vacancy for a new detective.'

'We only have one detective position. And it's taken.'

'Not any more. Goodyear just resigned.'

'Are you serious? Why?'

'Call it a personal crisis. So he'll have to be replaced. They could bring someone in from the outside, I guess. But someone local would be better. Someone who cares about the town. Who has a string of recent arrests to her name. You know anyone like that?'

Rule thought for a moment. 'Time for me to get back to the courthouse. Make that letter disappear.' She got halfway around the hood of her car then turned back to Reacher. 'What about you? Where are you going?'

'I have no particular place in mind.'

'How about my place? You know where it is. It's Friday evening. We could get some carry out. I have some beer. Some wine.'

'What about your neighbours? They would be bound to see me.'

'Screw them. What are they going to do? Mess with the town's soon-to-be only detective?'

THIRTY

Rusty Rutherford emerged from his apartment on Monday morning, exactly two weeks after he got fired.

He wasn't normally the type of guy who dawdled in his local coffee shop. He went to the same one every day. Purely for the caffeine. He didn't go in search of conversation. He wasn't interested in finding new company. He stood quietly in line. Placed his order. Collected his drink as soon as it was ready. And left. Even after the week he spent with Jack Reacher it proved a difficult habit to break.

The adjustment process wasn't made any easier by the response he received from the other patrons. Everyone was pleased to see him. He felt like a magnet with the right polarity. The surrounding customers crowded in closer than usual. By the time he reached the counter he had exchanged kind words with a dozen other people. And he had seen how the barista dealt with the two men in front of him when they stepped up to order. She had slammed their cups on the counter. Slopped coffee into the saucers then slid them forward, spilling even more. But she smiled at Rusty when it was his turn, and asked if he wanted his regular.

'House blend, medium, no room for milk, right?' she said.

'Right,' Rusty said. 'To go.'

'It's on the house,' she said. 'See you tomorrow?'

The same time Rusty Rutherford was leaving the coffee shop, Jack Reacher was standing at the side of the street. He was half a block from the town's only set of traffic lights, which were working perfectly. He watched Rutherford set off, heading east. Not hurrying. Not dawdling. Just drifting along in his own little bubble. Following a familiar route. Comfortable with his surroundings. Heading home. Where he belonged.

A car drew up alongside Reacher and stopped. It was new and shiny and bland. A rental. Driven by the insurance guy Reacher had met the week before. He was still wearing his plain, dark-coloured suit. But he no longer seemed panic-stricken. More like he was on top of the world.

'Need a ride?' the guy said.

'Where are you going?' Reacher said.

'Nashville. Meeting at the office. Giving a presentation about how I negotiated the ransom down forty per cent, and still got the town's systems back up and running. All apart from some archive thing, but whatever. History. Who cares?'

Reacher thought for a moment. He had just left Nashville, and he had a rule. Never go back. It rarely ends well. But he had been making a few exceptions recently. They had all worked out OK. And if he made another one now he could go to a club.

Catch a band.

Make sure they got paid.

Read on for a Q&A with

Lee Child
and
Andrew Child

How did you find collaborating on *The Sentinel*?

LC: Sitting down together to write *The Sentinel* felt like the final phase of a twenty-five-year process. When I finished the first Reacher book, *Killing Floor*, I showed it to my wife and daughter, who were loyal and enthusiastic, but neither of them was a natural thriller reader, so next I showed it to Andrew, for what I felt would be an informed opinion. I knew it would have been really tough for him to criticize his big brother's work, but equally I knew he would if necessary. He's like that. But fortunately he approved, and from then on Reacher became a kind of family property . . . almost like another brother. So in the end the collaboration felt pretty easy.

AC: I found the writing hard – Lee sets a very high bar! – but the collaboration part came much more naturally than I'd expected. I haven't written anything with anyone else for years – decades! – because in the past when I tried I always felt like I was swimming against the tide. I was always out of step with my partners and none of my ideas seemed to mesh with theirs. But with Lee we were in sync from minute one and remained that way throughout.

What was it like writing a novel during the Covid-19 lockdown?

LC: A lot of it was mapped out and written before lockdown, but those enforced nothing-else-to-do months were really helpful, actually, in terms of focus and concentration.

AC: The lockdown meant that we had less face-to-face contact than I'd expected while we were writing, meaning more had to be done via Zoom and text, etc., but I agree that the opportunity for total immersion in the creative process was very beneficial.

Andrew, what was Lee like growing up?

AC: I have few memories of us living together due to the difference in our ages but there is one incident that will always stay with me. I was about five and my father was mad with me due to some childish misdemeanour I'd committed. Lee was the only one who took my side, and in the aftermath we struck a deal: he would always stand up for me, and I would always stand up for him. I had very little in common with the rest of my family so as I grew up I saw Lee very much as a beacon of hope – proof that it was possible to find your own path in life, have fun, and be a success.

And Lee, same question about Andrew!

LC: I was a teenager when he was born. I had girlfriends and was going to gigs and parties all the time. But he was a cute baby, and soon developed a fascinating personality . . . stubborn, obstinate, opinionated, but funny, too. From the start he had to carve out his own space in a crowded house. I had a good time hanging out with him. And he was good practice for having my own kid later. One time I babysat for him when he was a few months old, he wouldn't sleep because he had a cold. So I held him upside down by the ankles until all the snot drained out, and then he slept like a log. A useful technique. Then I left home, so really he grew up a friend rather than a brother, because we weren't under the same roof all the time, with all the usual sibling issues.

There's quite an age gap between you. Did you find that creatively useful?

LC: Totally, and that's very much the point of the transition. As a writer I'm aware now of the world passing me by somewhat, and I wanted the series to get a shot of more contemporary energy. Having Andrew on board is like mysteriously waking up fifteen years younger, full of ideas and passion. It's like meeting a younger me.

AC: The situation is a complete turnaround for me. As the youngest in the family I was always aware of being the slowest, the least qualified, the least experienced. And now, for the first time in my life, being younger has turned to my advantage and given me something different to contribute.

Was there anything you disagreed on?

LC: Not really. We both knew what we were aiming for.

AC: The opposite, actually. I was always clear where I thought the story should go but didn't always know how to get there, so having Lee to constantly steer us in the right direction was invaluable.

It's well known that you both love coffee. Who is the bigger addict?

LC: You know how some folks take a glass of water to bed? Andrew went through a phase of taking a cup of black coffee, so probably he's the bigger addict, although how his head doesn't therefore explode is a mystery to me.

AC: I still do that, some nights. If I haven't had enough coffee during the day I end up with a headache and can't sleep. A friend once bought me a mug with a diagram of all the veins and arteries in the human body on it with the caption, 'There's too much blood in my caffeine system.' That pretty much sums me up.

Do you have the same favourite Reacher books?

LC: I have a certain quiet pride in some of them, but ultimately my favourite is always the next one, because theoretically it could be the perfect one ... but then I worry that if an author was totally satisfied with a book, where's the motivation for carrying on?

AC: There are two that particularly stand out for me. *Killing Floor*, because it was the first and I will never forget how I felt after reading the manuscript. The joy of tearing through such a magnificent book. The relief of seeing how great it was, knowing how much was at stake for my brother. And in addition, a sense of connection. The narrative is written in the first person and we don't learn Reacher's name for quite some time, but long before it was revealed I thought, I know this guy on a deep, fundamental level. The other book I think is particularly special is *Make Me*. It has all the ingredients that make us love Reacher – the captivating location, the pervading sense of mystery, the fabulous characters, the intriguing (and particularly disturbing) plot, the propulsive prose, the action, the sense of justice done – but I feel that this time out, the language was even more lyrical and aesthetically satisfying.

How do you hope people will feel when they finish reading this book?

LC: Relieved and satisfied that justice has been done, and that the bad guys got more than just a stern talking-to.

AC: All the above – and wanting more!

What does the future hold for Jack Reacher?

LC: As always, that's up to the readers. If they want more, we'll supply it!

AC: With the greatest pleasure!

Read on for an exclusive first chapter from

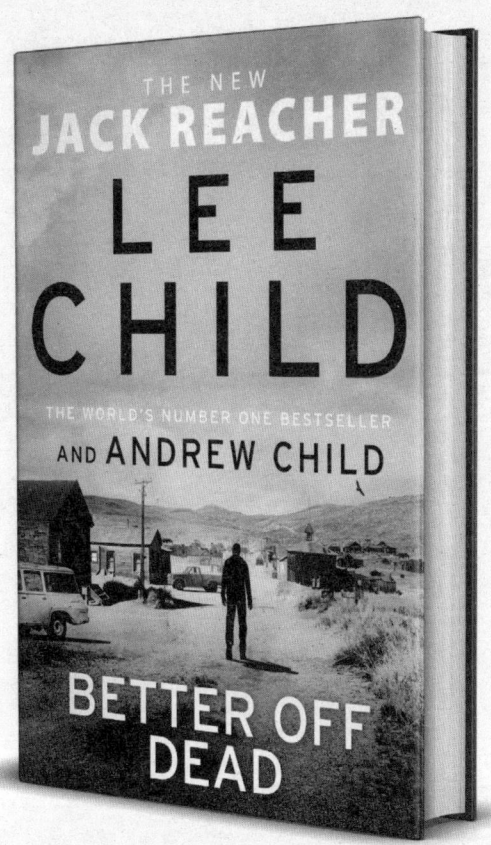

Coming 26 October 2021

Available to pre-order now
in hardback, ebook and audiobook

ONE

The stranger got into position under the street-light at eleven p.m., as agreed.

The light had been easy to find, just like he'd been told it would be. It was the only one in the compound that was still working, all the way at the far end, six feet shy of the jagged metal fence that separated the United States from Mexico.

He was alone. And unarmed.

As agreed.

The car showed up at 23:02. It kept to the centre of the space between the parallel rows of lock-up garages. They were made of metal, too. Roofs warped by the sun. Walls scoured by the sand. Five on the right. Four on the left. And the remains of one more lying torn and corroded ten feet to the side, like something had exploded inside it years ago.

The car's lights were on bright, making it hard to recognize the make and model. And impossible to see inside. It continued until it was fifteen feet away then braked to a stop, rocking on its worn springs and settling into a low cloud of sandy dust. Then its front doors opened. Both of them. And two men climbed out.

Not as agreed.

Both the car's back doors opened. Two more men climbed out.

Definitely not as agreed.

The four men paused and sized the stranger up. They'd been told to expect someone big and this guy sure fit the bill. He was six feet five. Two hundred and fifty pounds. Chest like a gun safe and hands like backhoe buckets. And scruffy. His hair was coarse and unkempt. He hadn't shaved for days. His clothes looked cheap and ill-fitting, except for his shoes. Somewhere between a hobo and a Neanderthal. Not someone who was going to be missed.

The driver stepped forward. He was a couple of inches shorter than the stranger, and a good fifty pounds lighter. He was wearing black jeans and a black sleeveless T-shirt. He had on black combat-style boots. His head was shaved, but his face was hidden by a full beard. The other guys followed, lining up alongside him.

'The money?' the driver said.

The stranger patted his jacket pocket.

'Good.' The driver nodded toward the car. 'Back seat. Get in.'

'Why?'

'So I can take you to Michael.'

436

'That wasn't the deal.'

'Sure it was.'

The stranger shook his head. 'The deal was, you tell me where Michael is.'

'Tell you. Show you. What's the difference?'

The stranger said nothing.

'Come on. What are you waiting for? Give me the money and get in the car.'

'I make a deal, I stick to it. You want the money, tell me where Michael is.'

The driver shrugged. 'The deal's changed. Take it or leave it.'

'I'll leave it.'

'Enough of this.' The driver reached behind his back and took a pistol from his waistband. 'Cut the crap. Get in the car.'

'You were never going to take me to Michael.'

'No shit, Sherlock.'

'You were going to take me to someone else. Someone who has questions for me.'

'No more talking. Get in the car.'

'Which means you can't shoot me.'

'Which means I can't kill you. Yet. I can still shoot you.'

The stranger said, 'Can you?'

A witness would have said the stranger hardly moved at all but somehow in a split second he had closed the gap between them and had his hand on the driver's wrist. Which he pulled up, like a proud fisherman

437

hauling something from the sea. He forced the guy's arm way above his head. He hoisted it so high the guy was raised up on his tiptoes. Then he drove his left fist into the guy's side. Hard. The kind of punch that would normally knock a man down. And keep him down. Only the driver didn't fall. He couldn't. He was suspended by his arm. His feet slid back. The gun fell from his fingers. His shoulder joint ripped apart. Tendons stretched and snapped. Ribs shattered. It was a grotesque cascade of injuries. Each one devastating in its own right. Each one enough to sideline the guy for weeks. But in the moment he hardly noticed any of them. Because his entire upper body was convulsing in agony. Searing bolts of pain shot through him, all stemming from one place. A spot just below his armpit, where a dense tangle of nerves and lymph nodes nestled beneath the skin. The exact spot that had just been crushed by the stranger's massive knuckles.

The stranger retrieved the driver's fallen gun and carried him over to the hood of the car. He laid him back, squealing and gasping and writhing on the dull paintwork, then turned to the other three guys. 'You should walk away. Now. While you have the chance.'

The guy at the centre of the trio stepped forward. He was about the same height as the driver. Maybe a little broader. He had hair, cropped short. No beard. Three chunky silver chains around his neck. And a nasty sneer on his face. 'You got lucky once. That won't happen again. Now get in the car before we hurt you.'

The stranger said, 'Really? Again?'

But he didn't move. He saw the three guys swap furtive glances. They had to decide what to do, but with their leader out of commission their command structure was disrupted. He figured that if the guys were smart, they'd opt for a tactical retreat. Or if they were proficient, they would attack together. But first they'd work one of them around to the rear. He could pretend to check on the injured driver. Or to give up and get in the car. Or even to run away. The other two could create a distraction. Then, when he was in place, they would all rush in at once. A simultaneous assault from three directions. One of the guys was certain to take some damage. Probably two. But the third might have a chance. An opening might present itself. If someone had the skill to exploit it.

They weren't smart. And they weren't proficient. They didn't withdraw. And no one tried to circle around. Instead, the centre guy took another step forward, alone. He dropped into some kind of generic martial arts stance. Let out a high-pitched wail. Feinted a jab to the stranger's face. Then launched a reverse punch to the solar plexus. The stranger brushed it aside with the back of his left hand and punched the guy's bicep with his right, his middle knuckle extended. The guy shrieked and jumped back, his axillary nerve over-loaded and his arm temporarily useless.

'You should walk away,' the stranger said. 'Before you hurt yourself.'

The guy sprang forward. He made no attempt at disguise this time. He just twisted into a wild roundhouse punch with his good arm. The stranger leaned back. The guy's fist sailed harmlessly past. The stranger watched it go then drove his knuckle into the meat of the guy's tricep. Both his arms were now out of action.

'Walk away,' the stranger said. 'While you still can.'

The guy lunged. His right leg rose. His thigh first, then his foot, pivoting at the knee. Going for maximum power. Aiming for the stranger's groin. But not getting close. Because the stranger countered with a kick of his own. A sneaky one. Straight and low. Directly into the guy's shin. Just as it reached maximum speed. Bone against toecap. The stranger's shoes. The only thing about him that wasn't scruffy. Bought in London years ago. Layer upon layer of leather and polish and glue. Seasoned by time. Hardened by the elements. And now as solid as steel.

The guy's ankle cracked. He screamed and shied away. He lost his balance and couldn't regain it without the use of his arms. His foot touched the ground. The fractured ends of the bone connected. They grated together. Pain ripped through his leg. It burned along every nerve. Way more than his system could handle. He remained upright for another half second, already unconscious. Then he toppled onto his back and lay there, as still as a fallen tree.

The remaining two guys turned and made for the car. They kept going past its front doors. Past its rear doors. All the way around the back. The trunk lid popped open. One of the guys dropped out of sight. The shorter one. Then he reappeared. He was holding something in each hand. Like a pair of baseball bats, only longer. And thicker and squarer at one end. Pickaxe handles. Effective tools, in the right hands. He passed one to the taller guy and the pair strode back, stopping about four feet away.

'Say we break your legs?' The taller guy licked his lips. 'You could still answer questions. But you'd never walk again. Not without a cane. So stop dicking us around. Get in the car. Let's go.'

The stranger saw no need to give them another warning. He'd been clear with them from the start. And they were the ones who'd chosen to up the ante.

The shorter guy made as if to swing, but checked. Then the taller guy took over. He did swing. He put all his weight into it. Which was bad technique. A serious mistake with that kind of weapon. All the stranger had to do was take a step back. The heavy hunk of wood whistled past his midriff. It continued relentlessly through its arc. There was too much momentum for the guy to stop it. And both his hands were clinging to the handle. Which left his head exposed. And his torso. And his knees. A whole menu of tempting targets, all available, all totally unguarded. Any other day the stranger could have taken his pick. But on this occasion he had no time. The taller guy got off the hook. His buddy bailed him out. By jabbing at the stranger's gut, using the axe handle like a spear. He went short, aiming to get the stranger's attention. He jabbed a second time, hoping to back the stranger off. Then he lunged. It was the money shot. Or it would have been, if he hadn't paused a beat too long. Set his feet a fraction too firm. So that when he thrust, the stranger knew it was coming. He moved to the side. Grabbed the axe handle at its mid-point. And pulled. Hard. The guy was dragged forward a yard before he realized what was happening. He let go. But by then it was too late. His fate was sealed. The stranger whipped the captured axe handle over and around and brought it scything down, square onto the top of the guy's head. His eyes rolled back. His knees buckled and he wilted, slumping limp and lifeless at the stranger's feet. He wouldn't be getting up again any time soon. That was for sure. After that kind of a blow he might not be getting up ever.

The taller guy glanced down. Saw the shape his buddy was in. And swung his axe handle back the opposite way. Aiming for the stranger's head. Looking to knock it off his shoulders. He swung harder than before. Wanting revenge. Hoping to survive. And he missed. Again. He left himself vulnerable. Again. But this time something else saved him. The fact that he was the last of his crew left standing. The only available source of information. He now had strategic value. Which gave him the chance to swing again. He took it, and the stranger parried. The guy kept going, chopping left and right, left and right, like a crazed lumberjack. He managed a dozen more strokes at full speed, then he ran out of gas.

'Screw this.' The guy dropped the axe handle. Reached behind him. And pulled out his gun. 'Screw answering questions. Screw taking you alive.'

The guy took two steps back. He should have taken three. He hadn't accounted for the length of the stranger's arms.

'Let's not be hasty.' The stranger flicked out with his axe handle and sent the gun flying. Then he stepped closer and grabbed the guy by the neck. 'Maybe we will take that drive. Turns out I have some questions of my own. You can— '

'Stop.' It was a female voice. Confident. Commanding. Coming from the shadows near the right-hand row of garages. Someone new was on the scene. The stranger had arrived at 8 p.m., three hours early, and searched every inch of the compound. He was certain no one had been hiding then.

'Let him go.' A silhouette broke free from the darkness. A woman's. She looked to be around five ten. Slim. Limping slightly. Her arms were out in front and there was the squat outline of a matt-black pistol in her hands. 'Step away.'

The stranger didn't move. He didn't relax his grip.

The woman hesitated. The other guy was between her and the stranger. Not an ideal position. But he was six inches shorter. And slightly to the side. That did leave her a target. An area on the stranger's chest. A rectangle. It was maybe six inches by ten. That was big enough, she figured. And it was more or less in the right position. She took a breath. Exhaled gently. And pulled the trigger.

The stranger fell back. He landed with his arms spread wide, one knee raised, and his head turned so that he was facing the border fence. He was completely still. His shirt was ragged and torn. His entire chest was slick and slimy and red. But there was no arterial spray. No sign of a heartbeat.

No sign of life at all.

The tidy, manicured area people now called *The Plaza* had once been a sprawling grove of trees. Black walnuts. They'd grown, undisturbed, for centuries. Then in the 1870s a trader took to resting his mules in their shade on his treks back and forth to California. He liked the spot, so he built a shack there. And when he grew too old to rattle back and forth across the continent he sold his beasts and he stayed.

Other people followed suit. The shanty became a village. The village became a town. The town split in two like a cell, multiplying greedily. Both halves flourished. One to the south. One to the north. There were many more years of steady growth. Then stagnation. Then decline. Slow and grim and unstoppable. Until an unexpected shot in the arm was delivered, in the late 1930s. An army of surveyors showed up. Then labourers. Builders. Engineers. Even some artists and sculptors. All sent by the WPA.

No one local knew why those towns had been chosen. Some said it was a mistake. A bureaucrat misreading a file note and dispatching the resources to the wrong place. Others figured that someone in D.C. must have owed the mayor a favour. But whatever the reason, no one objected. Not with all the new roads that were being laid. New bridges being constructed. And all kinds of buildings rising up. The project went on for years. And it left a permanent mark. The towns' traditional adobe arches became a little more square. The stucco exteriors, a little more uniform. The layout of the streets, a little more regimented. And the amenities, a lot more generous. The area gained schools. Municipal offices. Fire houses. A police station. A courthouse. A museum. And a medical centre.

Some of the facilities became obsolete over the years. Some were sold off. Others demolished. But the medical centre was still the main source of healthcare for miles around. It contained a doctor's office. A pharmacy. A clinic, with half a dozen beds. And thanks to the largesse of those New Deal planners, even a morgue. It was tucked away in the basement. And it was where Dr Houllier was working, the next morning.

Dr Houllier was seventy-two years old. He had served the town his whole life. Once he was part of a team. Now he was the only physician left. He was responsible for everything from delivering babies to treating colds to diagnosing cancer. And for dealing with the deceased. Which was the reason for that day's early start. He'd been on duty since the small hours. Since he received the call about a shooting on the outskirts of town. It was the kind of thing that would attract attention. He knew that from experience. He was expecting a visit. Soon. And he needed to be ready.

There was a computer on the desk, but it was switched off. Dr Houllier preferred to write his notes longhand. He remembered things better that way. And he had a format. One he'd developed himself. It wasn't fancy, but it worked. It was better than anything those Silicon Valley whizz-kids had ever tried to foist on him. And it was sure as hell cheaper. He sat down, picked up the Mont Blanc his father had bought him when he graduated medical school, and started to record the results of his night's work.

There was no knock. No greeting. No courtesy at all. The door just opened and a man came in. The same one as usual. Early forties, tight curly hair, tan linen suit. *Perky,* Dr Houllier privately called him, because of the bouncy way the guy walked. He didn't know his real name. He didn't want to know.

The guy started at the far end of the room. The cold storage area. The meat locker as Dr Houllier thought of it, after decades of dealing with its contents. There was a line of five steel doors. The guy approached, examined each handle in turn, but didn't touch any of them. He never did. He moved on to the autopsy table in the centre. Crossed to the line of steel trolleys against the far wall, near the autoclave. Then he approached the desk.

'Phone.' He held out his hand.

Dr Houllier passed the guy his cell. The guy checked to make sure it wasn't recording, slipped it into his pants pocket, and turned to the door. 'Clear,' he said.

Another man walked in. *Mantis*, Dr Houllier called him, because whenever he looked at the guy with his long skinny limbs, angular torso, and bulging eyes he

446

couldn't help but think of the insect. Although he did know this guy's real name. Leo Dendoncker. Everyone in town knew it, even if they'd never met him.

A third man followed Dendoncker in. He looked a little like Perky, but with straighter hair and a darker suit. And with such an anonymous face and bland way of moving that Dr Houllier had never been inspired to find him a nickname.

Dendoncker stopped in the centre of the room. His pale hair was almost invisible in the harsh light. He turned through 360 degrees, slowly, scanning the space around him. Then he turned to Dr Houllier.

'Show me,' he said.

Dr Houllier crossed the room. He checked his watch, then worked the lever that opened the centre door of the meat locker. He pulled out the sliding rack, revealing a body covered by a sheet. It was tall. Almost as long as the tray it lay on. And broad. The shoulders only just fitted through the opening. Dr Houllier pulled the sheet, slowly, revealing the head. It was a man's. Its hair was messy. The face was craggy and unnaturally pale, and the eyes were taped shut.

'Move.' Dendoncker shoved Dr Houllier aside. He pulled the sheet off and dropped it on the floor. The body was naked. If Michelangelo's *David* was made to embody masculine beauty, this guy could have been another in the series. But at the opposite end of the spectrum. There was nothing elegant. Nothing delicate. This one was all about brutality. Pure and simple.

'That's what killed him?' Dendoncker pointed to a

447

wound on the guy's chest. It was slightly raised. Its edges were rough and ragged and they were turning brown.

'Well he didn't die of sloth.' Dr Houllier glanced at his watch. 'I can guarantee that.'

'He'd been shot before.' Dendoncker pointed at a set of scars on the other side of the guy's chest. 'And stabbed.'

'The scar on his abdomen?' Dr Houllier shook his head. 'Like some kind of sea creature? I don't think that's a knife wound. More likely shrapnel.'

'Whatever.' Dendoncker turned away. 'I guess death was tired of waiting for him. He pushed his luck one time too many. What else do we know about him?'

'Not much.' Dr Houllier snatched up the sheet and spread it loosely over the body. 'I spoke to the sheriff. Sounds like the guy was a drifter. He had a room at a motel outside of town. He'd paid through next weekend, in cash, but he had no belongings there. And he'd registered under a false address. One East 161st Street, the Bronx, New York.'

'How do you know that's false?'

'Because I've been there. It's another way of saying Yankee Stadium. And the guy used a false name, too. He signed the register as John Smith.'

'Smith? Could be his real name.'

Dr Houllier shook his head. He moved back to his desk, took a Ziploc bag from the top drawer, and handed it to Dendoncker. 'See for yourself. This was in his pocket.'

Dendoncker popped the seal and fished out a passport. It was crumpled and worn. He turned to the second page. *Personal Information.* 'This has expired.'

'Doesn't matter. The ID's still valid. And look at the photo. It's old, but it's a match.'

'OK. Let's see. Name: Reacher. Jack, none. Nationality: United States of America. Place of birth: Berlin, West Germany.' Dendoncker glanced at the body then tossed the passport in a trash can next to Dr Houllier's desk. 'Burn that.' He turned to the two guys he arrived with. 'All right. I've seen enough. Get rid of the body. Dump it in the usual place.'

Choose your next Jack Reacher novel

The Reacher books can be read in any order, but here they are in the order in which they were written:

KILLING FLOOR

Jack Reacher gets off a bus in a small town in Georgia. And is thrown into the county jail, for a murder he didn't commit.

DIE TRYING

Reacher is locked in a van with a woman claiming to be FBI. And ferried right across America into a brand new country.

TRIPWIRE

Reacher is digging swimming pools in Key West when a detective comes round asking questions. Then the detective turns up dead.

THE VISITOR

Two naked women found dead in a bath filled with paint. Both victims of a man just like Reacher.

ECHO BURNING

In the heat of Texas, Reacher meets a young woman whose husband is in jail. When he is released, he will kill her.

WITHOUT FAIL

A Washington woman asks Reacher for help. Her job? Protecting the Vice-President.

PERSUADER

A kidnapping in Boston. A cop dies. Has Reacher lost his sense of right and wrong?

THE ENEMY

Back in Reacher's army days, a general is found dead on his watch.

ONE SHOT

A lone sniper shoots five people dead in a heartland city.
But the accused guy says, 'Get Reacher'.

THE HARD WAY

A coffee on a busy New York street leads to a shoot-out
three thousand miles away in the Norfolk countryside.

BAD LUCK AND TROUBLE

One of Reacher's buddies has shown up dead in the California
desert, and Reacher must put his old army unit back together.

NOTHING TO LOSE

Reacher crosses the line between a town called
Hope and one named Despair.

GONE TOMORROW

On the New York subway, Reacher counts
down the twelve tell-tale signs of a suicide bomber.

61 HOURS

In freezing South Dakota, Reacher hitches
a lift on a bus heading for trouble.

WORTH DYING FOR

Reacher runs into a clan that's terrifying the Nebraska locals,
but it's the unsolved case of a missing child that he can't let go.

THE AFFAIR

Six months before the events in *Killing Floor*,
Major Jack Reacher of the US Military Police goes
undercover in Mississippi, to investigate a murder.

A WANTED MAN

A freshly-busted nose makes it difficult for Reacher to hitch a
ride. When at last he's picked up by two men and a woman, it
soon becomes clear they have something to hide . . .

NEVER GO BACK

When Reacher returns to his old Virginia headquarters he is
accused of a sixteen-year-old homicide and hears these words:
'You're back in the army, Major. And your ass is mine.'

PERSONAL

Someone has taken a shot at the French president.
Only one man could have done it – and Reacher
is the one man who can find him.

MAKE ME

At a remote railroad stop on the prairie called Mother's
Rest, Jack Reacher finds a town full of silent, watchful
people, and descends into the heart of darkness.

NIGHT SCHOOL

The twenty-first in the series takes Reacher back to
his army days, but this time he's not in uniform.
In Hamburg, trusted sergeant Frances Neagley at
his side, he must confront a terrifying new enemy.

NO MIDDLE NAME

Published in one volume for the first time, and
including a brand-new adventure, here are all the
pulse-pounding Jack Reacher short stories.

THE MIDNIGHT LINE

Reacher tracks a female officer's class ring back to its owner in
the deserted wilds of Wyoming, on a raw quest for simple justice.

PAST TENSE

Deep in the New England woods, Reacher spots a sign to the
town where his father was born, while two young Canadians
are stranded at a remote, sinister motel . . .

BLUE MOON

On a Greyhound bus, Reacher rescues an old man from a mugger.
Elsewhere in the city, two rival criminal gangs are competing for
control – will Reacher be able to stop bad things happening?

**Alternatively, you can find a list of the books
in the order of events in Reacher's life, at
www.deadgoodbooks.co.uk/ReacherBooks**

If you enjoyed THE SENTINEL
unravel another mystery in TRIPWIRE

Reacher spends his days digging swimming pools
by hand and his nights as a strip club bouncer
in the Florida Keys.

He doesn't want to be found.

But someone has sent a private detective to
seek him out. It's time to work out who is trying
to find him and why.

**AVAILABLE NOW IN PAPERBACK,
EBOOK AND AUDIOBOOK**

Turn back the clock to meet a younger Reacher in THE ENEMY

A soldier is found dead in a sleazy motel bed.
Reacher is the Military Policeman on duty.
The soldier turns out to be a two-star general.
The situation is bad enough, then Reacher finds
the general's wife.

AVAILABLE IN PAPERBACK, EBOOK AND AUDIOBOOK

Another close shave for Reacher in
THE VISITOR.

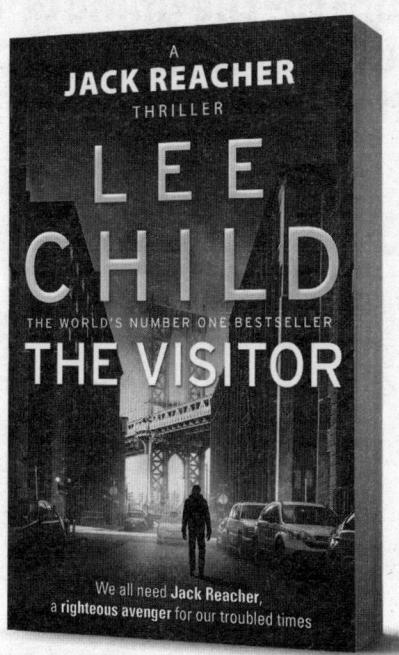

Two women are found dead in their own homes,
naked, in a bath full of paint.
Apparent victims of an army man. A loner, a smart
guy with a score to settle, a ruthless vigilante.
A man just like Jack Reacher.

AVAILABLE IN PAPERBACK,
EBOOK AND AUDIOBOOK

For up-to-the-minute news about Lee & Andrew Child find us on Facebook

Find out more about the Jack Reacher books at www.JackReacher.com

- Take the book selector quiz
- Enter competitions
- Read and listen to extracts
- Find out more about the authors
- Discover Reacher coffee, music and more . . .

PLUS sign up for the monthly Jack Reacher newsletter to get all the latest news delivered direct to your inbox.